NEW AMERICAN LIBRARY

THE
LEFT HAND
of GOD

Paul Hoffman

New American Library
Published by New American Library, a division of
Penguin Gro up (USA) Inc., 375 Hudson Street,
New York, New York 10014, USA
Penguin Group (Canada), 90 Eglinton Avenue East, Suite 700, Toronto,
Ontario M4P 2Y3, Canada (a division of Pearson Penguin Canada Inc.)
Penguin Books Ltd., 80 Strand, London WC2R 0RL, England
Penguin Ireland, 25 St. Stephen's Green, Dublin 2,
Ireland (a division of Penguin Books Ltd.)
Penguin Group (Australia), 250 Camberwell Road, Camberwell, Victoria 3124,
Australia (a division of Pearson Australia Group Pty. Ltd.)
Penguin Books India Pvt. Ltd., 11 Community Centre, Panchsheel Park,
New Delhi - 110 017, India
Penguin Group (NZ), 67 Apollo Drive, Rosedale, Auckland 0632,
New Zealand (a division of Pearson New Zealand Ltd.)
Penguin Books (South Africa) (Pty.) Ltd., 24 Sturdee Avenue,
Rosebank, Johannesburg 2196, South Africa

Penguin Books Ltd., Registered Offices:
80 Strand, London WC2R 0RL, England

Published by New American Library, a division of Penguin Group (USA) Inc. Previously
published in a Dutton edition.

First New American Library Printing, July 2011
10 9 8 7 6 5 4 3 2 1

Copyright © Paul Hoffman, 2010
Excerpt from *The Last Four Things* copyright © Paul Hoffman, 2011
All rights reserved

REGISTERED TRADEMARK—MARCA REGISTRADA

New American Library Trade Paperback ISBN: 978-0-451-23188-8

The Library of Congress has catalogued the hardcover edition of this title as follows:

Hoffman, Paul, 1953–
The left hand of God/Paul Hoffman.
p. cm.
ISBN 978-0-525-95131-5
1. Teenage boys—Fiction. 2. Monasteries—Fiction.
3. Religious fanaticism—Fiction. I. Title.
PR6058.O446L44 2010
823'.914—dc22 2010000830

Printed in the United States of America

Set in Adobe Caslon
Designed by Spring Hoteling

For Victoria *and* Thomas Hoffman

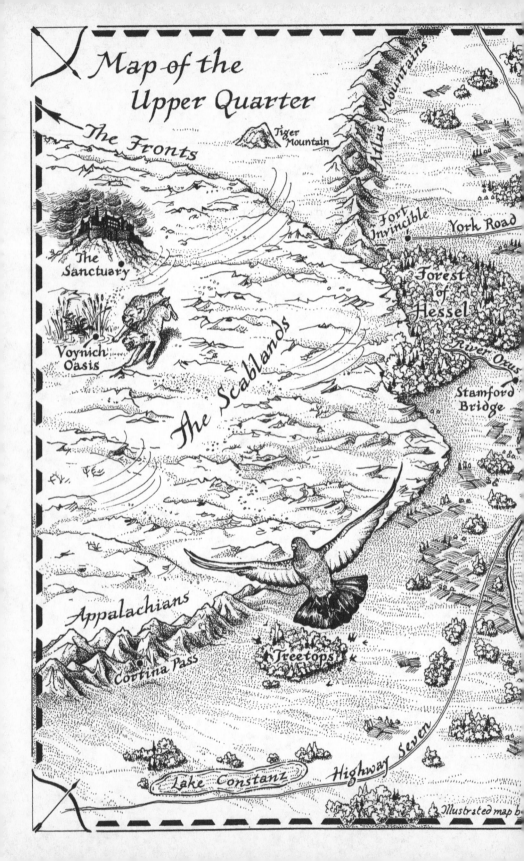

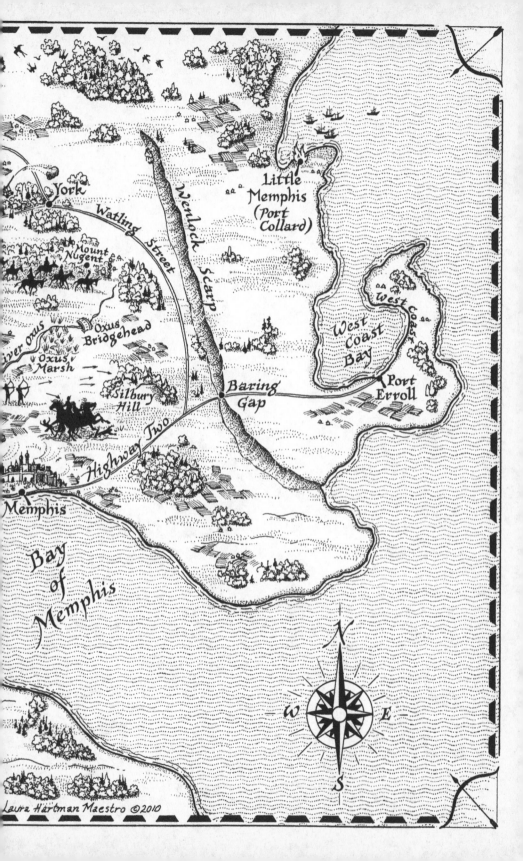

THE LEFT HAND *of* GOD

Listen. The Sanctuary of the Redeemers on Shotover Scarp is named after a damned lie, for there is no redemption that goes on there and less sanctuary. The country around it is full of scrub and spindly weeds and you can barely tell the difference between summer and winter—which is to say that it is always bloody freezing no matter what the time of year. The Sanctuary itself is visible for miles when there is no filthy smog obscuring it, which is rare, and is made of flint, concrete and rice flour. The flour makes the concrete harder than rock and this is one of the reasons that the prison, for this is what it truly is, has resisted the many attempts to take it by siege, attempts now considered so futile that no one has tried to take Shotover Sanctuary for hundreds of years.

It is a stinking, foul place and no one except the Lord Redeemers go there willingly. Who are their prisoners, then? This is the wrong word for those who are taken to Shotover, because "prisoners" suggests a crime and they, none of them, have offended any law made by man or God. Nor do they look like any prisoner you will ever have seen: those who are brought here are all boys under the age of ten. Depending on their age when they enter, it may be more than fifteen years before they leave and then only half will do so. The other half will have left in a shroud of blue sacking and been buried in Ginky's Field, a graveyard that begins under the walls. This graveyard is vast, spreading as far as you can see, so you will have some idea of the size of Shotover and how very hard it is even to stay alive there. No one knows his way round all of it and it is as easy to get lost within its endless corridors that twist and turn, high and low, as in any wilderness. There is no change in the way it looks—every part of it looks much the same as every other part: brown, dark, grim and smelling of something old and rancid.

Standing in one of these corridors is a boy looking out of a window and holding a large, dark blue sack. He is perhaps fourteen or fifteen years old. He is not sure and neither is anyone else. He has forgotten his real name because everyone who comes here is rebaptized with the name of one of the martyrs of the Lord Redeemers—and there are many of them on account of the fact that, time out of mind, everyone they have failed to convert has hated their guts. The boy staring out of the window is called Thomas Cale, although no one ever uses his first name, and he is committing a most grievous sin by doing so.

What drew him to the window was the sound of the Northwest Gate groaning as it always did on one of its rare openings, like some giant with appallingly painful knees. He watched as two Lords in their black cassocks stepped over the threshold and ushered in a small boy of about eight, followed by another slightly younger and then another. Cale counted twenty in all before another brace of Redeemers brought up the rear and slowly and arthritically the gate began to close.

Cale's expression changed as he leaned forward to see out of the closing gate and into the Scablands beyond. He had been outside the walls on only six occasions since he had come here more than a decade before—it was said, the youngest child ever brought to the Sanctuary. On these six occasions he was watched as if the lives of his guards depended on it (which they did). Had he failed any of these six tests, for that was what they were, he would have been killed on the spot. Of his former life he could remember nothing.

As the gate shut, he turned his attention to the boys again. None of them was plump, but they had the round faces of young children. All were wide-eyed at the sight of the keep, its immense size, its huge walls, but, though bewildered and scared simply by the strangeness of their surroundings, they were not afraid. Cale's chest filled with deep and strange emotions that he could not have given a name to. But, lost in them as he was, his talent for keeping one ear alive to whatever was going on around him saved him, as it had so many times in the past.

He moved away from the window and walked on down the corridor.

"You! Wait!"

Cale stopped and turned round. One of the Redeemers, hugely fat with folds of skin hanging over the edge of his collar, was standing in one of the doorways off the passage, steam and odd sounds emerging from the room behind him. Cale looked at him, his expression unchanged.

"Come here and let me see you."

The boy walked toward him.

"Oh, it's you," said the fat Redeemer. "What are you doing here?"

"The Lord of Discipline sent me to take this to the drum." He held up the blue sack he was carrying.

"What did you say? Speak up!"

Cale knew, of course, that the fat Redeemer was deaf in one ear, and he had deliberately spoken quietly.

Cale repeated himself, this time shouting loudly.

"Are you trying to be funny, boy?"

"No, Redeemer."

"What were you doing by the window?"

"The window?"

"Don't play me for a fool. What were you doing?"

"I heard the Northwest Gate being opened."

"Did you, by God?"

This seemed to distract him.

"They're early." He grunted with annoyance and then turned and looked back into the kitchen, for that was who the fat man was: the Lord of Vittles, overseer of the kitchen from which the Redeemers were well fed and the boys hardly at all. "Twenty extra for dinner," he shouted into the evil-smelling steam behind him. He turned back to Cale.

"Were you thinking when you were by that window?"

"No, Redeemer."

"Were you daydreaming?"

"No, Redeemer."

"If I catch you loitering again, Cale, I'll have the hide off you. Hear me?"

"Yes, Redeemer."

The Lord of Vittles turned back into the room and began to close the door. As he did so, Cale spoke softly but quite distinctly, so that anyone not hard of hearing would have picked it up.

"I hope you choke on it, you lardy dritsek."

The door slammed shut, and Cale headed off down the corridor dragging the large sack behind him. It took nearly fifteen minutes, running most of the way, before he came to the drum located at the end of its own short passageway. It was called the drum because that was what it looked like, as long as you disregarded the fact that it was six feet tall and embedded in a brick wall. On the other side of the drum was a place sealed off from the rest of the Sanctuary where, it was rumored, there lived twelve nuns who cooked for the Redeemers only and washed their clothes. Cale did not know what a nun was and had never seen one, although from time to time he did talk to one of them through the drum. He did not know what made nuns different from other women, who were spoken of rarely and only then with distaste. There were two exceptions: the Hanged Redeemer's Holy Sister and the Blessed Imelda Lambertini, who at the age of eleven had died of ecstasy during her first communion. The Redeemers had not explained what ecstasy was, and no one was foolish enough to ask. Cale gave the drum a spin, and then it turned on its axis, revealing a large opening. He dumped the blue sack inside and gave it another spin, then he banged on the side, causing it to emit a loud boom. He waited for thirty seconds, and then a muffled voice spoke from the other side of the drum wall:

"What is it?"

Cale put his head next to the drum so he could be heard, his lips almost touching the surface.

"Redeemer Bosco wants this back by tomorrow morning," he shouted.

"Why didn't it come with all the others?"

"How the hell would I know?"

There was a high-pitched cry of muffled rage from the other side of the drum.

"What's your name, you impious pup?"

"Dominic Savio," lied Cale.

"Well, Dominic Savio, I'll report you to the Lord of Discipline and he'll have the hide off you."

"I couldn't care less."

Twenty minutes later Cale arrived back at the Lord Militant's training buroo. It was empty except for the Lord himself, who did not look up or give any sign that he had seen Cale. He continued to write in his ledger for another five minutes before speaking, still without looking up.

"What took you so long?"

"The Lord of Vittles stopped me in the corridor of the outer banks."

"Why?"

"He heard a noise outside, I think."

"What noise?" Finally, the Lord Militant looked at Cale. His eyes were a pale, almost watery blue, but sharp. They did not miss much. Or anything.

"They were opening the Northwest Gate to let in the freshboys. He wasn't expecting them today. I'd say his nose was out of joint."

"Hold your tongue," said the Lord Militant, but mildly by his unforgiving standards. Cale knew that he despised the Lord of Vittles, and hence he felt it less dangerous to speak in such a way of a Redeemer.

"I asked your friend about the rumor they'd arrived," said the Redeemer.

"I have no friends, Redeemer," replied Cale. "They're forbidden."

The Lord Militant laughed softly, not a pleasant sound.

"I have no worries about you on that score, Cale. But if we must plod—the scrawny blond-haired one. What do you call him?"

"Henri."

"I know his given name. You have a moniker for him."

"We call him Vague Henri."

The Lord Militant laughed, but this time there was the echo of some ordinary good humor.

"Very good," he said appreciatively. "I asked him what time the freshboys had arrived and he said he wasn't sure, sometime between eight bells and nine. I then asked him how many there were and he said fifteen or so, but it might have been more." He looked Cale straight in the eyes. "I thrashed him to teach him to be more specific in future. What do you think of that?"

"It's all the same to me, Redeemer," replied Cale flatly. "He deserved whatever punishment you gave him."

"Really? How very gratifying you should think so. What time did they arrive?"

"Just before five."

"How many were there?"

"Twenty."

"What ages?"

"None younger than seven. None older than nine."

"Of what kind?"

"Four Mezos, four Uitlanders, three Folders, five half-castes, three Miamis and one I didn't know."

The Lord Militant grunted as if only barely satisfied that all his questions had been answered so precisely. "Go over to the board. I've set a puzzle for you. Ten minutes."

Cale walked over to a large table, twenty feet by twenty, on which the Lord Militant had rolled out a map, which fell slightly over the edges. It was easy to recognize some of the things drawn there—hills, rivers, woods—but on the remainder there were numerous small blocks of wood on which were written numbers and hieroglyphs, some of the blocks in order, some apparently chaotic. Cale stared at the map for his allotted time and then looked up.

"Well?" said the Lord Militant.

Cale began to set out his solution.

Twenty minutes later he finished, his hands still held out in front of him.

"Very ingenious. Impressive, even," said the Lord Militant. Something in Cale's eyes changed. Then with extraordinary speed the Lord Militant lashed the boy's left hand with a leather belt studded with tiny but thick tacks.

Cale winced and his teeth ground together in pain. But quickly his face returned to the watchful coldness that was these days all that the Redeemer ever saw from him. The Lord Militant sat down and considered the boy as if he were an object both interesting and yet unsatisfactory.

"When will you learn that to do the clever thing, the original thing, is merely your pride controlling you? This solution may work, but it's unreasonably risky. You know very well the tried solution to this problem. In war a dull success is always better than a brilliant one. You had better learn to understand why."

He banged the table furiously.

"Have you forgotten that a Redeemer has the right to kill instantly any boy who does something unexpected?"

There was another crash as he hit the table again, stood up and glared at Cale. Blood, not a great amount, dripped from the four holes in Cale's still-outstretched left hand. "No one else would have indulged you the way I have. The Lord of Discipline has his eye on you. Every few years he likes to set an example. Do you want to end up as an Act of Faith?"

Cale stared ahead and said nothing.

"Answer me!"

"No, Lord."

"Do you think you are needful, you useless Zed?"

"No, Lord."

"This is my fault, my fault, my most grievous fault," said the Lord Militant, striking his breast with his hand three times. "You have twenty-four hours to consider your sins and then you will debase yourself before the Lord of Discipline."

"Yes, Redeemer."

"Now, get out."

Dropping his hands to his side, Cale turned and walked to the door.

"Don't bleed on the mat," called out the Lord Militant.

Cale opened the door with his good hand and left.

Alone in his cell the Lord Militant watched the door close. As it clicked shut, his expression changed from that of barely constrained rage to one of thoughtful curiosity.

Outside in the corridor Cale stood for a moment in the horrible brown light that infected the entire Sanctuary and examined his left hand. The wounds were not deep, because the studs in the belt had been designed to cause intense pain without taking long to heal. He made a fist and squeezed, his head shaking as if a small tremor were taking place deep inside his skull as the blood from his hand dripped heavily onto the floor. Then he relaxed his hand, and in the grim light a look of horrible despair crept over his face. In a moment it was gone, and Cale walked on down the corridor and out of sight.

None of the boys in the Sanctuary knew how many of them there were. Some claimed there were as many as ten thousand and growing more with every month. It was the increase that occupied the conversations most. Even among those nearing twenty years old there was agreement that, until the last five years, the number, whatever it was, had remained steady. But since then there had been a rise. The Redeemers were doing things differently, itself an ominous and strange thing: habit and conformity to the past were to them like air to those who breathe. Every day should be like the next day, every month like the next month. No year should be different from another year. But now the great increase in numbers had required change. The dormitories had been altered with bunks of two and even three tiers to accommodate new arrivals. Divine service was held in staggered rosters so that all might pray and store up every day the tokens against damnation. And now meals were taken in relays. But as for the reasons behind this change, the boys knew nothing.

Cale, his left hand wrapped in a dirty piece of linen previously thrown away by the washerserfs, walked through the huge refectory for the second sitting carrying a wooden tray. Late to arrive, though not too late—for this he would have been beaten and excluded—he walked toward the large table at the end of the room where he always ate. He stopped behind another boy, about the same age and height but so intent on eating that he did not notice Cale standing behind him. It was the others at the table whose raised heads alerted him. He looked up.

"Sorry, Cale," he said, shoving the remains of his food into his mouth at the same time as he stepped out from behind the bench and hurried off carrying his tray.

Cale sat down and looked at his supper: there was something that looked like a sausage, but was not, covered in a watery gravy with some indeterminate root vegetable bleached by endless boiling into a yellowy pale mush. In a bowl beside it was porridge, gelatinous and cold and gray as week-old slush. For a moment, starving as he was, he couldn't bring himself to start eating. Then someone pushed his way onto the bench beside him. Cale didn't look at him but started to eat. Only the slight twitch at the edge of his mouth revealed what filthy stuff it was.

The boy who had pushed in next to him started to speak, but so low was his voice that only Cale could hear. It was unwise to be caught speaking to another boy at mealtimes.

"I found something," said the boy, the excitement clear even though he was barely audible.

"Good for you," replied Cale without emotion.

"Something wonderful."

This time Cale did not react at all, instead concentrating on getting the porridge down without gagging. There was a pause from the boy.

"There's food. Food you can eat." Cale barely raised his head, but the boy next to him knew that he had won.

"Why should I believe you?"

"Vague Henri was with me. Meet us at seven behind the Hanged Redeemer."

With that the boy stood up and was gone. Cale raised his head, and a strange look of longing came over his face, so different from the cold mask he usually showed the world that the boy opposite stared at him.

"Don't you want that?" said the boy, eyes bright with hope as if the rancid sausage and waxy gray porridge offered more joy than he could easily comprehend.

Cale did not reply or look at the boy but began eating again, forcing himself to swallow and trying not to be sick.

When he had finished, Cale took his wooden tray to the cleanorium, scrubbed it in the bowl with sand and put it back in its rack. On his way out, watched by a Redeemer sitting in a huge high chair from which he could survey the refectory, Cale knelt in front of the statue of the Hanged Redeemer, beat his breast three times and muttered, "I am Sin, I am Sin, I am Sin," without the slightest regard for what the words meant.

Outside it was dark and the evening fog had descended. This was good; it would make it easier for Cale to slip unnoticed from the ambo into the bushes that grew behind the great statue.

By the time he arrived Cale was unable to see more than fifteen feet in front of him. He stepped down from the ambo and onto the gravel in front of the statue.

This was the largest of all the holy gibbets in the Sanctuary, and there must have been hundreds of them, some of them no larger than a few inches, nailed to walls, set in niches, decorating the tubs of holy ashes at the end of every corridor and on the spaces above every door. They were so common, so frequently referred to, that the image itself had long ago lost any meaning. Nobody, except the freshboys, really noticed them for what they were: models of a man hanging from a gallows with a rope around his neck, his body hatched with scars from the torture before his execution, his broken legs dangling at strange angles beneath him. Holy gibbets of the Hanged Redeemer made during the Sanctuary's founding a thousand years before were crude and tended to a straightforward realism: a terror in the eyes and face for all the lack of carving skill, the body twisted and wracked, the tongue protruding from the mouth. This, said the carvers, was a horrible way to die. Over the years the statues had become more skilled but also milk-and-water. The great statue, with its huge gallows, its thick rope and twenty-foot-tall savior dangling from it, was only thirty years old: the weals on his back were pronounced but neat and bloodless. Rather than being agonizingly smashed, his legs were held in a pose as if he were suffering more from cramp. But it was the expression on his face that was oddest of all—instead of the pain of strangulation he had a look of inconvenienced holiness, as if a small bone was stuck in his throat and he was clearing it with a demure cough.

Nevertheless, on this night in the fog and the dark the only things that Cale could see of the Redeemer were his huge feet dangling out of the white mist. The oddness of this made him uneasy. Careful not to make any noise, Cale eased himself into the bushes that obscured him from anyone walking past.

"Cale?"

"Yes."

The boy from the refectory, Kleist, and Vague Henri emerged from the bushes in front of Cale.

"This better be worth the risk, Henri," whispered Cale.

"It is, Cale. I promise."

Kleist gestured Cale to follow into the bushes against the wall. It was even darker here and Cale had to wait for his eyes to adjust. The two others waited. There was a door.

This was astonishing—while there were plenty of doorways in the Sanctuary, there were few doors. During the Great Reformation two hundred years before, more than half the Redeemers had been burned at the stake for heresy. Fearing that these apostates might have contaminated their boys, the victorious sect of Redeemers had cut their throats just to be on the safe side. After the restocking of freshboys, the Redeemers had made many changes and one of them had been to remove all the doors wherever there were boys.

What, after all, could be the purpose of a door where there were sinners? Doors hid things. Doors were about many devil-type things, they decided, about secrecy, about being alone or with others and up to something. The very concept of a door, now that they thought of it, began to make the Redeemers shake with rage and fear. The devil himself was no longer just depicted as a horned beast but almost as often as a rectangle with a lock. Of course this antipathy toward doors did not apply to the Redeemers themselves: the very sign of their own redemption was the possession of a door to their place of work and their sleeping cells. Holiness for the Redeemers was measured by the numbers of keys they were allowed to hold on the chain around their waists. To jangle as you walked was to show that you were already being tolled to heaven.

This was why the discovery of an unknown door was something amazing.

Now that his eyes were becoming accustomed to the dark, Cale could see a pile of broken plaster and crumbling bricks piled next to the door.

"I was hiding from Chetnick," said Vague Henri. "That's how I found this place. The plaster on the corner there was falling away, so while I waited I picked at it. It was all crumbling—water had got in. It only took half a mo."

Cale reached out toward the edge of the door and pushed carefully. Then again, and again.

"It's locked."

Kleist and Vague Henri smiled. Kleist reached into his pocket and took out something Cale had never seen in a boy's possession—a key. It was long and thick and pitted with rust. All their eyes were shining with excitement now. Kleist put the key in the lock and turned, grunting with the effort. Then, with a *clunk!* it shifted.

"It took us three days of shoveling in grease and stuff to get it to open," said Vague Henri, his voice thick with pride.

"Where did you get the key?" asked Cale. Kleist and Vague Henri were delighted that Cale was talking to them as if they had raised the dead or walked on water.

"I'll tell you when we get in. Come on." Kleist put his shoulder to the door, and the others did the same. "Don't push too hard. The hinges might be in bad shape. We don't want to make any noise. I'll count to three." He paused. "Ready? One, two, three."

They pushed. Nothing. It wouldn't budge. They stopped, took a deep breath. "One, two, three."

They heaved, and then with a screech the door shifted. They stepped back, alarmed. To be heard was to be caught, to be caught was to be subject to God knows what.

"We could be hanged for this," said Cale. The others looked at him.

"They wouldn't. Not a hanging."

"The Militant told me that the Lord of Discipline was looking for an excuse to set an example. It's been five years since the last hanging."

"They wouldn't," repeated Vague Henri, shocked.

"Yes, they would. This is a *door*, for God's sake. You have a *key*." Cale turned to Kleist. "You lied to me. You've got no idea what's in there. It's probably a dead end, nothing worth stealing, nothing worth knowing." He looked back at the other boy. "It isn't worth the risk, Henri, but it's your neck. I'm out."

As he started to turn, a voice called from the ambo, angry and impatient.

"Who's there? What was that noise?"

Then they heard the sound of a man stepping onto the gravel in front of the Hanged Redeemer.

2

Sheer terror would be mild compared to what Kleist and Henri felt as they heard that sound, the knowledge of the cruelty coming to them for their stupidity—the vast and silent crowd waiting in the gray light, their screams as they were dragged to the gallows, the terrible hour-long wait as Mass was sung and then the rope and being hauled into the air, choking and kicking.

But Cale had already moved over to the door and with one silent surge of effort lifted the door up from its collapsing hinges and pushed. It swung open almost silently. He reached for the shoulders of the two motionless boys and pushed them into the gap. Once they were in, he squeezed himself in after them and with another huge effort shut the door behind him, again almost silently.

"Come out! At once!" The sound of the man's voice was muffled, but still clear.

"Give me the key," said Cale. Kleist handed it over. Cale turned to the door and felt for the lock. Then he paused. He did not know how to use a key. "Kleist! You!" he whispered. Kleist felt for the lock and then slipped in the heavy key.

"Quietly," said Cale.

With a trembling hand that knew that what it was doing was death or life, Kleist twisted the key.

It turned with what seemed to them the clang of a hammer on an iron pot.

"Come here now!" demanded the muffled voice. But Cale could hear that there was uncertainty in it. Whoever was out there in the fog was unsure of what he had heard.

They waited. In the silence only the light rasp of the breathing of the fearful. Then they could just make out the muffled crunch of gravel as the man turned away, the sound quickly swallowed up.

"He's gone for the Gougers."

"Perhaps not," said Cale. "I think it was the Lord Vittles. He's an idle fat bastard and he wasn't sure what he heard. He could have searched the bushes but he wouldn't make the effort. He'll be wary of getting the Gougers out with the dogs when he wasn't even ready to check behind a few bushes because of the strain on his lardy carcass."

"If he comes back tomorrow when it's light, he'll find the door," said Vague Henri. "Even if we escape now, they'll come after us."

"They'll come after *someone* and they'll make sure they find them, whether they're guilty or not. There's nothing to connect us with this place. Someone will take it in the neck but there's no reason it should be us."

"What if he has gone for help?" said Kleist.

"Unlock the door and let's get out."

Kleist felt for the door and patted his way down to the key sticking out of the lock. He tried to turn it but it wouldn't budge. Then he tried again. Nothing. Then he twisted as hard as he could. There was a loud *snap!*

"What was that?" demanded Vague Henri.

"The key," said Kleist. "It's broken off in the lock."

"What?" said Cale.

"It's broken. We can't get out. Not this way."

"God!" swore Cale. "You half-wit. If I could see you, I'd wring your neck."

"There might be another way out."

"And how are we going to find it in the pitch black?" said Cale bitterly.

"I have a light," said Kleist. "I thought we'd need one."

There was a pause, with only the ruffling of Kleist searching his cassock, dropping something, finding it again and then some more ruffling. Then there were sparks as he struck a flint onto some dry moss.

Quickly it began to flame, and in its light they could see Kleist touching it to the wick of a carrying candle. In a moment he had inserted it into its glass cap and they could look around for the first time.

It's true that there was not much to be seen in the light of the carrying candle, only a poor illumination is to be had from the yellow rendered fat of animal meat, but it was clear to the boys as soon as they looked around that this was not a room but a blocked-off corridor.

Cale took the light from Kleist and examined the door.

"This plaster isn't that old—a few years at most."

In the corner something scuttled and the three of them had the same thought: rats.

The eating of rats was forbidden to the boys on religious grounds, but this was at least one taboo with a good reason behind it—they were disease on four legs. Nevertheless, the meat of a rat was considered a great treat by the boys. Of course, not everyone could be a rat butcher. The skill was much prized and was passed from butcher to trainee in exchange only for expensive swag and mutual favors. The rat butchers were a secretive lot and charged half the rat for their services—a price so high that from time to time some catchers had decided to dispense with them and try butchering for themselves, often with results that encouraged the others to pay up and be grateful. Kleist was a trained butcher.

"We don't have time," said Cale, realizing what was on his mind. "And the light isn't good enough to prepare one."

"I can skin a rat in the pitch black," replied Kleist. "Who knows how long we'll be stuck?" He pulled up his cassock and removed a large pebble from a pocket hidden in the hem. He took careful aim and then lashed it into the semidark. In the corner there was a squeal and a horrible scuttling. Kleist took the candle from Cale and walked toward the sound. He reached into his pocket and with great care unfolded a small piece of cloth and used it to get hold of the creature. With a flick of his wrist he snapped its neck and then put it in the same pocket.

"I'll finish later."

"This is a corridor," said Cale. "It must've led somewhere once, maybe it still does." As the one with the candle, Kleist took the lead.

After less than a minute Cale began to revise his opinions. No doorways, bricked up or otherwise, appeared as Cale had hoped.

"This isn't a corridor," said Cale at last, still keeping his voice low. "It's more like a tunnel."

For more than half an hour they walked on and moved quickly, despite the dark, because the floor was almost completely smooth and clear of rubbish.

Eventually it was Cale who spoke.

"Why did you tell me there was food when you'd never even been here?"

"Obvious," said Vague Henri. "You wouldn't have come otherwise, would you?"

"And how stupid that would have been. You promised me food, Kleist, and I was idiot enough to trust you."

"I thought you were famous, you know, for not trusting people," said Kleist. "Besides, we have a rat. I didn't lie. Anyway, there is food."

"How do you know?" said Henri, his voice betraying his hunger.

"There are lots more rats. Rats need to eat. They have to get it from somewhere."

Kleist stopped suddenly.

"What's the matter?" asked Henri.

Kleist held out the candle. In front of them was a wall. There was no door.

"Maybe it's behind the plaster," said Kleist.

Cale felt the wall with the palm of his hand and then tapped it with his knuckle. "It's not plaster. It's rice flour and concrete. Same as the outer walls." There would be no breaking through this.

"We'll have to go back. Maybe we missed a door in the side of the tunnel. We weren't looking for that."

"I don't think so," said Cale. "And besides . . . how long will the candle burn for?"

Kleist looked at the tallow he was holding. "Twenty minutes."

"What'll we do?" said Vague Henri.

"Put the candle out and let's have a think," said Cale.

"Good idea," said Kleist.

"Happy you think so," muttered Cale, and he sat down on the floor.

Having sat down himself, Kleist opened the glass and extinguished the flame between thumb and forefinger.

They sat in the dark, all three of them distracted by the smell of the animal fat from the candle. For them the stench of burned rancid tallow was a reminder of one thing: food.

After five minutes, Vague Henri spoke.

"I was just . . ." His sentence trailed off. The other two waited. "This is one end of a tunnel . . ." Again he paused. "But there has to be more than one way to get into a tunnel . . ." His voice faltered again. "Just a thought."

"A *thought*?" said Kleist. "Don't flatter yourself."

Henri did not reply, but Cale got to his feet.

"Light the candle."

It took a minute for Kleist with his moss and flint, but soon they were able to see again. Cale sank onto his haunches.

"Give it to Henri and get on my shoulders."

Kleist handed the candle over and then clambered onto Cale's back and settled his legs around his neck. With a grunt Cale pushed him into the air.

"Take the light."

Kleist did as he was told.

"Now look up by the roof."

Kleist raised the candle, looking for something without any idea what it was. "Yes!" he shouted.

"Be quiet, damn you!"

"It's a hatch," he whispered, overjoyed.

"Can you reach it?"

"Yes. I don't even have to stretch hardly."

"Be careful—just a gentle push. There might be someone around."

Kleist placed his palm at the nearest edge of the hatch and pushed.

"It moved."

"Try and push it away. Try and see something."

There was a scraping sound.

"Nothing. It's dark. I'll put the candle up there." There was a pause. "I still can't see much."

"Can you get up?"

"If you push my feet. When I grab the edge. Now!"

Cale grabbed his feet and heaved upward. Kleist slowly moved and then pulled away to the sound of the hatch clattering above them.

"Keep it quiet!" hissed Cale.

But Kleist was gone.

Cale and Henri waited in the dark, illuminated by the faint glow from the hatch above. Even this grew dim as Kleist searched his surroundings. Then it went dark.

"Do you think we can trust him not to clear off?"

"Well," said Vague Henri. "I think." He paused. "Probably."

But he didn't finish. The light appeared in the hatch again, followed by Kleist's head.

"It's some sort of room," he whispered. "But I can see light through another hatch."

"Get on my shoulders," said Cale to Vague Henri.

"What about you?"

"I'll be fine—just both of you wait up there to pull me up."

Vague Henri was much lighter than Kleist, and it was easy enough to lift him up to the hatch, where Kleist could haul him through.

"Hang the candle as far down as you can."

Kleist lowered himself while Vague Henri held on to his feet.

Cale went to the wall of the tunnel, reached up to a crack in the wall and pulled himself up. Then he found another and another until he was able to reach toward Kleist's hand.

They clasped each other's wrists.

"You all right for this?"

"Worry about yourself, Cale. I'm going to give Henri the candle."

He turned his hand back to Vague Henri, half his body length dangling out of the hatch, and the light disappeared back up into the darkness.

"On my count of three." He paused. "One, two, three."

Cale let go and swung out into midair—a hefty grunt from Kleist as he took his weight. He hung for a moment, waiting for the swinging to stop. Then with his free arm he reached up and pulled on Kleist's shoulder as Henri heaved on his legs. They shifted only six inches, but it was enough for Cale to grab the edge of the hatch and ease the weight on Kleist and Henri. He held for a moment and then was pulled through the hatch and onto the wooden floor.

The three of them lay there panting with the effort. Then Cale stood up.

"Show me the other hatch."

Getting to his feet, Kleist picked up the now nearly vanished candle and went over to the other side of a room that looked to Cale to be about twenty feet by fifteen.

Kleist bent down next to a hatch followed by the other two. There was, as he'd said, a crack to one side. Cale put his eye as close as he could, but beyond the fact that there was light, he was able to see nothing in detail. Then he put his ear to the crack.

"What do you . . . ?"

"Be quiet!" hissed Cale.

He kept his ear to the floor for a good two minutes. Then he sat up and went to the hatch. There was no obvious way to lift it, so he felt around the edges until he found enough of a gap to pull the hatch itself toward the fixed lip. It gave slightly, making a grating noise. Cale winced with irritation. There wasn't room enough for even a finger, so he had to push his fingernails into the wood to get any kind of purchase. It hurt as he pulled at the edge, but then he eased it upward enough to get his hand underneath. He lifted the hatch away from its frame and then all three of them looked down.

About fifteen feet below them was a sight unlike anything they had ever experienced; indeed, more than they had ever dreamed of.

3

Absolutely still, absolutely silent, the three boys continued to stare down into the kitchen, for that was what it was. Every surface was covered in plates of food: there was roast chicken with its crispy skin rubbed in salt and ground pepper, beef in thick slices, pork with crackling so crisp to bite it would make the sound of a dry stick being broken. There was bread, sliced thick with the crust so dark it was almost black in places; there were plates piled high with onions tinged with purple, and rice with fruits, fat raisins and apples. And there were puddings: meringues like mountains, custards of a deep yellow and bowls of clotted cream.

The boys had no words for most of what they saw: why have a word for custard when you had never even imagined the existence of such a thing, or think that the slabs of beef and breasts of sliced chicken bore any relation to the scraps of giblets and feet and brain boiled together and minced into offal tubes that were their only taste of meat. Think of how strange the colors and sights of the world would be for a blind man abruptly made to see, or a man deaf from birth hearing the playing of a hundred flutes.

But confused and amazed as they were, hunger drove them out of the hatch like monkeys, swinging away from the table and into the middle of the kitchen. All three stood astonished at the abundance around them. Even Cale almost forgot that the hatch had to be closed. In a daze of smells and sweet colors he took some of the plates off the table and stood up on it. With his hands stretched to their farthest limit, he was just able to push the hatch across so that it fell into place.

By the time he was back on the floor, the other two were already plundering the food with the skill of long-practiced scavengers. They took only one thing from each place and rearranged the gap so it appeared that nothing was gone. They couldn't resist a few bits of chicken or bread, but most of what they took went into the forbidden pockets that they had stitched into their cassocks to hide any contraband they came across that could be easily stolen and hidden.

Cale felt sick with the rich smells that seemed to surge in his brain and make him want to faint, as if they were baited with strange vapors.

"Don't eat. Just take what you can hide." He was instructing himself as much as the others. He took his share and hid what he filched, but there were few pockets to hide it in. They had no need of many hiding places, the pickings in their ordinary life being so thin and scanty.

"We have to get out. Now." Cale walked toward the door. As if they had been woken from a deep sleep, Kleist and Vague Henri began to realize how much danger they were in. Cale listened at the door for a moment and then eased it open. It was a corridor.

"God knows where we are," he said. "But we have to find cover." With that he pulled the door open and walked out, the others warily following.

They moved quickly, keeping close to the walls. Within a few yards they came across a staircase leading upward. Cale shook his head as Vague Henri made his way over to it. "We need to find a window or get outside and see if we can find out where we are. We have to get back to the sleepshed before candle out or they'll know we're gone." They moved on, but as they approached a door on the left it began to open.

In an instant they turned and fled back to the stairs and ran to the top. All three flattened themselves on the landing as they heard voices pass beneath them along the corridor. They heard the sound of another door being opened, and Cale raised his head, only to see a figure heading into the kitchen from which they had just come. Vague Henri moved beside him. He looked confused and afraid.

"Those voices," he whispered. "What was wrong with them?"

Cale shook his head, but he too had noticed how strange they were and felt a peculiar movement in his stomach. He stood up, scanning the place where they were hiding. There was nowhere to go except through a door behind them. Quickly he turned the handle and eased into the room behind it. Except that it wasn't a room. It was a balcony of some kind with a low wall ten feet or so from the door. Cale crawled toward it with the others doing the same until they were all crouched behind the wall.

From the space overlooked by the balcony there was a burst of laughter and applause.

It was not just the laughter that spooked the three boys—for all that laughter was something rarely heard in that place and never in such volume and with such easy joy—it was much more the pitch and sound of it. Like the voices they had heard in the corridor a few moments before, it set off an alien thrill deep inside them.

"Look and see," whispered Vague Henri.

"No," mouthed Cale.

"You must, or I will."

Cale grabbed his wrist and squeezed.

"If we're caught, we're dead."

Vague Henri, reluctant, eased back against the balcony wall. There was another burst of laughter, but this time Cale kept his eye on Vague Henri. Then he noticed that Kleist had moved onto his knees and was looking down, fascinated at the source of so much careless joy. Laughter for an acolyte was something droll, laconic, bitter. Cale tried to pull him back, but Kleist was much stronger than Vague Henri, and it was impossible to budge him without using so much force that they would have revealed themselves instantly.

Cale slowly raised his head over the balcony wall and looked down on something far more shocking and disturbing than the sight of the food in the kitchen. It was as if everything inside him were being battered with a hundred of the Redeemers' nail sticks.

Below in a large hall were about a dozen tables, all covered in the same food they'd seen in the kitchen. The tables were arranged in a circle so that everyone seated could see one another, and it seemed obvious that two girls dressed in pure white were the cause of this celebration. One of these girls in particular was striking, with long dark hair and deep green eyes. She was beautiful but also as plump as a cushion. In the middle of the circle of tables was a large pool full of hot water, mists of steam clinging to its surface. It was the half dozen or so girls in the pool who froze the wide-eyed expression on Cale's and Kleist's faces, a look as shocked and bewildered as if they had come upon a sight of heaven itself.

The girls in the pool were naked. They were pink or brown according to their origin, but all were curved and voluptuous. But it was not their nakedness that so amazed the boys so much as the fact that they had never seen a woman before.

Who could capture what they felt? The poet does not exist who could put it into words, the terrible joy, the shock and awe.

There was a gasp, this time from Vague Henri, who now was beside the two others.

The noise brought Cale back to his right mind. He slumped down and rested against the wall. In a few seconds the others, pale and distraught, did the same.

"Wonderful," whispered Vague Henri to himself. "Wonderful, wonderful, most wonderful."

"We have to go or we're dead."

Cale slipped onto his hands and knees and crawled to the door, the others following. They slipped out and crept to the edge of the landing and listened. Nothing. Then they made their way down the stairs and began to walk down the corridor. Luck was with them because there was nothing left of the skilled and cautious boys who had made their way to the balcony and the shocking scenes beneath. But in this shaken and enraptured state they made it to a doorway that led to another corridor. They turned to the left because they had no better reason to go to the right.

Now the three of them, with just half an hour to get back to the sleepshed, broke into a run, but in less than a minute they came to a sharp turn. It was twenty feet long, and at the end was a thick door. Their faces fell in despair.

"Dear God!" whispered Vague Henri.

"In forty minutes they'll have the Gougers out looking for us."

"Well, it won't take them long, will it? Stuck in here."

"And then what? They won't let us tell what we've seen here," said Kleist.

"Then we have to leave," said Cale.

"Leave?"

"As in go away and never come back."

"We can't even get out of here," said Kleist, "and you're talking about escaping from the Sanctuary altogether."

"What choice do we—" But Cale's reply was cut short by the sound of the key turning in the lock of the door in front of them. It was a huge door and at least six inches thick, so there were a few seconds for them to find a hiding place. Except that there wasn't one.

Cale signaled the other two to flatten themselves against the wall where the opening door would hide them, if only until it was shut. But they had no choice: to run back was to be stuck where they were until their absence was discovered, followed by quick capture and a slow death.

The door swung open, the result of some effort if the swearing and groan of irritation were anything to go by. Accompanied by more bad-tempered muttering, the door moved toward them and then stopped. Then a small wedge of wood was forced under the door to keep it open. More cursing and groaning followed, and then there was the sound of a small cart being pushed down the corridor. Cale, who was on the edge side of the door, looked out and saw a familiar figure in a black cassock limping away as he pushed the cart and then disappeared around the corner. Cale signaled the others out and moved quickly through the door.

They were outside in the cold fog. There was another cart filled with coal waiting to be taken in. That was why Under Redeemer Smith, lazy bastard as always, had jammed the door open rather than lock it as he must have been instructed to do.

Normally they would have stolen as much coal as they could carry, but their pockets were full of food and they were too afraid in any case.

"Where are we?" asked Vague Henri.

"No idea," replied Cale. He moved down the ambo trying to get used to the fog and the dark in order to find a landmark. But now the relief at their deliverance was fading. They'd walked a long way in the tunnel. They could be anywhere in the Sanctuary and its maze of buildings and ambos and corridors.

Then a huge pair of feet loomed out of the fog. It was the great statue of the Hanged Redeemer they had left behind more than an hour ago.

Within less than five minutes they, separately, joined the queue for the sleepshed, more formally known as the Dormitory of the Lady of Perpetual Succor. What any of this meant they knew not and cared less. They began chanting along with the others: "What if I should die tonight? What if I should die tonight? What if I should die tonight?" The answer to this dismal question had been made pretty clear to the acolytes all their lives by the Redeemers: most of them would go to hell because of the disgusting black state of their souls and be burned for all eternity. For years when the subject of their dying in the middle of the night came up, and it came up often, Cale was frequently hauled to the front of the group, and the Redeemer in charge would raise his cassock up to reveal his naked back and show the bruises that covered it from nape to sacroiliac. The bruises were of many sizes, and while going through the various states of healing, his back was sometimes beautiful to behold with so many variations of blue and gray and green, vermilioned reds and almost golden purple yellows. "Look at these colors!"

the Redeemer would say. "Your souls, which should be as white as a turtle's wing, are worse than the blacks and purples on this boy's back. This is what all of you look like to God: purple and black. And if any one of you dies tonight, you don't need me to tell you what line you'll be forming. As for what's waiting at the end of that line—there are beasts to eat you and shit you out and eat you yet again. There are metal ovens waiting, heated red, and you'll be baked to cinders for an hour, then rendered down to fat, then kneaded by a devil, ash and lard together like an ugly dough, and then be born again and then be burned again and born and burned for all eternity."

Once, a visiting dignitary, one Redeemer Compton, who was opposed to Bosco, had witnessed this demonstration and also seen one of the beatings that had caused the bruises. "These boys," said Redeemer Compton, "are being shaped to fight the blasphemy of the Antagonists. Violence so extreme against a child no matter how much he has become the devil's playground will break his spirit long before it will make it tough enough to help us wipe their sacrilege from the sight of God."

"He is not unruly and he is very far from being the playground of the devil." Bosco, always so very guarded when it came to discussing Cale, was instantly angry with himself at being provoked even to so enigmatic an explanation.

"Then why do you allow this?"

"Do not ask the reason. Be satisfied."

"Tell me, Redeemer."

"I say I will not."

And at this, Redeemer Compton, wiser for once than Bosco, held his tongue, but later he instructed two of his paid squealers at the Sanctuary to pick up whatever they could about the purple-backed boy.

"What if I should die tonight? What if I should die tonight? What if I should die tonight?" As Cale and the others muttered their way to bed, the chant that years of repetition had rendered almost empty of meaning renewed the dreadful power it had had over them as young children, when they would lie awake all night convinced that merely the closing of their eyes would see them feeling the hot mouth of the beast or hearing the charred clash of the metal oven doors.

Within ten minutes the huge shed was full and the door locked as five hundred boys in absolute silence prepared to sleep in the vast, freezing and dimly lit barn. Then the candles were put out, and the boys began to prepare for a sleep that came quickly, for they had been awake since five o'clock that morning. The dormitory settled into a noisy mixture of snores, weeping, yelps and grunts as the boys fled into whatever comfort or horror waited for them in their dreams.

Three boys, of course, did not fall asleep quickly, nor did they do so for many hours.

4

Cale woke early. This had been his habit for as long as he could re-member. It gave him an entire hour to be on his own, as far as anyone could be alone with five hundred sleeping boys in the same room. But in the dark before dawn no one talked to him, watched him, told him what to do, threatened him or looked for an excuse to beat or even kill him. And even if he was hungry, he was at least warm under his blan-ket. And then, of course, he remembered the food. His pockets were full of it. It was reckless to reach for the cassock hanging by his bed, but he was driven by something irresistible, not just hunger, because he lived with that constantly, but delight, the thought, the unbearable pleasure of eating something that tasted so wonderful. Taking his time, he reached into his pocket and took the first thing he found there, a kind of plain biscuit with a custard layer, and shoved it in his mouth.

At first he thought he would go wild with delight, the flavors of sugar and butter exploding not only in his mouth but in his brain, in-deed, in his very soul. He chewed on and swallowed, pleasure beyond words.

And then, of course, he felt sick. He was no more used to food like this than an elephant is to flying through the air. Like a man dying of thirst or from lack of food, he needed to be fed stingy drops and mor-sels or his body would rebel and die of the very thing it so desperately needed. Cale lay there for half an hour and tried very hard not to vomit.

As he began to recover he could hear the sound of one of the Re-deemers walking his rounds before wake-up. The hard soles of his shoes clacked on the stone floor as he circled the sleeping boys. This went on for ten minutes. Then suddenly a quickening of pace and loud claps. GET UP! GET UP!

Cale, still queasy, eased himself upright and began to pull on his cassock, careful not to let anything spill from his overfull pockets as the five hundred groaned and staggered their way to their feet.

A few minutes later they marched through the rain to assemble in the great stone Basilica of Eternal Mercy, where they spent the next two hours muttering prayers in response to the ten Redeemers holding Mass, using words that had long ago become empty from repetition. Cale didn't mind this; he had learned as a small boy to sleep with his eyes open and mutter along with the rest, only a small part of his mind keeping wary, alert for Redeemers on the lookout for slackers.

Then it was breakfast, more gray porridge and dead men's feet, a kind of cake made from many kinds of animal and vegetable fat, usually rancid, and numerous varieties of seed. It was revolting but highly nutritious. It was only because of this disgusting mixture that the boys survived at all. The Redeemers wished them to have as little pleasure in life as possible, but their plans for the future, for the great war against the Antagonists, meant that the boys had to be strong. Those who lived, of course.

It was not until eight o'clock, as they queued for practice on the Field of Our Redeemer's Absolute Forgiveness, that the three were able to talk again.

"I feel sick," said Kleist.

"Me too," whispered Vague Henri.

"Nearly threw up," admitted Cale.

"We're going to have to hide it."

"Or throw it away."

"You'll get used to it," said Cale. "Anyway, I'll have yours if you don't want it."

"I have to fold the vestments after practice," said Vague Henri. "Give me the food and I'll hide it in there."

"Talking. You boys. Talking." In his usual, almost miraculous, way, Redeemer Malik had appeared behind them. It was unwise to be doing anything wrong when Malik was around, because of his strange ability to creep up on people. His unannounced taking over of the training session from Redeemer Fitzsimmons, known universally as Fitz the Shits because of the dysentery that had plagued him since his time in the Fen campaigns, was just bad luck. "I want two hundred," said Malik, fetching Kleist a hefty clip round the back of his head. He made the entire line, not just the three of them, get down on their knuckles and start to do their allotted press-ups. "Not you, Cale," said Malik. "Balance on your hands." Cale moved easily into a handstand and started to push up and down, up and down. With the exception of Kleist, the faces of the others in the line were already frowning under the strain, but Cale kept moving up and down as if he might never stop, his eyes blank, a thousand miles away. Kleist merely looked bored, though completely at ease, while moving twice as fast as the others. When the last of them had finished, exhausted and in pain, Malik made Cale do twenty more for showing bodily pride. "I told you to balance on your hands, not do press-ups as well. The pride of a boy is a tasty snack for the devil." This was a moral lesson lost on the acolytes in front of him, who stared at him blankly: the experience of a light but refreshing meal between other meals, tasty or otherwise, was something they had never imagined, let alone experienced.

When the bell rang to signal the end of practice, five hundred boys walked as slowly as they dared back to the basilica for morning prayers. As they passed by the alley leading into the back of the great building, the three boys slipped away. They gave all the food in their pockets to Vague Henri, and then Kleist and Cale rejoined the long queue that jammed the square in front of the basilica.

Meanwhile, Vague Henri shoved the latch on the sacristy door with his shoulders, his hands being full of bread, meat and cake. He pushed it open and listened out for Redeemers. He moved into the dark brown of the dressing place, ready to back out if he saw anything. It seemed to be empty. Now he rushed over to one of the cupboards, but he had to dump some of the food onto the floor in order to open it. A bit of dirt, he reflected, never harmed anyone. With the door open, he reached inside the cupboard and lifted a plank of wood from the floor. Underneath was a large space in which Vague Henri kept his belongings—all of them forbidden. The acolytes were not permitted to own anything, in case it made them, as Redeemer Pig put it, "lust after the material things of this world." (Pig, it should be added, was not his real name, which was Redeemer Glebe.)

It was Glebe's voice that now rang out behind him.

"Who's that?"

Three-quarters hidden by the cupboard door, Vague Henri shoveled the food in his arms and the chicken legs and cake from the floor into the cupboard and, standing up, shut the door.

"I beg your pardon, Redeemer?"

"Oh, it's you," said Glebe. "What are you doing?"

"What am I doing, Redeemer?"

"Yes," said Glebe irritably.

"I . . . uh . . . well." Vague Henri looked round as if for inspiration. He seemed to find it somewhere up in the roof.

"I was . . . putting away the long habiliment left by Redeemer Bent." Redeemer Bent was certainly mad, but his reputation for forgetfulness was largely due to the fact that whenever they got the chance the acolytes blamed him for everything that was misplaced or was questionable about whatever they were doing. If ever they were caught doing something or being somewhere that they shouldn't, the acolytes' first line of defense was that they were there at the command of Redeemer Bent, whose poor short-term memory could be relied upon not to contradict them.

"Bring me my habiliments."

Vague Henri looked at Glebe as if he had never heard of such things.

"Well? What?" said Glebe.

"Habiliments?" asked Vague Henri. As Glebe was about to step forward and give him a clout, Vague Henri said brightly, "Of course,

Redeemer." He turned and walked over to another of the cupboards and flung it open as if with huge enthusiasm.

"Black or white, Redeemer?"

"What's the matter with you?"

"The matter, Redeemer?"

"Yes, you idiot. Why would I wear black habiliments on a weekday during the month of the dead?"

"On a weekday?" said Vague Henri as if astonished by such a notion. "Of course not, Redeemer. You'll need a thrannock, though."

"What are you talking about?" Glebe's querulous tone was also uncertain. There were hundreds of ceremonial robes and ornaments, many having fallen into disuse over the thousand years since the founding of the Sanctuary. He had, it was clear, never heard of the thrannock, but that didn't mean such a thing did not exist.

Vague Henri went over to a drawer and pulled it open, watched by Redeemer Glebe. He searched for a moment and then pulled out a necklace made of tiny beads, on the end of which was a small square made out of sacking. "It's to be worn on Martyr Fulton's day."

"I've never worn anything like that before," said Glebe, still uncertain. He walked over to the Ecclesiasticum and opened it at that day's date. It was, indeed, Martyr Fulton's day, but then there were so many martyrs and not enough days—as a result, some of the minor ones were celebrated only every twenty years or so. Glebe sniffed irritably.

"Get a move on. We're late."

With due solemnity, Vague Henri placed the thrannock around Glebe's neck and helped him into the long, white, elaborately decorated habiliment. This done, he followed Glebe out into the basilica proper for morning prayers, and spent the next half an hour pleasurably reliving the episode with the thrannock, something that did not exist outside Vague Henri's imagination. He had no idea what the square of sack on the end of the beaded string was for, but there were numerous such unknown bits and bobs in the sacristy whose religious significance had been long forgotten. Nevertheless, he had, and not for the first time, taken an enormous risk just for the pleasure of making a fool out of a Redeemer. If he were ever found out, they would have the hide off his back. And this was no figure of speech.

His nickname, given to him by Cale, had caught on, but only the two of them realized what it truly meant. No one except Cale realized that Henri's elusive way of answering or repeating any question he was asked was not due to his inability to understand what was said to him, or to give clear replies, but merely a way of defying the Redeemers by pushing his response to them to the very limit of their not very great tolerance. It was because Cale had come to see what Henri was up to and admire its spectacular recklessness that he had broken one of his most important rules: make no friends, allow no one to make friends with you.

At that moment Cale was making his way into a spare pew in Basilica Number Four, looking forward to catching up on his sleep during the Prayers of Abasement. He had perfected the art of dozing while lambasting himself for his sins, sins of turpitude, of delectatio morosa, sins of gaudium, of desiderium, sins of desire efficacious and inefficacious. In unison the five hundred children in Basilica Four vowed never to commit transgressions that would have been impossible for them even if they had known what they were: five-year-olds swore solemnly never to covet their neighbor's wife, nine-year-olds vowed that under no circumstances would they carve graven images and fourteen-year-olds promised not to worship these images even if they *did* carve them. All of this under pain of God punishing their children even to the third or fourth generation. After a satisfying forty-five-minute doze, the Mass ended and Cale filed out silently with the others and made his way back to the far end of the training field.

The field was never empty during the day now. The huge increase in the number of acolytes under instruction in the last five years had meant that almost everything now was done in shifts: training, eating, washing, worship. For those thought to be falling behind, training took place even at night, when it was particularly hated because of the terrible cold, the wind off the Scablands like a knife even in summer. It was no secret that this increase in acolytes was to provide more troops for the war against the Antagonists. Cale knew that many of those who left the Sanctuary were not going permanently to the Eastern Front but were being held most of the time in reserve and rotated for six months to either front, with up to a year or longer back in reserve in between. He knew this because Bosco had told him.

"You may ask two questions," said Bosco after he had informed him about this strange deployment. Cale had considered for a moment.

"The time they spend in reserve, Lord—do you plan to increase it and keep on increasing it?"

"Yes," said Bosco. "Second question."

"I don't need a second question," replied Cale.

"Really? You'd better be right, then, hadn't you?"

"I heard Redeemer Compton say to you that there was stalemate at the fronts."

"Yes, I could see you earwigging at the time."

"And yet you both talked around it as if it wasn't a problem."

"Go on."

"You've trained a girt number of priests militant in the last five years—too many. You're trying to give them a go at the fighting, but you don't want the Antagonists to know that you've been building up your forces. That's why the time in reserve has been increasing. We're always being told that there are Antagonist traitors everywhere at the fronts. Is that true?"

"Ah." Bosco smiled, not a pleasant sight. "A second question while all the time boasting that you needed only one. Your vanity will destroy you, boy, and I don't mean that for the good of your soul. I have . . ." He stopped, and it was as if he were uncertain what to say next, something that Cale had never seen before. It was disturbing. "I have *expectations* of you. Demands will be made. It would be much better if you were thrown off the walls of this place with a millstone round your neck than if you failed to meet those demands and those expectations. And it is your pride that most worries me. Every other Redeemer from here to eternity will tell you that pride is the cause of all the other twenty-eight deadly sins, but I have bigger fish to fry than your soul. It distorts your judgment and makes you put yourself in situations that you could have avoided. I gave you two questions, and for no reason but vain superbia you wanted to best me and risked a punishment for failing that you need not have risked. It makes you weak in such a way that I wonder whether you have deserved my protection all these years." He stared at Cale, and Cale stared at the floor, all the while hating and sneering at the idea of Bosco protecting him. Strange and perilous thoughts went through his mind as he waited.

"The answer to your second question is that there are Antagonist spies and intelligencers at the fronts, but only a few. Enough, however."

Cale kept his eyes on the floor. Pretend not to resist. Minimize the punishment. Yet all the while the raging resentment that Bosco was right and that he might have avoided what was coming.

"You are building up reserves for a great attack on both fronts, and yet you must keep numbers there at more or less the same level or they'll see what's coming. You want the reserves to get experience, but there are now too many—so they have to spend more time away from the front. And yet you need many more soldiers to finish off the Antagonists, but they must be battle-hardened and there aren't enough battles. You're in a bind, Lord."

"Your solution?"

"I'll need time, Redeemer. There may not be a solution that isn't another problem."

Bosco laughed.

"Let me tell you, boy, the solution to every problem is *always* another problem."

Then, without warning, Bosco lashed out at Cale. Cale blocked it as easily as if it were aimed by an old man. They looked at each other.

"Put your hand down."

Cale did as he was told.

"I will hit you again in a moment," said Bosco softly, "and when I do you will not move your hands and you will not move your head. You will let me strike you. You will allow it. You will consent."

Cale waited. Bosco this time made a clear show of his preparations for the blow. Then he hit out again. Cale flinched, but the blow did not land. Bosco's hand stopped a fraction from Cale's face. "Don't you move, boy." Bosco drew his hand back and again lashed out. Yet again Cale flinched. "DON'T YOU MOVE!" screamed Bosco, his face red with rage except for two very small white spots in the center of his cheeks that grew whiter as the skin on his face went ever darker. Then another blow, but this one landed as Cale stood still as stone. Then another and another. Then a blow so hard it dropped a stunned Cale to the floor. "Get up," so softly that he was barely audible. Cale got to his feet, shaking as if from intense cold. Then the blow. He fell again, stood up; another blow, and then he got to his feet again. Bosco changed hands. With his weaker left it took five more blows before Cale fell to the floor again. Bosco stared down at him as he started to get to his feet. Both of them were shaking now. "Stay where you are." Bosco was almost whispering. "If you get up, I won't answer for what will happen. I'm going." He seemed almost bewildered, exhausted by the dreadful intensity of his anger. "Wait for five minutes and then leave." Then Bosco went to the door and was gone.

For a full minute Cale did not move. Then he was sick. It took another minute of rest and then three more to clean up the mess. Then, slowly, shaking as if he might never reach it, he got out into the corridor and, supporting himself by feeling his way along the wall, made his way out into one of the blind alleys off a courtyard and sat down.

"KEEP YOUR WAIST STRAIGHT! NO! NO! NO!" Cale snapped back from what had become almost a trance. The noises and sights of the training field had vanished as he'd gone missing in his memories of the past. It was something that was happening to him more often, but it was not a good idea to become so distracted in a place like the Sanctuary. You paid attention here or pretty quickly something unpleasant happened. All around him the sights and sounds of training were vivid now. A line of twenty acolytes, soon to leave, were practicing an attack in formation. Redeemer Gil, known as Gil the Gorilla because of his ugliness and terrible strength, was complaining routinely about the sloppiness of his trainees: "Have the gates of death been shown to you, Gavin?" he said wearily. "They will be if you keep exposing your left side like that." The acolytes in the line smiled at Gavin's discomfort. For all his physical power and brute ugliness, Redeemer Gil was as close to being a decent man as a Redeemer ever got. Except for Redeemer Navratil, and he was a peculiar case. "Night training for you," Gil said to the hapless Gavin. The boy next to him laughed. "And you can join him, Gregor. And you, Holdaway."

Just beyond the line a small boy, no more than seven years old, was hanging by his arms from a wooden frame about seven feet off the ground. A belt of heavy weights in canvas was strapped around his shins and he was grimacing, tears of pain rolling down his contorted face. The Under Redeemer beneath him kept insisting that unless he raised his weighted feet to make a perfect L-shape every time, none of his efforts would count. "Crying won't do any good—only doing it right will do any good." As the child struggled to do as he was told, Cale noticed the extreme definition of the six muscles of his stomach as he strained, bulging and powerful as those of a grown man. "Four!" counted the Under Redeemer.

Cale walked on past boys of five, some laughing like little boys anywhere, and eighteen-year-olds who looked like middle-aged men. There were groups of eighty or so practicing pushing one another back and forth, shouting in a rhythm as if they were one giant grunting against another; an additional rank of five hundred or so marched in formation without a sound, turning as one to the signaling of flags: left then right, then stopping dead, then retreating, then stopping again and moving forward. By now Cale was about fifty yards from the great wall around the Sanctuary, at the edge of the archery range where Kleist was giving lip to a squad of ten acolytes easily four years older than himself. He was abusing them for their uselessness, their ugliness, their lack of skill, the poor quality of their teeth and the fact that their eyes were too close together. He stopped only when he saw Cale.

"You're late," he said. "Lucky for you that Primo is sick or he'd have your hide."

"You could always try, if you like."

"Me? I couldn't care if you were here or not. Your loss."

Cale's faint shrug in response indicated a reluctant acknowledgment that this was probably true. Kleist was stripped to the waist, revealing a remarkable, if odd, body shape. He seemed to be all back and shoulders, as if the upper body of an adult male had been inserted between the legs and head of a fourteen-year-old. His right arm and shoulder in particular were so much more knotted with muscle than his left side that he looked almost deformed.

"Right," said Kleist, "let's have a look at what's wrong." He was clearly enjoying the chance to demonstrate his sense of superiority and very keen that Cale should know he was enjoying it too.

Cale raised the longbow Kleist had handed him, pulled back the drawstring to his cheek, aimed, held for a second, then loosed the arrow to its target eighty yards away. He groaned even as it left the bow. The arrow arced toward the target, the size and shape of a man's body, and missed by several feet.

"Shit!"

"Oh dear, oh dear," said Kleist, "I haven't seen anything like that since . . . Well, I can't remember. You used to be adequate—where on earth did you pick up a set of shanks like that from?"

"Just tell me what I need to do to put them right."

"Oh, that's easy enough. You're plucking the bowstring when you should just be letting it go—like this." He twanged at the string of his own bow to show what Cale was doing wrong and then showed him, with enormous pleasure, how it should be done. "You're also opening your mouth when you shoot and dropping the elbow of your string arm before you let loose." Cale started to protest. "And," interrupted Kleist, "you're letting your string hand creep forward at the same time."

"All right, I get the point. Just talk me through it. I've just got into some bad habits, that's all."

Kleist drew in his breath through his teeth as melodramatically as possible.

"I'm not sure, myself, if it's as simple as a few bad habits. I think you're probably a choker." He pointed to his head with a finger. "I think you've lost it up here, mate. Now that I think about it, yours is the worst case of the yips I've ever seen."

"You just made that up."

"You've got the yips all right, the staggers, the twitches. No known cure. All that mouth gaping and elbow dropping—just an exterior mark of the state of your soul. The real problem's in your spirit." Kleist put an arrow in his bow, drew back the string and let it loose in one elegant movement. It arced beautifully and landed with a satisfying *thwack* in the chest of the target. "You see, perfect—an outward sign of inward grace."

By now Cale was laughing. He turned back to the quiver of arrows lying on the bench behind him, but as he did so he saw Bosco walking through the middle of the field and approach Redeemer Gil, who immediately gestured an acolyte forward. Cale heard a soft "Zut!" behind him and turned his head to see Kleist furtively aiming his bow at the distant Bosco and making the sound of an arrow on its way.

"Go on. I dare you."

Kleist laughed and turned back to his pupils sitting and talking some distance away. One of them, Donovan, had as usual taken advantage of any pause to begin sermonizing on the evils of the Antagonists. "They don't believe in a purgatory where you can burn away your sins and then go to heaven. They believe in justification by faith." There was a gasp of disbelief from some of the acolytes who were listening. "They claim that each one of us is saved or damned by the unalterable choice of the Redeemer and there is nothing you can do about it. And they take the tunes from drinking songs and use them for their hymns. The Hanged Redeemer that they believe in never existed, and so they will die in their sins because they have a horror of confession, and so will depart this life with all their transgressions printed on their souls and be damned."

"Shut your gob, Donovan," said Kleist, "and get back to work."

Once the acolyte had left with his message for Cale, Bosco waved Redeemer Gil to one side so they could not be heard.

"There are rumors that the Antagonists are talking to the Laconic mercenaries."

"Are they solid?"

"They're solid by the standard of rumors."

"Then we should be worried." A thought struck Gil. "They'll need ten thousand or more to break us. How will they pay?"

"The Antagonists have found silver mines at Laurium. Not a rumor."

"Then God help us. Even we have no more than a few thousand troops . . . three, maybe . . . capable of going up against Laconic hired men. Their reputation isn't exaggerated."

"God helps those who help themselves. If we cannot deal with men who fight only for money and not the glory of God, then we deserve to fail. It's a test and to be expected." He smiled. "In spite of dungeon, fire and sword—isn't that right, Redeemer?"

"Well, My Lord Militant, if it is a test, it's one I don't know how to pass, and if *I* don't—pardon the sin of pride—there's no other Redeemer who does."

"Are you quite sure? About the sin of pride, I mean."

"What are you saying? It's not necessary to be obscure with me. I deserve better at your hands."

"Of course. My apologies for my own presumption." He beat himself gently on the chest three times. "*Mea culpa. Mea culpa. Mea maxima culpa.* I have been expecting this, or something like it, for some time. I have always felt that our faith would be tested and tested harshly. The Redeemer was sent to save us and mankind replied to that divine gift by hanging my love from a gibbet." His eyes began to mist over as he stared into the distance as if at something he had witnessed himself, though a millennium had passed since the Redeemer's execution. He sighed deeply again as if at a terrible and recent grief and then looked directly at Gil. "I can't say more." He touched his arm lightly and with true affection. "Except that if this report is true, then I haven't been idle in my search for an end to the apostasy of the Antagonists and to putting right the awful crime of doing murder to the only messenger of God." He smiled at Gil. "There is a new tactic."

"I don't understand."

"Not a military tactic—a new way of seeing things. We should no longer think just of the problem of the Antagonists—but of an ultimate solution to the problem of human evil itself."

He urged Gil closer and lowered his voice still further.

"For too long we have been ready to think only about the Antagonist heresy and our war with them—what they do, what they don't do. We have forgotten that they're of secondary importance to our purpose to allow no god but the One True God and no faith but the One True Faith. We've allowed ourselves to become stuck in this war as if it were an end in itself—we have let it become one squabble in a world filled with squabbles."

"Forgive me, Lord, but the Eastern Front covers a thousand miles and the dead can be numbered in hundreds of thousands—that's not a squabble."

"We are not the Materazzi or the Janes, interested in war only for gain or power. But that's all we have become. One power amongst many in the war of all against all because, like them, we desire victory but fear defeat."

"It's sensible to be leery of defeat."

"We are the representatives of God on earth through His Redeemer. There is a single purpose to our existence and we've forgotten it because we're afraid. So things must change: better to fall once than be forever falling. Either we believe that we have God on our side or we do not. If that's what we truly believe rather than what we affect to believe, then it follows that we must pursue absolute victory or none at all."

"If you say so, Lord."

Bosco laughed, a sweet sound, genuinely amused.

"I do say so, friend."

Both Cale and Kleist were aware of the acolyte as he walked up to them, pleased at the chance to deliver what he clearly felt was unpleasant news. As he started to speak, Kleist interrupted.

"What do you want, Salk? I'm busy."

This put Salk off the slow malice with which he'd intended to spin out his news.

"Tough titty, Kleist. It's got nothing to do with you. Redeemer Bosco wants to see Cale in his rooms after night prayers."

"Fine," said Kleist, as if this were utterly routine. "Now piss off."

Taken off guard both by the hostile lack of curiosity and by the fact that Cale was staring at him oddly, Salk spat on the ground to show his own indifference and walked away. Cale and Kleist looked at each other. Because Cale was Bosco's zealot, calls for him to go and see the Lord Militant, something that would have terrified any other boy, were not uncommon. What was unusual, and therefore disturbing given the events of the day before, was that Cale had been called to his private rooms and not until late evening. This had never happened before.

"What if he knows?" said Kleist.

"Then we'd be in the House of Special Purpose already."

"It'd be just like Bosco to make us think that."

"I suppose. But there's nothing we can do about it now." Cale drew back the bow, held for a second and then loosed the arrow. It arced toward the target and missed by a good twelve inches.

The three had already agreed to escape dinner. Normally to be anywhere but where you were supposed to be was dangerous, but it was
unheard of for an acolyte to be absent from a mealtime because they
were always hungry, however repellent the food. As a result, the Redeemers were at their least vigilant at the evening meal, something that
made it easier for Cale and Kleist to hide behind Basilica Number Four
and wait for Vague Henri to bring them their food from the sacristy.
They ate the food more slowly this time, and not much of it, but ten
minutes later they were all sick.

Half an hour later Cale was waiting in the dark corridor outside the
Lord Militant's rooms. An hour later he was still there. Then the cast-
iron door opened and the tall figure of Bosco stood watching him.

"Come in."

Cale followed him into rooms only slightly less gloomy than the
corridor. If he had expected to see anything of the private man after all
these years, Cale would have been disappointed. There were doors
leading off the room he entered, but they were shut and all there was
to see was a study and with little in it. Bosco sat down behind his desk
and examined a piece of paper in front of him. Cale stood and waited,
knowing that it might be a requisition for the withdrawal of a dozen
blue sacks or his own death warrant.

After a few minutes Bosco spoke, but without looking up and in a
tone of mild inquiry.

"Is there anything you want to tell me?"

"No, Lord," replied Cale.

Still Bosco did not look up.

"If you lie to me, there's nothing I can do to save you." He looked
Cale straight in the eyes, his gaze infinitely cold and infinitely black. It
was death itself looking at him. "So, I ask you again. Is there anything
you want to tell me?"

Holding his gaze, Cale replied. "No, Lord."

The Lord Militant did not look away, and Cale felt his will begin to dissolve as if some acid were being poured over his very soul. A horrible desire to confess began to grow in his throat. It was dread, the knowledge that had been with him since he was a small boy, that the Redeemer in front of him was capable of anything, that pain and suffering were the constant companions of this man, that anything that lived grew quiet in his presence.

Bosco looked back at the paper in front of him and signed his name. Then he folded the paper and sealed it with red wax. He handed it to Cale.

"Take this to the Lord of Discipline."

A cold wind swept through Cale.

"Now?"

"Yes. Now."

"It's dark. The dorm will be locked in a few minutes."

"Never mind about that. It's been seen to."

Without looking up, Redeemer Bosco began writing again.

Cale did not move. The Redeemer looked up again.

Instinct fought instinct in Cale. If he confessed, the Redeemer might help. He was his zealot after all. He might save him. But other creatures in Cale's soul were screaming at him, "Never confess! Never admit guilt! Never! Always deny everything. Always."

Cale turned and walked to the door, fighting his urge to run. Once outside he closed the iron door and stared back into the room as if it were as transparent as glass, eyes filled with hatred and loathing.

He walked to the nearest adjoining corridor and stopped under the dim light from a candle set into the wall. He knew that it was a deliberate test by Bosco, that he was offering him the chance to open the letter, an offense that would lead to his immediate execution. If Bosco knew about yesterday, it was possible this was an instruction to the Lord of Discipline to have him killed—it would be Bosco's way to arrange for Cale to deliver his own death warrant. But it might be nothing, just another of the endless attempts by the Lord Militant to test him whenever he could.

He took a deep breath and tried to see things as they were, uncolored by fear. It was, of course, obvious: there might be nothing deadly in this letter, although its consequences were bound to be unpleasant and painful—but to open it would mean certain death. With that, he started walking toward the office of the Lord of Discipline, though all the time there were hammers beating in his brain about what he would do if the worse came to the worst.

Within ten minutes, having once become briefly lost in the warren of corridors, he approached the Chamber of Salvation. For a moment in the deep gloom he stood in front of the great door, heart beating with fear and anger. Then he noticed it was unlocked and very slightly ajar.

Cale paused for a moment, thinking about what to do. He looked at the document he was holding and then pushed the door open enough so that he could see inside. At the far side of the room he could see the Lord of Discipline bent over something and singing to himself.

> Faith of our fathers, living still
> In spite of dungeons, fire, and sword
> Da dum de dum de dum de dum dum
> Da dum de dum de dum de dum
> Faith of our fathers, dum de dum
> We will be true to thee till death.

Then he stopped singing and humming, needing to concentrate particularly hard on something. That part of the room was as well lit as anything could be by candlelight, and it seemed as if the Lord of Discipline was enclosing the light in a kind of dome of warm brightness bounded by the shape of his body. As Cale's eyes adjusted, he could see that the Lord was leaning over a wooden table about six feet by two and there was something lying on it, though the end of it was wrapped in cloth. Then the humming started again, and the Lord of Discipline turned aside and dropped something small and hard onto an iron plate. Picking up a pair of scissors next to it, he turned back to his work.

> How sweet would be their children's fate,
> If they, like them, could die for thee!
> Da dum de dum de dum de dum de dum
> Da dum de dum de dum de dum

Cale moved the door farther ajar. Over in the darkest part of the room he could see another table, also with something lying on it, but this time obscured by the gloom. Then the Lord of Discipline stood upright again and walked over to a low cupboard on his right and began rooting about in a drawer. Cale just stared, unable to grasp what was on the table even though he could now see quite clearly what the Lord had been doing. On the table was a body on which the Lord of Discipline was performing a dissection. The chest had been cut open with great skill and down all the way to the lower stomach. Each section of skin and muscle had been carefully, precisely, cut back and held away from the incision with some sort of weight. What had so shocked Cale, apart from the sight of a body displayed in this way, what had made it so difficult to take, despite the fact that he had seen many dead bodies before, was that this was a girl. And she was not dead. Her left hand hanging over the side of the table twitched every few seconds as the Lord of Discipline kept rooting in the drawer, still humming to himself.

Cale felt as if spiders were crawling along the skin of his back. And then he heard a groan. The light no longer held in by the Lord of Discipline, he could now see what was on the other table. It was another girl, tied and gagged, trying to call out. And he knew her. She was the more striking of the two girls who had been dressed in white and laughing with delight at the center of the celebrations the day before.

The Lord of Discipline stopped humming, stood up straight and looked over at the girl.

"Be quiet, you," he said, almost gently.

Then he bent back down, started singing again and continued searching.

Cale had seen many dreadful things in his short life, terrible acts of cruelty, and had endured suffering almost beyond description. But for that moment he was stunned by what he was seeing and could not make sense of the dissected girl, her hand moving now less and less. And then, very slowly, Cale moved back out of the room, into the corridor and began to walk away as silently as he had come.

5

Ah!" said Redeemer Picarbo, the Lord of Discipline, to himself with deep satisfaction as he found what he was looking for, a long, thin skewer with a sharp pincer on the end. "Praise God." He tested it. *Snap! Snap!*

Satisfied, he turned back to the girl on the table and peered thoughtfully into the terrible but beautifully made wound. He reached down and, taking gentle hold of her hand, now lifeless, he placed it at her side. Then he took the skewer in his right hand and was about to continue when the girl in the corner started to try to scream again. This time he spoke more firmly, as if he had run out of patience.

"I told you to be quiet." He smiled. "Don't worry. I'll get to you in good time."

Whether he heard something or whether it was just the instinct born of long experience, the Lord of Discipline turned and raised his arm to block the blow aimed at the back of his head by Cale. The Redeemer caught Cale just below the wrist, a blow of such force that the half brick in his hand shot across the room and hit one of the cupboards with a crash, shattering into a dozen pieces. Cale was off balance, and the Lord of Discipline shoved him violently to the left, sending him flying into the base of the table where the bound girl was lying. She let out another muffled scream.

The Lord stared at Cale in utter astonishment. It was just not possible that an acolyte could attack him, not here, not in this place, not at any time at all. In a thousand years no such thing had ever been heard of. For a moment they stared at each other.

"Are you mad? What are you doing here?" demanded the Lord in a furious rage. "You will be hung for this . . . hung and quartered. You will be strangled and disemboweled while you are still alive and have your guts burned in front of you. And . . ."

He stopped after the fast torrent of words, again overtaken by astonishment that he had been attacked. Cale was white with shock. The Lord of Discipline turned to one side and picked up what looked like, and indeed was, a butcher's knife.

"I'll do it now, you little shit-bag." He moved toward the prone boy and raised the knife, standing over him, legs apart. And then Cale struck out with the skewer that had fallen beside him in the struggle, taking the Lord of Discipline on the inside of his thigh.

The Lord staggered back, not because he was hurt, but out of an even deeper astonishment than he thought it possible to feel.

"You struck me!" he said. Astonishment. Incredulity. Wonder. "You struck me." He looked down at the boy. "By God, you'll die slowly. By all that's—" The Lord stopped, quite suddenly, mid-flow. A puzzled expression came over his face, as if he had been asked a difficult question. He cocked his head to one side as if listening for something.

He sat down, slowly, as if pushed by a giant but benevolent hand. He looked at Cale as the boy moved back, shifting away from him. Then the Lord looked down at his legs. A large pool of blood was staining the skirt of his cassock. Cale suddenly seemed not to be either a frightened boy or an enraged murderer. An odd calm had fallen on him, and now he looked more like a curious child watching something of considerable but not overbearing interest. Redeemer Picarbo continued pulling at his cassock, bewildered, now revealing his undertrousers massively stained with red. He drew his hand back as if affronted, looked at Cale as if to say, "Do you see what you've done?" then reached down and tore the undertrousers away from the wound to expose the skin of his thigh. Blood was pumping out of the small wound in spurt after spurt. He stared down at it, utterly perplexed, then looked at Cale with the same expression. "Bring me a towel," he said, gesturing over to a pile of large swabs on the table near the dead girl. Cale responded by standing up but stayed where he was. It was as if only part of what he was seeing was real. The Redeemer in front of him trying to stem the bleeding with his fingers and sighing in irritation as if he had sprung a small but deeply inconvenient leak—the black stain of blood spreading relentlessly across the floor. The sight and what it meant for him were impossible to take in. The part of him not able to grasp what he had done was thinking that it would be possible to go back and things would be like they were less than a minute before, and that the longer he waited to change things back the harder it would be. But he also knew there was nothing to be done. Everything was changed, utterly changed, horribly changed. A line he had heard a hundred times from the *Redeemers' Book of Proverbs* came back to him and kept repeating itself over and over in his head: "We are like water spilled on the ground that cannot be gathered up again." And so he kept on looking, paralyzed, as Picarbo leaned back as if terribly tired, resting first on his elbow and then on his back.

Cale continued watching as the breath of the Lord's body stopped and the light in his eyes failed. Redeemer Picarbo, the fiftieth Lord of Discipline of that name, was dead.

6

Kleist woke up with the sensation of being smothered and held down. This was for a simple reason: Cale had his hand over his mouth and Vague Henri had his hands pinned to his side.

"Shhhh! It's Cale and Henri." Cale waited until Kleist stopped struggling and then took away his hand. Henri let his grip relax. "You have to come with us now. If you stay, you're dead. Are you coming?"

Kleist sat up and looked at Vague Henri in the moon-illuminated dark.

"Is this true?"

Henri nodded. Kleist sighed and stood up.

"Where's Spider?" asked Kleist, looking around for the sleepshed Redeemer.

"He's gone for a smoke. We have to go."

Cale turned and the others followed. Cale stopped and bent low over the bed of a boy who was pretending to be asleep. "You say anything to Spider, Savio, and I'll disembowel you, you little shit, all right?" The not-sleeping boy nodded without opening his eyes and Cale moved on.

Outside the door, which Spider had left unlocked with his usual carelessness, Cale led them into the ambo and, keeping to the wall side, made toward the large statue of the Hanged Redeemer and the entrance that they had uncovered the day before.

"What's going on?" asked Kleist.

"Be quiet."

Cale pushed open the door and ushered the other two inside. Then he lit a candle, much brighter than anything they had ever seen before.

"How did you get the door open?" said Kleist.

"A crowbar."

"Where did you get that candle?"

"The same place I got the crowbar."

Kleist turned to Vague Henri.

"Do you know what's going on?" Vague Henri shook his head. Cale moved over to the far left of the tunnel and raised the candle.

"God!" said Kleist as he looked at the terrified figure crouching on the floor.

"It's all right," said Cale as he leaned down toward the girl. "They're here to help," he added, without much conviction.

"Tell me what's going on," said Kleist, "or we're going head-to-head here and now."

Cale looked at him and smiled, if a little grimly.

"Listen . . . ," he said, and blew out the flame. Twenty minutes later he had finished his story and relit the candle.

The two boys stared at him and the girl in turn, appalled at what they had heard and yet fascinated by the girl. It took a moment for Kleist to come to himself.

"*You* killed him, Cale—why drag us into this?"

"Don't be stupid. Once they realize it was me, they'll torture Henri because they know we're friends. Then they'll connect Henri to you. This way you have a chance."

"But I had nothing to do with this."

"What difference will that make? You've been seen talking to me at least twice over the last few days. They'll kill you to make a point and to be on the safe side."

"Does this mean you have a plan?" said Henri, afraid but trying to calm himself down.

"Yes," said Cale. "It'll probably fail. But we have a chance." He blew out the candle and told them what he'd come up with.

"You're right," said Kleist when he'd finished. "It probably *will* fail."

"If you've got anything better . . . ?" Cale left the sentence unfinished. He lit the candle again and took it close to the girl, who was staring into the distance, shaking and holding herself in her arms.

"What's your name?" said Cale. She didn't seem to hear him at first; then her eyes turned to look into his face. But she said nothing.

"Poor thing," said Vague Henri.

"What's she to you to make you sorry for her?" said Kleist bitterly, torn between his own fear and the strange creature huddled in the corner. "It's yourself you should be worrying about."

Cale stood up, handed the candle to Vague Henri and moved to the door.

"Now," he said.

Henri blew it out. There was the sound of the door opening and closing and Vague Henri, Kleist and the girl were left in utter darkness.

The shock of the events of that night were beginning to wear off as Cale made his way through the Sanctuary for the third time. He was, of course, keeping to the shadows, but he was calmer now. He was beginning to realize that the habits of his lifetime—the awareness that you were always being watched, that there were always eyes prepared to note and report on every movement—no longer applied. The Redeemers had made an assumption, and for good reason, that their skill in watching the acolytes along with the viciousness of their response to disobedience in thought or word would keep order among them. They had made an assumption that at night, with the acolytes locked in their dorms, exhausted and rightly fearing the consequences of trying to get out, they could relax their deranged vigilance. On this third trip through the Sanctuary at night, in a few hours Cale had seen only one Redeemer in the distance.

A strange exhilaration spread through Cale. The people he hated and who seemed so invulnerable and powerful were not. He had outwitted Bosco, killed the Lord of Discipline and now he was moving easily about the Sanctuary. A warning sounded deep in his heart not to become cocky—"Be watchful, or else you'll swing for this."

Still, however much he thought about it, however much it smacked of recklessness, it made sense to return to the Lord of Discipline's rooms. He had taken a few things before he'd left with the girl, but if the four of them were to have any chance outside, they would need . . . In fact he didn't know what they would need, but there was a chance to find many things to help in the dead man's rooms, and it would be foolish not to take the chance. Given luck, there would be another four hours before the dead Redeemer was found.

Ten minutes later he was standing over Picarbo's dead body again. He paused for a moment and then began to search. It was an odd experience because there was so much. Acolytes were not permitted to own anything. Even Redeemers were supposed to own only seven things, though why not eight or six nobody knew. Picarbo's rooms were filled with stuff. Cale did not know what many of the things were, and he would have liked to spend time just rolling them over in his hands and speculating about their purpose—how peculiar and pleasant to the touch a shaving brush made of badger hair, and how wonderful the smell and slippery feel of a bar of soap. But death soon damped down his curiosity, and he began to pick and choose what would go into the rucksack he had found: knives, a telescope—a fabulous thing he had seen being used by Bosco from the battlements—a sharpening tool for Picarbo's medical instruments, a linen bag, some herbs he had seen used for the treatment of wounds, fine-bore needles, thread, a ball of string. He searched the cupboards, but most of them contained tray upon tray of preserved specimens of bits of women's bodies. Cale did not, of course, recognize most of them. Not that he felt any need to justify killing Picarbo, a man he'd seen beat many children in formal punishments and even kill one. But the carefully dried body parts made him feel disgust as well as dread.

Then he tried one of the doors leading off the room, avoiding looking as he did so at the poor creature on the dissection table.

He opened it, and at once a strong smell of stale priest afflicted his nostrils. He had noticed before whenever he was in the midst of more than two Redeemers in a confined space that they smelled odd. But this room seemed to be stained in its very walls with the odor—something rotten, as if everything inside them, the very living spirit, was in the process of becoming rank. On his way out, Cale did not want to look at the body of the girl, but something drew him toward it. He looked only for a moment at the careful and meticulous mutilation of the beautiful young woman. He felt an unaccustomed surge of pity that something so soft and delicate should be laid to waste in such a way. Then his eye caught the small, hard object in the metal dish that the Lord of Discipline had removed from the girl's stomach just before Cale left the first time. It was not bone or anything that looked very gruesome—it was the shape and texture of a small pebble washed smooth by long exposure to a fast-flowing stream. It was milkily transparent, and a golden brown color. Wary, Cale touched it with his forefinger. Then he picked it up and looked at it. Then he sniffed. The smell almost overpowered him, as if every cell in his brain was taken over by its strange but wonderful perfume. He stood for a moment, dazed and ready to faint. But he had to move on. He took a deep breath and continued searching, taking a few more things he thought could be useful and a few things he just liked the look of; then he was out the door and off to his hiding place.

7

For nearly two years Cale had been planning his escape. This was not a plan that he ever intended to use if it could be avoided, because the chance of success was so very poor. The Redeemers moved heaven and earth to recapture runaways, for whom the punishment was to be hung, drawn and quartered. No one, as far as Cale knew, had ever succeeded in evading the Dogs of Paradise, and his long-term plan to escape the Redeemers involved patience, waiting until he was twenty and sent to the frontier and taking his chance as it came. Still, he thought to himself, well done for preparing for this. He tried, as he crept along the ambo, not to think of the chances of success. Nevertheless he could not stop the resentment at what it had cost to intervene. Saving the girl was *pointless*. All he had achieved was his own almost certain death, as well as, though less important, the deaths of Vague Henri and Kleist. Stupid! He took a deep breath and tried to calm himself. But she had looked so happy the night before, her smile so . . . what? It was hard to describe what he felt about happiness, watching someone actually being happy. That was what had come back to him as he tried to leave and stood in the dark corridor, trembling at what he had seen in the Lord of Discipline's room and the horror of the disgusting cruelty. It had made him livid with anger and he was used to that, but this time, for the first time in his life, he had given way to it. *But you didn't do any good*, he thought to himself. *No good at all.*

But now he had arrived. He was in a small niche off the main ambo that had a gap at one end, not an entrance but just where one part of an internal wall did not quite meet with the main Sanctuary external battlements. He slid sideways into it, breathing in and struggling to push himself inside. In a few months he would be too big to squeeze through. But he reached out and grasped a handhold he had dug out of the wall when he was smaller, and just about managed to pull himself inside. It was too dark to see, but the space was tiny and the hiding place familiar to his touch. He squatted down and pulled out one loose brick and then the one next to it, then shifted the two half bricks resting on top.

Then he reached inside and pulled out a long rope braided with painstaking care, at the end of which was a bent iron hook. Then he stood up straight and squeezed back between the walls.

Back in the niche he listened for a moment. Nothing. He reached up and felt around the rough surface of the main wall and jammed the hook into a small crevice he had made months before, just after he had finished making the rope. He had made the rope not of jute or sisal but from the hair of the acolytes and Redeemers he had collected from the washrooms over the years during his time as cleaner—a disgusting task, sure enough, and one that had made him gag many times, but one he had steeled himself to as a possible chance for life. He tugged on the rope to make sure it was fixed. Then he pulled himself up and jammed himself between the two walls of the niche, back against one wall, feet against the other. He loosened the hook, reached up with it again for another crevice and repeated the move again and again. Over the next hour, moving no more than two feet at a time and often less, he hooked and jammed his way to the top of the Sanctuary battlements.

As he rolled onto the top, he let out an exhausted grunt of delight. He lay there for five minutes, his arms like deadweights, lifeless except for being agonizingly painful. He daren't wait any longer. Reaching down, he pulled the unfurled rope up behind him and placed the hook into the largest crevice he could find. Then he fed the rope over the side.

He hoped it would make a sound when it hit the ground, but there was nothing clear about the noise it made as he jerked it up and down. The rope was half as long again as the wall on the Sanctuary side but, for all he knew, this part of the wall might have been built on the edge of a cliff.

He looked down into the fathomless dark and paused for a moment. Then with his right hand he felt for the rope and pulled it taut so that the hook was forced to bite into the crevice. With one hand on the wall, the other holding the rope taut, he paused once more as he realized how appalling his situation was. *Still, better to go this way than being hanged and fried.* And with this consoling thought, he let go of the wall, let the rope take the strain and slipped over the edge.

With his legs crossed over the rope, Cale let himself down hand over hand. This was the easy part, with his weight doing the work for him. Indeed, he would have felt exultant if it were not for the fact that the rope was untested and might snap or come apart from rubbing against the rough walls—and also the unpleasant thought that it might not be long enough and he could be left dangling a hundred feet from the ground. Even a ten-foot drop onto rocks would break his leg. But what was the point in worrying about it? It was too late now.

8

*E*very few minutes Kleist and Vague Henri would light the candle Cale had stolen from the Lord of Discipline and look at the girl. They had agreed it was best to keep an eye on her every now and again. After all, there were nine candles, so they could afford to be generous. They had seen people go quiet in the way the girl was quiet and with that odd sightless stare, usually in boys who had taken more than a hundred strokes. If they stayed like that for more than a few days, they were taken away and never came back. Those who pulled themselves to-gether often used to start screaming in the middle of the night, weeks or even months later—in Morto's case it had been years. Then they vanished too.

This, they told themselves, was why they kept checking on the girl. If she started screaming, maybe someone would hear.

Every time they lit the candle, Vague Henri would say to her, "It's going to be all right." She did not respond except by shivering every now and again. The third time they lit the candle, Henri remembered something from the very distant past, a phrase that came into his head, something comforting he had once heard and long forgotten. "There, there," he said. "There, there."

But there was another reason they kept lighting the candle besides checking on the girl: they couldn't stop themselves from looking at her. They had both come into the Sanctuary as seven-year-olds from a life that now seemed as remote as the moon. Vague Henri's parents had been dead since not long after he was born. Kleist's parents had sold him for five dollars to the Redeemers, and had been only a little less brutal toward him. They had not seen a girl or a woman since they came through the great gates of the Sanctuary, and all that the Re-deemers had told them was that women and girls were the devil's playground. If, by any chance, they were to see one when they left the Sanctuary for the frontier or the Eastern Breaks, they were immediately to cast their eyes down. "The body of a woman is a sin in itself, crying out to the heavens for vengeance!" There was only one woman who was to be regarded without disgust and alarm: the mother of the Hanged Redeemer who, alone among her sex, was pure. She was the source of compassion, perpetual succor and solace—though what these virtues entailed the boys had no idea, none of these qualities ever having come their way. About what it involved, this business of women being the devil's playground, the Redeemers were equally vague. As a result, Kleist and Vague Henri were driven to watch the girl by an intense curiosity, mixed with fear and no little awe. Anyone who could get the Redeemers into such ecstasies of loathing and hatred had to be very powerful indeed and, therefore, in ways they could not begin to guess at, worth being afraid of.

At the moment, shivering and terrified in the candlelight, the girl did not seem like something fearful. She was still, however, fascinating. She was, for one thing, such an extraordinary shape. She was wearing a linen shift of fair quality, much better than anything the boys had ever worn, tied around her waist with a cord.

Kleist gestured to Vague Henri to move away and bent his head to whisper in his ear.

"What are those humps on her chest?" he asked.

Vague Henri, with as much deference as possible, considering he had no knowledge of how to behave toward a woman, held the candle toward her breasts and looked at them thoughtfully.

"I don't know," he whispered at last.

"She must be fat," whispered Kleist. "Like that shit-bag Vittles." There were, of course, no fat boys at the Sanctuary. There was barely an ounce between all ten thousand.

Vague Henri considered this.

"Vittles is saggy and round. She goes in and out."

"Go on, then," said Kleist.

Vague Henri thought about this for a moment.

"No, I think we should leave her alone. I suppose," he added, "he must have given her a beating."

Kleist let out a deep breath as he considered the girl.

"She doesn't look like she could take a hiding, not one like the kind Picarbo can hand out."

"*Used* to hand out," corrected Vague Henri. They both grunted with a strange satisfaction, given that his death had put them in so much danger. "I wonder why he beat her."

"Probably," said Vague Henri, "for being the devil's playground."

Kleist nodded. It seemed plausible.

"What's your name?" asked Vague Henri, not for the first time. Again she did not reply.

"I wonder how long Cale will take," said Vague Henri.

"Do you think he really has a plan?"

"Yes," said Vague Henri, with a tone of complete certainty. "If he says something, he means it."

"Well, I'm glad you're so sure. I wish I was."

Then the girl said something, but so softly they couldn't hear.

"What did you say?" asked Vague Henri.

"Riba." She took a deep breath. "My name is Riba."

✠

limbing down in the deep black, Cale's two worst fears became real. First, his feet hit the large knot he had made at the end of the rope still leaving him in midair with no idea how far he had left to fall. Second, he could feel that the strain had been too much for the iron hook holding his weight in the cranny at the top of the wall. Even at this distance he could feel it begin to give. "You're going to fall anyway," he said to himself, and with one push out with both feet from the rock face, he raised his arms to protect his head and began to fall.

Fall, that is, if a drop of less than two feet can be described as such. A delighted Cale stood and raised his hands in triumph. Then he pulled out one of the candles he had stolen from the Lord of Discipline and tried to light it with dried moss and a flint. In time he got a flame and lit the candle, but as he held it up to the vast darkness, its light was so feeble he could barely see anything. Then the wind blew it out.

The dark was absolute, with thick clouds blotting the moon. If he tried walking, he would fall, and even a minor injury that slowed him down in the course ahead would mean death. It was better to wait the two hours or so until dawn. With that decision made, he wrapped his cassock around himself, lay down and went to sleep.

Nearly two hours later he opened his eyes to find that the dark gray dawn had given him enough light to see by. He looked back at the rope hanging from the walls, now showing the place where he had begun his escape like a huge pointing finger. But there was nothing to be done about it, or about his regret that he was leaving behind something that had taken him eighteen months, and much retching, to make. It looked, although Cale had never seen such a thing, like a two-hundred-foot ponytail. He turned and in the rising light made his way down the rocky, pathless slant of Sanctuary Hill, happy that it might be another hour before they found the body of the Lord of Discipline and, with luck, another two before they came across the rope.

He had luck on neither count. The body of Redeemer Picarbo had been discovered half an hour before dawn by his servant, whose hysterical screams had the entire Sanctuary, enormous as it was, awake and in ferment within a few minutes. Quickly every dormitory was roused and roll call taken, and it soon became clear that three of the acolytes were missing.

Pathfinder Brunt, dog ostler and the Redeemer charged with catching the very few acolytes who were foolish enough to escape, was sent immediately to Redeemer Bosco and for the first time in his life was shown into his offices immediately.

"I want all three of them returned alive, by which I mean you will do everything in your power to do so."

"Of course, Lord Militant. I always—"

"Spare me," interrupted Bosco. "I'm not *asking* you to be careful. I'm *telling* you. Under no circumstances, not at the price of your own life, is Thomas Cale to be harmed. I suppose if Kleist and Henri are killed, then so be it, though I'd prefer them alive as well."

"May I ask why Cale's life is so precious, Lord?"

"No."

"What shall I tell the others? They won't understand and they're in a powerful rage."

Bosco realized what Brunt was driving at. Holy rage could overcome even the most obedient Redeemer faced with an acolyte who had done something so unthinkably dreadful. He sighed with irritation. "You may indicate that Cale is working on my behalf and has been forced to go with these murderers while attempting to uncover a most terrible conspiracy involving a plot by the Antagonists to murder the Supreme Pontiff." It was, thought Bosco, pitiful stuff, but good enough for Brunt, who instantly went pale with distress. He was exceptional for his brutality even by the low standards of Redeemer dog ostlers, but the deep protectiveness of Brunt's feelings for the Pontiff, like that of a child for his mother, would have been plain to anyone.

Cale's rope of hair was quickly found, its scent given to the Dogs of Paradise, and then the great doors were rolled open and a hunting party was on its way with Cale less than five miles in front of them. But in its most important respect his plan was a success: it had not occurred to anyone that only one acolyte had made his escape, and so no search of any kind was made inside the Sanctuary. For the moment, Vague Henri, Kleist and the girl were safe. Assuming, of course, that Cale kept his promise.

Cale had moved another four miles by the time he heard the faint sound of the dogs drifting on the wind. He stopped and listened in the silence. For a moment there was just the cold wind scratching over the sandy rock. Distant though it was, it was clear enough that he was in for trouble, and sooner rather than later. It was a strange, high-pitched noise, not like the usual yelping of pack hounds but a constant squeal of rage that sounded something like a pig having its throat cut with a rusty saw. They were hefty like pigs too, even more bad tempered than a boar and with a set of fangs that looked as though someone had poured a bag of rusty nails into their mouths. The sound died away again as Cale looked to see if there was any sign of the Voynich oasis. Nothing stood out from the endless stretch of crusty, diseased-looking hillocks from which the Scablands got its name. He started running again, now faster than before. There was a long way to go, and with the hounds this close, he knew he would be lucky to make it past midday. Move too slowly and the hounds would have him, too fast and exhaustion would give him up. He shut all this out and listened only to the rhythm of his own breathing.

"How long have you been here, Riba?"

For a moment she seemed not to have heard Vague Henri; then she looked at him as if trying to bring him into focus.

"I've been here for five years." The boys looked at each other in astonishment.

"But why are you here?" said Kleist.

"We came here to learn to be brides," she said. "But they lied. He killed Lena, that man, and he would have killed me. Why?" It was a bewildered appeal. "Why would anyone do that?"

"We don't know," said Kleist. "We don't know anything about you. We had no idea you existed."

"Start from the beginning," said Vague Henri. "Tell us how you came here, where you're from."

"Take your time," said Kleist. "We have plenty of it."

"He's coming back for us, isn't he, that other one?"

"His name is Cale."

"He's coming back for us."

"Yes," said Vague Henri. "But it might be a long wait."

"I don't want to wait here," she said, furious. "It's cold and dark and horrible. I won't!"

"Keep your voice down."

"Let me out—now—or I'll scream."

It was not that Kleist had no idea how to treat a member of the opposite sex; it was that he had no idea how to deal with anyone behaving in such an emotional way. Expressing uncontrolled anger usually meant a visit to Ginky's Field and a three-foot hole. Kleist raised his arm to shut her up, but Henri pulled him back.

"You have to be quiet," he told Riba. "Cale will come back and we'll take you somewhere safe. But if they hear us, then we are dead things. You must understand."

She stared at him for a moment, looking as if madness itself were whispering in her ear. Then she nodded her head.

"Tell us where you came from, and as much as you know about why you're here."

In her great agitation, Riba had stood upright, a tall and shapely girl, if plump. She sat down again and took a deep breath to calm herself.

"Mother Teresa bought me in the serf market in Memphis when I was ten. She bought Lena as well."

"You're a slave?" said Kleist.

"No," said the girl at once, ashamed and indignant. "Mother Teresa told us we were free and we could leave whenever we wanted."

Kleist laughed. "Why didn't you, then?"

"Because she was kind to us and gave us presents and pampered us like cats, and fed us wonderful food and many rich things and taught us how to be brides and told us that when we were ready we would have a rich knight in shining armor who would love us and take care of us forever." She stopped, almost breathless, as if what she was saying were actually happening and the horrors of the last day just a dream. That she stopped was just as well, because very little of it made sense to the boys.

Vague Henri turned to Kleist. "I don't understand. It's against the faith to own slaves."

"None of this makes sense. Why would the Redeemers buy a girl and do all these things for her and then start to butcher them like—"

"Be quiet!" Vague Henri looked at the girl, but she was lost in her own world for the moment. Kleist sighed with irritation. Vague Henri pulled him away and lowered his voice. "How would you feel if it was you who had to watch that happening to someone you'd been with for five years?"

"I'd thank my lucky stars that there was a half-wit around like Cale to rescue me. You need," he added, "to spend more time worrying about us and less about the girl. What's she to us or we to her? God knows we all get what's coming to us—no need to go looking for it."

"What's done is done."

"But it isn't done, is it?"

As this was true, Vague Henri lapsed into silence for a moment.

"Why would the Redeemers, of all people," he said at last in a whisper, "bring someone who was the devil's playground into the Sanctuary, feed them, care for them, tell them wonderful lies and then cut them into pieces while they were still alive?"

"Because they're bastards," said Kleist sullenly. But he was no fool and the question interested him. "Why have they increased the numbers of acolytes by five, maybe even ten times as much?" Then he swore and sat down. "Tell me something, Henri."

"What?"

"If we knew the answer—would you feel better or worse?" And with that, he shut up for good.

Cale was urinating over the edge of one of the Scabland hillocks that had half-collapsed. The screaming yelp of the dogs was close and continuous now. He finished and hoped that the smell would attract them away from his true line for a few minutes. His breathing was labored, despite the rest, his thighs heavy and beginning to drag him down. By his calculations from the map he had found in Redeemer Bosco's bureau, he should have been at the oasis already. But there was still no sign, just the hillocks and rocks and sand stretching as far as he could see. It was now that he faced the possibility that he had carried with him since the moment he found the map—that it was a trap set for him by the Lord Militant.

There was no point in pacing himself now; the dogs would be on him in a few minutes. That there had been no letup in their noise meant that they had missed or ignored the smell of his urine. He ran as fast as he could now, although he was too exhausted after four hours to increase his speed by much.

Now the dogs were baying fit to kill, and Cale was beginning to slow as he knew that he could never outrun them. His breath rasped as if sand were being scraped inside his lungs, and he began to stumble. Then he fell.

He was on his feet in an instant, but the fall had made him look at his surroundings. Still the same hillocks and rocks, but now the sand had lanky weeds and grass in clumps. Where there was grass, there was water. Immediately there was a surge in the howls of the dogs as if they had been lashed with a nailed whip. Cale raced off in search of the oasis, hoping to God he was heading for it and not just skirting its edge and heading only for more desert and death.

But the grass and weeds became thicker, and as he leapt over a ridge and nearly took a fall, there in front of him on the other side was the Voynich oasis. The dogs were screaming now as they sensed their hunt was over. Cale ran on, stumbling as his body began to rebel. He knew not to look back, but he couldn't help himself. The hounds were pouring over the lip of the ridge like coals from a sack, yelping and howling in their desperation to tear him apart, getting in one another's way and snarling and biting.

He scrambled on as the dogs bounded toward him, all hunched shoulders and teeth. Then he was into the first few trees of the oasis. One of the dogs, faster and more vicious than the others, was already on him. The creature knew its task and clipped Cale's heel with its front paw, throwing Cale off balance and sending him sprawling.

That should have been that—but, too eager for its prey, the dog had overbalanced as well. Unused to the damper and looser surface of the oasis, it could find no grip and went headlong, tail over head, and crashed into a tree, fetching a hefty wallop to its spine. It screamed in rage, but its desperation to get to its feet only made things worse, as it scrabbled to gain a purchase on the unstable ground. Cale ran toward the lake at the center of the oasis and was already fifteen yards ahead before the animal was on its feet and after him. But it would not be a long chase at four times the speed of the exhausted boy. Quickly the dog gained and was about to leap when Cale leapt before him, a long arc in the air and then a huge splash as he hit the surface of the lake.

A scream of rage from the dog as it stopped shy of the edge. Then another dog found him, and another, all of them baying at him with a sound like the end of the world—hatred and fury and hunger.

It was five minutes before the pathfinder and his men arrived on their ponies to find the dogs at the edge of the water that fed the oasis. They were still barking, but there was nothing to be seen. The pathfinder stood on the bank for some time, looking and thinking—his face, never a pretty sight, black with frustration and suspicion. At last one of his men spoke.

"Are you sure it's them, Redeemer? These imbeciles," he said, look-ing at the dogs, "it wouldn't be the first time they've taken chase after a deer or a wild pig."

"Be quiet," said Brunt softly. "They could still be here. They're good swimmers, by all accounts. Set guards and the better dogs around the perimeter. If they're here, I'll have them. But Cale's not to be harmed, by God." In fact, Brunt had told his men nothing of Bosco's fantasy of a plot against the Pontiff. He had not exactly lied to Bosco about the rage of his men. They were angry all right, but they would do as they were told simply because he had told them. To be the only ordinary Redeemer to know about the terrible threat to the Pontiff made him feel an ever deeper love for His Holiness, and this love was not to be squandered by sharing it with others.

He gestured—a slight nod, no more—and in a moment the men around him began to move. Within the hour the oasis was shut up tighter than a mouse's ear.

In the secret corridor in the Sanctuary, Riba was asleep. Kleist had gone hunting for rats, and Vague Henri was watching the girl, intrigued by her strange curves and feeling puzzling new impulses along with the hunger and fear. He did well to be frightened. The Redeemers never stopped looking for escapers until they were caught, no matter how long. When they were recaptured, an example would be made of them that would freeze the blood in the veins of every acolyte for a thousand years, make their hearts miss a beat, their hair stand on its end like the quills upon a fretful porcupine. The cruelty and agony of their punish-ment and eventual death would become a legend.

Despite keeping himself busy with the rats, Kleist was feeling much the same. The other feeling they shared was a growing suspicion that Cale was halfway to Memphis and never coming back. In fact Kleist was certain of it, but even the loyal Vague Henri was unsure of what Cale would do. He had always wanted to be friends with Cale, although he could not really say why. Fear of the Redeemers' anathema to friendship kept the acolytes cautious of one another, not least because the Redeemers set traps. Certain boys, those with charm and a capacity for treachery, were trained by the priests to be even more charming and treacherous. Known as chickens, these boys would tempt the unsuspecting into exchanging confidences, talking, playing games and other signs of friendship. Those who responded to their overtures were given thirty strokes with a spiked glove in front of their entire dorm and left there to bleed for twenty-four hours. But not even such dire consequences would prevent some acolytes from becoming the strongest friends and allies in the great battle to keep themselves alive or be swallowed up by the Redeemers' faith.

But when it came to Cale, Vague Henri was always unsure whether theirs was a real friendship. Henri had gone out of his way to intrigue Cale by going through his insolent routines in front of him with various Redeemers, hoping to impress with his wit and reckless daring. But for months he had no sense that Cale realized what he was doing or, if he did, that he couldn't care less. Cale's expression was always the same: a laconic watchfulness. He never expressed an emotion, no matter what the circumstances. His victories in training seemed to give him no pleasure, just as the harsh punishments for which Bosco often singled him out seemed to cause him no pain. He was not exactly feared by the acolytes, but neither was he liked. No one could make him out; he neither rebelled nor was he one of the faithful. Everyone left him alone, and Cale, insofar as it was possible to tell, preferred it that way.

"Penny for your thoughts." It was Kleist, back from his rat hunt, the tailless results dangling from a string at his waist. Five of them. He undid a loop and dropped them on a stone and started to skin them.

"Better get them sorted before she wakes up," said Kleist, smiling. "I don't suppose she'd take to them baked in their skins."

"Why don't you leave her alone?"

"You know she's going to get us killed, don't you? Not that we've got much of a chance anyway. Your friend's got twelve hours to get back or—"

"Or what?" interrupted Vague Henri. "If you've got a plan, let's hear it. I'm all ears."

Kleist sniffed as he started gutting. "If I couldn't look forward to eating these," he said, gesturing at the rats, "I'd be feeling really bad by now. About our chances, I mean. Our chances of ever seeing Cale again."

Having emerged from one of the reed beds at the side of the lake, Cale had moved about five hundred yards into the diggings. For fifteen years the Redeemers had been coming to the oasis and carrying away tons of the rich loam that formed under the tree canopy. It was magical stuff, capable of enriching even the dead earth of the Sanctuary's vegetable gardens. So fertile was it that its use alone had allowed the Sanctuary to expand the numbers of acolytes it trained more than tenfold. But Cale had discovered that the soil of the oasis had another property. Working in the gardens one day and being guarded by the dogs who were set on any acolyte who stole, Cale had stopped during a short break and taken out a piece of dead men's feet he had found on the floor of the refectory. As soon as he sniffed it, he realized it had not been dropped but discarded: it was rancid and completely inedible. He noticed one of the dogs sleeping nearby, with his handler looking the other way. He threw it to him, not out of kindness but hoping the creature, who, like all the hounds, would eat anything, would gobble it down and be sick—and serve the shit-bag right. The piece of dead men's feet landed just near the dog, on a small pile of oasis loam just by its head. The dog raised himself up at the sound—alert and ready. But despite the fact that there was food lying under its nose, and it was a nose that could smell gnat's pee at a thousand yards, it didn't look at the food at all. Instead it glared at Cale, yawned, scratched itself, then settled down and went back to sleep. Later, when the guard and his dog were gone, Cale picked up the piece of dead men's feet and sniffed it. It stank to high heaven. Puzzled, he picked up a handful of loam and wrapped it around the morsel. Then he sniffed again, and all he could smell this time was a rich, dark, peaty smell. Something in the loam had done more than mask the smell of rotten fat: it had made it vanish. But only as long as it was in contact.

Over the next few days in the garden he tried out an experiment with the dogs as the piece of dead men's feet grew more and more fetid. Not once did the dogs smell a thing. Finally, he dropped it, wiped free of loam, on the flint path, and in a couple of minutes one of the dogs, drawn by its stink, scarfed it down. To Cale's great satisfaction, ten minutes later he could see the dog hurling up its prodigious guts in the corner.

It was more dangerous than difficult to find references to the source of the loam in the library archive. There were maps and files in there he often fetched for the Lord Militant, and all he needed to do was be patient for an opportunity to take the right file and even more patient for the chance to return it. If getting caught doing this was unlikely, the consequences of being so would have been nasty, perhaps fatal if the Redeemers worked out that his interest in the documents about the oasis was inspired more by a plan to escape than, say, an enthusiasm for gardening and fertilizer.

Shortly after he emerged from the lake, a soaking wet Cale was still able to hear the baying of the hounds. Once into the trees, he could not be seen or smelled, but he knew that would not be the case for long. Almost immediately after he began walking, he was into the Redeemers' digging grounds. The harvesting of the loam had left a long field of hollows rather than straight trenches, because the loam was too soft to sustain straight-sided walls like ordinary earth, though not so soft that it couldn't trap and asphyxiate a man by collapsing on top of him, as the records from the archive made clear. A satisfying thought when Cale had read it, given that a dozen Redeemers had died mining the stuff— not so satisfying as he looked for something to dig in and hide himself from sight and scent.

Picking his spot, a light hollow at the base of one of the hillocks, he scooped out as deep a hole as he dared, gathered some loose loam from around about so the searchers would not detect signs of recent digging and eased himself into the deepened hollow, pulling the loam around him and carefully dragging it down from above. It did not take long and he felt vulnerable so near the surface, but he dared not dig deeper and risk a collapse. What he tried to keep in mind was that he only needed not to be seen or smelled. The Redeemers' confidence in their animals was their weakness—to them, if their dogs didn't smell anything, it wasn't there. They wouldn't bother with even a simple search, because it wasn't necessary. Cale lay back and tried to sleep, aware that there was nothing else to do. He needed the rest. And, in any case, it would not be a deep sleep. He had taught himself a long time ago to be awake in a moment.

Fall asleep he did, and woke up in an instant also, alert to the sound of dogs and Redeemers, barking and shouting. They came closer and closer, the barking settling down to a snuffling yelp as the dogs concentrated on the slower search and not a chase. Closer and closer came the sound until one of them must have started sniffing a few inches away. But the dog didn't stay long. Why would it? The loam did its job, blotting out everything but itself. Soon the snuffling and occasional bark faded and Cale allowed himself a moment of delight and triumph. He had, however, to stay where he was for hours yet. He relaxed and went to sleep.

When he woke again, he was stiff from the effects of his long run, and his left knee in particular, pained by an old injury, throbbed. He was also freezing. He eased his right arm through the loam and cleared away enough to see it was dark. He waited. Two hours later he could hear birds singing, and soon after came the lightening of the sky. Slowly he emerged, ready to vanish back into his hole at the first sign of the Redeemers. But there was nothing but the sound of the birds in the tall trees and the rustle of small creatures in the undergrowth. He took out the linen bag he had taken from the Lord of Discipline's room and began shoveling in loam, pressing it down so he could pack in as much as possible.

Then he swung it over his back and went off in search of the Redeemers and their dogs.

He found them about three hours later. It was not difficult—there were twenty Redeemers and forty dogs. Besides, they had no reason to cover their tracks: no one within two hundred miles would by choice go near even a lone Redeemer, let alone a score of them with dogs. They searched for others; others did not search for them. For ten minutes after he caught up with them, Cale considered whether he should forget about the three waiting for him in the Sanctuary and make his escape to Memphis while he still could. He owed Kleist nothing, Vague Henri only a little, and he had saved the girl's life once already. As when the octopus changes its colors in the face of tooth and claw, reds and yellows sweeping under its skin like waves, Cale's urge to leave or stay swept over him, back and forth, muddy and clear and mixed. Reasons to vanish now were obvious, reasons to return were hazy and obscure, but it was the undertow of the last that drove him, with great reluctance and much blaspheming, back toward the searching dogs and priests.

Even though he was covered in dirt from the loam, Cale stayed downwind of the dogs, approaching no closer than half a mile. Two hours later, as he'd hoped, they halted the search and turned about, heading for the Sanctuary. Cale knew they hadn't given up. This was only the primary search, sent out to catch a fugitive quickly. Usually it worked, but if they lost the trail within thirty hours, the first search would return and be replaced by as many as five secondary teams, fully equipped and self-sufficient, who would stay on the hunt for years if necessary. They had never had to. Two months was the longest anyone had evaded capture, and his punishment when caught had been infandous.

Still keeping his distance and still downwind, Cale shadowed the Redeemers for the next twelve hours, moving gradually closer and closer, waiting for any sign of the dogs catching his scent. He followed them all the way back to the Sanctuary and was so close by then that all he had to do was join on the end of the now exhausted group and, hood up over his face, follow them as they went, in the now pitch dark, through the great gates. There was no security check. What madman, after all, man or boy, would ever try to break into the Sanctuary?

After a day's wait in the secret corridor, the three sat in the dark, each with their own thoughts, always similar, always grim. When they heard the light tap on the door, they went to it desperately hopeful, but also possessed by the fear that it might be a trap.

"What if it's them?" whispered Kleist.

"Then they're coming in one way or another, aren't they?" replied Vague Henri. They both set to and began to pull the door open.

"Thank God, it's you," said Vague Henri.

"Who were you expecting?" said Cale.

"We thought it might be those men."

It was the first time that Cale had been spoken to by a woman face-to-face. Her voice was soft and low, and if his expression had been visible in the dark, it would have shown intense surprise and fascination.

"If the Redeemers come for us, they won't knock first."

"We've had enough," said Kleist. "Tell us what you've been doing and if we can get out of here alive."

"Light a candle—we'll need it."

In two minutes they could see one another as the gentle light made the scene almost beautiful—the four huddled together.

"What's that smell?" said Vague Henri. Cale dropped the bag of loam on the floor. "The dogs can't smell you if you rub this over your body and clothes. I'll explain what happened while you get on with it."

In other places in the world, what followed might have been awkward. Riba, shocked by this, was about to protest that she must have privacy, but the three boys all turned their backs to her and to one another. To be naked in the presence of another boy was an offense that cried out to heaven for vengeance, as the late Lord of Discipline was fond of saying. There were many offenses for which heaven bawled for noisy reprisals.

The boys moved into the darkness to undress as a matter of ingrained habit. Left standing on her own, there was no one Riba could see to protest to. So she grabbed a handful of the pungent loam and she too went into the dark.

"Are you ready?" mocked the voice of Cale. "Then I'll begin."

Five hours later, as a grubby dawn bled through the murk, Brunt ordered his five secondary search parties, each comprising a hundred men with dogs, out of the main square. As the last group left, four others hooded against the cold tacked themselves onto the end of the column and followed them out of the gates, down the cinder road and to the arid plain below. Here the five hundred Redeemers split into their separate groups and headed out to all points.

The four kept behind the column heading to the south. For an hour they kept pace with them as the preceptor chanted the marching song of shame:

"Holy Redeemer!"

"BANISH OUR SINS!" came the groaning response from a hundred and four voices.

"Holy Redeemer!"

"CHASTISE OUR CRIMES!"

"Holy Redeemer!"

"SCOURGE OUR LUST!"

"Holy Redeemer!"

"THRASH OUR . . ."

And so it went on until a sharp bend around the first hillock of the Scablands, when a hundred and four voices became merely a hundred.

From the battlements the Lord Militant watched as the five hundred emerged from the low fog and after a mile or two began to split into five. He stood until the last one was out of sight and then turned back to go to breakfast, his favorite—a bowl of black tripe and a hard-boiled egg.

The boys would have made forty or even fifty miles before night but for the fact that Riba was a liability. Beautiful, plump and pampered, she had in the last five years barely moved at all, walking only from massage table to hot bath and from there, and four times more in a day, to a dining table filled with stuffed vine leaves, pig's feet in aspic, spice cake and anything else fattening you could think of. As a result she could no more walk forty miles than she could fly thirty. At first Kleist and Cale were just irritated and told her to move herself, but when it was clear that bullying, threats and even pleading could not push the poor girl to go another step, they sat down and Vague Henri began to get her to tell them about her daily life in the hidden realms of the Sanctuary.

It was not just a wonderful story of luxury and comfort, of body spoiling, of care and warmth. It was also incomprehensible. Every time Riba added a new detail of a way in which she and the other girls were petted, mollycoddled, pampered and indulged, the three acolytes became more mystified about why the Redeemers would behave in such a way to anyone, least of all to creatures who were the devil's playground. And how did this astonishing kindness make any sense at all in the light of the hideous practices performed on Riba's friend Lena, a cruelty so grotesque not even the boys would have credited such a thing to the Redeemers. But it would be a long time before any of them could begin to put together the terrible story of which the three acolytes, Riba and the Lord Militant were now a part—and not least since Cale had put the sweet-smelling object he had found in the dissecting dish in one of his rarely used pockets and forgotten all about it.

But they had more pressing matters than the fate of mankind to deal with: how to stay alive while hauling along the beautiful but hefty Riba. They made ten miles that day, something of a tribute to Riba's willpower, as the most strenuous work she had done in her life before this was to raise a piece of fried chicken to her lips or turn over on a massage table to have rich foams and unguents stroked into her smooth skin. Needless to say, this determination on Riba's part was not much appreciated by the three boys. Exhausted, she fell asleep on the ground as soon as they stopped for the night. Then as they ate the dried meat prepared by Kleist, the boys discussed what to do with her.

"Let's leave her here and run away," said Kleist.

"She'll die," said Vague Henri.

"We'll leave water. Let's face it," said Kleist, scanning her overfed body, "it'll be a long time before she dies of starvation."

"She'll die anyway if we move at this rate, and us with her." This time it was Cale who spoke, not so much forming an argument as pointing out a simple fact.

Vague Henri tried flattery. "I don't think so, Cale. Look, you've fooled them completely. They already think we're miles away. They'll probably think we had help to get away that easily."

"Who the hell would help us against the Redeemers?" said Kleist.

"What does it matter? They think we've got away. And we have. They're not going to realize for a long time how we did it, if they ever do. We can afford to go slowly."

"It's a lot better if we don't," said Cale.

"They'll catch us at this rate," said Kleist. "It'll take more than a trick and some badger shit to keep them off our trail."

"We've gone through all of this to save her. We can't let her die now."

"Yes, we can," said Kleist. "The kindest thing is to cut her throat while she's sleeping. Best for her and us."

Cale let out a brief sigh, not especially regretful.

"Henri's right. What's the point if we let her die now?"

"What's the point?" shouted an exasperated Kleist. "The point, stupid bastards, is that we get away. Free. Forever."

The other two said nothing. It was true enough.

"Let's vote," said Vague Henri.

"No, let's not vote. Let's use our brains."

"Let's vote," said Cale.

"Why bother? You've made up your minds. We keep the girl."

There was a bad-tempered silence.

"There's something else we should do," said Cale at last.

"What now?" groaned Kleist. "Go and find enough goose feathers to make that fat beezle a mattress?"

"Keep your voice down," said Vague Henri. Cale ignored Kleist.

"We have to decide who's to do it if the Redeemers catch us."

It was an unpleasant thought, but they knew he was right. None of them wanted to be taken alive back to the Sanctuary.

"We'll draw straws," said Vague Henri.

"There isn't any straw," said Kleist, miserable.

"Then we'll draw stones." Vague Henri searched for a minute and came back with three stones of different sizes. He showed the others, who nodded their agreement. "Smallest loses." Henri put the stones behind his back and then held out his left hand, fist clenched in front of him. There was a pause—suspicious as always, Kleist was unwilling to choose. Cale shrugged and held out his hand, palm up, eyes closed. Without letting Kleist see, Vague Henri dropped the stone, and Cale closed his fist around it. He opened his eyes. Then Henri brought out the remaining two stones, one in each fist. Still Kleist was wary of making a decision in case he should, in some way he couldn't quite put his finger on, be taken advantage of.

"Get a move on," said Vague Henri, unusually irritable. With great reluctance Kleist tapped Henri's right hand and closed his eyes. Now they all had one stone each.

"On a count of three. One, two, three."

The three boys opened their fists. Cale was holding the smallest stone.

"Well, at least you know it'll be done properly."

"You needn't have worried, Cale," said Kleist. "I wouldn't have had any problems slotting you."

Cale looked at him, but the trace of a smile was still there.

"What are you doing?" Riba had woken up and had been watching them.

Kleist looked over at her. "We've been discussing who we eat first when we run out of food." He looked at her meaningfully, as if to suggest that the answer was pretty obvious.

"Don't listen to him," said Vague Henri. "We were just deciding who'd take the first watch."

"When is it my turn?" said Riba.

All three of the acolytes were surprised at the defiant, even irritable note in her voice.

"You need all the rest you can get," said Vague Henri.

"I'm ready to do my share."

"Of course. In a few days when you're more used to this. For now we need you as rested as possible. It's best—you can see that."

It was, of course, hard to argue.

"Would you like something to eat?" said Vague Henri, holding up a piece of dried rat. It did not look appetizing, least of all to a girl raised on cream and pastries, chicken pie and delicious gravies. But she was very hungry.

"What is it?" she said.

"Um. Meat," said Vague Henri vaguely.

He moved toward her and shoved it under her nose. It smelled very much as a dead rat might be expected to. Her delicate nose wrinkled in involuntary disgust.

"Ugh, no." Though she quickly added, "Thank you."

"Going without for a bit won't do her any harm," muttered Kleist under his breath, but loudly enough for the girl to hear. Riba, however, was not aware that she was in any way less than perfect. She had been told so all her life, and as a result Kleist's remark, although she was aware it was hostile, conveyed no specific insult to her at all.

"I'll take first watch," said Cale, and with that he turned and walked to the top of a nearby scab. The two remaining boys lay down and within minutes were asleep. Riba, however, could not settle and she began to sob quietly. Kleist and Vague Henri were dead to the world. Cale, however, on the top of the scab, could hear the sound of her crying and considered it carefully before finally she too fell asleep.

The next morning the boys woke at five as usual, but there was no point in striking camp, such as it was. "Let her sleep," said Cale. "The more rested she is the better."

"Without her we could be eighty, perhaps a hundred, miles from here," muttered Kleist. A knife thudded point-down at his feet.

"I took it from Picarbo. Cut her throat, if you like. Anything, so long as you stop whining." His tone was matter-of-fact, not angry at all. Kleist stared at Cale, eyes cold and full of dislike. Then he turned away. Vague Henri wondered if he had really been ready to kill the girl or perhaps use the knife on Cale—or whether he just liked having something to complain about. Cale, at any rate, was wise enough not to imply any kind of victory when he spoke again.

"I've an idea. Perhaps we can make use of the problem with the girl."

Kleist turned back, sullen—but he was listening.

"If we can't put distance between us and the search parties to east and west of us, it's best if we track them to make sure we don't cross them by accident."

He bent down and picked up the knife and started drawing in the sand. "If Henri and the girl move south in a straight line and don't do more than twelve miles a day, then Kleist and me will always know where you are, pretty much. Kleist goes west, I'll go east, and find the two nearest search parties." He gestured to the straight line he'd drawn for Henri and Riba. "If we think they're going to hit the search parties as they zigzag, then we return and take them off in the other direction."

Kleist looked thoughtful as well as dubious.

"Suppose you come back and take them off somewhere. How am I supposed to find you when you're not at the meeting point?"

Cale shrugged. "You'll have to decide whether to track us or make your own way to Memphis. Wait for us there as long as you think best."

Kleist sniffed and looked away. It was an agreement of sorts.

"Does that suit you?" asked Cale, nodding to Henri.

"Yes," said Vague Henri. "There are a lot of things I want to find out from the girl."

Within five minutes, having split the food and water, Kleist and Cale were moving off to east and west. In five minutes more they'd vanished from sight.

Vague Henri was sitting down eating his breakfast and looking at the girl as she slept, observing the beautiful pale skin, the red lips and the long eyelashes, the sense of beautiful peace. He was still watching, fascinated, an hour later when she woke up. She was startled at first to find Vague Henri looking straight at her, not more than three feet away.

"Didn't anyone ever tell you it's rude to stare?"

"No," said Vague Henri truthfully.

"Well, it is."

Henri looked down at his feet and now felt awkward.

"I'm sorry," she said. "I didn't mean to be so harsh."

At this, Vague Henri forgot his awkwardness and burst into laughter.

"What's so funny?" she said, angry again.

"For us, being harsh means dragging you out in front of five hundred people and the Redeemers stringing you up."

"What do you mean?"

"Hanging you by the neck. You know, like the Hanged Redeemer."

"Who's the Hanged Redeemer?"

This shut him up. He looked at her as if she had asked what the sun was, or if animals could talk. He said nothing for some time, but there were hammers beating in his brain about what this could possibly mean.

"The Hanged Redeemer is the son of the Lord of Creation. He sacrificed himself to wash our vile sins away with His blood."

"Uuugh!" she said. "Whatever for?"

His look of astonishment made her instantly regret her reaction. "I'm sorry, I didn't mean to offend you. It's just such a strange idea."

"What is?" he said, still openmouthed.

"Well . . . what sins? What did you do?"

"I was born sinful. Everyone is born full of revolting sin."

"What a ridiculous idea."

"Is it?"

"How can a baby have done anything wrong, let alone anything dreadful?"

Neither of them said anything for a moment. "And why would you wash something away in blood?"

"It's a symbol," he said, defensive and wondering why.

"I'm not stupid," she replied. "I can see that. But why? Why would you use blood as a symbol of something like that?"

Vague Henri was, by nature, someone who thought carefully about everything. But these ideas had been so much a part of him and for so long that she might just as well have questioned the point of his arms or the meaning of his eyes.

"Where are the others?" she said.

Still reeling over what he had heard, his answer was distracted. "Oh, they've gone."

"They've left us?" she said, eyes widening in alarm.

"Only for a few days. They're going to track down the searchers on either side of us and make sure we don't walk into them."

"How will they find us again?"

"They're very good at tracking," Henri said evasively.

"I don't understand," she said. "I thought you said you hardly ever left the Sanctuary?"

"Um . . . we better get going. I'll explain as we go along."

Redeemer Bosco raised his walking stick and rapped twice on the door.

It was nearly thirty seconds before it opened, but he did not show any sign of impatience, or indeed any sign at all. Finally the door opened and a tall man, another Redeemer, stood in front of the Lord Militant.

"Do you have an appointment?" said the tall man.

"Don't be foolish," replied Bosco, terse and dismissive. "The High Redeemer asked to see me. Here I am."

"The High Redeemer commands. He does not ask any—"

Bosco pushed past him. "Tell him I'm here."

"He's displeased with you. I've never seen him so angry." Bosco ignored him as the tall man went over to an inner door, knocked and went in. There was a short pause, the door opened again, and the tall man returned, smiling, though nothing pleasant was intended.

"He is ready to see you now."

Bosco walked into a room so dark that even the gloom-accustomed eyes of the Lord Militant found it hard to see. It was something more, though, than the small shuttered windows and the dark tapestries murkily retelling stories of ancient and hideous martyrdoms. The center of the darkness seemed to come from the bed in the corner. A man was sitting up, propped by at least a dozen uncomfortable cushions. Bosco had to move very close before he could make out the face, the skin pale to the point of being white and hanging down from cheek and neck in endless scrawny folds. The eyes were watery, as if the mind had long gone. But when he caught sight of Bosco something bright flashed there, a light full of hate and great cunning.

"You kept me waiting!" said the High Redeemer, the voice distant but sharp.

"I came as soon as I could, Your Grace." He was not believed, nor did he expect to be.

"When I summon you, Bosco, you drop everything instantly and damned quick." He laughed. It was a particularly unpleasant sound that only, perhaps, Bosco in all the Sanctuary would not have been unnerved by. It was the sound of something dead, animated only by an intense malice and anger.

"What did you wish to see me about, Your Grace?"

The High Redeemer stared at him for a moment. "That Cale boy."

"Yes, Your Grace?"

"He's made a fool of you."

"How so, Your Grace?"

"You had plans for him."

"You know that I did, Your Grace."

"He must be brought back."

"You and I differ on nothing, Your Grace."

"Brought back and scourged."

"Of course, Your Grace."

"Then hanged and quartered."

Bosco did not respond at first.

"He murdered a Redeemer. He must become an Act of Faith."

Bosco looked thoughtful for a moment.

"My investigations have made it clear that it was the two other acolytes who were responsible. It seems likely that they coerced Cale into leaving with them. They were armed; he was not. If this is true, then Cale should be punished merely as an example. The quartering, however, seems unnecessary to me. The others will do, given the fault is theirs."

There was a snort of contempt that might have been mistaken for choking.

"Ha! Pity is nothing of kin to you, Bosco. This is just your vanity talking. It doesn't matter whether Cale or these other two killed Picarbo. By God, I've half a mind to burn the entire dormitory along with them."

The High Redeemer had allowed himself to become rather too excited and was now choking on his own spittle. He gestured toward a mug of water on his bedside table. Taking his time, Bosco handed it to him. He drank noisily. Finally, he handed back the now sloppy wet mug. Bosco replaced it on the table with a look of fine distaste.

Gradually the High Redeemer's sucking breath began to slow and return to normal. The light of malevolence, however, had only increased.

"Tell me about this business with Picarbo."

"Business, Your Grace?"

"Yes, *business*, Bosco, the business of the Lord of Discipline being found in his rooms with a disemboweled slut!"

"Ah," said Bosco thoughtfully. "That business."

"You think because I'm old and sick that I don't know what's going on here? Well, not for the first time, you're wrong. Sick as I am, you still can't get up early enough to catch me out, Bosco."

"No one of any intelligence would underestimate your wisdom and experience, Your Grace, but . . ." He let out a regretful sigh. "I had hoped to spare you the revolting nature of what we found in Redeemer Picarbo's rooms. It would be a pity if a reign as distinguished as your own should be overshadowed by something like this."

"I'm too old for that flannel, Bosco. I want to know what he was doing with her. It wasn't just fucking, was it?"

Even Bosco, a man apparently unmoved by anything, was unsettled by the use of the term. Such direct reference to the sex act was never heard, it usually being spoken of only using such circumlocutions as "beastliness" and "uglification"—though, even then, rarely.

"Perhaps his soul had gone bad. Evil is always at work, Your Grace. He had perhaps taken pleasure in the just punishments meted out to the acolytes. It has been known before, I think."

The High Redeemer grunted. "How did he get hold of a girl out here?"

"As yet I have been unable to find out. But he had many keys. You and I alone would be permitted to ask questions of a Lord of Discipline. It will take time."

"He couldn't have done this without help. This could be about more than beastliness—it might be a heresy."

"The thought had occurred to me, Your Grace. There are twenty of

his cronies in isolation in the House of Special Purpose. The more senior deny—so far—that they knew anything, but the ordinary Redeemers admit they created a further cordon around the convent under
Picarbo's orders by sealing up farther layers of corridors so no one would
suspect anything. The convent was already completely isolated from the
Redeemers, after all. No one was ever supposed to see the brides' faces.
Picarbo disguised their activities in and out of the place by moving the
kitchen and laundry used for higher Redeemers inside the cordon. Everything goes in and out by a great drum. Because Picarbo had the Lord
of Vittles and the Master of the Laundry as part of his little set of heretics, there was no problem drawing off food or anything else."

"But we're opening up the old corridors by the mile. Molloy would
have found them sooner or later."

"Unfortunately the Master of Reclamation was one of them."

"My God! That sanctimonious pismire Molloy was helping turn
the Sanctuary into a whorehouse?" The High Redeemer lay and gasped
at the horrible enormity of it all. "We need a purging, we need Acts of
Faith from here to the end of the year . . . we must disem—"

"Your Grace," interrupted Bosco, "it is by no means clear that uglification was the purpose of this harem. I'm not sure it was a harem at
all, more a place of isolation. From what I have been able to decipher
from his writings, mad as they are, Picarbo was looking for something,
something very specific."

"What would he find in the bowels of some fat slut?"

"I can't say as yet, Your Grace. Purging may be required, and a great
deal of it, but we should wait until I've got to the bottom of this before
we start lighting the candles to God." Lighting candles to God had
nothing to do with wax or wicks.

"You watch out, Bosco. You think that you're the better for knowing things, but I know . . . " He jabbed a finger at Bosco and raised his
voice, "I KNOW that knowledge is the root of all evil. That bitch Eve
wanted to know things and that was what brought sin and death down
upon all of us."

Bosco stood up and moved to the door.

"Redeemer Bosco!"

Bosco turned and looked at the shriveled old priest.

"When you bring Cale back here, he is to be executed. And I will issue an order to that effect today. And you forget about digging into that shit Picarbo's debauchery. You cleanse everyone who had dealings with him. I don't care if they might be innocent. We can't take the chance of heresy—burn them and let God sort them out. The blameless will get a better reward of eternal life."

An observer of the kind on whom nothing was lost might have seen the Lord Militant blink as if he had considered something and made a decision. But it might merely have been a trick of the lack of light. He stepped forward and bent down as if to plump up the pillows around the High Redeemer. But instead he took one of them and placed it carefully and firmly around his tiny old face, all of it done with such speed and so little fuss that it was only in the fraction of a second before the pillow closed over his mouth that the Lord High Redeemer realized the horror of what was happening.

Two minutes later Bosco emerged from the bedroom and saw the tall Redeemer instantly stand up to go into his master.

"He fell asleep while we were talking. Not like the High Redeemer at all. Perhaps you should take a look at him."

Bosco had not only murdered the High Redeemer—he'd lied to him. He had not told him the true extent of Picarbo's collection of young women or of his growing suspicions about the aims of the late Lord of Discipline's disgusting experiments. There would need to be a period of assessment concerning what to do with the women, but in due course they would make an extremely useful pretext for his next move to take complete control of the Sanctuary and an object lesson for Cale on his return.

By the third day Cale had caught up with the Redeemers and had watched them turn west, taking them away from Vague Henri and

Riba. And after another day they turned east, which would have taken them dangerously close to the pair. It was while following and hoping they would turn again that the only truly unusual experience of his watch took place.

He was approaching the end of one of the Scabland hillocks, one that had collapsed and formed a jagged edge. As he turned the corner, he bumped into a man coming the other way. Cale was so surprised he almost lost his feet on the loose gravel, but the man, standing on a steeper section, could get no purchase and crashed onto his back with a hefty thud.

It gave Cale time to pull the knife he had stolen from the Lord of Discipline and stand over the man with him at his mercy. The man, however, quickly got over his surprise at the strange sight and groaned as he started to get to his feet. Cale waved the knife at him to make it clear he should stay where he was.

"So," said the man with weary amiability, "first you bump into me and now you want to cut my throat. Not very friendly."

"People do say that about me. What are you doing out here?"

The man smiled. "What everyone does in the Scablands—trying to get out."

"I won't ask you a second time."

"I don't think that's really any of your business."

"I'm the one with the knife, so I'll decide what's my business or not."

"A good point. May I get up?"

"You'll do where you are for the moment."

The man looked as if he'd seen a few odd things in his life, but he was clearly puzzled by the presence of someone so young and so self-possessed in the middle of the Scablands.

"You're a long way from home, aren't you, boy?"

"Never mind about me, Granddad. You need to be more worried about where you're going to buy a walking stick all the way out here."

The man laughed.

"You're a Redeemer's acolyte, aren't you?"

"What's it to you?"

"Nothing, really. It's just that on the few occasions I've seen an acolyte they were in rows of two hundred and there were a couple of dozen Redeemers watching them with whips. Never seen one on his own before."

"Well," said Cale, "there's a first time for everything."

The man smiled.

"Yes, I suppose there is." He held his hand out. "IdrisPukke, currently in the service of Gauleiter Hynkel."

Cale didn't take his hand. IdrisPukke shrugged and lowered it.

"Perhaps you're not as young as you look. It's wise to be careful out here."

"Thanks for the advice."

IdrisPukke laughed again.

"You don't compromise, do you, boy?"

"No," said Cale flatly. "And don't call me boy."

"As you prefer. What should I call you?"

"You don't need to call me anything." Cale nodded toward the west. "You're going that way. Try to follow me, IdrisPukke, and then you'll see just how uncompromising I can be." He gestured that he should get up. IdrisPukke did as he was told. He looked at Cale for a few moments, as if carefully considering what he would do. Then he sighed, turned round and went off in the direction Cale had signaled.

For the next twelve hours Cale remained intensely suspicious of the meeting with IdrisPukke. Was he a Redeemer in disguise, for example? Not likely. Too much liveliness of soul came off him for one of them. A bounty man? Again, not likely. The Redeemers kept things like this to themselves. On the other hand he had killed a Lord of Discipline, a sin of such foulness that they might be ready to do anything to get him back. So it was on this thread that he stayed while he tracked the Lord

Redeemers and hoped they would change direction. A day later they did so, heading west again. Usually the hunters would stay that way for at least twenty-four hours. It was time to get back to the others. If he could find them.

Twelve hours later he was on the line they had planned for Henri and the girl to take. But ten miles ahead, just in case. Then he started to walk back down the line to make sure he didn't miss them, all the while keeping as hidden as he could so that the Redeemers Kleist was supposed to be spotting didn't blunder into him or he into them. It was only a few hours before he found all three of them standing in a large hollow surrounded by some twenty mutilated bodies, some cut into small pieces. The others saw him from a hundred yards away and waited, without moving, as he walked through the scatter of dead bodies. He nodded to all three of them.

"The Redeemers have gone to the west," he said.

"Last time I was with mine, they'd turned east."

Then there was silence.

"Any idea who they are?" said Cale, nodding at the dead.

"No," said Vague Henri.

"They've been dead for about a day, I'd say," said Kleist.

Riba had something of the same stunned look about her Cale had seen when he rescued her from Picarbo—a look that said: this isn't happening.

"How long have you been here?" he asked softly.

"About twenty minutes. We met Kleist on the way here a couple of hours ago."

Cale nodded. "We'd better search them. Whoever did this hasn't left much, but there might be some salvage."

The three boys started to search among the remains, finding the occasional coin, a belt, a torn coat. Then Vague Henri spotted something shiny in the sand next to a severed head and quickly brushed the sand away, only to discover it was a brass knuckle duster. He was disappointed, but it was at least useful.

"Help me," groaned the severed head.

With a cry Henri leapt backward.

"It spoke to me, it spoke to me!"

"What?" said Kleist, irritable.

"The head. It spoke."

"Help me," groaned the head.

"See!" said Vague Henri.

Carefully Cale approached the head with his knife and poked it in the temple. The head groaned but did not open his eyes.

"They've buried him up to his neck," he said after a moment of careful consideration. The three boys, familiar with human atrocity, realized now that nothing supernatural was involved. They all looked down at the buried man and considered what was to be done.

"We should dig him out," said Vague Henri.

"No," said Kleist. "Whoever did this went to a lot of trouble. I can't see they'd take kindly to us ruining their efforts. We should leave well enough alone."

"Help me," whispered the man again.

Vague Henri looked at Cale. "Well?" he said.

Cale said nothing, thinking carefully.

"We haven't got all day, Cale," said Kleist. By now Cale was looking into the distance.

"No, we haven't." Cale's tone of voice was odd, alarming. The other two looked up, following his flat gaze. At the top of the nearest hillock, about three hundred yards away, a line of Redeemers was looking down at them. Then the line began to move.

The boys, all three of them pale, stood still. There was nowhere to run. Riba moved first, running forward to get a better look at the line of men marching toward them.

"No. No. No," she said, over and over again.

Vague Henri, white as flour, looked at Cale.

"You drew the small stone," he said.

Cale stared at his friend, eyes expressionless. There was a moment's pause, and then Cale took out his knife and walked quickly toward Riba, who was still staring at the line of advancing men. As Cale moved to grab her hair and expose her neck, Kleist called out.

"Wait!"

At this Riba turned round. Cale had lowered the knife, but even in her terrified state she could see that something odd was happening.

"They're not Redeemers," said Kleist. "Whatever they are. Best just to let's see what happens."

As they watched, more men came over the top of the hillock, but they were on horses and leading behind them thirty more. The riders caught up with the men on foot, who then themselves mounted, and within less than a minute, fifty or so bad-tempered cavalrymen surrounded the four of them. Half of them dismounted and began examining the remains of the bodies. The others, swords drawn, just stared at the four.

One of the cavalrymen looking at the bodies called out: "Captain, it's the Embassy from Arnhemland. This is Lord Pardee's son."

The captain, a large man on an enormous horse nearly twenty hands high, moved it forward and dismounted. He walked over to Cale and without pausing fetched him such a hefty blow to the face that the boy crashed heavily to the ground.

"Before we execute you, I want to know who ordered this."

Dazed and in pain, Cale did not answer. The captain was about to add a kick of encouragement when Vague Henri spoke up.

"It was nothing to do with us, Lord. We only came on them just now. Do we look as if we could have done this?" Henri thought it best to tell the truth. "We only have one knife between us. How could we?"

The captain looked at him and then back at Cale. Then he delivered a hefty kick to Cale's stomach.

"Fair enough. We won't cut your throats for murder—we'll do it for looting."

He looked over at the small pile of things they had collected from whatever the killers had missed—a bag, a plate, some kitchen knives and dried fruit as well as the brass knuckle duster. Henri could see that it looked bad.

"One of them's still alive. We were just about to dig him out." Henri pointed to the now unconscious man who, more than ever, looked like a severed head in the dust.

Quickly the soldiers surrounded him and began digging at the sand and gravel.

"It's Chancellor Vipond," said one of them. The captain waved them to stop and knelt down, taking out a flask of water. Gently he poured a little into the unconscious man's mouth. He coughed, spitting all the water back.

By now one of the soldiers had brought forward a pair of shovels, and within five minutes they had eased the man out of the sand and laid him on the ground. There was much listening to his heart and checking him for wounds.

"We were going to save him," said Henri, as Cale looked at the captain malevolently from his pitch in the dust.

"That's what you say. All I know for sure is that you're a bunch of thieves. No reason not to sell the girl and kill you three."

"Don't be unreasonable, Captain Bramley, darling," called out a man's voice from behind a mounted cavalryman's horse. That he was not one of them was clear from the fact that he did not wear a uniform and that both his hands were tied and hung from a rope knotted to the saddle of the horse in front of him.

"Shut your big gob, IdrisPukke," said the captain.

But IdrisPukke was clearly not a man to do as he was told.

"Be wise for once, Captain, darling. You know that Chancellor Vipond and me go back time out of mind. He wouldn't take kindly, I'd say, to you killing three young men who'd tried to save him. What do you think?"

The captain looked uncertain for the first time. IdrisPukke dropped the mocking tone. "He'd want the chance to make up his own mind. That's for certain."

The captain looked down at the unconscious man, now being put onto a stretcher with a rolled blanket under his head. He looked back at IdrisPukke.

"One more word out of you and, I swear to God, I'll disembowel you where you stand. Understand me?"

IdrisPukke shrugged but wisely, thought Vague Henri, said nothing. "Grady! Fog!" the captain called out to two soldiers. "Stay close to this gobshite. And if he even looks like he's going to try and escape, blow his bloody head off."

$\mathcal{C}$aptain Bramley just tied the hands of the three boys and let them walk and occasionally run behind the horses. However, as a punishment for IdrisPukke, he kept him tied to a saddle and, in response to his mocking pleas to be allowed to ride in the arms of a cavalryman like the girl, administered numerous kicks for his trouble.

They made camp about half an hour before dark. Riba was left free with the cavalrymen, who were given a bad-tempered warning by Bramley not to touch her. These were hard men who had seen and done much, a great deal of it too unpleasant to tell, but the warning was barely needed for most of them. While some would happily have done mischief to the beautiful young girl, most seemed entranced by her as she chatted and joked with them, artlessly flirting and opening her eyes in amazement at the endless supply of stories that any soldier delighted in telling. Despite a number of sympathetic looks over at the boys, she had been told to steer clear of them and that any attempt to talk would mean she'd be tied up.

Instead they had IdrisPukke as a companion, all four of them chained to the axle of a carriage that had joined up with the cavalry shortly after their capture. The boys had been fed but not IdrisPukke, who was given a kick instead of bully beef and soda bread. They were starving and began to gobble the lot as quickly as dogs.

"What about sharing some of that?"

"Why should we?" said Kleist from behind a stuffed mouth.

"Oh, because I interceded on your behalf when that bastard Bramley wanted to spill your guts onto the oh so hungry sands of the Scablands."

Kleist quickly finished his last mouthful.

"Sorry about that—but thanks for this afternoon."

The other two were more gracious, even if Cale was only willing to offer his soda bread because he wanted to question IdrisPukke.

Unlike the boys, IdrisPukke took his time over the bread and the small amount of bully beef left by Vague Henri.

"Do you know anything about the killings?" asked Cale.

"Me?" said IdrisPukke. "I was going to ask you the same thing." He took another bite of the soda bread. "Were you going to help Vipond?"

There was a pause as Vague Henri and Cale looked at each other.

"We were thinking about it," said Cale.

"Very wise. Always think carefully before doing anyone a favor. Good advice. In your friend's case," he added, nodding at Kleist, "I wish I'd taken it."

"You'd have gone without your dinner if you had."

IdrisPukke laughed softly. "Not much of an exchange—two pieces of bread for three lives. I'd say you still owed me."

"There's nothing we can do for you," said Vague Henri.

"Perhaps not. But in future I may have to call it in. I hope you're honorable men."

Cale laughed.

"Are you an honorable man?"

"You'd be laughing on the other side of your face if I wasn't."

Vague Henri thought it best to change the subject.

"What do you think they'll do to us?"

IdrisPukke shrugged. "They'll take you to Memphis. If Vipond lives, you should be all right." He smiled. "As long as you stick to your story."

"And if he doesn't?" asked Vague Henri.

"Depends. They might put you on trial or they might just throw you in the bypass."

"What's that?"

"Somewhere you get forgotten about."

"We didn't do anything," said Cale.

"So I gather." He laughed again. "But don't tell them that."

"Who do you think killed them?"

IdrisPukke considered.

"There are lots of hooligans in the outer Scablands, but not many would think of touching an armed embassy from the Materazzi."

"Who are they?"

"My God, don't they teach you anything at that place?"

All three looked at him, stony of expression.

"Right. Well, the Materazzi rule Memphis and everywhere up to the Scablands and down as far as the Great Bight—which I can see you've never heard of either."

"What's Memphis like?"

"Wonderful. The greatest show on earth. There's nothing you can't get in Memphis, nothing that can't be bought or sold, no crime that hasn't been committed, no food they haven't eaten, no practice"—he paused— "unpracticed. You're in for a treat as long as they don't kill you or forget you—and of course as long as you have money."

"We don't," said Cale.

"Then you must get it. If you have no money in Memphis, there's no point to you. And if there's no point to you in Memphis, someone will soon find one for you."

"What do you—"

"Enough questions. I'm sore and tired. We'll talk in the morning." He winked. "If I'm still here." And with that IdrisPukke turned over and within five minutes was snoring.

They assumed he was joking as he so often and so puzzlingly seemed to be, but next morning when they woke up IdrisPukke had gone.

Captain Bramley was furious and gave all three boys a good kicking, and though it did make them feel considerably worse, it didn't seem to make him feel better. Riba had rushed over and begged him to stop.

"Why would they help him to escape and stay behind themselves?" she pointed out desperately. "It isn't fair!"

The boys, being old hands at unfairness, stoically kept their mouths shut and tried to keep their more tender portions away from the point of Captain Bramley's boot. Fortunately for them he was a railer and a flailer rather than one of the skillful sadists they were used to. Unfairness was as familiar to them as water, not least because a beating was often preceded by a reference to the Hanged Redeemer's direst warning that anyone who hurt a child would be better off being cast into the sea with a millstone around his neck. When the boys first arrived they were frequently told stories and parables about the kindness of the Holy Redeemer and his particular regard for the young, whose care and happiness were always being recommended to those around him. At first the fact that they were often beaten for no good reason prior to these homilies of love and kindness, and often afterward too, was the cause of bewildered resentment. Over the years, however, the contradictions ceased to exist and the words of comfort and joy went in one ear and out the other. They were just words, bereft of meaning to all concerned.

Having worked out his initial burst of rage on the boys, Bramley turned to his sergeant and corporal, who stood by with weary patience for their turn.

"You!" he shouted at the sergeant. "You big fat sack of shit. And you!" he said, looking at the corporal, a much smaller man. "You scrawny *little* sack of shit. Get ten of your best men and find that bastard IdrisPukke. And if you come back without him, and alive, you bring your dinner, both of you, because when I've finished with you you're going to bloody need it."

And with this he stamped off toward his tent.

"Keep interrogating the prisoners," he yelled over his shoulder.

The sergeant let out a deep breath of disdain and patient irritation. "You heard what the man said, Corporal."

The corporal approached the three boys, now backed against the wheel of the wagon, knees drawn up to protect themselves.

"Do you know anything about the escape of the prisoner?"

"No!" yelled back a furious but frightened Kleist.

"The prisoner says no," reported the corporal calmly.

"Ask him if he's sure, Corporal."

"Are you sure?"

"Yes, I'm sure," said Kleist. "Why, in God's name, would he tell us where he was going?"

"He has a point, Sergeant."

"Yes," said the sergeant wearily. "Yes, he does." There was a pause. "Mount up Seven Platoon and wake up Scout Calhoun. We'll be on our way in ten minutes."

With that the soldiers around them dispersed and the boys and Riba were left alone as if nothing had happened. She knelt down beside them and looked at them with heartbreaking pity—an emotion, it has to be said, that they barely appreciated. Firstly, they were more concerned with their own bruises, and secondly, they were not capable of understanding that she could actually feel for their pain. Except for Vague Henri, perhaps, who when they had been together for the week in the Scablands had stripped to the waist to wash when they'd come across one of its few streams. He had caught her surreptitiously looking at his back and the numerous scars and gouges and weals that covered it. Even though he had never encountered feminine sympathy before, he was, in a confused way, it's true, alive to its strange power.

Then the camp itself started to move. The prisoners were fed on porridge and they were off. Before she was taken away, Riba whispered excitedly that in two days they would be in Memphis. The three of them were unable to share her enthusiasm, given the uncertainty of the welcome that awaited them.

"The old guy," said Kleist to Riba, "the one we were about to rescue. Is he dead?"

"I don't think so."

"Try to do something useful and find out," said Kleist.

Her eyes opened wide at this rebuke and started to mist.

"Leave her alone," said Vague Henri.

"Why?" said Kleist. "They're going to hang us if he dies—so I don't see how she can be riding to Memphis on her fat arse and not finding out what we need to know."

The mistiness was instantly replaced by indignation.

"Why do you keep saying that I'm fat? I'm supposed to be like this."

"No more arguments," said Cale irritably. "Kleist—leave her alone. You—find out what's happened to the old man."

Riba looked at Cale, shocked and angry, but said nothing.

"March or die! March or die!" The corporals cried out, the threat no longer significant, because this was called every time they struck camp and moved on. The cart to which the boys were tied lurched and moved on, and they left Riba behind, staring at them furiously. Later that day, however, she walked by them, nose still clearly out of joint, and said as if it were a matter of no possible consequence:

"He's still alive."

The Scablands came to an end quite suddenly within a hundred meters. They moved from grit, ash, stones and scruffy hillocks to a green and fertile plain already spotted with farms, houses and the huts of workers. People emerged from behind hedges and clumping barrows to take a look at them. Not for long, though—the sight of the soldiers, baggage and prisoners was enough to make them curious, but after a gawp of twenty seconds or so everyone but the children went back to what he was doing.

For the rest of the day and all the next the number of houses and people grew denser. First villages, then towns, then the suburbs of Memphis itself. But it was still two hours more before they saw its great Citadel.

They had stopped because of traffic jams, and one of the corporals, seeing them stare, amazed, at the city, moved his horse forward.

"Those walls are the greatest in the world—fifty foot thick at the weakest and twice five miles around." The boys looked at him.

"That'd be ten miles, then," said Kleist.

The corporal's face fell and he spurred the horse onward.

11

The last two miles up to the great gates of the Citadel of Memphis consisted entirely of markets of one kind or another. The noise and the smells and the colors left the boys wide-eyed and almost overwhelmed with delight. Any traveler would have considered it an experience to take with him until the Day of the Dead—but for three boys whose staple food was something called dead men's feet, varied by an occasional rat, this was heaven itself, only a heaven rich and strange beyond imagining. Each drawn-in breath came with the smell of cumin and rosemary and along with it the sweat of a herder selling goats, a housewife dashed with oil of tangerine, a whiff of urine and the smell of roses. There were calls and cries from every direction: the squawk of cooking parrots, the meow of the gourmet's favorite—the Memphis boiling cat—the cooing of sacrificial doves, the bark of dogs raised in the hills around the city for roasting on holidays; pigs squealed, cows groaned, and a huge shout went up as a pike about to be gutted flapped its way loose from a fishmonger and flailed its way to freedom in a sewer. A cry of tragic loss from the monger, derisive laughter from the crowd.

On they moved through the traders' incomprehensible cries, "Widdee, Widdee, Wee!" called out a man who seemed to be selling bright pink cow tails from a casket, shaved of skin and the color of candy floss. "Etchy-Gudda-Munda," shouted another, displaying his vegetables with a hand swept out with all the smugness of a magician who had just made them appear from thin air. "Buyee myah vegetables ah! Rhyup tommies. Deliciosa pinnapules. Buy ah my herbage, my gorgheous botany."

Some stalls were on sites filling half an acre—and on one corner an old man, half-naked, held out a ragged cloth, trying to sell the two speckled eggs it contained and hopping from foot to foot.

Gawping around to his left, Vague Henri saw a train of boys of around nine years, linked by chain round their necks, being led toward a gate watched over by huge men in leather jackets, who nodded them through. The boys seemed unconcerned, but what truly alarmed Vague Henri was that the lips of the boys were painted red and their eyelids powdered in a delicate blue.

Vague Henri called over to one of the soldiers next to him. He nodded at the boys and the building through the gate, gaudily painted and even more crowded than the market.

"What's going on there?"

The solider looked at the boys and his face paled over with disgust.

"That's Kitty Town. Never go there." He paused and looked sadly at Vague Henri. "Not if you have a choice."

"Why is it called Kitty Town?"

"Because it's run by Kitty the Hare. And so you don't ask any more questions, he ain't no woman and he ain't no hare. Stay away."

As they entered past the guards into the city of Memphis proper, the change was instant: from the crush and noise and smell of the market into the deep cool of the tunnel. Within thirty yards of near darkness under the walls they were out in the light again. And then again it was another world. Unlike the Sanctuary, where brownness and uniformity made everywhere look like everywhere else, in the citadel there was endless variety: a palace with spiky copper minarets blooming with green stood next to a manor house of yellow and purple brick. There were tailor-perfect boulevards with trees whose trunks were painted white with chalk, and leading off them warped and ancient lanes so narrow even a cat would think twice before entering. Hardly anyone looked at the boys: it was as if they were not so much ignored as unseen. Except by the younger children, who ogled them from behind the delicate iron railings of the garden squares, all curls and golden hair.

Then there was a burst of activity from one of the roads above them, and twenty household cavalry in red and gold uniforms clattered into the square escorting a decorated carriage. They headed urgently toward the caravan and pulled up around the covered wagon in which Lord Vipond lay unconscious. The carriage opened its two wide doors and three important-looking men rushed toward the wagon and disappeared inside. The boys all stood for five minutes and waited in the cool breeze and the shadows of the trees that lined the square.

A small girl, perhaps five years old, walked unseen by her gossiping mother up to the rail nearest the three acolytes.

"Hey, you, boy."

Cale looked at her with all the considerable unfriendliness he could muster.

"Yes, boy, you."

"What?" said Cale.

"You have a face like a pig."

"Go away."

"Where have you come from, boy?"

He looked at her again.

"From hell, to take you away in the night and eat you."

She considered this for a moment.

"You look like an ordinary boy to me. A dirty, ordinary boy."

"Looks can be deceiving," said Cale. By this time Kleist was interested.

"You'll see," he said to the little girl. "Three nights from now we're going to break into your room, but very quiet-like so your mother can't hear. And then we'll put a gag in your mouth and then we'll probably eat you there and then. And then all we'll leave behind is some bones."

Her confidence in their ordinariness seemed to waver. But she was not a girl to be easily frightened.

"My dada will stop you and kill you dead."

"No, he won't, because we'll eat him too. Probably first, so you'll know what's coming."

Cale laughed aloud at this and shook his head at Kleist's pleasure in the exchange.

"Stop encouraging her," he said, smiling. "She looks like a snitch to me."

"I am *not* a snitch!" said the little girl indignantly.

"You don't even know what a snitch is," said Kleist.

"Yes, I do."

"Quiet!" whispered Cale.

The girl's mother had finally missed her and was hurrying over to her.

"Come away, Jemima."

"I was just talking to the dirty boys."

"Be quiet, bold girl! You mustn't talk about these unfortunate creatures like that. I'm sorry," she said to the boys. "Apologize now, Jemima."

"I won't."

She started to drag her away. "Then there will be no pudding for you!"

"What about us?" Kleist called. "What about pudding for us?"

Now there was movement ahead, and six household soldiers were lifting down Chancellor Vipond while the three men looked on with worried faces. He was taken to the carriage and carefully lifted inside. Within a minute the carriage had left the square, and the caravan moved on slowly behind.

Three hours later they were inside the last keep, had been taken down to the cells, stripped, searched and had three buckets of freezing water thrown at them, smelling of unpleasant chemicals unfamiliar to them. Then they'd been given back their clothes, dusted in itchy white powder and locked in a cell. They sat in silence for thirty minutes until Kleist gave a sigh and said, "Whose idea was this? Oh, yes, Cale's. I forgot."

"The difference between here and the Sanctuary," replied Cale, as if barely interested enough to reply, "is that here we don't know what's going to happen. If we were back there we would, and it would involve a lot of screaming." It was hard to argue with this, and within a few minutes they were all asleep.

For three days Lord Vipond drifted closer and closer to death. Many were the balms and medicines given to him, the aromatic herbs burned day and night; tinctures of this and that were smoothed on his wounds. Each one of these treatments was either useless or positively harmful and only Vipond's natural vigor and good health pulled him through, despite the best efforts of the finest physicians Memphis could provide. Just when his heirs had been told to prepare for the worst (or, from their point of view, the best), Vipond woke up and croakingly demanded that the windows be opened, the noxious herbs removed and his body washed in boiled water.

In a few days, no longer deprived of cool fresh air and with his natural defenses able to do their work, he was sitting up and giving an account of the events that led to him being buried up to his neck in the sandy grit of the Scablands.

"We were about four days from Memphis when we were hit by a sandstorm, though it was more gravel than sand. That was what scattered the caravan, and before we could regroup Gurriers attacked us. They killed everyone as they stood—but for some reason they decided to leave me as you found me."

The man he was speaking to was Captain Albin, head of the Materazzi's secret service—a tall man with the blue eyes of a young girl. This striking feature was in great contrast to the rest of his appearance, which was precise (he looked as if he had just been ironed) and cool.

"You're sure," asked Albin, "that it was just Gurriers?"

"I'm not an expert on bandits, Captain, but that was what Pardee told me before he died. Do you have any reason to think otherwise?"

"Some odd things."

"Such as?"

"The way the columns were attacked seemed too organized, too deft for Gurriers. They're opportunists and butchers, and they rarely band together in the numbers needed to take soldiers of the quality who were guarding you—even if they were scattered by the storm."

"I see," said Vipond.

"And also, the fact that they left you alive. Why?"

"Barely alive."

"True. But why risk it? At all?" Albin walked over to the window and looked down on the courtyard below.

"You were found with a folded paper pushed into your mouth."

Vipond looked at him, and an unpleasant sensation came back to him of his jaws being forced open and having to fight for breath before he lost consciousness.

"I'm sorry, Lord Vipond. This must be upsetting. Would you like me to come back tomorrow?"

"No. It's all right. What was on the paper?"

"It was the message you were carrying from Gauleiter Hynkel to Marshal Materazzi promising that there would be peace in our time."

"Where is it?"

"Count Materazzi has it."

"It's worthless."

"Ah," said Albin, thoughtfully. "You think so? That *is* interesting."

"Because?"

"Leaving you alive with a message of some importance stuffed in your mouth looks like someone trying to make a point."

"Such as what?"

"An obscure point. Deliberately perhaps. It certainly doesn't seem like Gurriers. They're interested in rape and thieving, not political messages—clear or otherwise."

"If it was a message—shouldn't it have been clearer?"

"Not necessarily. Hynkel thinks of himself as something of a prankster. It would amuse him, no doubt, to disguise such an attack on a minister of the Materazzi, while also unsettling us by making us think there was more to it." Albin smiled, self-deprecatingly. "But you've met him more recently: perhaps you disagree?"

"Not at all. He was a good-humored host but he twinkled a good deal too much. Like many clever men, he thinks that everyone else is a fool."

"That's certainly what he thinks of our ambassador."

There was a slight pause and Albin wondered if he had gone too far. Vipond looked him over carefully.

"You seem to know a great deal," said Vipond, careful yet inviting him to go on.

"A great deal? I wish that were true. But something. In a few days I may have news that could clear this up one way or the other."

"I would be extremely grateful if you would keep me informed. I have resources also that might be of use."

"Of course, my lord."

Albin was pleased with what looked like an arrangement. It was not a question of whether Vipond could be trusted, because he most certainly could not. The court at Memphis was a nest of vipers, and no one without sharp teeth full of venom could have occupied a place as important as Vipond's. It was unreasonable to expect otherwise. Still, he felt there was progress toward an understanding, the understanding being that he could depend on Vipond not to betray him until it was seriously in his interests to do so.

"There are one or two other matters I'd like to discuss with you, my lord. But of course if you're too tired, I can return tomorrow."

"Not at all. Please . . ."

"There's the odd matter of four young persons that Bramley found standing over you when you were . . ." He paused.

"Buried up to my neck?"

"Well, yes."

"I thought," said Chancellor Vipond, "that was a dream. Three boys and a girl."

"Yes."

"What were they doing?"

"Ah, we thought you might be able to answer. Bramley wants to execute the boys and sell the girl."

"What on earth for?"

"He thinks they were part of the Gurrier band who attacked you."

"They attacked us at least twenty-four hours before I was found. What in God's name would they be doing there if they had anything to do with the Gurriers?"

"Bramley still wants to execute them. He says we need to send a message that anyone who attacks a minister of the Materazzi should know what's coming to them."

"He's a bloodthirsty bastard, this Bramley of yours."

"Oh, he's not one of mine—God forbid."

"What do these children have to say for themselves?"

"That they'd just arrived and were about to dig you up."

"And you don't believe them?"

"There were no signs of digging." Albin paused. "And I wouldn't say they were children exactly. The three boys are thirteen or fourteen, but hard-looking creatures. The girl, on the other hand, looks as if she'd been stored in soft soap. And what were they doing in the middle of the Scablands?"

"What did they have to say for themselves?"

"They said they were gypsies."

Vipond laughed. "There haven't been any gypsies in this part of the world since the Redeemers wiped them out sixty years ago."

He looked thoughtful for a moment. "I'll talk to them myself in a few days when I feel better. Pass me that cup of water. There's a good fellow."

Albin reached to the table beside the bed and handed Vipond the cup. He was looking very pale now.

"I'll leave you, Chancellor."

"You said there were two things?"

Albin stopped. "Yes. Before Bramley found you he caught Idris-Pukke skulking about four or so miles away."

"Excellent," said Vipond, his eyes alight with interest. "I'll talk to him tomorrow."

"Unfortunately he escaped."

Vipond gasped with irritation. He did not speak for nearly a minute.

"I want IdrisPukke. If he ever comes under your hand, you will bring him to me, and tell no one else."

Albin nodded. "Of course." He left Vipond's room a satisfied man.

It was the sixth day of their captivity in the cells underneath Memphis, but despite the uncertainty the three boys were in good spirits. They had three good meals a day, which is to say that by the standards of a normal person they had three revolting meals a day; they were able to sleep as long as they liked, and they did so for as much as eighteen hours, as if making up for the deprivations of a lifetime. At about four in the afternoon their jailer unlocked the cell door and showed in Albin, who had interrogated them once before, along with a clearly much-revered man in his late fifties.

"Good afternoon," said Lord Vipond.

Vague Henri and Kleist looked at him carefully from their beds. Cale was sitting on his with his knees drawn up to his chest and his hood drawn over his face.

"On your feet when Lord Vipond enters the room," said Albin quietly. Slowly Vague Henri and Kleist stood up. Cale did not move.

"You, stand up and remove your hood—or I'll get the guards to do it for you." Again Albin's voice was quiet, unthreatening, matter-of-fact.

There was a pause, and then Cale sprang to his feet as if rising from a refreshing sleep and flicked back his hood. He stared at the floor as if he found what was in the dust of immense interest.

"So," said Vipond. "Do you recognize me?"

"Yes," said Kleist. "You're the man we tried to rescue in the Scablands."

"That's right," said Vipond. "What were you doing there?"

"We're gypsies," said Kleist. "We got lost."

"What kind of gypsies?"

"Oh, the usual kind," said Kleist, smiling.

"Captain Bramley thinks you were trying to rob me."

Kleist sighed. "He's a bad man, that Captain Bramley, a very bad man. All we were doing was trying to save an important person like yourself and he chains us up like criminals and puts us in here. Not very grateful."

There was a strange and alarming gaiety about the way Kleist was cheeking the great man in front of him, as if not only did he not expect to be believed, but he did not care whether he was or not. Vipond had met this kind of insolence from only one other source: men he had accompanied to the gallows who knew that nothing could save them.

"We were going to help you," said Vague Henri—and of course from his point of view he was telling the truth.

Vipond looked over at Cale.

"What's your name?"

Cale did not respond.

"Come with me." Vipond walked to the door. The jailer quickly opened it. Vipond turned back to Cale. "Come on, boy. Are you deaf as well as insolent?" Cale looked at Vague Henri, who nodded, as if urging him to agree. Cale did not move for a moment but then slowly walked to the cell door.

"Follow us, if you'd be so kind, Captain Albin." Vipond set off with Cale behind him and Albin hanging back, his finger loosening the clasp holding his shortsword in its scabbard. Kleist moved to the bars as the cell was locked.

"What about me? I fancy a walk too."

Then the two boys heard the outer door being unlocked and Cale was gone.

"Are you sure," asked Vague Henri, "that you're all right in the head?"

Cale found himself in a pleasant courtyard with an elegant lawn at its center. They began to walk along the path that followed the walls, Cale keeping in step with Chancellor Vipond.

"I've always believed in the principle," said Vipond, after they had been walking for a minute or so in silence, "that you should never tell your best friend anything you wouldn't be prepared to tell your worst enemy. But now is a time, as far as you're concerned, when honesty is very much the best policy. So I don't want to hear any nonsense about gypsies, or indeed any other nonsense. I want the truth about who you are and what you were doing in the Scablands."

"You mean the truth like I'd tell my best friend."

"I may not be your best friend, young man, but I am your best hope. Tell me the truth and I might be prepared to take a generous view of the fact that, while the girl and the slow-witted one wanted to help me, you and that other guttersnipe wanted to leave me there."

Cale looked at him. "Since we're telling the truth, Lord, wouldn't you have thought about what you were getting into—if you were in our shoes?"

"Indeed. Now get on with it. And if I think you're lying, I'll hand you over to Bramley as quick as two shakes of a lamb's tail and no questions asked."

Cale said nothing for a few seconds and then sighed as if he had made a decision.

"The three of us are Redeemers' acolytes from the Great Sanctuary at Shotover."

"Ah, the truth," said Vipond, smiling. "It has a ring about it, don't you find? And the girl?"

"We were looking for food in the combs—tunnels and hallways the Redeemers had closed off. We stumbled across her in a place we've never heard of. There were others like her."

"Women in the Sanctuary? How very strange! Or perhaps not."

"We were seen with the girl and we had no choice. We had to go on the lam."

"A very great risk, I understand."

"There was no risk at all if we'd stayed."

"Quite so." He thought about what he had heard for a minute or so as the two walked slowly in step around the courtyard, side by side. "And the Scablands?"

"It was the best place to hide—you can't see far because of all the hillocks and eskers that break it up."

"The Redeemers hunt with dogs. I've seen one—ugly as death but great sniffers."

"I'd worked out how to stop them." Cale explained, omitting the detail of his double escape. The fact of their escape may have been true, but whatever Vipond said, the events leading up to it did not *sound* true. And besides, they had all agreed to keep their story simple after Kleist's half-witted attempt to claim they were gypsies. It was clear that whatever the Redeemers had told them about the gypsies was a lie: there had been no treacherous attack on the Sanctuary sixty years before followed by a punitive but restrained expedition to teach the gypsies to behave themselves in future. They must have massacred them to the last child.

"Will you hand us over to the Redeemer search party?"

"No."

"Why not?"

Vipond laughed. "Good question. But we've no reason to. We don't even have diplomatic relations. We only deal with them through the Duena."

"Who are the Duena?"

"Do you know what a mercenary is?"

"Someone who kills for pay."

"The Duena are mercenaries who are paid to negotiate instead of kill. We have so little in the way of dealings with the Redeemers it's cheaper to pay someone else to do it on our behalf. Time for a change, I think. We've been remiss in remaining ignorant. You could be very useful. Their war in the Eastern Breaks has kept them busy for a hundred years. Perhaps they are planning something here—perhaps elsewhere. It's time we knew more." He smiled at the boy. "So perhaps you can trust me, because you can be of use."

"Yes," said Cale thoughtfully. "Perhaps."

By now they had returned to the outer door of the cells. Vipond gave it a hefty thump with his fist and it opened immediately. He turned to Cale.

"In a few days you will be moved somewhere more comfortable. Until then you will be made more welcome—decent food and exercise."

Cale nodded and went through the door, which shut quickly behind him.

Vipond turned as Albin came up behind him. "How very curious, my dear Albin—not like any children I've ever met. If any Redeemers turn up looking for them, they are to be told nothing and kept in the outskirts. The boys are to have house-arrest status."

And with that Vipond walked away, calling out over his shoulder, "Bring the girl to me tomorrow at eleven."

So, Riba," said Vipond, affable as a kindly schoolmaster, "until these three young men stumbled upon this attempt by a Redeemer to assault you and during which he was knocked unconscious, you were completely unaware of the presence of men in the Sanctuary?"

"Yes, sir."

"And yet you had lived there since you were ten years old and had been treated, from what you say, like a little princess? That's very strange, don't you think?"

"It was what I was used to, sir. We were given nearly everything we wanted, and the only strict rule, for which the punishment would be terrible, was not to leave our grounds. They were very large and the walls impossible to climb. And we were happy."

"Did the women in charge of you explain why you were being treated with such kindness and generosity?"

Riba sighed for the death of a long-held dream.

"They said that when we were fifteen we would be taken to become brides in a place more wonderful even than the Sanctuary, and we would be blissfully happy forever. But only if we became as perfect as possible."

"Perfect? In what way?" asked the now slightly startled Vipond.

"Our skin must be without flaw, our hair shiny and manageable, we must have wide, bright eyes, our cheeks pink, our breasts round and large, our buttocks large and smooth and between our legs, under our arms, nor anywhere else except our heads were we to permit the growth of a single hair. We must be always interested and charming and always smell of flowers. We must never be angry or scold or be critical of other people, but be kind and affectionate and always ready with kisses and tenderness."

Both Albin and Vipond were men of considerable experience and had seen and heard many strange things, but when Riba had finished, neither of them could think of a thing to say. It was Albin who finally spoke.

"To go back to the assault on you by this Redeemer. You'd never seen him before?"

"No, nor any man."

"How," asked Vipond, "did you practice your . . . tenderness? If you had no men."

"On each other, sir." This startled the two men even more.

"We would take it in turns and pretend to be tired and bad-tempered and shout a lot and bang doors, and one of the others would calm us down and be kind until we were happy." She looked at them and realized that her answer had fallen short in some way. "Then there were the dolls."

"The dolls?"

"Yes, the man dolls. We dressed them and massaged them and treated them like kings."

"I see," said Vipond.

"Me and Lena . . ." She stopped for a moment. "Lena was the girl the Redeemer killed—we were told we had been chosen to be sent to be married and live happily ever after. But then we were taken to that man's room by our aunties—that's what we called the women who brought us up and told us we were going to be married. But then that man came and he killed Lena."

"Your aunties, they knew about what would happen to you?"

"Why would they do that, having been so kind to us? They must have been tricked."

"Wasn't it a strange coincidence," said Albin, not now sure if they weren't being led up the garden path, though she was, he thought, a brilliant liar if this was so, "that you should have come across this Redeemer and Cale all in twenty-four hours and that Cale should have arrived in the nick of time to save you?"

"Yes. I thought that—even at the time. How strange to come across four men at the same time after all those years—and one so cruel and the others risking their lives for me, for someone they didn't know. Are such things common?"

"No," said Vipond. "Not common. Thank you, Riba. That will be all for the moment." He rang a bell in front of him. The door opened and in walked a young woman. She had about her the air of cool pride of any sixteen-year-old member of the aristocracy, as if she had seen everything and little of it held interest. But her eyes goggled when she saw Riba with her dark hair and enormous plump curves. Standing next to each other, they seemed to be creatures only distantly related.

"Riba, this is Mademoiselle Jane Weld, my niece. She is going to be looking after you for the next few days."

Mademoiselle Jane, still boggled, nodded slightly. Riba just smiled nervously.

"Albin. Would you wait outside with Riba while I have a word with Mademoiselle Jane?"

Albin ushered Riba outside and closed the door. Vipond looked at his startled niece.

"Close your mouth, Jane. The wind may change and you'll have to stay like that."

Mademoiselle Jane's mouth shut with a snap that was almost audible, only for her to open it again almost immediately.

"Who on earth was that creature?"

"Sit down and listen and for once try and do as you're told!"

Resentfully Mademoiselle Jane did so. "You are to befriend Riba and to get her to tell you again everything she has already told me and anything else. Write it down and send it to me, omitting no detail, however trivial or strange . . ." He looked at the young girl. "And it will be strange.

"When you have heard her story, you will see if she can be trained to keep quiet about it and pretend she comes from the Southern Isles or some such. She has manners enough of her own, but you will teach her ours. Perhaps if she does well, she will make a personal maid or even a companion."

"You expect me to train a maid?" said Mademoiselle Jane indignantly.

"I expect you to do whatever I tell you. Now get out."

13

Redeemer Stape Roy, pathfinder of the southern hunting party, rode into Memphis having left his hundred men and dogs in a town thirty miles away, his mind as uneasy as at any time in his life. This unease was no mean thing, given that Stape Roy had undergone many hellish experiences, and caused a fair number too. But now as he approached Kitty Town, he felt he was coming as close to hell itself as could ever be found on earth. As he approached the gaudily lit entrance to the nightmarish suburb of Memphis, he stopped, got down off his horse and led him the last few yards. Even this late there were still tourists and locals streaming past the guards, who ignored most, searched some.

"You can't bring that in here," said one of the guards, gesturing to the horse. "Are you armed?"

To the teeth, thought Stape Roy. "I don't want to come in. I have a letter for Kitty the Hare," he said.

"Never heard of him. Now bugger off!"

Slowly, watched intently by the guards, Stape Roy reached into his saddlebags and brought out two purses, one much bigger than the other. He reached out with the smaller one. "This is for you to share. The other one is for Kitty the Hare."

"Hand them over. I'll see he gets them." The guards, five of them, huge and carefully chosen for their lack of charm, began to move to encircle Stape Roy. "You come back tomorrow or, better still, the day after."

"I'll keep my money till then."

"No. I don't think so," said the guard. "It'll be safe with us."

He moved toward Stape Roy as quickly as any man of twenty stone could and reached for the money. Stape Roy seemed to have given in. His shoulders sagged as if in utter defeat. Then, as the guard pushed him in the chest, he simply folded his own hands across the guard's and pushed them down. There was a not particularly loud *crack!* and a scream of agony as the guard fell to his knees. The others, taken aback at the suddenness of this, now rushed forward. But they had hardly moved when they saw that Stape Roy was holding a shortsword point at the guard's neck. The scream from the guard to tell them to step back was hardly necessary.

"Now bring me someone in authority and be quick about it. I have no intention of staying in this cesspit any longer than I have to."

Twenty minutes later Stape Roy was sitting in an anteroom, and despite the fact that it was one of the most pleasant rooms he had ever been in—lined with cedar and sandalwood, it spoke of rich simplicity and smelled of something so subtle and easing to the senses he considered trying to cut some of it out and take it with him—he remained uneasy. Not because of the fight at the gates of Kitty Town but because of what he had seen after he had been allowed inside. The man who had supervised the massacres at Odessa and Polish Wood, notorious even in the roll call of malice that characterized the wars in the Eastern Breaks, was unnerved by the things he had seen in the last few minutes. Then a door opened at the far end of the room and an old man stepped forward and said politely, "Kitty the Hare will see you now."

Even as the door slid open, a curious odor wafted toward him. It was only slightly unpleasant and even sweet, though a sweetness that raised the hairs on Stape Roy's neck. He was certain he had never smelled it before, and yet something was warning Stape Roy, something was signaling and making him uneasy for all his vicious courage. Already deeply upset by the scenes in Kitty Town, he walked toward the door and then the old man, staying in the anteroom, closed it behind him.

The room was dark but carefully lit so that the floor was easy to see. Above waist height nothing was properly visible except as the dimmest shape. There was someone sitting at a desk in the center of the room, but it was as if that person were made of shadow.

"Please make yourself comfortable, Redeemer."

That voice. It was like nothing he had ever experienced. There was no cruel edge, no hissing sibilance of malice, no threat or menace, all tones of voice he was familiar with time out of mind. This was like the cooing of a dove, a sighing note as if of great sadness, a deep mewling. It was, by some way, the most horrible thing he had ever heard. The sound seemed to resonate in his stomach like the deepest unheard note of the organ in the great cathedral at Kiev. He felt that he was going to be sick.

"You do not look well, Redeemer," cooed the voice. "Would you care for water?"

"No. Thank you."

The voice of Kitty the Hare sighed as if deeply worried. It was, to Stape Roy, like being kissed by something unimaginably foul.

"To business, then."

It took all of the Redeemer's strength of purpose to answer, a strength of purpose proved many times in the burning of apostates and the general slaughter of the innocent.

To breathe deeply did no good. There was only more of that horrible smell of sweetness.

"It is true," said Kitty the Hare, "that the four young persons you are looking for are being kept in Memphis."

"Can you reach them?"

"Oh, Redeemer, anyone can be reached. You want them brought out alive?"

"Can you do that?" Poor Stape Roy could barely stop himself from fainting.

"I do not choose to, Redeemer. It does not suit, you see."

Then he made a sound that might have been a gentle laugh, or might not. The door opened and the old man who had ushered Stape Roy in said, "If you come this way, Redeemer, I will finish our business."

Ten minutes later and still green around the gills, Redeemer Stape Roy was recovering from his horrible interview with Kitty the Hare.

"Are you feeling better, Redeemer?" asked the old man. Stape Roy looked at him.

"What kind—"

"Do not ask questions that might be considered offensive," interrupted the old man. "To be insulting about that kind of thing in this place is unwise." The old man took a deep breath. "This is the score. You wish us to remove these four persons from the old city. This is possible, but it will not be done, because it will interfere with interests very close to our hearts."

"Then I will leave and inform my master. He insists on hearing bad news immediately."

"Don't be unreasonable, Redeemer," said the old man. "More haste, less speed. We will keep an eye on them. At some time they must leave the city. We will let you know. Then as a gesture of goodwill we will return them to you unharmed. This is a promise."

"How long?"

"As long as it takes, Redeemer. We will do as we say—but let me be clear. If you make any attempt to take them yourselves, Kitty the Hare will consider this an attack upon his interests."

There was a knock on the door.

"Come in."

It opened and two guards entered. "These men will escort you to the gates of Kitty Town. Your horse has been fed and watered as a gesture of our good intent. Good-bye."

As Redeemer Stape Roy emerged from the building, the air of Kitty Town hit him like a blow to the face. The noise! The people! He felt like a blind man whose first sight was of the rainbows of hell, a deaf man whose hearing is restored to the sound of the end of the world. There were bawlers with their loozles, mawleys with their ya-yas hanging out for all to see; there were benjamins in jemimas calling out, "Yellow, come and get get." There were burtons and their naked pikers, middlemen calling for agony, aunts with their bung nippers covered in rouge and shouting for a half-and-half. There were Huguenots selling bum-baileys to the highest bidder and nutty lads with long tongues looking for a pigeon in a packet of two.

Struck by horror and stunned into immobility, Redeemer Stape Roy suddenly let loose a cry of utter loathing and disgust. Then, to the astonishment of the two guards escorting him, he took to his heels and ran his scorched soul to the gates of Kitty Town and out into the night.

Thirty miles from the last village protected by Memphis, IdrisPukke sat in a ditch and was rained on. There was nothing dry with which to light a fire, and even if there had been, it was too dangerous to do so. All he had eaten in the last twenty-four hours was half a potato, and one slimy with rot at that. How had a man who had commanded three armies, had the ear of kings and emperors, disgraced almost an entire generation of the beautiful daughters of the Nabob of this, the Satrap of that—how had he come here, to this? A good question, but one to which IdrisPukke knew the answer. The luck that most people might push once too often, IdrisPukke pushed on an almost daily basis. He had reaped where he had not sown, been given an inch and taken a mile; he had made six fortunes and lost seven. His nine lives were long ago exhausted. There was no denying his brilliance as a soldier in the field, his wit, his skill at arms and his political judgment admired everywhere in the known world—which is to say everywhere there was a death sentence against him, not including all those places where such matters as trials and sentences were considered tiresome formalities. In short there was no state to which IdrisPukke could flee where he was not liable to be boiled, disemboweled, burned or hanged, and often all four several times over. The greatest mercenary the world had ever seen was now reduced to hiding from one of dozens of bounty hunters and soldiers in a ditch, wet, tired and suffering terrible indigestion after his last moldy meal.

Twice in the previous month he had been captured and escaped almost immediately. But the real problem was that there was nowhere to escape *to*. All IdrisPukke had to do was close his eyes to hear the flapping wings of chickens coming home to roost.

SNAP!

Without thinking, IdrisPukke was on his knees and scrambling along the ditch as fast as he could go.

"Torches. Lights. He's seen us!"

From all around the blaze of torches lit up the pitch black of the field. But what helped them helped IdrisPukke, and now he could see a cloud of trees thirty yards ahead. He scrambled on, fast as a dog, but slipping and sliding in the mud.

"There!"

He'd been seen. As he scrambled on, he could see the light of the torches moving together toward him. Anytime now—the arrow or sword and the agonizing death. Panting, afraid, he scrambled on. Still he was free and moving. He needed to break to the trees. He climbed up the bank, slipping and sliding, and just as he rose above its edge, a blow.

CRACK!

He stood for a moment. The world had stopped in a flash of lightning and pain. Then another blow and he was falling back. Before he hit the bottom of the ditch, fetching his head another terrible clout, he was already unconscious.

When he woke up, a huge, hairy gorilla had both his feet gripped firmly in one hand and was swinging his head casually into a brick wall like a housewife wearily beating a carpet. Then it stopped and the gorilla raised him up, face-to-face, and stared him in the eyes. He knew it was a gorilla because he had seen one at a circus in Arnhemland. This one was much bigger—its breath was hot and wet and smelled of month-old rotting meat, and huge streams of green snot were pouring out of its nose.

"Still alive, then," said the gorilla. It was only then, and with some relief, that IdrisPukke realized he was still unconscious and dreaming.

Then the gorilla continued lazily to bang his head against the brick wall.

When he forced his eyes open, the scene around him dissolved and became a farmer's cart where he was bound, hand and foot, with his head banging against the wooden sidewall with every jolt as the cart moved over rutted land.

He breathed in deeply to stay conscious and moved his head away into the center of the cart. It was true, he thought: it is nice when you stop banging your head against a wall. Then the pain shrieked back and he stopped being grateful. He groaned.

"You're awake, then, are you?"

It was a soldier and not a bounty hunter, which at least suggested that he had fallen into the hands of people who might want to go through some formalities before inflicting any unpleasantness. That meant a chance of escape. The soldier gave him a swift jab in the stomach with the butt of his short spear. "I asked you a civil question and I want a civil answer."

"Yes, I'm awake," groaned IdrisPukke. "Where am I going?"

"Shut your gob. They told me I wasn't to talk to you, not on any account, but I don't see why. You don't look like much to me." And with another jab to his stomach with the spear butt, the soldier sat back and did not speak again.

"hat do you want me to do with them?" asked Albin.

Vipond looked up from his desk and considered. "They interest me. But I think it's time we squeezed them a little more. I want you to oversee their questioning about the Redeemers. We need to create a better picture of the Sanctuary and whether what the Redeemers are up to has any significance for us. In the meantime put the boys out as apprentices to the Mond."

"Solomon Solomon won't be happy about that."

"Good God," gasped Vipond. "Doesn't anyone do as they're told anymore? If he doesn't like it, he can lump it."

"The Mond are an arrogant collection, Chancellor. It won't be easy for the three of them."

"I realize. But I want you to keep a close eye on them. I want to know how they react to their treatment. I don't blame them for lying to me—I'd do the same in their place—but I want to get to the bottom of this business."

And that was how two days later Cale, Kleist and Vague Henri found themselves in the Square of the Field of Excellence, along with forty-seven other apprentices, watching the same number of young Materazzi aristocrats warming up in front of Solomon Solomon, comptroller of martial arts at the Mond. He was a big man with a shaved head and bad-tempered eyes.

The new apprentices stood and admired the young men, fourteen- and fifteen-year-olds, as they stretched and eased their muscles on the field. In general their appearance was uniform—they were tall, astonishingly supple, blond and slim. Confidence and self-belief shimmered in the air about them as they stretched their long limbs into impossible contortions or performed one-handed push-ups as if magical engines powered their lithe arms. Forty-seven of the apprentices looked on awestruck, the sons of wealthy merchants who had paid Solomon Solomon a good deal of money to allow mere trade the opportunity to have daily contact with the Materazzi. The late substitution of the three yobs from the Scablands had cost Solomon Solomon more than a thousand dollars a year. This was why his icy heart was very much icier than usual.

Each of the apprentices had been placed under a different shield of arms, and while Cale had no idea what these were, he could see from the Materazzi warming up near him that each one had a badge on his chest and that they were the same as the coat of arms he could see behind some of the apprentices. It was a while before he could make out the owner of the badge that matched his own shield. He was like the others, only much more so: taller, blonder, more graceful, stronger. He moved with great speed as he mock-fought several opponents, pulling his blows but still putting each one on his backside. Cale took a few seconds to look back and scan the vast array of weapons for each one of the Mond—half a dozen kinds of sword, short, medium and long spears, axes, as well as several other kinds of weapons he had never seen before.

"You! YOU! STAND WHERE YOU ARE!" It was Solomon Solomon and he was staring at Cale. Solomon Solomon stepped down from the rough stage filled with combat dummies, from which he had been surveying the warm-up, and marched directly over to Cale, not taking his eyes from him for a moment, until he stood directly in front of him. On the field the warm-up came to a halt as the young Materazzi watched to see what would happen. They did not have to wait long. As soon as Solomon Solomon reached Cale, he fetched him a huge palm-open blow across the side of his head. Some of the Mond laughed in a kind of heartless sympathy, as you might on seeing an athlete take a terrible tumble in a race or a weak boxer walk into a punch that would knock him unconscious for hours.

Although Cale staggered, he did not go down as Solomon Solomon expected. Nor, as his head came back into line, did he protest or look Solomon Solomon angrily in the face—Cale had too much experience of arbitrary acts of violence and the incomprehensible bad temper of those in authority over him to make either mistake.

"Do you know what you've done?"

"No, sir," said Cale.

"No, sir? You dare to tell me that you don't know?" This was said with all the pent-up fury of a miser who had lost a thousand dollars a year without an acceptable explanation. He hit Cale again. When the third blow came, Cale realized his mistake. At the Sanctuary, falling down under a blow was only cause for another blow; here it was now clear that the opposite was true. He duly fell to the floor. "In future," screamed Solomon Solomon, "you keep your eyes to the front, you watch your master and do not take your eyes from him. DO YOU UNDERSTAND?"

"Yes, sir."

With that, Solomon Solomon turned and marched back to his podium. Cale slowly got to his feet, his head ringing. All of the other apprentices were staring ahead in terror, except for Vague Henri and Kleist, who stared ahead because they knew what was required. One person, however, was looking at him: the tallest and most graceful of the Materazzi, the one in front of whose shield Cale was standing. Those around him were laughing, but the blond Materazzi was not. He was almost bright red with anger.

Not even the beating he had handed out to Cale improved Solomon Solomon's temper; the loss of so much money had been a deep blow to the heart. "Attend to your apprentices. Shortswords."

The Mond walked toward the line of apprentices and stood opposite. The tall young Materazzi looked at Cale and spoke softly. "Make an exhibition of yourself like that again and I'll make you wish you'd never been born. Do you hear?"

"Yes, I hear," replied Cale.

"I am Conn Materazzi. You call me Boss from now on."

"Yes, Boss, I hear."

"Give me the shortsword."

Cale turned around. There were three swords hanging from a wooden bar, with blades of equal length but different shapes, from straight to curved. To Cale, a sword was a sword. He picked one.

"Not that one." This was followed by a kick in the arse. "The other one." Cale reached for the sword next to it. He took another kick. There was much laughter from Conn Materazzi's cronies and some of the apprentices. "The *other* one," said Conn. Cale picked it out and handed it to the smiling young man. "Good. Now say thank you for that instructional kick." There was quiet at this, the quiet of expectation that perhaps the apprentice might be foolish enough to protest or, even better, strike back.

"Thank me," repeated Conn.

"Thank you, Boss," said Cale, almost pleasantly, much to the relief of Vague Henri and even Kleist.

"Excellent," said Conn, looking at his pals. "A lack of backbone, I like to see that in a servant." The ingratiating laughter was cut short by another barked order from Solomon Solomon. For the next two hours Cale watched, head aching, as the Mond went through their training routines. When it was over, they left the field, laughing, to bathe and eat. Then several older men, the scouts, came out and instructed the apprentices in the use and care of the weapons stacked behind them.

Later, the three sat and talked, Vague Henri and Kleist surprisingly more miserable than Cale.

"God," said Kleist, "I thought we'd finally had a bit of luck turning up here." He looked at Cale bitterly. "You have a real talent, Cale, for getting under people's skin. It took you, what, twenty minutes to pick a fight with the two biggest smells in what looked like being a really cushy number."

Cale considered this thoughtfully, but said nothing.

"Do you want to leave tonight?" asked Vague Henri.

"No," replied Cale, still thoughtful. "I'll need time to steal as much stuff as I can."

"It isn't wise to wait. Think what might happen."

"It'll be all right. Besides, there's no need for you two to leave. Kleist is right—you've landed on your feet here."

"Ha!" said Vague Henri. "Once you're gone, they'll move on to us anyway."

"They might, they might not. Perhaps Kleist is right—it's something about me that makes people angry."

"I'll come with you," said Vague Henri.

"Don't."

"I said I'll come."

There was a long silence, finally broken by Kleist. "Well, I'm not staying here on my own," he said, and stormed off in a sulk.

"Perhaps," said Cale, "we could leave before he gets back."

"It makes sense for us to stick together."

"I suppose so, but why does he have to whine so much?"

"He just does. It's his way. He's OK."

"Really?" asked Cale, as if only mildly curious.

"When do you want to leave?"

"A week—there's a lot of stuff worth filching here. We need to stock up."

"It's too dangerous."

"It'll be fine."

"I don't agree."

"Well, it's my head and my arse, so it's my decision."

Vague Henri shrugged. "I suppose so." He changed the conversation. "What did you think of the Mond—full of themselves, wouldn't you say?"

"Pretty good, though."

"Well," said Vague Henri, smiling, "pretty, anyway." After a pause he said, "Do you think Riba will be all right?"

"Why shouldn't she be?"

It was clear that Vague Henri was truly worried. "The thing is," he said, "she's not like you and me. She couldn't take a beating or anything. She wasn't brought up to that."

"She'll be fine. Vipond has seen us all right, hasn't he? What Kleist said is true—if it wasn't for me, you'd be in clover here." He didn't in fact know what clover was, but he'd heard the saying a couple of times and liked the sound of it. "Riba knows how to get on with people. She'll be all right."

"Why can't you get on with people, then?"

"I don't know."

"Just try and stay out the way, and if you can't, stop looking like you want to slit their throats and feed them to the dogs."

But the next day Vague Henri's hope that things might blow over with Solomon Solomon and Conn Materazzi was disappointed. Solomon Solomon found another excuse to continue the hefty beating of the day before, but this time in the middle of the field so that everyone could have a good look and be encouraged to find an excuse to do likewise. Conn Materazzi, however, more subtle than his fighting master and unwilling to be seen merely to be copying him, continued kicking Cale on the slightest pretense but putting hardly any force into it. The young man had a talent for humiliation, treating Cale as if he were an amusing burden that was his lot to deal with as kindly as possible. With his long and flexible legs and after a lifetime of practice, he could hit Cale on the back of the leg, his arse or give him a gentle clip around the ear, as if using his hands on someone like Cale was to take him too seriously. After four days of this, it was Conn's effect on Cale that began to worry Vague Henri more than the rough treatment handed out by Solomon Solomon. Cale was used to a brutality more extreme than anything Solomon Solomon could come up with. But mockery, being made to look ridiculous, was outside their experience. Henri began to worry that Cale might be provoked into striking back.

"He seems calmer than ever to me," said Kleist as Vague Henri sat beside him worrying.

"As quiet as a haunted house until its demon be up." They both laughed at this often-repeated line from the Redeemers.

"Just two more days."

"Let's get him to leave tomorrow."

"All right."

Conn Materazzi continued to develop his role as the tolerant master of a ridiculous fool with ever greater malice—and was much admired by his friends for doing so. In between the hefty beatings handed out by Solomon Solomon, he would ruffle Cale's hair over some pretended mistake, as if he were an old family pet, incontinent yet much pitied. There were endless provoking gentle slaps to the back of his head, light taps on the buttocks with the flat of his sword blade. And all the time Cale became quieter and quieter. And Conn would see this—see that the hefty beatings seemed to leave no impression, but that, however carefully disguised, his mockery was slowly penetrating through this very hard soul. Conn Materazzi was a monster, but no fool.

The Materazzi were famous for two things: the first, their supreme skill in the martial arts and a reckless courage to go with it; the second, the extraordinary beauty of the Materazzi women, matched by their extraordinary coldness. Indeed, it was said that it was impossible to understand the Materazzi's willingness to die in battle until you had met one of their wives. The Materazzi individually and collectively were a terrifying war machine. But if you really did encounter one of their wives, you would certainly be met with a condescension, pride and dismissal such as you would never have experienced before. But you would also have been thunderstruck by her beauty—and, like the Materazzi men, been willing to endure almost anything for a smile or a patronizing kiss. Although the Materazzi held nearly a third of the known world in the solid grip of their military, economic and political power, the conquered could always console themselves with the thought that, however great their ascendancy, the Materazzi were slaves to their women.

As the beatings and the harassment of Cale continued, all three of the former acolytes were spending as much time thieving as possible. This was not particularly difficult or dangerous—the Materazzi had what, to the boys, was a bizarre attitude toward their possessions. They seemed ready to throw things away almost as soon as they had bought them. As acolytes forbidden possessions of any sort, this baffled them. At first they would steal objects they thought would be useful—a clasp knife, a sharpener, then money left casually lying about in their bosses' bedrooms, often in astonishingly large amounts. Then it became easier to ask the boss if he wanted something tidied up or put elsewhere, because often they were told just to get rid of it. Inside four days they had stolen and been "given" more stuff than they could use, or even knew how to use: knives, swords, a light hunting bow with a nick easily repaired by Kleist, a small field kettle, bowls, spoons, rope, twine, preserved foods from the kitchens and a fair amount of money, of which there would be more when they sucked their bosses' rooms dry just before they left. This was all hidden carefully in an assortment of nooks and crannies, but there was little chance of discovery because no one missed any of it. The realization that you could live the life of Riley in this place just off the things that other people didn't want made Kleist and Vague Henri deeply sad that they had to leave. But Vague Henri saw with every mocking taunt by Conn Materazzi, and every humiliating poke and prod, that Cale became more and more quiet. Conn would flick Cale's ears and pull his nose as if he were a mischievous small boy.

On the afternoon of the fifth day, Cale was on the search to steal something useful in a part of the keep where, as an apprentice, he was forbidden to go. "Forbidden" in Memphis meant something different from "forbidden" in the Sanctuary—there an infraction might mean, say, forty strokes with a metal-studded leather belt from which you might easily bleed to death. Here it meant something you shouldn't do that might mean a vaguely unpleasant punishment or something you could easily talk your way out of. In this instance, if caught, Cale would apologetically explain that he was lost.

He was moving now through the oldest part of the great keep, indeed the oldest part of Memphis. Much of this wall, with its interior rooms now used for storage, had been demolished and replaced by the elegant houses with their huge windows so beloved by the Materazzi. But this old part of Memphis was dark, the only light from the passageways entering and exiting at the walls' limits, often sixty feet apart. It was designed for siege, not casual passage. As Cale went carefully up one set of dark stone steps without any guard or banister to stop him falling forty feet or more onto the flagstones below, he heard someone hurrying down the stairs toward him. He could not see because of a curve in the stairwell, but whoever it was was carrying a lantern. He stepped back into a recess on the stairs and hoped to be missed as the person passed by. The hurried steps and the faint light moved on and then someone appeared. He pressed himself back into the wall and the girl did not see him as she rushed past. But the light was poor in this great dim place and the stones uneven. She had come around the curve too fast and, already unbalanced, clipped her heel on an uneven flagstone. For a moment she started to twist and was held in balance as she hovered over a forty-foot drop onto hard stone. There was a brief cry from the girl as she threw the lantern over the edge and was about to go with it, when Cale snatched her by the arm and pulled her back.

She cried out in terror at this astonishing appearance from nowhere.

"My God!"

"It's all right," said Cale. "You were going to fall."

"Oh!" she said, and looked down at the lantern, broken but still burning the oil that had spilled. "Oh," she said again. "You frightened me."

Cale laughed. "Lucky you're still alive to *be* frightened."

"I would have been fine."

"No, you wouldn't."

She looked down at the steep drop and then back at Cale in the dim light. He was not like any boy or man she had ever seen—of only medium height and with deep black hair—but it was the expression in his eyes, old and dark and something else she could not place.

Suddenly she was afraid.

"I have to go," she said. "Thank you." And then she started to run swiftly down the stairs.

"Careful," said Cale, so softly that he could not possibly be heard. And then she was gone.

Cale felt as though he had been struck by lightning. Even the oldest and wisest head was liable to have been turned by the girl Cale had chanced upon, and, when it came to women, Cale was very far from either. She was Arbell Materazzi, daughter of Marshal Materazzi, Doge of Memphis. But no one, except her father, thought of Arbell by her given surname. To everyone else she was always Arbell Swan-Neck, and she was recognized by all as the most beautiful woman in Memphis, and probably all of its vast territories. Describe her beauty? Think of a woman like a swan.

How different history would have been had Cale not encountered her inside the great wall that afternoon, or had lacked the deftness in that dark and slippery place to pull her back and, as certainly would have been the case, she had broken her oh-so-beautifully long and elegant neck on the flagstones below.

Within hours a lovestruck Cale had told one bemused and one resentful companion that he had changed his mind about leaving Memphis. He did not, of course, explain the real reason, telling them that he had taken worse beatings than those handed out by Solomon Solomon all his life and that he had decided just to ignore Conn Materazzi's nonsense. Why should he let the stupid jokes of a spoiled brat worry him when they had so many good reasons to stay? Puzzled though they were, Vague Henri and Kleist had no reason to doubt him. Nevertheless, Vague Henri did so.

"Do you believe him?" he said later when he was alone with Kleist.

"Why should I care in any case? It suits me if he wants to stay. I just don't like him acting like God Almighty all the time."

Over the next few days Vague Henri watched as the beatings and mockery continued. As always it was the ridicule of Cale that concerned him most. Conn Materazzi might have been a spoiled brat, but he was also a martial artist of formidable skill. Only the oldest and most experienced of the Materazzi men-at-arms ever beat him in the painfully realistic fights that took place every Friday and lasted the whole day. And these defeats against soldiers of deadly skill and ruthlessness became fewer and fewer as the weeks passed. He was renowned, it was as simple as that, and for good reason. It was no surprise at all that in the last week of his formal training he was awarded a prize given only rarely to anyone passing out into the Materazzi army: the Forza or Danzig Shank, known popularly as The Edge. Made by Martin Bacon, the great armorer, a hundred years before, it was a weapon forged from a steel of unique strength and flexibility, a secret sadly lost when Bacon killed himself over a young Materazzi aristocrat who did not care for him. Peter Materazzi, the then doge for whom he had made the sword, was inconsolable at his death and refused for the rest of his life to believe that a man of Bacon's genius could have killed himself for such a reason. "A girl!" he exclaimed in disbelief. "I'd have given him my wife if he'd only asked." Given the reputation of Materazzi women for coldness, the effectiveness of such an offer remains doubtful.

At any rate, the superintendence of The Edge was a signal honor for Conn and had not been awarded for more than twenty years.

The award ceremony and passing-out parade was as splendid as might be imagined: vast crowds, hats waved, cheers, music, pomp and splendor, speeches and all the rest. The Mond arrayed in front of their forebears were nearly five thousand strong. These should not be confused with mere soldiers—these were an armored elite, the best trained and equipped in the world, each one of high rank and aristocratic birth.

And at the center of it all, Conn Materazzi: sixteen years old, six feet tall, blond, muscular, slender and beautiful—the observed of all the observers, the very center of attention, the darling of the crowds, the pride of the Materazzi. How full of himself he was as he acknowledged the cheers and applause as The Edge was presented to him. As he raised it high about his head, there was a roar like the end of the world.

Vague Henri clapped in order not to call attention to himself. Kleist enthusiastically expressed his dislike by exaggerating his applause and cheering as loudly as if Conn were his twin brother. But despite a nudge from Kleist and a whispered plea from Vague Henri, Cale looked on impassively, a reaction not missed by his master, for all Conn's feelings that he had been struck by a heavenly lightning.

Given his already high opinion of himself—one reinforced by his set of sycophantic admirers—Conn's sense of his own wonderfulness had expanded to dizzying new heights. Even two hours later, after the crowds had dispersed and he had returned to the seclusion of the great keep, his brain still buzzed like a hive of excited bees. Nevertheless, after the compliments and adoration of his friends and the cream of Materazzi society began to die away, he had returned sufficiently to the real world to remember the calculated insult offered him by Cale's refusal even to applaud his triumph. This spectacular act of insubordination was not to be endured, and he sent off one of the servants to call his arms apprentice to come at once.

It took the servant some time to find Cale, not least because when he arrived at the apprentices' dormitory he had the misfortune to ask Vague Henri where Cale could be found. His talent for evasion had not been needed for some time, but under direct questioning his natural slipperiness reasserted itself.

"Cale?" he said as if he was not even sure what such a thing might be.

"Lord Conn Materazzi's new apprentice."

"Lord who?"

"He's got black hair. So high." The servant, believing he was dealing with someone dense, stuck his hand out at about five feet six. "Miserable looking."

"Oh, you mean Kleist. He's down in the kitchens."

Perhaps, thought the servant, he *was* looking for Kleist. He thought Conn Materazzi had said Cale, but it might have been Kleist, and given the mood he was in, he didn't much fancy going back and asking him. Unfortunately Cale came into the dormitory hoping to get some sleep, and Vague Henri's plan to send the servant halfway toward the Sanctuary in his search came to nothing.

"That's him," said the servant to Vague Henri.

"That's not Kleist," replied Vague Henri triumphantly, "that's Cale."

By the time Cale arrived in the summer garden, the crowd around Conn had thinned and vanished. However, one last and by far the most important visitor, as far as Conn was concerned, finally arrived: Arbell Swan-Neck. Because she had been brought up to treat men with disdain modified only by condescension, it was a matter of some difficulty for Arbell to give the impression that she had any personal regard for Conn beyond, at best, indifference. In fact, she was no more indifferent to his beauty and achievement than would most young women have been, however swanlike and beautiful. Had it been anyone else but Conn, she would have known instinctively to turn up halfway through the proceedings, offer him an unenthusiastic compliment and disappear. But it was not quite as easy as usual to be indifferent. Not even the chilliest of the Materazzi female elite could remain entirely indifferent to the gorgeous young warrior, the roar of the crowds and the glorious and rare power of the ceremony. Arbell Swan-Neck was, in fact, considerably less disdainful than she appeared, and to her great confusion she was actually shaking at the moment Conn had raised The Edge to the crowd and the crowd roared its approval to the magnificent young man. As a result, her talent for appearing utterly indifferent to young men, even magnificent young men, had rather deserted her and her indecisiveness had led her both to arriving far too late and even blushing (not enough for Conn to notice) when she complimented him on his great achievement. There were only two people that Conn regarded with any degree of deference—his uncle and his uncle's daughter. He was completely in awe of Arbell because of both her staggering beauty and her apparent total contempt for him. Despite a day that had endowed the already swollen-headed youth with even more power and majesty, Conn was still thrown into confusion by her arrival and would not have noticed her discomfort short of her having thrown her arms around his neck and smothered him with kisses. He listened to her congratulations in such a state of awkwardness that he barely understood what she was saying, let alone the unsteady tone in which she said it. It was just as they bowed to each other and Arbell Swan-Neck turned to leave that Cale arrived.

Normally Arbell would no more pay attention to an apprentice than to a gray moth. But, already in something of a state, she was startled into yet deeper confusion by suddenly encountering the strange boy who had saved her from falling in the old wall only a few days before. Under such strain Arbell's face froze into a look of utter blankness.

Only the greatest and most experienced lovers in history, the legendary Nathan Jog, perhaps, or the fabled Nicholas Panick, could have seen through such an expression to the now seething young woman within. Poor Cale, of course, was very far from either of these great lovers and saw only what he feared to see. To Cale, her expression spoke only of cold affront: he had saved her life and fallen in love and she did not even recognize him. Even in her deep state of confusion, Arbell Swan-Neck's exit from this unexpected meeting was clear enough. She simply turned around and began walking toward the gate some hundred yards away at the other end of the garden. By now there were only seven people in the garden besides these three: four of Conn Materazzi's close friends and three bored guards dressed in full ceremonial armor and carrying three times as many weapons as they would ever bring into a real battle. There was now also one observer: Vague Henri, worried for his friend, had made his way onto the roof overlooking the garden and was watching from behind a chimney.

Conn Materazzi now turned to his apprentice, but whatever he was going to do was overtaken by one of his friends who, the worse for drink, thought he would amuse everyone by copying Conn's habit of treating Cale as if he were soft in the head. He reached out his hand and gave Cale a gentle couple of slaps on the face. The others, except Conn, began laughing loud enough to make Arbell Swan-Neck look back at them and see a third mocking slap. She was appalled by what she saw but Cale could only see yet more evidence of disdain in her expression.

It was on the fourth slap to his face that, it could be said, the world itself changed. Hardly seeming to make any great effort, Cale caught the young man's wrist in his left hand and his forearm with his right and then twisted. There was a loud *snap!* and a scream of agony. Cale kept up his apparently slow movement and, grabbing the screaming adolescent by the shoulders, threw him at the startled Conn Materazzi, knocking him down. Cale took a pace backward, enclosed his right fist in his left hand and rammed his elbow into the face of the nearest Materazzi. He was unconscious before he hit the ground. Now the remaining two had overcome their astonishment and drawn their ceremonial daggers before stepping back into a fighting stance. They did not just look formidable, but were so. Cale kept moving toward them but stooped low as he did so and scraped up a handful of lime dust and gravel, which he flung into the faces of his two opponents. In agony they twisted away, Cale fetching a punch to the kidneys of the nearest and another to the sternum of the second. He picked up the two daggers and turned to face Conn, who now had untangled himself from his still-screaming friend. This had all taken no more than four seconds. Now there was a long silence as Conn and Cale faced each other. Conn Materazzi's expression was controlled but furious; Cale's face was utterly blank.

By now the three soldiers had run over from the cloister where they had been trying to keep cool in their full armor.

"Let us deal with him, sir," said the sergeant-at-arms.

"You'll stay where you are," said Conn evenly. "If you move to take him, I swear to God you'll be clearing out horse shit for the rest of your life. You are obliged to obey me."

This was true enough. The sergeant eased back but signaled one of the others to fetch more guards. *I hope,* thought the sergeant, *that jumped-up little prick gets his arse kicked.* But he knew this was not going to happen. Conn Materazzi was a uniquely skillful soldier, already a master even at sixteen. Prick he might be, but you had to hand it to him.

Conn drew The Edge. Other than for the ceremony on this particular day, it was far too valuable not to be safely displayed in the great hall. It was certainly far too valuable to be used in a fight. But Conn knew he could argue that he had no choice, and so for the first time in forty years The Edge was drawn with the intention of killing someone.

"Stop it!" called out Swan-Neck.

Conn ignored her—in a matter of this kind, not even she could have a say. Cale gave no sign he had even heard. Up on the roof Vague Henri knew there was nothing he could do.

Then it began.

Conn swept The Edge forward with enormous speed followed by another cut and another as Cale slowly retreated, blocking each blow with his two ornamental knives that were soon as toothed as an old saw. Conn moved and parried and blocked with grace and speed, as much like a dancer as a swordsman. Cale kept retreating, just managing to block each stroke as Conn jabbed and thrust at his head, his heart, his legs, anywhere he could see a gap. And it was all in silence except for the odd music of the clash of the almost tuneful Edge and the dull response of the daggers.

Conn Materazzi pressed on and Cale blocked, high to this thrust, low to the next, always moving back. Finally Conn had forced him against the wall and there was no retreating for Cale. Now that he had him trapped, Conn stepped back, covering any movement Cale could make to either side.

"You fight the way a dog bites," he said to Cale. But Cale's expression, flat and without emotion, did not change. It was as if he hadn't heard.

Conn moved from side to side and made a few elegant passes signaling to those watching that he was now preparing to kill. His heart surged, shocked by the ecstasy of knowing he would never be the same again.

By now another twenty soldiers, archers among them, had come into the garden and had been drawn up by the sergeant-at-arms in a semicircle a few yards back from the fight. The sergeant could see, along with everyone else, where this was going. Despite Conn's orders, he knew very well there would have been trouble if any harm had come to him. He felt truly sorry for the boy pinned back against the wall as Conn raised his sword for his last stroke. But Conn held it there waiting—searching out the fear in Cale's eyes. But Cale's expression never changed—blank and absent as if there was no soul inside him anymore.

Get on with it, you little shit, thought the sergeant.

Then Conn struck. It is not possible to say how fast The Edge cut through the air—lightning moved slowly compared to it. Cale did not block the blow this time—he simply moved to one side, barely at all. The stroke of the sword missed—but only by the breadth of a gnat's wing. Then another stroke and another miss. Then a jab that Cale sidestepped, snake-fast though it was.

Then, for the first time, Cale struck a blow himself. Conn parried, but only just. Stroke after stroke now pushed him backward until they were almost back where the fight started. Conn was breathing heavily now, and growing fear made him gasp the harder—his body, unused to the terror and presence of death, rebelled against his great skill and years of training; nerves frayed and guts melted.

Then Cale stopped.

He stepped back out of striking range and looked Conn up and down. There was a beat of a second or two, and then a desperate Conn struck once more, The Edge hissing as it cut the air. But Cale was moving even before the blow began, blocking The Edge with one knife and stabbing the other deep into Conn's shoulder.

With a cry of pain and shock, Conn dropped the sword as Cale twisted him around and held him around the neck with his forearm, pointing the remaining knife at Conn's stomach.

"Keep still," he whispered softly in Conn's ear, and then loudly to the soldiers as they moved to stop him, "As you are or I'll butterfly the little creep," and he gave Conn a sharp jab in the stomach to make his point. The sergeant, terrified now, motioned his men to stop.

Throughout all this Cale had been squeezing Conn around the neck ever harder so that he could not breathe. Again he whispered in his ear.

"Just before you go, Boss, something to take with you: fighting isn't an art."

With that Conn collapsed into unconsciousness and hung limply from Cale's now loosening grip around his neck.

"He's still alive, Sergeant, but he won't be if you do anything courageous. I'm going to pick up the sword—so behave yourself."

Taking Conn's considerable weight, Cale slowly sank down and reached for The Edge. Once it was in his grasp, he stood up again, keeping a weather eye on the soldiers. More were coming in through the outer gates now, until there must have been nearly a hundred.

"Where are you going to go, son?" said the sergeant.

"You know," said Cale, "I hadn't really thought about it."

It was then that Vague Henri shouted down from the roof.

"Promise you won't hurt him and he'll let him go."

Startled, the soldiers responded to this first attempt at negotiation with three arrows in Henri's direction. Vague Henri ducked and disappeared from view.

"Delay that!" shouted the sergeant. "Next one who moves without an order gets fifty and a year cleaning the shithouse!"

He turned back to Cale. "What about it, son? Let him go and you'll come to no harm."

"And after?"

"I can't say. I'll do what I can. I'll tell them these boys were moithering you—whether they'll listen . . . What choice do you have?"

"Cale! Do what he says," shouted Vague Henri from the roof, careful this time to let only his head show over the roof's edge.

Cale waited for a moment, although it was perfectly clear what he had to do. Taking The Edge away from Conn's throat, he carefully looked around for somewhere to place it. He was in luck. Just two steps back, which he took with extreme care, there was an old part of the wall at just below knee height where two enormous foundation stones met. He slipped The Edge between the two stones to a depth of about ten inches.

"What are you doing, boy?" called out the sergeant.

And with that Cale dropped the unconscious Conn Materazzi to the ground, turned to the sword and with all his strength pushed it against the weight of the great stones. The Edge, perhaps the greatest sword in the history of all the world, bent then snapped with a sound of a bell being struck—PING!

There was a gasp from the soldiers as if from one person: Cale looked at the sergeant then calmly dropped the broken half of The Edge he was still holding. The sergeant walked toward him, taking a chain and lock from one of the soldiers next to him.

"Turn around, boy."

Cale did as he was told. As the sergeant cuffed his hands, he said softly in Cale's ear, "That's the last stupid thing you'll ever do, son."

One of the physician soldiers—one to every sixty men in the Materazzi army—was checking the unconscious Conn. He nodded to the sergeant and then went to check the others. Now Arbell Swan-Neck burst into the ring that surrounded Cale and knelt down next to Conn, checking his pulse. Satisfied, she stood up and looked at Cale, now pinioned between two soldiers. He stared back at her, expressionless and calm.

"I don't suppose you'll forget me a second time," he said, and with that he was dragged off by the soldiers. It was then that Cale had a stroke of luck. Vague Henri had not been alone on the roof. Just as curious, if less worried about what might happen to Cale, Kleist had followed Vague Henri. As soon as the fight had started Vague Henri had told Kleist to try to bring Albin.

Kleist had found Albin in the only place he knew where to look for him. In a moment he was out of his office door and calling for his men to go with him. And so it was that Albin arrived just as four soldiers were dragging Cale out of the garden and heading for the city jail, a place where he would have been lucky to make it through the night.

"We'll take care of this now," said Albin, backed by ten of his men dressed in their uniform of black waistcoats and black bowler hats.

"The sergeant-at-arms told us to take him to the jail," said the most senior of the soldiers.

"I am Captain Albin of Internal Affairs and responsible for security in the Citadel—so hand him over or else."

Albin's commanding presence as well as the ten hard-looking "bull-dogs," as they were not at all affectionately known, had cowed the soldiers, who were rarely allowed in the Citadel and were instantly ill at ease when challenged in such a strange place. Nevertheless the senior soldier tried once more.

"I'll have to ask the sergeant-at-arms."

"Ask who you like, but he's our prisoner and he's coming with us now." With that, Albin nodded his men forward and the disadvantaged soldiers uncertainly let Cale be taken. The senior soldier nodded to one of the others and he legged it back into the garden to fetch help—but by then the bulldogs had taken Cale and, picking him up, had started making their way into the labyrinth of alleys that wound in and out of the Citadel. By the time help arrived, they had vanished.

Within ten minutes Cale was locked inside one of Vipond's private cells and a jailer was working on the irons binding his hands. Twenty minutes later he was free and standing in the middle of the dimly lit cell as the door was locked behind him. There was a cell to either side of him, separated partly by a wall and partly by bars. Cale sat down and began to consider carefully what he had done. They were not happy thoughts, but after a few minutes they were interrupted by a voice from the cell to his right.

"Got a smoke?"

15

W henever we meet," said IdrisPukke, "it seems to be in unhappy circumstances. Perhaps we ought to change our ways."

"Speak for yourself, Granddad." Cale sat down on the wooden bed and pretended to ignore his fellow prisoner. It was too much of a fluke, meeting up with IdrisPukke again.

"Bit of a coincidence, this," said IdrisPukke.

"You could say."

"But I *do* say." There was a pause. "What brings you here?"

Cale thought carefully before replying.

"Got into a fight."

"Getting into a fight wouldn't bring you into Vipond's personal jail. Who were you fighting with?"

Again Cale thought about his reply—but what did it matter? "Conn Materazzi."

IdrisPukke laughed, but the delight and admiration were clear, and while Cale tried to resist the flattery, he was hardly able to.

"My God, Goldenbollocks himself. From what I've heard, you're lucky to be alive."

Cale should have realized he was being provoked, but for all his unusual gifts he was still only young.

"He's the one who's lucky. He should be coming round about now, and with a nasty pain in his head."

"Well, you're full of surprises, aren't you?" He said nothing for a moment. "Still—none of that explains why you're here. What's this got to do with Vipond?"

"Maybe it was because of the sword."

"What sword?"

"Conn Materazzi's sword."

"Why would his sword have anything to do with this?"

"It wasn't exactly *his* sword."

"Meaning?"

"It was really Marshal Materazzi's sword. The one they call The Edge." The silence was much deeper this time.

"After I dropped Conn, I jammed it between two stones and snapped it."

The silence from IdrisPukke was deep and cold. "A particularly mindless act of vandalism, if I may say so. That sword was a work of art."

"I didn't have time to admire it while Conn was trying to use it to cut me in two."

"But the fight was over by then—that's what you said."

The truth was that Cale had been regretting his impulse from the moment he snapped the sword.

"Do you want my advice?"

"No."

"I'll give it to you anyway. If you're going to kill someone, then kill them. If you're going to let them live, then let them live. But don't make a meal of it either way."

Cale turned his back on IdrisPukke and lay down.

"While you're sleeping, dream on this: everything you did, particularly breaking the sword, means you should be in the Doge's hands. None of it explains why you're here."

Half an hour later the sleepless Cale was disturbed by the sound of his cell door being unlocked. He sat up to see Albin and Vipond entering. Vipond looked at him balefully.

"Evening, Lord Vipond," called out IdrisPukke cheerfully.

"Shut up, IdrisPukke," replied Vipond, still looking at Cale. "Now tell me—and I want the whole truth, or by God I'll hand you over to the Doge this minute—tell me exactly what happened; and when you've finished, then tell me exactly who you are, and how it was possible that you beat Conn Materazzi and his friends so easily. I mean it—the truth, or I'll wash my hands of you as quick as boiled asparagus."

Cale did not, of course, know what asparagus was. The only difficulty was going to be in deciding how much he would have to tell Vipond in order to persuade him he was being completely honest.

"I lost my temper. That's what people do all the time, isn't it?"

"Why did you break the sword?"

Cale looked awkward. "That was a stupid thing to do—it was in the heat of a fight. I'll apologize to the Doge."

Albin laughed. "Oh, well, as long as you're sorry."

"Where did you learn to fight so well?" said Vipond.

"At the Sanctuary—all my life, twelve hours a day, six days a week."

"Are you telling me that Henri and Kleist can fight like that?"

This was awkward for Cale.

"No. I mean, they're trained to fight, but Kleist is a zip . . . a specialist."

"In what?"

"The spear and the bow."

"And Henri?"

"Supply, mapmaking, spying." This was true, but not entirely true.

"So neither of them could have done what you did today?"

"No. I told you."

"Are there others with the same skill as you in the Sanctuary?"

"No."

"What," asked Vipond, "makes you so special?"

Cale paused in order to give the impression he was reluctant to answer.

"When I was nine years old I was good at fighting—but not like now."

"So what happened?"

"I was in a training fight with a much older boy—no holds barred, real weapons, except the points and edges were blunted. I got the best of him, got him down on the ground—but I was too cocky and he managed to pull me down. Then he hit me on the side of the head with a rock. That was that. The Redeemers pulled him off me, which is why he didn't beat my brains out. I woke up a couple of weeks later, and two weeks after that I was back to normal except for a dent in my skull." He reached up and pointed with one finger to the left side of his skull toward the back. Then, again, he stopped as if reluctant to go on.

"But you weren't like before?"

"No. At first I couldn't fight as well as before. My timing was all wrong, but after a while whatever happened when he cracked my skull open, I got used to it."

"Used to what?" asked Albin.

"Every time you strike a blow it means you've already decided where it's going to land on your opponent. And you always give yourself away—where you're looking, the turn of your body, how you bend to stop from overbalancing as you strike. All of that tells your opponent where you're going to strike, and if he reads these signals badly then the blow lands; if he reads them well, he blocks it and avoids it."

"Any fighter, anyone who plays games, knows that," said Albin. "A good fighter, a good ball player, they can disguise a strike or a throw."

"They can't hide it from me, no matter what they do. Not now. I can always read whatever move someone is about to make."

"Can you show us?" asked Vipond. "Without hurting anyone, I mean."

"Ask Captain Albin to put his hands behind his þack."

Albin looked uneasy at this, something not lost on the, until now, silently watching IdrisPukke.

"I wouldn't trust him if I were you, Captain, darling."

"Shut your mouth, IdrisPukke." Albin looked closely at Cale and then slowly put his hands behind his back.

"All you need to do is decide which hand to point at me as quickly as you can. You can do whatever you want to make me guess wrong—

feint, move your body, try to make me choose the wrong way. It's up—"

Before Cale had finished his sentence Albin lashed his left hand toward him, only for Cale to catch it in his right hand as gently as if it were a ball thrown by a clumsy three-year-old. Six more times, try as hard as Albin might, the same thing happened.

"My turn," said Cale as Albin, peeved but mightily impressed, gave in. Cale put his hands behind his back and they began the same process in reverse. Cale struck out six times and six times Albin made the wrong choice.

"I can read what you're going to do," said Cale. "The instant you start to move. It's just a fraction faster than before my injury, but it's always enough. No one can read what I'm going to do, no matter how quick or experienced they are."

"And that's all there is to it?" said Albin. "A bang on the head?"

"No," replied Cale, angry and not sure why. "All my life I've been trained to do one thing. I could have taken Conn Materazzi anyway, good as he is, just not as easily and not four others at the same time. So no, Captain, that's not all there is to it."

"How did the Redeemers react when they realized what had happened?"

Cale grunted, a kind of laugh but without amusement.

"Not *the* Redeemers—one Redeemer: Bosco, the Lord Militant, responsible for all training in the martials."

"The martials—like our martial arts?"

Cale laughed, this time genuinely amused.

"There's no art in what I do—ask Conn Materazzi and his pals."

Vipond ignored the mockery. "This Bosco, what did he do when he found out the result of your injury?"

"He tested me for months, against others much older and stronger. He even brought in five veterans, skirmishers from the wars in the Eastern Breaks under sentence of death, he said." Cale stopped.

"And what happened?"

"Four days in a row he put me in a fight with them. 'Kill or die' was all he said to both of us. Then, after the fourth day, he stopped."

"Why?"

"He'd seen enough to be sure about me. A fifth time would be an unnecessary risk." He smiled, not at all pleasantly. "After all, you never know with a fight, do you? There's always a chance, isn't there—a sucker blow."

"And then?"

"Then he tried to copy me."

"How do you mean?"

"He spent days measuring the wound in my head and matching it with some skulls he'd taken from the graveyards. Then he made a clay model. Then he spent six months trying to make it happen again."

"I don't follow. How?"

"He took a dozen acolytes the same age and size as me and he tied them down and struck a chisel he'd had made the same shape as my wound—he struck it with a hammer into the same point on their skulls. Harder, then softer, then softer again."

For a moment no one said anything.

"What happened?" asked Vipond softly.

"What happened was that half of them died pretty much straight-away and the rest—well they weren't themselves afterward. Then no one ever saw them again."

"Taken somewhere else?"

"In a manner of speaking."

"And then?"

"Bosco started taking my training sessions himself. He'd never done that before. Sometimes he'd keep me going for ten hours a day—finding any weakness, giving me a good hiding when I failed and then putting it right. Then he disappeared for six months, and when he returned, it was with seven Redeemers who he said were the best at what they did."

"And that was?"

"Killing people mostly—people with armor, without, with swords, sticks, bare hands. How to organize a mass killing . . ." Cale paused.

"Of prisoners?"

"Not just prisoners—anybody. Two of them were sort of generals—one did tactics—battles, retreats, big set pieces. The other did the bandit stuff: small groups fighting in enemy territory, assassinations, how to terrify the locals into helping you and not your enemy."

"And what was all this for?"

"You know, I was never stupid enough to ask."

"Was it to do with the Redeemer wars in the East?"

"I told you, I didn't ask."

"You must have formed an opinion."

"Formed an opinion? Yes. That it was something to do with the wars in the East."

Vipond looked long and hard at Cale, who stared insolently back. Then it was as if the chancellor had made up his mind about something. He turned to Albin.

"Bring the other two to my house as soon as possible."

Albin signaled the jailer and then they were gone.

Cale sat down on his bed, and IdrisPukke moved next to the bars.

"Interesting life," he said to Cale. "You should write a book."

16

*O*nce Lord Vipond had finished talking to Vague Henri and Kleist, he made his way over to the palazzo of Marshal Materazzi, Doge of Memphis.

The Doge had many advisors because he was a man who loved to consult, to talk things over and at great length. The fact that he seldom took the advice was just a peculiarity of the kind that often afflicts those born into positions of enormous power. The one exception to this rule of talking without listening was Lord Vipond, who was himself immensely powerful by virtue of his own network of spies and informers and a hard-to-defy talent for being right. As the popular rhyme had it:

> Chancellor Vipond is either reaping or sowing,
> And what he doesn't know it isn't worth knowing.

It wasn't much of a rhyme, but it wasn't far wrong either. Marshal Materazzi was a man of considerable ruthlessness who had come to rule the largest empire the world had ever known. To have maintained control of it without challenge for twenty years required great military prowess, a talent for politics and considerable intelligence. But having had Vipond as his chancellor through nearly all of this, he had never quite managed to understand how Vipond had himself become almost as powerful. One day, about three years into his reign, he began to realize, to his horror, that Vipond had become indispensable. At first he became deeply hostile to Vipond—such a thing was intolerable and left him exposed to assassination or, even worse, to his becoming some sort of puppet. But Vipond had made it clear to the Marshal that he would always be a loyal servant as long as he did not interfere with his role as chancellor or continue to be a damned nuisance. Their relationship since then had been not uneasy exactly, but, as the peasants around Memphis say, more frit.

Shown into Materazzi's presence, Vipond nodded and was invited to sit.

"How are you feeling, Vipond?"

"Very well, my lord. And yourself?"

"Oh, fine."

There was an awkward pause; awkward for the Marshal because Vipond simply sat there smiling benevolently.

"I understand you met with the Embassy from the Norwegians today."

"Indeed."

One of the border races conquered by Materazzi more than fifteen years before, the Norwegians had enthusiastically seized upon the advantages offered by occupation—roads, centrally heated palazzos and luxurious imports—without abandoning their ferocious appetite for fighting. Five years ago the now war-weary Marshal, increasingly irritated by the expense of maintaining his vast empire, had decided that it should expand no more. The Norwegians, while touchingly loyal to their conqueror, were always stirring up trouble and trying to expand their own territory northward whenever they could and despite repeated orders to do no such thing. Endlessly devious, the Norwegians provoked their neighbors and generally used every trick they could to claim they were being attacked and that they had no choice but to protect themselves by invading their aggressors. As Vipond well knew, these attacks were in reality made by Norwegian soldiers disguised as the forces of such of their neighbors as they were keen on plundering.

"What did they have to say for themselves?"

"Oh," replied Vipond, "the usual claim to be the victims—peaceloving victims, merely defending themselves and the empire of which they are such loyal subjects."

"And what did you say?"

"I told them that I wasn't born yesterday and if they didn't return their army to barracks, we might consider offering them independence."

"And how did they take that?"

"All six of them went white with horror and promised the army would withdraw within the week."

Materazzi looked carefully at Vipond.

"Perhaps we should offer them independence anyway, and to a fair few others as well. The cost of governing and policing is bloody ravenous. More than we get in taxes, am I right?"

"Very nearly—but then you'd have to either reduce our army and have a great many bad-tempered soldiers wandering about the place looking for mischief, or pay for them yourself."

Materazzi grunted.

"Between the devil and a hard place."

"Quite so, my lord. But of course, if you'd like me to do a proper study . . ."

"Why did you take the boy who broke my sword?"

These sudden changes of tack were an old tactic of the Marshal's to unsettle anyone who annoyed him.

"I am responsible for security in the city."

"You're responsible for matters dealing with sedition—you're not a policeman. This is nothing to do with you. He broke my sword—it's priceless—and he seriously wounded my nephew and the sons of four members of the court. They want his blood and, I'll tell you this for nothing, so do I."

Vipond looked thoughtful.

"It may be possible to repair The Edge."

"You don't know anything about it. Don't pretend you do."

"Indeed not—but I know a man who does. Prefect Walter Gurney has returned from his embassy in Riben."

"Why hasn't he reported to me?"

"He is unwell—not likely to last the year, I'd say."

"What's it got to do with my sword?"

"Gurney's report included a long section on the Ribens' mastery of metal. He says that he has never seen such work. I talked to him briefly, and he said that if The Edge could be repaired, the Riben sword makers could be the ones to do it." He paused. "This would, of course, be under my guarantee of its safety and at my expense."

"Why?" asked Materazzi. "What's this boy to you that you'd go to all this trouble and cost?"

"In your perfectly understandable annoyance at what has happened to a prized possession and the injuries to your nephew, you have, if I may be frank, overlooked the fact that a boy of fourteen managed to beat the living daylights out of five of the Materazzi's most promising soldiers, including one who's supposed to be the greatest in a generation. This isn't a matter of concern for you?"

"All the more reason to get rid of him."

"You're not interested in how he acquired his extraordinary talent?"

"How, then?"

"This young man, Cale, was trained by the Redeemers at the Sanctuary."

"They've never given us any problems."

"Not in the past—but what this boy tells me is that in the last seven years there's been a great change in the life and training at the Sanctuary. They are training more soldiers, and more ruthlessly."

"You're afraid they're going to attack us? They'd be very foolish if they did."

"Firstly, it is my duty to be afraid of such things. Secondly, how many kings and emperors thought the same about you thirty years ago?"

Materazzi sighed, irritated and uncomfortable: although he'd been a bloodthirsty holy terror while building his great empire, the truth was that in ten years of peace he had lost his appetite for war. The ruthless soldier who was once a byword for rapacious conquest had became a man in late middle age who wanted a quiet life where he would never have to be freezing cold one week, dying of thirst the next, or dreading, as he once had drunkenly admitted to Vipond, having his guts waved about on a billhook by some spavined peasant who managed to get in a lucky blow. He had never confessed as much to anyone, but his real distaste for war had set in after a winter spent starving in the ice fields of Stetl, where he had been reduced to eating the remains of his much-loved regimental sergeant major.

"So, what's your plan? I'm sure you have one—and it had better include some way of getting my brother off my back about Conn."

Vipond put a letter on the table. It was from Conn Materazzi. The Marshal opened it and began reading. When he finished, he put the letter back on the table.

"Conn Materazzi has many admirable qualities. I didn't realize a willingness to be the bigger man was one of them."

"Your good judge of character, Marshal, is a lesson to us all. How would vanity do? I had a word with Conn and pointed out that having Cale punished for defeating him would make him look ridiculous. He agreed."

"You can't have this boy of yours wandering about Memphis. The city fathers won't tolerate it and neither will I. I can't be seen to overlook this, Vipond."

"Of course not. But everyone knows he's in my custody. If he escapes, the criticism will fall on me."

"You want to let him go?"

"Indeed I do not. This boy has unique skills—besides, he and his friends are the only real sources of knowledge we have about the Redeemers and their intentions. We need to know much more. I've set this in train, but I need them to verify the information I receive. They are too valuable—more important than any sword or the bruised heads of a collection of spoiled bullies who got what they so richly deserved."

"Are you defying me, by God?"

"If I have displeased you, my lord, I will resign immediately."

There was a gasp of irritation from Materazzi.

"There you go! You're doing it again. No one can say boo to you without you going off like a firework. The older you get, Vipond, the more irritable."

"My apologies, Marshal," said Vipond with an insincere air of regret. "My injuries have perhaps made me more ill-tempered than I would like."

"Exactly! My dear Vipond, you must be careful. It was a terrible ordeal, terrible. I have kept you for too long—unforgivably selfish of me. You must rest."

Vipond stood up, nodded his acceptance of the Marshal's concern and then went to leave. But as he approached the door, Materazzi called out pleasantly.

"So you'll arrange for the repair of the sword at your expense and see to this other matter."

17

*T*wo days later IdrisPukke and Cale were slowly making their way along Highway Seven, one of the broad stone roads that led from Memphis, which, day and night, were packed with goods going in and out of this greatest of all centers of trade. After several hours of silence Cale asked a question.

"Were you put into the cells to spy on me?"

"Yes," said IdrisPukke.

"No, you weren't."

"Why did you ask, then?"

"I wanted to see if I could trust you."

"Well, you can't."

"Does Chancellor Vipond trust you?"

"About as far as he could throw me."

"So why did he make it a condition for keeping my friends safe that I have to stay with you?"

"You should have asked him."

"I did."

"And what did he say?"

"'Curiosity killed the cat.'"

"There you are, then."

Cale stayed silent for a moment. "What did he do to make sure you'd stay with me?"

"He paid me."

This wasn't entirely a lie, but what bound IdrisPukke to Cale was much more than money. For money to be of any use you had to have somewhere to spend it. And there was nowhere it was worth being that also didn't have a sentence on his life, or worse. Vipond had simply laid out the facts of IdrisPukke's future—which is to say that there wasn't one—and then offered him a possible way out. Firstly a reasonably comfortable place to hide for a few months and then, if he did as he was told, the chance of a series of temporary pardons that would at least keep him safe from execution by any official government under the rule of the Materazzi.

"What about the ones who want to kill me who aren't official?" he'd asked Vipond.

"That's your problem. But if you get close to the boy and learn something useful and keep him out of trouble, I might have something for you."

"It's a little thin, my lord."

"For a man in your position, which is to say no position at all, I think it's very generous," replied Vipond, waving him away. "If you have a better offer, my advice is that you take it."

"What," said Cale after another hour of silence, "are we going to do at wherever this place is we're going to?"

"Stay out of trouble—put you straight about a few things."

"Such as?"

"Wait till we get there."

"Did you know," said Cale, "we're being followed?"

"The ugly-looking brute in the green jacket?"

"Yes," said a disappointed Cale.

"A bit obvious, don't you think?"

Cale turned to look, as if the obviousness of their follower was also clear to him. IdrisPukke laughed.

"Whoever's behind this expects us to catch laughing boy and leave him in a ditch somewhere. The real tail is about two hundred yards back."

"What's he look like?"

"There's your first lesson. See if you spot him before I deal with him."

"You mean kill him?"

IdrisPukke looked at Cale.

"What a bloodthirsty little cutthroat you are. Vipond made it clear we should make ourselves invisible, and I don't think leaving a trail of dead bodies behind us counts."

"So what are you going to do?"

"Watch and learn, sonny."

Every five miles along the roads leading to Memphis there were small guardhouses manned by no more than half a dozen soldiers. It was at one of these that IdrisPukke, watched by an amused Cale, found himself in an argument with a corporal.

"For God's sake, man, this is a warrant signed by Chancellor Vipond himself."

The corporal was apologetic but firm.

"I'm sorry, sir. It looks official, but I've never seen one of these before. The C-in-C usually signs these kinds of warrants. I know what they look like and I know his signature. Try to see it from my point of view. I'll send for Lieutenant Webster."

"How long will that take?" said an exasperated IdrisPukke.

"Tomorrow, probably."

IdrisPukke groaned with frustration, then walked over to the window. After a minute or so he signaled Cale to come to him. "Wait outside," he whispered.

"I thought I was supposed to watch and learn?"

"Don't bloody well argue—just do it. Go out the back and don't let anybody see you."

Smiling, Cale did as he was told. At the back of the guardhouse were four soldiers sitting on a wall, smoking and looking bored. Five minutes later IdrisPukke emerged and nodded to Cale to join him as he led the horses down a back alley away from the main road.

"So," said Cale, "what's going on?"

"He's going to arrest our followers and keep them in the cells for a couple of days."

"What changed his mind?"

"What do you think?"

"I don't know, that's why I'm asking you."

"I bribed him. Fifteen dollars for him and five for each of his men."

Cale was genuinely shocked by this. Vicious, cruel and small-minded as the Redeemers might be, the idea that they would neglect their duty for money was unthinkable.

"We had a warrant," he said, indignant. "Why should we have to bribe them?"

"There's no point in getting bent out of shape about it," said IdrisPukke irritably. "Just look on it as a part of your education—a new fact to take on board in getting to know what people are really like. Don't imagine," he continued crossly, "that just because the Redeemers treated you like a dog that you know everything about what a rotten, corrupt bunch of bastards the human race are."

And on this bad-tempered note he walked on ahead and did not speak again for the rest of the day.

Perhaps it is easy to say why IdrisPukke was so annoyed, given that he was used to very much worse than being shaken down by a cynical grunt like the corporal. How many of us necessarily require a great disaster to put us in a fit of pique? To lose a key, step on a sharp stone or be contradicted in a matter of no importance is enough to send even a reasonable man or woman into a rage if they're in the mood for it. That's all there is to it—and whatever the limits to Cale's grasp of human nature as it applied to people who were not vicious fanatics, he had enough sense to leave IdrisPukke to himself until such time as he calmed down.

Nevertheless, if IdrisPukke had realized who was behind their being followed he would have been perfectly justified in feeling enraged—and scared as well, because he would have known that Kitty the Hare would not have allowed his spies to have been so easily discovered. Despite the fact that the two men spotted by IdrisPukke were locked up in a cell within an hour, they were decoys expressly sent out in order to be caught. As Cale and IdrisPukke made their way back onto the main road, and a day later turned off it and headed toward the White Forest, there were two more pairs of eyes following them, and this time with a great deal more cunning.

As they moved up into the mountains, the sun shone and the air was as clear as good water. IdrisPukke's temper of the day before was forgotten, and he returned to his more expansive ways, telling Cale all about his life and adventures and his opinions—of which he had a great many. You might have thought that Cale, capable as he was of grim rage and fearful violence, would have been irked by his companion setting himself up as a mentor and Cale as a disciple—but you must appreciate that Cale was still a young man, for all his iron qualities, and the range and nature of IdrisPukke's experience, his rises and falls, his loves and his opponents, would have enthralled even the most jaded listener. Not the least of his skills was in the way that IdrisPukke mocked himself and took responsibility for the majority of his falls from grace. An adult who laughed at himself was something more than unfamiliar to Cale: it was almost incomprehensible. Laughter to the Redeemers was an occasion of sin—a babbling inspired by the devil himself.

It was not that IdrisPukke had a cheerful view of the world in any way, but that his pessimism was expressed with a knowing delight and a willingness to include himself in his witty cynicism, a willingness that Cale found oddly comforting as well as amusing. Cale was not of a mind to listen to anyone who had a happy view of human beings—such a temperament could never chime with his daily experience. But he found his anger was easier to bear and even soothed by listening to someone who laughed at human cruelty and stupidity.

"There are few ways," IdrisPukke would proclaim, as if from nowhere, "of putting people in a good humor other than by telling them of some terrible misfortune that has recently befallen you."

Or again: "Life's a journey for people like you and me—one where we're never sure where we're going along the way. You see a new destination as you travel and a better one and so on until the place you had originally decided on is completely forgotten. We are like alchemists—starting out searching for gold—who along the way discover useful medicines, a sensible way of ordering things, and fireworks—the only thing they never discover is gold!"

Cale laughed. "Why should I listen to anything you say? The first time I met you, you fell over my feet, and both times after that you were a prisoner."

An expression of mild disdain crossed IdrisPukke's face, as if this were a familiar objection barely worth answering.

"Then learn from my mistakes, Master Wet-Behind-the-Ears—and then learn from the fact that while I've walked the corridors of power for forty years I'm still alive—which is a lot more than you can say about most of the people I've walked them with. And I daresay unless you show a good deal more sense than you have done until now—the same will be true of you."

"I've done all right so far."

"Have you?"

"Yes."

"You've been lucky, sonny, and very. And I don't care how good you are with your fists. That you've made it this far without swinging on the end of a rope is as much luck as judgment." He paused and sighed. "Do you trust Vipond?"

"I don't trust anybody."

"Any fool can say they don't rely on anyone. The trouble is that sometimes you have to. People can be noble and self-sacrificing and all those admirable qualities—they do exist, but the trouble is that these noble virtues tend to come and go in people. No one expects a good-humored man or a kind woman to be good-humored or kind every day and every moment—yet they're appalled when people are trustworthy for a month or a year and then they aren't for an hour or a day."

"If they're not to be relied on all the time, then you don't trust them."

"And can you be relied on?"

"No—I've learned, IdrisPukke, that I can do noble things. I can rescue the innocent," he smiled, mocking, "rescue them from the wicked and the unrighteous. But it's out of character—it was a good day, or a bad day, when I saved Riba. But it won't happen again in a hurry."

"Can you be sure of that?"

"No—but I'll do my best." They rode on in silence for another half hour. "Do *you* trust Vipond?" said Cale at last.

"It depends. What about?"

Cale shifted uncomfortably in his saddle.

"He promised that if I stayed with you and behaved myself then Vague Henri and Kleist would be all right. He'd protect them. Will he?"

"So . . . worried about your friends? Not as heartless as you try to pretend."

"Is that what you think? Try depending on my heart—see where it gets you."

IdrisPukke laughed. "The thing about Vipond is to remember that he's a great man and that great men have great responsibilities, and not keeping his promises is one of them."

"You're just trying to sound clever."

"Not at all. Vipond has a great many big fish to fry, and you and your friends are not very big fish at all. What if a hundred lives or the future safety of Memphis and all its million souls depended on breaking his word to three little tiddlers like you and your friends? What would you do in his place? You think you're such a hard case, tell me."

"Kleist isn't my friend."

"What do you think Vipond wants from you?"

"He wants me to learn to trust you, to tell you the whole truth about what happened with the Redeemers. He thinks they might be a threat."

"And is he right?"

Cale looked at him. "The Redeemers are a poxy curse on the face of the earth . . ." He looked as if he wanted to continue but with an effort had stopped himself.

"You were going to say something else."

"Yes, I was."

"What?"

"That's for me to know and you to find out."

"Suit yourself. As for trusting Vipond . . . you can, up to a point. He'll go out of his way to watch over your friend and the other one who isn't your friend unless it becomes important not to. Until they become significant in the wrong way, they're as safe as houses."

And as they rode on in silence, still neither of them realized that Kitty the Hare's eyes were watching and his ears listening.

At four that afternoon IdrisPukke dismounted and, signaling Cale to do the same, he turned off the trail into what looked like virgin forest. The going would have been tough even without the horses, and it took them the best part of two hours before the density of trees and bushes eased and then opened onto another clearly little-used track.

"I'd say you knew the way," observed Cale to IdrisPukke's back.

"I can see there's no hiding anything from you, Mister Know-It-All."

"How's that, then?"

"I used to come here to Treetops all the time with my brother when I was a boy."

"And who's he?"

"Chancellor Leopold Vipond."

18

*C*ale might have thought that the next two months at Treetops Lodge were the happiest of his life, if he'd had another happy experience to compare it with. But, given that two months spent in the Seventh Circle of Hell would have been an improvement on his life in the Sanctuary, his happiness was not to be compared to anything. He was merely happy. He slept twelve hours a day and often more, drank beer and in the evening would enjoy a smoke with IdrisPukke, who took great pains to assure him that once he got over his initial dislike, smoking would be both a great pleasure and one of the few truly dependable consolations that life had to offer.

They would sit in the evening outside the old hunting lodge, on its large wood veranda, while listening to the *ribbit-ribbit* of the insects and watching the swallows and bats diving and ducking and tumbling at the day's end. Often they would sit for hours in silence, punctuated from time to time by one of IdrisPukke's drolleries about life and its pleasures and illusions.

"Solitude is a wonderful thing, Cale, and in two ways. First, it allows a man to be with himself, and second, it prevents him being with others." Cale nodded his agreement with a sincerity that was only possible for someone who had spent every waking and sleeping hour of his life with hundreds of others and always being watched and spied upon.

"To be sociable," IdrisPukke continued, "is a risky thing—even fatal—because it means being in contact with people, most of whom are dull, perverse and ignorant and are really with you only because they cannot bear their own company. Most people bore themselves and greet you not as a true friend but as a distraction—like a dancing dog or some half-wit actor with a fund of amusing stories." IdrisPukke had a particular dislike of actors and was frequently to be heard declaiming on their shortcomings, a distaste lost on Cale because he had never seen a play: the idea of pretending to be someone else for money was incomprehensible.

"Of course, you are young and have yet to feel the strongest impulse of all: the love of women. Don't get me wrong—every woman and every man should feel what it means to love and be loved—a woman's body is the best picture of perfection I've ever known. But to be perfectly honest with you, Cale—not that it will make any difference to you—to desire love, as some great wit once said, is to desire to be chained to a lunatic."

He would then open another beer, pour a quarter—never more and never too many times—into Cale's mug and refuse to give him any more tobacco, pointing out that when it came to smoking, you could have too much of a good thing, and that in excess it could damage a young man's wind.

And after that, sometimes long into the early morning, Cale looked forward to what had become almost his greatest pleasure—a warm bed, a soft mattress and all utterly, completely on his own—no groaning and crying out and snoring and the smell of farts of hundreds—just wonderful silence and peace. Bliss was it in those days for Cale to be alive.

He began wandering aimlessly in the woods for hours at a time, vanishing as soon as he had woken up and only returning to the hunting lodge as night closed in. The hills, the occasional meadow, rivers, the wary deer and the pigeons cooing in the trees during the hot afternoons—the wonderful bliss of just wandering on his own was a more intense pleasure even than beer or tobacco. The only thing to mar his happiness was the thought of Arbell Swan-Neck, whose face would come unbidden to him late at night or in the afternoon lying by the river, where the only sounds were of an occasional fish jumping, the song of birds and the faint wind in the trees. The feelings he had when she came into his mind were odd and unwelcome—they clashed unpleasantly with the wonderful peace he felt. She made him angry and he didn't want to feel angry ever again, he just wanted to feel like this—free, lazy, answerable to no one in the warmth and green beauty of the great summer forest.

The other great delight he discovered was eating. To eat to live, to have intense hunger satisfied just by filling your stomach was one thing, but for a boy whose diet had for much of his life consisted of dead men's feet, the possibility of good food in his new life meant that something people often took for granted could become a source of wonder.

IdrisPukke was a great food lover and, having lived at one time or another almost everywhere in the civilized world, considered himself, as on most subjects, an expert. He loved preparing meals almost as much as he loved eating them, but unfortunately his desire to teach his willing pupil about the world had some false starts.

His first attempt to introduce Cale to the great art of eating ended badly. Cale had returned to the lodge one day after a ten-hour absence and ravenous enough to eat a priest, only to be confronted by the Emperor's Feast—IdrisPukke's improvised version of the most spectacular meal he had ever eaten, a specialty of the House of Imur Lantana in the city of Apsny. Many of the ingredients had to be substituted: pork pizzles because they were not to be found in the mountains as the locals considered pigs to be unclean; saffron because it was too expensive and no one had ever heard of it anyway. Also, a dish considered by many to be the highlight of the meal was missing: IdrisPukke, though no sentimentalist, could not bring himself to drown ten baby larks in brandy before roasting them in a hot oven for less than thirty seconds.

When Cale arrived, brown-faced from the sun and starving, he laughed aloud at the delicacies laid before him by a proud IdrisPukke.

"Start there," said the smiling cook, and Cale almost literally launched himself at a plate of minced freshwater prawns fried on white bread with a sauce of sour wild raspberries. After five of these IdrisPukke nodded to the grilled duck and plum sauce fingers and then, along with a gentle warning to slow down, fried chicken wings in bread crumbs and strips of deep-fried potato.

Cale was soon, of course, violently sick. IdrisPukke had seen many people vomit during his life and had frequently done so himself. He had witnessed the disagreeable Kvenland habit of interrupting thirty-nine-course banquets with visits to the bilematorium or spew-parlor, visits that were necessary every ten courses or so if you were to finish and thereby avoid the deadly insult to your hosts implied in not making it to course thirty-nine. Cale's heavings were on an epic scale as his overburdened stomach expelled everything he had eaten in the previous twenty minutes and, as it appeared to IdrisPukke, pretty much everything else in his entire life.

Finally the exhausted boy was finished and he went to bed. The next morning Cale came outside with a greeny white tinge to his face that IdrisPukke had previously seen only on a three-day-old corpse. Cale sat down and took, with considerable caution, a cup of weak tea without milk. In a wan voice he began to explain to IdrisPukke the reason he had been so violently ill.

"Well," said IdrisPukke after Cale had finished telling him about the Redeemers' way with food. "If I'm ever disposed to think badly of you, I shall try to excuse you on the grounds that little should be expected of a child brought up on dead men's feet." There was a short silence. "I hope you don't mind me giving you some advice."

"No," said Cale, too weak to be affronted.

"There's a limit to how much we should expect of the capacity for acceptance of other people. It might be better, should the subject ever arise in good company, not to mention the rats."

19

Vague Henri and Kleist had seen Cale for only a few minutes before his hurried departure, so they had barely time to register the deeply suspicious reappearance of IdrisPukke, let alone receive a satisfactory account of all that had happened to Cale after he had been dragged out of the summer garden. Kleist, to his considerable irritation, didn't even have time to point out to Cale that his lack of discipline and general selfishness had left the two of them stranded up shit creek. But as it turned out, Kleist's reasonable fear that Cale had drawn down hostile interest from everyone around them turned out not to be entirely the case. There was hostility, certainly, but the ferocious beating Cale had handed out to the cream of the Mond had made those anxious for revenge extremely wary of Vague Henri and Kleist in case they were similarly gifted. It was not that the Mond were afraid of violent injury or death so much as the humiliation of being given a hammering by people who were so obviously their social inferiors.

Vipond had the two of them reassigned to the kitchens, where there was no chance of them encountering anyone who mattered. The lengthy and repeated curses Kleist brought down on Cale's head for leaving him washing dishes for ten hours a day hardly need to be imagined. However, there was an unexpected benefit in that servants with a grudge against the Mond for their cockiness and arrogance, and there were many of them, regarded the two of them with admiration; enough, anyway, after a month or so to let them help with more interesting tasks than washing dishes. Kleist offered to help in the meat bay, and they were impressed by his abilities as a butcher: "A natural." He was wise enough not to be specific about the small animals on which he had learned his skill. "Me," said Kleist to Vague Henri as he happily dismembered an enormous Holstein cow, "I like to work on a bigger scale."

Vague Henri had to make do with feeding animals and taking the occasional message to the servants' doors of the surrounding palazzos. This gave him the chance to see Riba, now pretty much always on his mind. When he saw her, it was never for long, but her face would light up and she would talk excitedly, touching his arm and smiling at him with her beautiful little white teeth. But, as he began to notice, hardly anyone passed without receiving the same smile, the same show of pleasure. It was in her nature to be open and winning toward everyone, and people responded to her, often surprising themselves at how much they came to value that lovely smile. Vague Henri, however, wanted it just for himself.

He had been nursing a dark secret about Riba for some time, since they had been alone in the Scablands for nearly five days. At first he had treated her with astonished deference, the way someone might while on a walking trip with an angel. All men have been entranced by the beauty of a woman, but imagine the fascination for someone who had grown up never seeing or imagining such a creature. After a few days of her company, he had started to calm down a little, if only at the emergence of baser feelings than reverence and adoration. He took meticulous care not to treat this divine presence in a way that might demean his own wonder (though what demeaning it might involve he was profoundly unclear about). Things stirred deep inside for which he had no name. After a few days they had come to a small oasis with a spring, luckily in full spate, that had created a small pool. She laughed in delight and Vague Henri's natural delicacy had caused him to offer to withdraw to the other side of a small hillock alongside the pool. He lay on his back and slowly began his first truly great struggle with the devil. Opportunities for great temptations in the Sanctuary were scant. Redeemer Hauer, his spiritual advisor for nearly ten years, would have been mortified to discover how weak was Vague Henri's resistance, how ineffectual the endless harassment about the certainty of hell for those who committed crimes against the Holy Spirit. (It was, for reasons never explained, the Holy Spirit who was particularly traumatized by sinful desires of this kind.) Henri's will was suddenly owned by the devil, and he turned onto his stomach and slowly crawled like the reptile servant of Beelzebub he had become to just below the brow of the hill. Had temptation given in to ever been so richly rewarded? Riba stood with the water up to her mid-thighs and lazily splashed herself. Her breasts were huge, not that Henri had anything to compare them to, and the areolae that covered the tips were an extraordinary rose pink unlike anything he had ever seen before. They moved when she moved but shivered with a grace that made him gasp. Between her legs . . . but we must not go there—though this was not a ban that Vague Henri countenanced even for a moment. The devil had taken him entirely. His breathing stopped, utterly struck at this most secret place. Henri had many images of hell branded into his soul, but until this divine moment not a single image of heaven. It was a picture of grace in softly folded skin never to be surpassed, still vibrant, still ringing in his soul until the day he died. So it was that Vague Henri, transfigured with holy terror, slowly slid back below the brow of the hill. The transgressed-against Riba carried on for many more minutes, unaware of the epiphany going on just over the hill. Had Henri simply stayed by the pool and watched, she would not have thought it amiss. She loved to give pleasure to men. This was what she had been raised for, after all. As for poor Vague Henri, he had been struck like a tuning fork and months afterward was still vibrating. Nature had given him intense desire, but his life had left him bereft of any experience or understanding that might make it possible to deal with it.

Riba had been a good deal luckier than the boys when it came to employment. She had started as maid to the maid of Mademoiselle Jane Weld's personal maid, a position, however lowly in the cutthroat world of ladies' maidships, that could take upward of fifteen years' service in the field to obtain. Chancellor Vipond's niece had taken on Riba with a particular sense of resentment that she should have, and be seen to have, an under-undermaid who was of so little standing. However, her resentment began to lessen (and with it the already intense resentment of the other maids to increase) when it became clear that Riba had in fact a genius for the skills for which ladies' maids are much valued: she was a hairdresser of great delicacy and skill; she could squeeze a spot or blackhead, causing as little damage to the complexion as was humanly possible, and then disguise the redness so that it was invisible; complexions blossomed under treatment from Riba's homemade creams and lotions, in the manufacture of which she was a magician; unsightly fingernails became elegant; eyelashes became thick; lips red; legs smooth (exfoliated as painlessly as possible, which is to say one degree below agony). In short, Riba was a find.

This left the problem for Mademoiselle Jane of what to do with her two other, now redundant, personal maids, the most senior of whom had been with her since she was a child. Mademoiselle Jane, though a cold beauty in many respects, had a sensitive side and could not bring herself to tell old Briony that she was no longer required. She knew that her ex-nanny would be deeply upset, and she was also rather concerned, now that she thought of it, about the numerous confidences that she had shared with Briony, confidences that a resentful person might be willing to reveal if she were given sufficient motive. Mademoiselle Jane spared Briony, therefore, the painful experience of being let go after twelve years' faithful service by having Briony's bags packed while she was sent off to buy a tub of rosemary cold cream. On the unfortunate maid's return, she found only a bare room and a servant holding an envelope. The envelope contained twenty dollars and a note thanking her for her faithful service and informing her that she was being sent to become maid to a distant relative in a far-off province, and in recognition of the said service she was to be accompanied on her very long journey by the servant bearing the envelope, who was instructed to stay with her and protect her at all times until she reached her destination. Mademoiselle Jane wished her good luck and expressed her hope that she would make the very best of her good fortune. Within twenty minutes Briony was on her horse and, with her protector, off to a new life, never to be heard from again.

The other maid, just in case Briony had been as indiscreet as her mistress, was similarly dispersed, and Mademoiselle Jane was left to contemplate a life where spots, pimples, blackheads, thin lips and unmanageable hair were a thing of the past.

For several months the young aristocrat was in heaven. Riba's skill in the arts of beautification made the very best of her only moderately good looks. Even more suitors came to call, enabling her to treat these would-be lovers—as was required by Materazzi traditions of courtship—with ever greater disdain and derision. As she well knew, no drug, however rare and expensive, offers the wonderful pleasure of being the center of another's dreams and desires while being able, with only a smile and a look, to shatter them completely.

Though at first lost in the delight of knowing that she was breaking more hearts now than even the detested Arbell Swan-Neck, Mademoiselle Jane started to become uncomfortably aware of something so strange and unfamiliar that she was for some weeks sure she was imagining it.

Some of the young aristocrats who came calling, and only some, seemed not quite as shattered by her continuous rejection as she had come to expect. They groaned and lamented and pleaded for her to reconsider as much as the others, but she was, as we have seen, a sensitive girl (if only to herself) and began to suspect that their protestations were not entirely sincere. What could this possibly mean? Perhaps, she thought, she was becoming used to breaking hearts and the pleasure was diminishing, as pleasures too frequently indulged usually do. But it was not this, because she continued to feel exactly the same intense rush of feeling with those who really were heartbroken by her coldness. Something was going on.

Mademoiselle Jane always set aside the late morning for breaking hearts and she gave her suitors generous slots, sometimes as long as thirty minutes if they were particularly good at lamenting her beauty, heartlessness and cruelty. She decided to set the entire morning aside for those she was suspicious of in order to see if she could get to the bottom of her disturbing qualms. Her chambers were constructed in such a way that she could spy easily on her suitors as they arrived and left and she duly spent the morning doing so.

By the middle of the morning she was in a furiously bad temper, with all her fears confirmed even though in a manner that beggared belief. It was all the fault of that ungrateful slut Riba.

Three times that morning she had endured the lying protestations of heartbreak from young men who, it was now clear, had been coming to see her only because it gave them the opportunity to arrive early to go through the motions of groveling before Mademoiselle Jane, and then leave as quickly as possible only so that they could make cow eyes at that fat whore Riba. It was unthinkably humiliating; not only were they deceiving the most beautiful and desired woman in Memphis (something of an exaggeration—she was number fifteen at best—but allowance must be made for her understandable outrage), but also they were doing so with a creature the size of a house who wobbled like a blancmange whenever she walked.

This insult—and for a Materazzi female to call a woman fat was a deadly one—was by no means entirely accurate either. Certainly Riba made a striking contrast to her mistress, and indeed to all the Materazzi women, but she had never wobbled like a blancmange; besides, in the two months she had been at Memphis, Riba had been so busy that she no longer had either the means to eat so much as she had at the Sanc-tuary, or the time. The result was that she had lost a considerable amount of her buttery pulchritude. What before had been too much of an unusual thing had now become a very enticing and unusual thing. Because they were used to the boyish slenderness and bad temper of Materazzi women, the curves and swaying undulations of Riba made more and more of the Materazzi men watch Riba with greater and greater interest as she sauntered past them with her disdainful mistress.

Almost as engaging was her cheerful smile and welcoming manner. The Materazzi men had been brought up on the rituals of a courtly love that involved a despairing and unrequited adoration for a distant object of affection who only ever treated all men like dirt. And so the quick conversion of a number of young men to a shapely good-looker who didn't look down on them as if they were something the cat had dragged in hardly needed much explanation.

In a dreadful state, Mademoiselle Jane ran down from her hiding place and through the door of her main apartment and into the reception hall where Riba had just closed the door behind a young Materazzi, who was ushered smiling into the street in a haze of desire and longing. Mademoiselle Jane screamed out for her housekeeper.

"Anna-Maria! Anna-Maria!"

An astonished Riba stared at her mistress, who had gone quite red with fury.

"What's the matter, mademoiselle?"

"Shut your mouth, you potbellied lump of lard," replied Mademoiselle Jane in a most unmademoiselle-like manner as Anna-Maria, astonished by the feral screaming, hurried into the room. Mademoiselle Jane looked at her housekeeper as if she might burst and then pointed to Riba.

"Get this treacherous bilker out of my house. I never want to see this beezle ever again."

Mademoiselle Jane was about to finish her tirade by fetching Riba a slap on the face but thought better of it as the young woman's expression turned from astonishment to anger at being so furiously insulted. "Get her out of my sight!" she yelled at Anna-Maria and hissed back into her chambers.

IdrisPukke had refused to give up trying to reeducate Cale's stomach. His new diet would at first have to be simple—and was not simplicity, after all, a test of a good cook's skill? The next time Cale returned to one of IdrisPukke's special meals, it was to fresh trout caught in the lake next to the lodge, lightly steamed and with boiled potatoes and herbs and leaves. Cale was cautious with the potatoes because they had a tiny amount of butter melted over them, but they stayed down and he even asked for more.

And so the days and nights passed. Cale continued on his long walks with and without IdrisPukke. They sat in silence for hours and talked for hours, although it was IdrisPukke who did most of the talking. He also taught Cale to fish, how to eat in civilized company (no belching, slurping, eat with your mouth shut), told him about his extraordinary life—along with many stories at his own expense, something that Cale continued to find bewildering. To laugh at an adult meant a vicious beating—for one to invite you to laugh at him defied belief. At night he would sometimes feel almost uncontainable bursts of joy for no reason at all. IdrisPukke also continued to offer Cale the benefits of his philosophy of life. "Love between a man and woman is the best possible example of the fact that all this world's hopes are an absurd delusion, and it is so because of the fact that love promises so excessively much and performs so excessively little." And again: "I know you don't need me to tell you that this world is hell, but try to understand that men and women are on the one hand the tormented souls in that hell and on the other the devils in it doing the tormenting." And yet more: "No one of real intelligence will accept anything just because some authority declares it to be so. Don't accept the truth of anything you have not confirmed for yourself."

In turn Cale told him about his life with the Redeemers.

"At first it wasn't just the beatings that scared us. In those days we believed what they said—that even if we weren't caught doing something wrong we were born evil and that God saw everything we did so we had to confess to everything. If we didn't and we died in a state of sin, we would go to hell and burn for all eternity. And we did die, every few months, and what they told us was that most of us went to hell and burned for all eternity. I used to lie awake at night in those days after the prayers that always finished 'What if you should die tonight?' Sometimes I was absolutely certain that if I fell asleep, I'd die and burn forever in agony." He stopped talking for a moment. "How old, IdrisPukke, were you before you knew what terror was?"

"A lot older than five, anyway. It was at the Battle of Goat River. I was, what, seventeen. We were ambushed on a scouting trip. My first time in a real fight. It wasn't that I hadn't been trained. And I was pretty good, third in my year. The Druse Cavalry came over the hill and then there was just confusion and noise and chaos. I couldn't speak, my tongue stuck to the roof of my mouth. I began to shake and I wanted to . . . well . . . I mean . . ."

"Shit yourself?" offered Cale.

"Why not be blunt? When it was all over, and it didn't last more than five minutes, I was still alive. But I hadn't even drawn my sword."

"Did anyone else see?"

"Yes."

"What did they say?"

"You'll get used to it."

"They didn't beat you?"

"No. But if it happened again, well, you weren't going to last long." There was another pause. "So you've never felt like that?" said IdrisPukke at last.

It was by no means a simple question. One of the conditions on which his brother, or, to be precise, his half brother, had released

IdrisPukke and put Cale in his control was that he must find out everything about the boy—and most important his apparent lack of fear and whether or not this was exceptional or in some way engineered by the Redeemers.

"I used to be afraid all the time when I was young," said Cale after a while. "But then it stopped."

"Why?"

"I don't know." This was not true, of course, or not entirely true.

"And now you're not afraid at all?"

Cale looked at him. The last few weeks had amazed him, and he was grateful to IdrisPukke and had felt many odd and unfamiliar emotions of friendship and trust. But it would take more than a few weeks of kindness and generosity to shake Cale's wariness. He considered whether or not to change the subject. But it didn't, on the face of it, seem to matter much if he told the truth.

"I feel afraid about things that can hurt me in general. I know what the Redeemers want to do to me. It's hard to explain. But fighting—it's different. What you were saying about the Battle of . . ." He looked at IdrisPukke.

"Goat River."

". . . That stuff about shaking and wanting to shit yourself."

"Don't think you have to spare my feelings at all."

"For me it's the opposite. I just go cold—everything becomes very clear."

"And afterward?"

"What do you mean?"

"Do you feel afraid?"

"No. Mostly I don't feel anything—except after I gave Conn Materazzi a good hiding. That felt pretty good. It still does. But when I killed the soldiers in the ring, I didn't feel good. After all—they never did me any harm." He paused. "I don't want to talk about this anymore."

And being wise, IdrisPukke did not push his luck. And so for the next few weeks Cale went back to his wandering, and in the evening they drank, smoked and ate together, the food slowly becoming richer as Cale was better able to take some fish fried in crispy batter, more butter on his vegetables, a drop of cream with his blackberries.

During the two months that Cale and IdrisPukke had been enjoying the calm and tranquillity of Treetops, a man and a woman had been watching over them. This should not imply care or concern—imagine the loving watchfulness of a mother over her child but without the love.

In stories of the good and bad it's only the good who are subject to dreadful luck, mischance and blundering. The bad are always sharp and act with discipline, have cunning plans only just thwarted in the nick of time. The evil are always on the cusp of winning ways. In real life bad as well as good make simple and easily avoidable mistakes, have dreadful days and go awry. The wicked have weaknesses other than their willingness to kill and maim. Even the bleakest, cruelest soul can have its tender spots. Even the harshest desert has its pools, its shady trees and gentle streams. It's not just the rain that falls on the just and the unjust alike, but good and bad luck, unlooked-for victories and unmerited defeats.

Daniel Cadbury, his back against a mulberry tree, closed the book he was reading, *The Melancholy Prince*, and grunted with satisfaction.

"Be quiet!" said the woman, who had been attentively facing away from him but, on hearing the snap of the book being shut, turned her head sharply in his direction.

"He's two hundred yards away," said Cadbury. "The boy heard nothing."

Checking briefly that Cale was still asleep on the banks of the river below, the woman looked back at Cadbury and this time merely stared. Had he been other than he was—murderer, former galley slave and sometime intelligencer to Kitty the Hare—Cadbury might well have been unnerved. She was not ugly, exactly, perhaps just extremely plain—

but her eyes, empty of everything but hostility, would have made almost anyone uneasy.

"Would you like to borrow it?" said Cadbury, gesturing at her with the book. "It's very fine."

"I can't read," she said, thinking that he was mocking her, which he was. Normally Cadbury would not have been so unwise as to taunt Jennifer Plunkett, a killer so admired by Kitty the Hare that he reserved her for none but his most difficult assassinations. Cadbury had groaned in dismay when Kitty the Hare had told him who was to partner him.

"Not Jennifer Plunkett, please."

"Not an amicable companion, I agree," gurgled Kitty, "but there are many very important persons interested in this boy, myself included, and it is my instinct that a good deal of mayhem of the kind at which Jennifer Plunkett so excels might be required. Abide her for my sake, Cadbury." So that was that.

It was boredom that caused Cadbury to goad the dangerously talented butcher still glaring at him. They had been watching the boy for nearly a month now, and all he had done was eat, sleep, swim, walk and run. Even the pleasures of *The Melancholy Prince*, a book he had enjoyed through a dozen readings in as many years, was not enough to stop him from growing restless.

"No offense, Jennifer."

"Don't call me Jennifer."

"I have to call you something."

"No, you don't." She did not look away and did not blink. There were limits to her tolerance and they were not very great. He shrugged to suggest that he was giving way, but she did not move. He began to wonder if he should get ready. Then, like an animal, not the kind that cared for human company, she turned her head away and went back to staring at the sleeping boy.

It's not just her eyes that are odd, thought Cadbury. *It's what's behind them. She's alive, but I can't put my finger on exactly how.*

Given his profession, Cadbury was entirely familiar with murderous persons. He was, after all, one himself. He killed when it was required, rarely with any pleasure and sometimes with reluctance and even remorse. Most murderers for hire took a certain pleasure, more or less, in what they did. Jennifer Plunkett was different in that he found it impossible to tell what was going on when she killed. His experience of watching her dispose of the two men IdrisPukke had bribed the soldiers to arrest was unlike anything he had witnessed before. On their release and unaware of their role as stooges, they had somehow blundered into the forest half a mile from Treetops and made camp. Without consulting him—professionally discourteous, but he'd decided to let the matter drop—she had walked toward them as they sat brewing up a pot of tea and stabbed them both. It was the lack of fuss that so astonished Cadbury. She killed them with as little effort as a mother might give to the picking up of her children's toys, a kind of bored distraction. By the time the men realized what was happening, they were already dying. Even the most vicious murderers in his experience had to, or wanted to, work themselves up to kill. But not Jennifer Plunkett.

His reverie was broken by the sound of the boy down by the river, who had now woken up and was on the move. He had backed away from the bank to a distance of twenty yards or so. He started calling out with a low "Whooooooo!" then launched himself at the river's edge, running faster and faster. Raising his voice to a high-pitched shout, he leapt from the bank, formed a bomb in midair and splashed in the water. Almost immediately he shot to the surface, screaming with laughter at the freezing cold, and thrashed his way back to the bank. Naked as the day, he danced up and down, laughing and shouting at the dreadful pleasure of the cold water and the warm summer air.

"Nice to be young, eh?" said Cadbury. It was impossible not to share in the boy's delight. And then with astonishment he saw how true this was. Jennifer Plunkett was smiling, her face transformed like a painting of a holy saint. Jennifer Plunkett was in love. As soon as she was aware of Cadbury looking at her, she vanished in an instant from whatever paradise the boy had taken her to. She looked at Cadbury, blinked like a hawk or a feral cat and then turned back to the river, her expression now utterly void.

"What do you think Kitty the Hare wants with him?" she said.

"No idea," said Cadbury. "But nothing good. It's a pity," he added, quite sincerely. "He seems such a happy little chap." He regretted saying this as soon as it was out, but he was still unnerved at what he'd witnessed. It was like seeing a snake blush. *That'll teach you*, thought Cadbury, *to think you know what's going on in other people*. Full of wonder at this strange turn of events, he sat down and laid his back again against the mulberry tree.

As it turned out, it didn't take long to find out. He appeared to Jennifer Plunkett to be asleep, but Cadbury had far too much nous not to be thrashing out this unforeseen development. He kept his not-quite closed eyes on Jennifer's back and drew his Mott knife and hid it, hand around the hilt, under his right thigh, the one farthest away from her. For fully thirty minutes he watched her motionless back while time and again he could hear the boy's repeated "Whooo!" and the splash and the scream of laughter. And then she turned and moved toward him, again without the least fuss, knife in hand, and began the killing blow. He blocked it with his left and stabbed upward with the Mott knife in his right. He marveled at her speed even as they rolled around in the dried-up autumn leaves that covered the forest floor. Back and forth, back and forth they rolled in their dreadful clutch, only the two of them hearing the hot low rasp of each other's breath and the rustle of dead leaves as, almost lip to lip, they stared into each other's eyes. And slowly his greater strength began to tell. She wriggled and squirmed and writhed with all her sinewy might, but Cadbury had her pinned and she was done. But Jennifer had one more weapon beyond her hatred and her rage that she could call on: her dreadful love. How could she give him up and die? And with a heave she slipped to one side, unbalanced Cadbury, wrenched free of his left hand's grasp and was up and haring down the hill to her darling boy.

"Thomas Cale! Thomas Cale!" she cried. The boy looked up as he climbed naked onto the mossy riverbank. Openmouthed, he gawped at the screaming harpy racing desperately down the hill and calling his name over and over: "Thomas Cale! Thomas Cale!"

In a life cursed with many extraordinary sights, this was one of the strangest of them all: a wild-faced sexless thing was shouting his name, waving a knife and rushing toward him with a dreadful madness in its eyes. Astonished, he ran for his clothes, fumbled for his sword, dropped it, picked it up again and raised it to strike as she was almost upon him, shouting wildly. Then he heard a sharp buzz, and a hollow thud like the slap of a man's hand on a horse's flank. Jennifer gave a sharp cough and went flying head over arse past the terrified Cale and hit the trunk of a sawtooth oak with a wallop.

Cale legged it behind a tree, his heart thumping and fluttering like a just-trapped bird. At once he started looking for an escape. Surrounding the tree there was a rough arc of cover-free ground varying between forty to sixty yards in width. He looked at the body. He could see now it was a woman, and she was lying crumpled against the base of a tree with her backside in the air and to one side. She had what looked like a three-ounce arrow in her back, the tip just emerging from her chest. Her nose was bleeding, a single drop falling to the ground every three or four seconds. It would have been no easy shot, hitting a moving target like that, but neither was it exceptional. She'd been running away from the direction of the arrow, whereas if he went now, immediately, he would be running across the line of fire. From a standing start it would take five or six seconds to reach cover. Enough for one shot, not more, and it would have to be a fine one. But then maybe he was as good as Kleist. Kleist could make a shot like that three times out of four.

"Hey! Sonny Jim!"

About two hundred yards and dead ahead, thought Cale.

"What do you want?"

"How about 'thank you'?"

"Thank you. Now why don't you piss off?"

"You ungrateful little shit, I just saved your life."

Was he moving? It sounded like it.

"Who are you?"

"Your guardian angel, mate, that's who I am. She was a very bad girl, that one, a very bad girl."

"What did she want?"

"She wanted to cut your throat, mate. That's what she did for a living."

"Why?"

"No idea, mate. Vipond sent me to keep an eye on you and his ne'er-do-well brother."

"Why should I believe you?"

"No reason. Don't care, anyway. I just don't want you coming after me. I wouldn't want to have to put one in you, not after all the trouble I've taken to keep you alive. So you just stay there for the next fifteen minutes, and during that period of patience I'll be on my way and no harm done. All right?"

Cale thought about this: make a run for it, follow him, catch him, beat the truth out of him. Or along the way get an arrow in his back. He sounded, this man, as if he knew what he was up to. Anyway, there was an alternative.

"All right. Fifteen minutes."

"Word of honor?"

"What?"

"Never mind. How about that 'thank you,' then?"

And with that, both Cadbury and Cale were on the move. Cadbury was yomping it back into the deepest part of the forest, and Cale, using the tree as a screen, had slipped into the river and was carefully swimming along its edge and away.

Three hours later Cale and IdrisPukke were back by the river examining the body of the dead woman under the cover of a cloud of trees. They had spent two hours searching for any sign of Cale's alleged savior but had found nothing. IdrisPukke frisked the body and quickly discovered three knives, two garrotes, a thumbscrew, a knuckle duster and, in her mouth, alongside the left gum, a flexible inch-long blade wrapped in silk.

"Whatever she was up to," said IdrisPukke, "she wasn't trying to sell you clothes pegs."

"Do you believe him?"

"Your savior? Sounds plausible. I don't know about whether I believe him, exactly. But let's face it, if he'd wanted to kill you, he could have done it at any time during the last month. Still—it stinks."

"You really think Vipond sent him?"

"It's possible. Lot of trouble to go to on account of someone like you. No offense."

The reason Cale was not affronted by IdrisPukke's remark was because he'd been thinking the same thing.

"What about the woman?" he said at last.

"Dump her in the river."

So that's what they did and that was the end of Jennifer Plunkett.

That evening the two of them were eating inside the lodge to be on the safe side and discussing what to do about the day's strange events.

"The thing is," said IdrisPukke, "what can we do? If whoever killed that young woman wanted to do the same to you, they would already have done it. Or they could do it tomorrow."

"You said it stinks."

"It's entirely possible that Vipond sent someone to keep an eye on us, even if it was for his own reasons. It is also possible that one of the Mond you humiliated so publicly paid someone to encoffin you. They have the money and the bile. It looked like the woman was coming to attack you: she had a knife in her hand. This man stopped her and then cleared off. Those are just facts. They're obviously not all the facts, and subsequent discoveries may make us come to see those facts that we have in an entirely different light. But until then, speculation is just that. Stay here or go somewhere else—we remain entirely vulnerable to anyone with a good aim and malice or a reward in their heart. We assume what the facts we know tell us because we might just as well do so. Have you any alternative?"

"No."

"There we are, then."

Realizing there wasn't much point in skulking inside, Cale went outside for a smoke. He could see the sense of IdrisPukke's fatalism, but it wasn't, after all, his fate that was the one in question. As IdrisPukke was always saying himself, every philosopher can stand the toothache except for the one who has it. Preoccupied, he barely registered there was a sleek pigeon walking up and down the terrace table eating stale bread crumbs.

"Don't move," said IdrisPukke softly from just behind him, and holding out a piece of bread he slowly approached the bird and began feeding it, carefully putting his hand around its body and then grasping it tightly. Turning the pigeon over, IdrisPukke began removing a small metal tube attached to one of its legs. Cale looked on, utterly bemused.

"It's a messenger pigeon," said IdrisPukke. "Sent by Vipond. Here, hold it." He handed Cale the bird and unscrewed the tube, removed a piece of rice paper and began reading. As he did so his face became grim.

"A troop of Redeemers has taken Arbell Swan-Neck."

Cale's face reddened in astonishment and confusion.

"Why?"

"It doesn't say. The point is that she was staying at Lake Constanz. It's about fifty miles from here. The quickest route back to the Sanctuary is through the Cortina pass—that's about eighty miles north of here. If that's the way they're going, we have to find them and get word to the troops Vipond is sending behind us." He looked worried and confused. "This doesn't make any sense. It's a declaration of war. Why would the Redeemers do this?"

"I don't know. But there's a reason. This wouldn't have happened without Bosco's nod. And Bosco knows what he's doing."

"Well, there's no moon, so they can't travel at night, and neither can we. We'll pack now, get some sleep and start at dawn." He drew in a deep breath. "Though God knows we've got little chance of catching them."

✠

The next day IdrisPukke would not start until it was light enough to see clearly. Cale argued it was necessary to take the risk, but IdrisPukke would not budge.

"If one of these horses goes lame blundering about in the dark, we're stuck."

Cale realized he was right, but he was desperate to be on the move and groaned in dismissive irritation. IdrisPukke ignored him for a further twenty minutes and then they were on their way.

For the next two days they stopped only to rest the horses and eat. Cale continually urged IdrisPukke to go faster. IdrisPukke calmly insisted that the horses, and he himself, could not take it even if Cale could. All four of them needed to catch the Redeemers, if indeed they were to be caught. And they had to have one of the horses at least in a fit state to ride quickly back to the Materazzi to give the information about numbers and direction.

"You don't seem worried about the girl," said Cale.

"It's precisely because I am worried that we're doing this my way—because I'm right. Besides, what's Arbell Swan-Neck to you?"

"Nothing at all. But if I can help to stop the Redeemers, then the Marshal will have a good reason to feel more generous to me than he does. I have friends in Memphis who are hostages too."

"I didn't think you had any friends—I thought it was just circumstances that brought you together."

"I saved their lives—I'd have thought that was pretty friendly."

"Oh," said IdrisPukke. "I thought you were a reluctant hero in all of this."

"So I was."

"So what are you, then, Master Cale, noble by calling or merely by circumstance?"

"I'm not noble at all."

"So you say. But I wonder if there isn't an incipient hero growing in there somewhere."

"What does 'incipient' mean?"

"Something beginning to appear, something beginning to exist."

Cale laughed, but not pleasantly.

"If that's what you think, let's hope you aren't in the position where you're going to find out."

And with this, IdrisPukke decided to be quiet.

On the second day, they descended onto the main road to the Cortina pass. It wasn't much of a road.

"No one uses it these days and they haven't for sixty years—not since the Redeemers shut the borders."

"How far to the Sanctuary from the pass?" asked Cale.

"You don't know?"

"The Redeemers didn't leave maps lying around—nothing to make it easier for us to escape. Until a few months ago I used to think Memphis was thousands of miles away."

Had IdrisPukke not been distracted by a beautiful vermilion and gold dragonfly, he would have seen a liar's expression on Cale's face, just in the moment he thinks he's given himself away. "I mean," added Cale, "before I came here and realized it wasn't." Now IdrisPukke noticed the awkward tone.

"What's the matter?"

"Nothing's the matter."

"If you say so."

Terrified that he had revealed something he was very anxious not to reveal, Cale stayed wrapped in alarmed silence for the next ten minutes. When IdrisPukke next spoke, it was as if he had forgotten the whole thing—which indeed he had.

"The Sanctuary is a good two hundred miles from the pass—but they don't need to get that far. There's a garrison twenty miles from the border—Martyr Town."

"I've never heard of it."

"Well, it's not so big, but its walls are thick. It would need an army to take it."

"What then?"

"Nothing. Materazzi adores the girl. He'll give them what they want."

"How do you know they want something?"

"It doesn't make sense otherwise."

"What makes sense to you and what makes sense to the Redeemers is a white horse of a different color."

"So, you've come up with an idea—I mean about what they're doing?"

"No."

"It doesn't have anything to do with you?"

Cale laughed. "The Redeemers are a bunch of bastards—but do you really think they'd start a war with Memphis over three kids and a fat girl?"

IdrisPukke grunted. "Not if you put it like that. On the other hand, you've been lying to me for the past two months."

"And who are you to be demanding the truth?"

"The best friend you've got."

"Is that so?"

"Yes—as it happens. So there's nothing you want to tell me?"

"No." And that was that.

Twenty minutes later they came across the remains of a fire.

"What do you think?" asked Cale, as IdrisPukke sifted the ashes through his fingers.

"Still hot. A few hours, that's all." He nodded at the flattened grass and lightly scuffed earth. "How many?"

Cale sighed. "Probably not less than ten—not more than twenty. Sorry, I'm not much good at this kind of thing."

"Neither am I." He looked around, thoughtful and uncertain. "I think one of us should ride back and tell the Materazzi what the score is."

"Why? Will it make them ride quicker? And even if it does, what are they going to do when they get here? Any kind of pitched battle and the Redeemers will kill her. They won't surrender, I can tell you that."

IdrisPukke sighed. "So what are you suggesting?"

"Catch them up, stay out of sight. Once we know the notch-up, we can work out what to do. Bring in a small number of Materazzi and do it quietly. That's what I think until we catch them up. Things might be different then."

IdrisPukke sniffed and spat on the ground.

"All right. You know them best."

Five hours later, as it was getting dark, Cale and IdrisPukke crept toward the top of a small hill just before the entrance of the Cortina pass—a huge cleft in the granite mountain that marked out the northern border between the Redeemers and the Materazzi.

The hill overlooked a depression about twenty feet deep and eighty yards long in which they could see six Redeemers preparing camp. In the middle of the group sat Arbell Materazzi, presumably tied because she did not move once while they watched. After five minutes the two of them drew back to a clump of bushes about two hundred yards away.

"Just in case you were wondering why there are only six, there'll be another four guarding the rim at least," said Cale. "They'll have sent a rider ahead to the garrison to meet them on the other side."

"I'll ride back and try and get the Materazzi," said IdrisPukke.

"What for?"

"If they're close, they'll take the risk of riding in the dark. Even if the Materazzi lose half the horses on the way, there are only a dozen Redeemers at most."

"And if you aren't here and deployed before dawn, they'll be into the pass and out of reach. And even if they're not—an attack in daylight means the girl is dead. We stop them before they leave or not at all."

"There are only two of us," pointed out IdrisPukke.

"Yes," replied Cale. "But one of the two of us is me."

"It's suicide."

"If it was suicide, I wouldn't do it."

"Then why are you?"

Cale shrugged. "If I rescue the girl then His Enormity, the Marshal, will be undyingly grateful. Grateful enough to give me money—a lot of money—and safe passage."

"Where to?"

"Somewhere it's warm, the food is good, and as far away from the Redeemers as you can get without falling off the edge of the world."

"And your friends?"

"Friends? Oh, they can come too. Why not?"

"The risk is too great. Better let her be a hostage, and Materazzi can buy her out with whatever it is the Redeemers want."

"What makes you so sure she's a hostage?" said Cale, his voice cold and irritable. IdrisPukke looked at him.

"So—now perhaps we get the truth."

"The truth is that you think the Redeemers are like you—nastier, madder—but that what you want and they want, well, it's the same underneath. But it isn't." He sighed. "It's not that I understand them, because I don't. I thought I did until what happened before I killed that shit-bag Picarbo—the Redeemer. I told you that I did it to stop him, you know, raking her."

"Raping."

Cale reddened, hating to be corrected. "Whatever it's called doesn't matter—that's not what he was doing. He was cutting her up." Then he told IdrisPukke exactly what happened that night.

"My God!" said an appalled IdrisPukke when he'd finished. "Why?"

"No idea. That's what I meant when I said I'd stopped thinking I knew what was going on in their nasty little minds."

"Why would they do that to Arbell Materazzi?"

"I told you, I don't know. Maybe they want to see what a Materazzi woman is like, you know . . ." He paused, awkward for once. "Inside. I don't know. But it doesn't make sense that they want her for money. *That* isn't their way."

"It makes even more sense if they want you back."

Cale gasped, almost laughing.

"They'd like to make an instance of me—a bonfire with all the trimmings. And I don't deny they'd go to extreme lengths to do it—but starting a war with the Materazzi over an acolyte? Not in a thousand years." He smiled, grim. "I guess the same thought has crossed the Marshal's mind. I'm prepared to bet the four of us would be on our way to the Sanctuary in two shakes of a lamb's tail just as a gesture of his goodwill. Don't you think so?"

IdrisPukke did not reply, because that was exactly what he'd been thinking. Both were silent for a couple of minutes.

"It is a risk. But it can be done," said Cale. "She's nothing to me," he lied. "I wouldn't throw my life away for some spoiled Materazzi brat. If the Redeemers take her, I've got everything to lose. If we get her back, everything to gain. You too, just as much as me. All you have to do is cover me. Even if I fail you've got a better than even chance of getting away. And nobody, let's face it, is going to thank you if they find out you caught up with her and let them go without doing anything."

IdrisPukke smiled. "The unfairness of life—always the best argument. Very well. Tell me your plan."

"There were three words Bosco beat into me nearly every day of my life—surprise, violence, momentum. Now he's going to wish he hadn't." Cale drew a circle in the dead pine needles that covered the forest floor.

"There'll be four guards around the circle—east, west, south, north. There's no moon tonight, so we can't move until first light. That's when you'll have to kill the guard at the west—as soon as you can make him out. Then I'll take the south guard. You have to hold the west guard's position because it's the only one where it's possible to get in a shot behind the rock the girl is next to. That's where I'm going to take her as soon as I cut her free. Do you know any birdcalls?"

"I can do an owl," said IdrisPukke doubtfully. "But there aren't any owls in this part of the world."

"The Redeemers probably don't know that." Cale paused. "What does an owl sound like?"

IdrisPukke gave him a demonstration. "What if the guard makes a noise while I'm trying to kill him?"

"*Trying?*" said Cale, appalled. "There won't be any *trying*. I don't want to hear anything about doing your best. Bungle it and I'm dead. Understand?"

IdrisPukke looked at Cale, piqued. "Don't worry about me, boy."

"Well, I do worry. So once I hear your signal, I'll kill the south guard. I'll need a minute to put on his cassock. Then I'll just walk into the camp as quietly as I can. Once the remaining guards work out what's happening . . ."

"Why don't we kill all the lookouts first?"

"There's no chance you'll be able to crawl around here for long without giving yourself away. This is the safest it's going to be. They'll be confused and I'll look just like the others in camp. It'll still be near dark. If you do your job properly, one way or the other, it isn't going to take long."

"So what do I do then?"

"You won't see where the lookouts are on the north and east unless they start shooting—if they do, then you shoot back—keep their heads down. I'll take the girl behind the rock here. They can't get us from anywhere but directly above." Cale smiled. "That's when this gets tricky. You have to stop them getting directly above and behind us until I can make a run for it. She'll be safe there as long as you can keep them from taking your position. Once I'm over the lip, it's two against two."

"That's forty yards in the open and up a steep climb for the last fifteen. If they're any good, I don't think much of your chances."

"They'll be good."

"Anyway, I can't see why I'm worrying about a suicidal dash—after all, you've got to kill six armed men single-handed first. This whole idea is ridiculous. We should wait for the Materazzi."

"They'll kill her before the Materazzi get to her. This is the only chance she has. Depend on it—I can do this quicker than I can tell you about it. They won't expect it so close to dawn, and they won't be able to tell me from one of their own in the dark. Once they've realized it's an attack, they'll be expecting Materazzi all over the place—they're not going to be expecting anything like this."

"Because it's too stupid to believe."

"It's my life here, not yours."

"And the girl's."

"The girl is worth something only if we're the ones who save her. Without this, you descend to a kind of nothing—or worse. The choice is simple enough, I'd say."

Six hours later IdrisPukke was standing over the body of the dead west guard.

In times gone by IdrisPukke had commanded numerous battles in which many thousands had died. But it had been a long time since he had killed a man face-to-face. He stood for a moment looking down at the glassy eyes and open mouth, lips pulled back over his teeth, and he could feel his whole body begin to shake.

As a result, his effort at impersonating an owl stuck in his throat and might have alarmed anyone who ever heard one before. But within less than a minute he could just make out the figure of Cale moving slowly down the slope, being careful not to make a noise or, if he was seen by the remaining two guards, to be in any kind of a hurry.

A profound dread began to fill IdrisPukke as he watched what, after all, was no more than a boy walk easily up to the six sleeping men and begin.

He had not been sure what to expect, but it was nothing like this. Cale drew his shortsword and in one movement stabbed downward at the first sleeping figure; the man neither moved nor cried out. Still unhurried, Cale moved on to the second man. Again the powerful downward strike and the lack of a cry. As he moved, the third Redeemer began to stir and even raised his head. Another strike—if he called out, IdrisPukke could not hear. Cale moved to the fourth man, who now sat upright and sleepily gazed at Cale, puzzled but not afraid. A downward jab into his throat and he fell back with a cry, strangled but loud.

The fifth and sixth of the sleepers woke—experienced men, hardened by battle and many surprises. The first shouted at Cale and came directly at him thrusting a short spear at his face. Cale aimed a blow at his neck but missed and struck him through the ear. The Redeemer screamed and went down bellowing in pain. The last of the sleepers lost his habitual presence of mind, the years of fighting no use to him now, and gazed in horror at his friend clutching the dead leaves of the forest covered in blood. He silently watched, stock-still as a tree stump, as Cale in a trance struck through his breastbone. A single gasp and then he fell, the man on the ground still roaring.

For the first time Cale started running, heading toward the girl, who had woken to see the last three killings. She was bound hand and foot, and he lifted her in one movement over his shoulder and ran to cover behind the great boulder against which she had been sleeping. An arrow zipped past his left ear and ricocheted among the rocks.

From directly over their heads IdrisPukke answered with an arrow of his own. There was an immediate reply from the second guard, zipping into the trees that hid IdrisPukke.

For the next few minutes arrows shot back and forth but IdrisPukke could see the pattern—one of the guards was stalking him while the

other provided covering fire. It was getting lighter now with every passing second, and with the rising dawn any chance of Cale making a
successful break was fading. IdrisPukke would have to move soon or be
cornered.

Cale gestured to Arbell to stay put and keep quiet; then he was
moving, running out from behind the rock and toward the rise out of
the hollow. IdrisPukke, bow drawn, hoped for a too-quick shot that
would give away the bowman's position as soon as he saw Cale on the
move. But the bowman was cool—he was going to wait until Cale
reached the rise that must slow him down, and catch him then. It took
the young boy only four seconds or so, and then he was climbing, his
feet and hands sinking into the surface layer of loose and dry pine
needles—and slowing all the time. Then three-quarters of the way up,
he slipped on a tree root covered by loam and slid to a halt, scrabbling
for a foothold. It was only a second, but it stopped his momentum and
gave the archer as much time as he needed. The shot came, zipping
like a wasp across the bowl, and struck Cale even as he made it over
the lip.

IdrisPukke's heart leapt—in the gloom it was hard to see where it had
hit, but the sound was unmistakable—a *thwack!* at once soft and hard.

Now he was in trouble himself. The two guards had only him to
worry about now—if he stayed, his chances were poor, but if he moved
away, they could take his present ground and merely lean over the lip
of the bowl and finish the girl—something that now there were only
two of them, they'd be sure to do. The bushes around him were dense,
and while this gave him cover, it would do the same for the guards.
Everything was now in their favor, nothing in his.

During the following five minutes many unpleasant thoughts
crossed his mind. The dreadful fact of approaching death and the temptation to cut and run. If he died here—as he surely would, his conscience devil pointed out—it would do the girl no good: two of them
would die instead of one. But then, of course, he would have to live

with himself. *But you could manage that*, said his devil conscience. *Better a live dog than a dead lion.*

And so IdrisPukke, sword stuck in the ground in front of him and a bow at the ready, waited and endured the thoughts hammering in his brains. And he waited. And he waited.

Pain was nothing new to Cale, but the arrow that had taken him just above his shoulder blade was an agony far beyond anything he had ever felt before. The sound he let out through gritted teeth was a whining noise, as unstoppable by courage or an act of will as the blood he could feel warmly pouring down his back. His body began shaking with the pain as if he were having a fit. He tried to breathe deeply but the pain kept hitting him and drew out a spasm of short gasps. He had to sit upright and bring it under control. He started crawling and whining, crawling and whining. Then he passed out. He woke up unsure how long he had been unconscious—seconds, minutes? They were coming for him and he had to get to his feet. He crawled to a pine tree and started to pull himself up. Too much. He stopped, then pushed on. Get on your feet or die. But it was as much as he could do to turn himself around and lean the unwounded part of his back against the tree. He vomited and passed out again. When he woke up, it was with a start and a grunt of pain, but this time from a fist-sized rock that a Redeemer standing about ten yards away had just thrown at him.

"Thought you might be playing possum," said the Redeemer. "Where are the others?"

"What did you say?" Cale knew he had to stay awake and keep talking.

"Where are the others?"

"They're over there." He tried to raise his hand to point away from IdrisPukke, but he lost consciousness again. Another rock, another start awake.

"What? What?"

"Tell me where they are or I'll put the next arrow in your groin."

"There are twenty . . . I know Redeemer Bosco . . . He sent me."

The Redeemer had drawn back his bow, deciding that he'd get no sense from Cale, but the mention of Bosco astonished him. How could anyone here know about the great Lord Militant? He lowered the bow and it was enough.

"Bosco says . . ." and Cale started to mumble his words as if he was going to pass out again, and the Redeemer, without really thinking, made a few steps forward to hear what he was saying. Then Cale lashed out with his good left arm, launching the rock so it took the Redeemer high on the forehead. His eyes rolled back in his head, mouth gaping, and he slumped to the ground. Cale fainted again.

IdrisPukke still waited in the small, roughly circular space surrounded on three sides by bushes so dense that he could not see out and no one else could see in. Behind him was the thirty-foot steep drop at the bottom of which still waited, he hoped, Arbell Materazzi. There was a faint rustle from beyond the bushes. He raised his bow, fully drawn, and waited. A stone dropped into the circle. He almost let loose the shot the thrower had hoped for. Moving the arc of the bow back and forth to cover a rushed entry he called out, voice shaking.

"Come in here and it's fifty-fifty you'll get an arrow in the gut!" He moved sideways three steps so as not to give away his position. An arrow zipped through the bushes and out over the edge of the bowl, missing IdrisPukke by the same three steps. "Leave now and we won't come after you." He ducked and shuffled again to one side. Another arrow. Again buzzing through almost exactly at the point he had been standing. Talking had been a mistake. Twenty seconds passed. Idris-Pukke's breathing sounded so loud in his ears that he was sure the Redeemer knew exactly where he was.

From about two hundred yards away there was a high-pitched skirling cry of pain and terror. Then it was silenced. Everything seemed to stop, only the wind hurrying through the leaves for what seemed like minutes.

"That was your friend, Redeemer. Now it's only you." Another arrow, another miss. "Run now and we won't come after you. That's the deal and you have my word."

"Why should I trust you?"

"It'll take my oppo about two or three minutes to get here—he'll vouch for me."

"All right. I agree to a covenant—but come after me and I swear to God I'll take one of you with me before I go."

IdrisPukke decided to stay quiet. With Cale out there, clearly alive and in a bad mood, all he had to do was wait. In fact, Cale had fainted again directly after he had killed the Redeemer just as he regained consciousness, and was in no state to do anything very much, let alone rescue IdrisPukke. But after ten minutes waiting, his anxiety slowly increasing, Cale spoke to him softly from beyond the bushes to his right.

"IdrisPukke, I'm coming in and I don't want you taking my head off when I do."

"Thank God," said IdrisPukke to himself, letting the bow sink downward and easing the bowstring.

There was a good deal of clumsy rustling and then Cale emerged in front of him.

IdrisPukke sat down, let out a long deep breath and started fiddling inside his pocket for his tobacco.

"I thought you might be dead."

"No," replied Cale.

"What about the guard?"

"He's dead, yes."

There was a grim laugh from IdrisPukke.

"You're a caution, and no mistake."

"I don't know what that means."

"Never mind." IdrisPukke finished rolling his tobacco and lit up. "Do you want one?" he said, gesturing with the cigarillo.

"To be honest," said Cale, "I don't feel very well." And with that he slumped forward in a dead faint.

Cale did not wake up for another three weeks, during which time he came close to death on more than one occasion. Partly this was due to an infection caused by the arrowhead that had lodged in his shoulder, but mostly it was because of the medical treatment given him by the expensive physicians who had tended him night and day and whose ruinously stupid methods (bleeding, scraping and defusculating) had very nearly achieved what a lifetime of brutality at the Sanctuary had failed to do. And they would have succeeded if a temporary easing of his fever had not allowed Cale to recover consciousness for a few hours. Confused and disorientated on opening his eyes, Cale found himself staring at an old man in a red skullcap gazing down at him.

"Who are you?"

"I am Dr. Dee," said the old man, who went back to placing a sharp and not especially clean knife to a vein in Cale's forearm.

"What are you doing?" said Cale, pulling his arm away.

"Be calm," said the old man reassuringly. "You have a bad wound in the shoulder and it has become infected. You need to be bled to let the poison out." He took hold of Cale's arm and tried to hold it still.

"Let go of me, you bloody old lunatic!" shouted Cale, though he was so weak it came out not much more than a whisper.

"Hold still, damn you!" shouted the doctor, and fortunately it was this that carried through the door and alerted IdrisPukke.

"What's the matter?" he said from the doorway. Then, seeing Cale was awake, "Thank God!" He came to the bed and bent down low over the boy. "I'm glad to see you."

"Tell this old fool to go away."

"He's your doctor—he's here to help."

Cale pulled his arm free again. Then winced at the pain in his shoulder.

"Get him away from me," said Cale. "Or by God I'll cut the old bastard's throat."

IdrisPukke signaled the doctor to leave, something he did with considerable show of hurt dignity.

"I want you to look at the wound."

"I don't know anything about medicine. Let the doctor come and look at you."

"Did I lose much blood?"

"Yes."

"Then I don't need some half-wit to help me lose any more." He rolled onto his right side. "Tell me what color it is."

Gently, though not without causing Cale considerable pain, IdrisPukke eased back the stained and grubby-looking bandage.

"Its got a lot of pus—pale green—and the edges are red." His face was grim now; he had seen killing wounds like this before.

Cale sighed.

"I need maggots."

"What?"

"Maggots. I know what I'm doing. I need about twenty. Wash them five times in clean water, drinking water, and bring them to me."

"Let me fetch another doctor."

"Please, IdrisPukke. If you don't do this for me, I'm finished. Please."

And so twenty minutes later, full of misgiving, IdrisPukke returned with twenty carefully washed maggots skimmed from a dead crow found in a ditch outside. With the help of a maid he followed Cale's detailed instructions: "Wash your hands clean, then wash with boiled water. Pour the maggots over the wound. Use a clean bandage and make the edges fast to the skin. Make sure to keep me on my stomach. Get as much water into me as you can." With that, he lost consciousness again and did not wake up for another four days.

When he opened his eyes again, a relieved IdrisPukke was by his bed.

"How are you?"

Cale took in a few deep breaths.

"Not bad. Am I hot?"

IdrisPukke put his hand to his forehead.

"Not too bad. For the first two days you were burning."

"How long have I been asleep?"

"Four days—though you weren't resting for much of it. You were making a lot of noise. It was hard to keep you on your front."

"Have a look under the bandage. It's itching."

Somewhat uncertainly IdrisPukke eased back the edge of the bandage, his nose twitching in disgusted anticipation of what he would find. He grunted in distaste.

"Is it bad?" asked an anxious Cale.

"Good God!"

"What?"

"The pus has gone—and the redness too—most of it, anyway." He eased the bandage back more, though this time the now fat maggots dropped in twos and threes into the bedding. "I've never seen anything like it."

Cale sighed—immense relief.

"Get rid of them—the maggots—then bring me some more. Same again." And with that he fell into a deep sleep.

hree weeks later IdrisPukke and a still yellow-looking Cale made their way up to the great keep of Memphis.

Secretly Cale had expected some sort of official welcome and—though he denied this to himself—he wanted one. He had, after all, killed eight men single-handed and saved Arbell Swan-Neck from a hideous death. It was not that he required much for enduring such dangers: a parade of several thousands throwing flowers and cheering his name, capped off by the tearful welcome of the beautiful Arbell, standing on a dais decorated in silk and beside a desperately grateful father so overcome with emotion that he could not speak would be enough.

Instead there was nothing, just Memphis going about its relentless pursuit of making and spending money—today under looming skies as a thunderstorm approached. As they were about to enter through the great gates of the keep, Cale's heart leapt as a sudden loud peal of bells rang out from the great cathedral, which was caught up in a wonderful ringing echo across the great city as the other churches followed suit. But his hopes were dashed by IdrisPukke.

"They ring the bells," he said, nodding at the approaching storm, "to keep the lightning away."

Ten minutes later and they were dismounting at Lord Vipond's manor house. A single servant was there to greet them.

"Hello, Stillnoch," said IdrisPukke to the servant.

"Welcome back, sir," said Stillnoch, a man whose face was so deeply lined and creviced that it reminded Cale of an old man's testicles. IdrisPukke turned to the exhausted but deeply disgruntled boy. "I'll have to go and see Vipond. Stillnoch will take you to your room. We'll have dinner tonight. I'll see you then." And with that he walked over to the main door. Stillnoch motioned Cale toward a smaller door at the far end of the manor.

Some stinking hovel, thought Cale to himself as his resentment blossomed.

But in fact his room, or rooms, turned out to be extremely pleasant. There was a sitting area with a soft couch and an oak dining table, a bathroom with its own jakes, something he had heard about but dismissed as a wild fantasy. And, of course, a bedroom with a large bed and a mattress stuffed with feathers.

"Would you care for luncheon, sir?" asked Stillnoch.

"Yes," said Cale, on the basis that it sounded as if it might be food. Stillnoch bowed. When he came back twenty minutes later with a tray of beer, pork pie, boiled egg and fried potatoes, Cale was asleep on the bed.

Stillnoch had heard the rumors. He put down the tray and looked the sleeping boy over carefully. With his yellow skin and drawn features caused by the infection that had so nearly killed him, he did not, thought Stillnoch, look up to much. But if he had given that cocky little bastard Conn Materazzi a bloody good hiding, then he deserved respect and admiration. And on this thought he drew the covers up over the sleeping boy, closed the curtains and left.

"He walked through their camp like Vile Death himself. I've seen some killers in my time, but nothing like this boy."

IdrisPukke was sitting opposite his half brother and drinking a cup of tea, and was clearly a troubled man.

"And is that all he is—a killer?"

"To be honest, if all I'd seen of him was that—well, I'd have got away from him as fast as I could. And I'd have told you to pay him off and get rid of him."

Vipond looked surprised.

"Good God, you've got very sentimental in your old age. Such people are useful—of course they are. But I'm asking you if he's more than a homicidal thug."

IdrisPukke sighed.

"Very much more, I'd say. And if you'd asked me before the fight at the Cortina pass, if you can call it a fight, I'd have told you he was a great find. He has suffered much, but he has wit and brains—though woefully ignorant about some things—and I would have said that there was a good heart in there. But I was shocked by what happened. There, that's all there is to it. I don't know what to make of him. I like him, but—to be blunt—he scares me."

Vipond sat back, thoughtful. "Well," he said at last, "he's won you golden opinions whatever your doubts and—to be fair—me also. And, God knows, you could do with them. Marshal Materazzi has forgiven all your sins and now you hang in his good favor like an icicle on a Dutchman's beard." He smiled at IdrisPukke.

"Indeed, if it wasn't for the need to keep this business secret, you'd both have had a parade and a band and all the fixings." Vipond smiled, this time mocking. "You'd have liked that, wouldn't you?"

"Yes, I would," said IdrisPukke. "And why wouldn't I? God knows it's been a long time since anyone was pleased to see me."

"And whose fault is that?"

"Mine, dear brother," laughed IdrisPukke. "All mine."

"You should perhaps explain to the boy why his reception has been so muted."

"To be honest, I don't think he gives a damn. Saving Arbell Swan-Neck was just a means to an end for him. He thought it was in his interests to risk his life—and that was all. He's never asked once about her. For all my misgivings, I praised his courage, and still he looked at me as if I were a fool. He wants money and a safe passage as far away from his old masters as the sea will carry him. This is not someone who cares for praise or blame. If he pleases or doesn't please, it's all the same to him."

"Then," said Lord Vipond, "he really is a most exceptional fellow." He stood up. "At any rate, whether you're right or not, the Marshal wishes to thank him personally tonight and, of course, Arbell Swan-Neck—though by the look on her face when he told her, she'd rather eat a weasel."

23

*F*or goodness' sake!" said the Marshal to his daughter. "Cheer up."

"He frightens me," said the deathly pale but beautiful young woman.

"Frightens you? He saved your life. What's the matter with you?"

"I know he saved my life—but it was horrible."

The Marshal gasped with irritation.

"I dare say it was horrible. Killing is a horrible thing. But he did what was necessary and he risked his own life—more than risked, given the odds—and you stand there whining about how terrible it was. What you need to do is think about how terrible things would have been if he hadn't saved you."

Arbell Swan-Neck, not used to being upbraided like this, looked even more miserable.

"I know he saved my life—but he still frightens me. You've never seen what he's like. I have—twice. He's not like anything I've ever seen—he's not human."

"Ridiculous—I've never heard anything so ridiculous. By God, you'd better be polite to him or there'll be trouble."

Neither was Arbell used to being threatened, and she was about to abandon her role as fearful girl for something more spirited when the door of the small dining room opened and a servant's announcement interrupted.

"Chancellor Vipond and guests, m'lud."

"Welcome, welcome," enthused the Marshal, attempting to dispel the coldness in the atmosphere with so much zeal that both Vipond and IdrisPukke were aware that there was some awkwardness in the room.

Cale was aware of nothing but the presence of Arbell Swan-Neck, who stood by the window looking beautiful and trying, unsuccessfully, not to shake. Cale, who had been in a state of longing and dread since he had learned that she was to be at the dinner, was also trying not to tremble.

"You must be Cale," said the Marshal, warmly grasping his hand. "Thank you, thank you. What you've done can never be repaid." He looked over at his daughter. "Arbell." His tone was at once encouraging and threatening. Slowly the beautiful young girl, effortlessly graceful, tall and slender, walked over to Cale and held out her hand.

Cale took it as if he barely knew what to do with it. He did not notice that Arbell's face (you would not have thought it possible) turned as pale as moonlight on snow.

"Thank you for everything you have done for me. I am very grateful."

It struck IdrisPukke that he had heard more life and enthusiasm in the last words of a condemned man going to the gallows. The Marshal looked fiercely at his daughter—and yet he could see that she was deeply afraid of the boy in front of her. To his irritation at her lack of manners was also added a genuine puzzlement. However deep his gratitude, and it went very deep indeed because he adored his daughter, he was, in truth, somewhat disappointed by Cale. He had expected—well, he wasn't sure what he had expected precisely—but someone, surely, given his fearsome reputation, with majestic presence, the charismatic power that any great man of violence always, in his experience, carried with him. But Cale looked like a young peasant, not bad-looking in an unrefined way, but as stupefied and stumped by the presence of royalty as peasants usually were. How such a creature could have battered the very best of the young Materazzi and killed so many men single-handedly was utterly mysterious.

"Let's eat. You must be very hungry. Come and sit by me," he said, taking Cale by the shoulders.

He was no sooner seated with Arbell opposite, her eyes downcast at the plate in front of her, than he became aware of the massed ranks of cutlery in front of him, a platoon of forks of various sizes, a matching squad of knives, sharp and blunt. Most disconcerting of all was an object that looked like something used for a particularly painful act of torture—the removal of a nose, say, or a penis. It looked like a tong—but it crossed over and back on itself at the end in an utterly mysterious way.

He already felt bad enough—an incomprehensible mixture of adoration and hatred for the woman seated across from him, who had taken his hand with as much enthusiasm as if it had been a dead fish. The ungrateful gorgeous bitch. Now he was certain to look something that he could not endure: foolish. Terrible pain and even death itself seemed to hold no fear for Cale—who, after all, could wield these two more skillfully than Cale himself?—but the prospect of feeling ridiculous made him almost weak with anxiety.

He nearly jumped as Stillnoch slid up behind him so silently that Cale was unaware of his presence—no mean feat—until a plate was put in front of him and the sympathetic Stillnoch whispered, "Snails!" into his ear.

Unaware of his heroic status in Stillnoch's eyes, Cale thought that "Snails!" must be some sort of withering insult from a servant who resented his presence among the great and good. On the other hand, he thought, trying to calm down, perhaps it was a warning. But, if so, of what kind? He looked down at the plate and his confusion deepened. Lying in front of him were six objects that looked like tiny, coiled soldiers' helmets with a horrible-looking flecked stickum oozing out of them. They certainly looked like something you needed to be warned against.

"Ah!" said IdrisPukke, sniffing the air like the worst actor in a pantomime. "Excellent. Snails in garlic butter!" Sitting next to Cale, he had noticed immediately the boy's alarm at the vast array of cutlery in front of him and the look of horror at the six snails in their shells. Now that he had Cale's attention, and, it must be said, the attention of the rest of the table, he raised the peculiar-looking tong instrument in his right hand and gave it a squeeze. The two spoonlike ends opened up, and he used them to cradle a snail shell. He loosened his squeeze on the handle and the spoons clamped shut, holding the shell firmly in their grasp. Taking up a small ivory-handled skewer, he poked inside the shell and adroitly, if theatrically so that Cale could see what he was doing, eased out what looked like (despite the garlic, parsley and butter in which it was smothered) a greeny gray piece of cartilage the size of an earlobe. Then he popped it into his mouth with another theatrical gasp of satisfaction.

Though at first bemused by this strange performance, the others around the table quickly realized what he was trying to do and studiously avoided looking at Cale as he stared down malevolently at his first course.

You might be surprised that a boy readily prepared to eat rat would turn his nose up at eating snail. But he had never seen a snail before, and who is to say that, all things being equal, you wouldn't choose to eat a glossy, well-fed vigorous rat over a snail oozing its pockmarked sluggy way from under a rotting log.

Surreptitiously double-checking his fellow guests as they seized their helmeted dinner, Cale picked up the tongs, grabbed a shell and, using the skewer, picked out the gray, soft-bodied moistness. He paused for a moment, studiously unwatched by the others, then put it in his mouth and began chewing with all the enthusiasm of a man eating one of his own testicles.

Fortunately the rest of the dinner was familiar enough, or at least looked like something he had eaten at IdrisPukke's table. By keeping an eye on his mentor, Cale was able to use the remaining cutlery more or less correctly—although forks remained a clumsily handled mystery. The three men did all the talking, nothing businesslike: reminiscences, stories of this or that common past event, though nothing of the touchy history of IdrisPukke's past indiscretions and expulsion.

Throughout dinner Arbell Swan-Neck did not once look up from her plate, though neither did she eat much. From time to time Cale shot her a look, and on each occasion she seemed more beautiful than the last—the long blond hair, the green and almond-shaped eyes and the lips! Red as a rosebud against her pale skin, a neck so long and slender that words and looks failed him. He turned back to his dinner, his soul ringing like a well-struck bell. But it was a bell that rang with more than joy and adoration—there was the sound there too of anger and resentment. She would not look at him because she did not want to be in his presence. She hated him and he (how could he not?) hated her in return.

As soon as the last dish was served—strawberries and cream—Arbell Swan-Neck stopped and said, "I'm sorry. I'm feeling unwell. May I leave?"

Her father looked at her, hiding his fury only for the sake of his guests. He merely nodded, hoping the irritable shake of his head made it clear: *I'll talk to you later.*

She quickly glanced around at the others, though not Cale, and then she was gone. Cale sat and seethed. What mountainous seas of feeling—of love and bitterness and wrath—burst and dashed upon this young man's rocky soul.

However, with the girl gone, there was no need to be careful about the matter of her kidnapping and its mysterious purpose. And it also became clear why there was a lack of crowds roaring their eternal gratitude for Cale's amazing bravery in rescuing Arbell Materazzi. Hardly anyone knew. The Marshal apologized to Cale but explained that had the kidnapping become known, the demand for war would have been irresistible. He and Lord Vipond were in agreement that they must know as much as they could about the Redeemers' unfathomable act before they took such a drastic step.

"We are blind," said Vipond to Cale. "And in being so are apt to stumble into such a great enterprise. IdrisPukke tells me you have no idea why they would do something so provocative?"

"No."

"You're sure?"

"Why would I lie? It makes no more sense to me than it does to you. All the Redeemers ever talked about was the war against the Antagonists. And all they said even then was that the Antagonists worshipped the Anti-Redeemer and were heretics who should be wiped from the face of the earth."

"And Memphis?"

"With disgust and hardly ever—it was a place of perversion and sin where anything at all could be bought and sold."

"Harsh," said IdrisPukke, "but you can see what they're driving at."

The Marshal and Vipond pointedly ignored him.

"So there's nothing you can tell us?" asked the Doge.

Cale realized he was about to be dismissed and that this was his only chance to shape his future among the powerful.

"Only this. If they've decided to do something, the Redeemers will not stop. I don't know why they want your daughter, but they'll keep coming for her no matter what it costs them."

At this the Marshal went pale. Cale kept his advantage.

"Your daughter, she's a very . . ." He paused, as if searching for the right word. "Prestigious person." He had liked the word when he heard it but had not quite got the hang of it. "I mean, everywhere in the empire they look on her—I've heard people say it—as its richest ornament. Everything that is to be admired about her is to be admired about the Materazzi. She stands for you, is that right?"

"What do you mean?" said the Marshal.

"If they wanted to send a message . . ." He let his voice trail.

"What kind of message?" asked the Marshal, more and more anxious.

"Kidnap Arbell Materazzi or kill her and show your subjects that the Redeemers can reach even the highest in the land." He paused, again only for effect. "They'll know that a second kidnapping will be impossible, probably, but in my opinion they won't let this go. They always finish what they start. It's as important for them to make that clear as letting you know they can reach anyone. They're trying to tell you that they absolutely will not stop."

By now the Marshal had gone white.

"She'll be safe here. We'll put a ring around her. No one will be able to enter."

Cale tried to look more awkward than he felt.

"She was protected, I was told, by a guard of forty when she was taken from the castle at Lake Constanz. Were there any survivors?"

"No," said the Marshal.

"And this time—it's just my opinion; I can't be sure—they'll only come to kill. Will eighty men or a hundred and eighty be sure to stop them?"

"If history teaches us one thing, my lord," said IdrisPukke, "it's that if you're prepared to sacrifice your own life, you can kill anyone."

Vipond had not seen the Marshal so uneasy and alarmed at any time in his life.

"Can you stop them?" said the Marshal to Cale.

"Me?" Cale looked as if the idea had not occurred to him. He thought for a moment. "Better than anyone else, I'd say. And I have Vague Henri and Kleist."

"Who?" said the Marshal.

"Cale's friends," observed Vipond, increasingly interested in what Cale was up to.

"They have your talents?" asked the Marshal.

"They have their own particular skills. Between us we can deal with anything the Redeemers send."

"You're very confident of your powers, Cale," said Vipond. "Given you've spent the last ten minutes telling us how invulnerable the Redeemers are."

Cale looked at him.

"I said their assassins were invulnerable to you." He smiled. "I didn't say they were invulnerable to me. I'm better than any soldier the Redeemers have ever produced. I'm not boasting. It's just a fact. If you don't believe me, sir," he said, looking at the Marshal, "then ask your daughter and IdrisPukke. And if they're not enough, then ask Conn Materazzi."

"Hold your tongue, you young pup," said Vipond, anger replacing his curiosity. "You never speak to Marshal Materazzi in such a manner."

"I've had worse things said to me," said the Marshal. "If you can keep my daughter safe, then I will make you rich and you can talk to me in private however you damn well please. But what you say had better be true." He stood up. "By tomorrow afternoon I want a written plan for her protection in front of me. Yes?"

Cale nodded.

"For now every soldier in the city is on duty. Now, if you wouldn't mind leaving us. You too, IdrisPukke."

The two of them stood up, nodded and left.

"That was quite a performance," said IdrisPukke as he shut the door. "Was any of it true?"

Cale laughed but did not reply.

Had he given IdrisPukke an answer, it would have been that very little of his dire warning was rooted in anything but his desire to force Arbell Swan-Neck to pay attention to him. He was furious at her ingratitude and more than ever in love with her. But she deserved to be punished for treating him in the way she did, and what could be better than to be able to decide when he wanted to see her and have endless opportunities to make her life a misery by his presence? Of course, the fact that his presence was so distasteful to her was a blow to the heart, but he was no less able to live with such painful contradictions than anyone else.

Anxiety for his daughter made the Marshal fear the worst, and he was an easy prey for Cale's ominous predictions. Vipond was no more convinced than IdrisPukke. On the other hand, he could see no harm in what Cale proposed. And the notion that the Redeemers might try to kill her was clearly not implausible. At any rate, it would allow the

Marshal to think that something was being done while Vipond worked day and night to get to the root of the Redeemers' intentions. He was sure that war of some kind was inevitable and was resigned to preparing for it, however surreptitiously. But for Vipond, to fight any war without knowing what precisely your enemy wanted was a disaster in the making. And so he was content for Cale to get up to whatever it was he was getting up to—though it was not difficult to see what it was. Cale clearly knew nothing of the motive behind the kidnapping, but having him as bodyguard to Arbell Materazzi would keep her safe. Vipond was, in his own less paternal way, as grateful to Cale for his rescue as her father: the political implications of having the most adored member of the royal family in the hands of such a murderous and brutal regime as that of the Redeemers did not bear thinking about. The news coming from the Eastern Front about the Redeemers' bitter stalemate with the Antagonists was terrible, so terrible indeed that it was hard to believe—except that the pitifully small number of those who had escaped over the borders into Materazzi territory all gave an alarmingly consistent story, one that gave the horrible ring of truth to the accounts Vipond's agents had been recording and sending him. If war was coming against the Redeemers, it promised to be like no other.

24

*T*ell me what you know about the Redeemer war against the Antagonists."

Vipond was looking grimly at Cale across his vast desk. IdrisPukke was sitting over by the window as if he were more interested in what was going on in the garden below.

"They are the Anti-Redeemers," said Cale. "They hate the Redeemer and all His believers and want to destroy Him and make His goodness perish from the earth."

"That's what you believe?" said Vipond, surprised at Cale's sudden movement from normal speech to a monotone rote.

"It was what we were taught to recite twice a day at Mass. I don't believe anything the Redeemers say."

"But what do you know about the Antagonists—about their beliefs?"

Cale looked puzzled and thought for a few moments.

"Nothing. We were never told that the Antagonists believed anything. All they cared about was destroying the One True Faith."

"You didn't ask?"

Cale laughed. "You didn't ask questions about the One True Faith."

"If you knew the Antagonists hated the Redeemers so much, why didn't you try and escape into the East?"

"We'd have had to travel fifteen hundred miles through Redeemer land and then try to cross seven hundred miles of trenches on the Eastern Front. And even if we had been stupid enough to try, we were always told that the Antagonists would martyr a Redeemer on sight. They were always telling us about Saint Redeemer George who was boiled alive in cows' urine or Saint Redeemer Paulus who was pulled inside out by having a hook forced down his throat and then tying it to a team of horses. They never stopped talking about dungeons, fire and sword, or singing about them. Like I said, it never really occurred to me that the Antagonists actually believed in anything except killing Redeemers and destroying the One True Faith."

"Did all your fellow acolytes think that way?"

"Some thought like me—a lot didn't. To them it was all they'd ever known, so they never questioned it. That's what the world was to them. They thought they'd be saved if they believed, and that if they didn't believe, then they'd burn in hell for all eternity."

Vipond started to become impatient.

"The war against the Antagonists has been going on since two hundred years before you were born. What you've consistently told me is that, along with being part of the One True Faith, all you were ever prepared for—and you in particular—was to fight, and yet you know nothing about victories or defeat or tactics or how this and that battle was won or lost? I find that hard to credit."

Vipond's skepticism was completely justified. Cale had gone over every battle and skirmish between the Redeemers and the Antagonists with Redeemer Bosco standing over him and hitting him with his belt every time he made an error in his analysis of what had gone well or badly. Cale had eaten and drunk the battles in the East four hours a day for ten years. But it was true, on the other hand, that he knew nothing about what the Antagonists believed. His decision to lie about what he knew about the war was based as much on instinct as calculation: if war between the Materazzi and the Redeemers was coming, then with it was coming terrible misery and death. He was not going to be a part of any such thing, and if he owned up to what he knew, then Vipond would pay any price to drag him into it.

"All they told us about were glorious victories and treacherous defeats. They were just stories—no details. You didn't ask questions. Me," he went on lyingly, "I was just trained to kill people. That's all—close combat and the three-second kill. That's all I know."

"What, in God's name," asked IdrisPukke from the window, "is the three-second kill?"

"What it says," replied Cale. "A real fight to the death is decided in three seconds, and that's what you aim for. Anything else—all that arty stuff you train the Mond in—that's just bollocks. The longer a fight goes on, the more chance comes into it. You trip, your weaker opponent gets in a lucky blow or he sees you have a weakness and he happens to have a strength. So—you kill in three seconds or take the consequences. The Redeemers at the Cortina pass died like dogs because I didn't give them a chance to die any other way."

Cale was being deliberately shocking. Since he was a small boy, he had been as proficient a liar as he was now a killer. And for the same reason: it was necessary to be so in order to live. He had deflected their interest in the one side of his past he did not want to reveal, by an admission of the truth elsewhere. And the more shocking, of course, even for such experienced hands as Vipond and IdrisPukke, the better. If the Materazzi believed that he was just a young and pitiless killer and no more, then encouraging them was in Cale's interest. It was true enough, which made him persuasive, but it was not the whole truth by a long chalk.

Vipond asked him a few more questions, but whether he believed Cale entirely or not, it seemed clear that the boy was giving nothing more away and so he went on to his plans for guarding the safety of Arbell Swan-Neck.

It was clear from his written arrangements for keeping her safe and his answers to Vipond's questions that Cale was as skilled in preventing death as he was in enabling it. Finally satisfied with Cale's answers, in this at least, Vipond took a thick file from his desk and opened it.

"Before you go, I want to ask you about something. I have had a number of reports from Antagonist refugees and double agents, and captured documents about a Redeemer policy they refer to as the Dispersal. Have you heard of this?"

Cale shrugged. "No." This time Vipond was convinced by the puzzled look on his face.

"These reports," continued Vipond, "are about something called
Acts of Faith. Is this a term familiar to you?"

"Executions for crimes against religion witnessed by the faithful."

"It's claimed that up to a thousand captured Antagonists at a time
are being taken to the centers of Redeemer towns and are being burned
alive. Those who recant their Antagonist heresy are shown mercy and
strangled before being burned." He paused, looking at Cale carefully.
"Do you think these Acts of Faith are possible?"

"Possible. Yes."

"There are other claims supported by captured documents that
these executions are only the beginning. These documents refer to the
Dispersal of all Antagonists. Some of my people say this is a plan
once victory is achieved to move the entire Antagonist population onto
the island of Malagasy. But some Antagonist refugees claim that the
Dispersal is a plan, once they are removed to the island, to kill the entire
Antagonist population in order to wipe out their heresy for good. I find
this difficult to believe—but you have more experience than any of us
as to the nature of the Redeemers. What do you think of such a thing?
Is it possible?"

Cale said nothing for some time, clearly torn between his loathing
of the Redeemers and the enormity of what he was being asked. "I don't
know," he said at last. "I never heard of anything like that."

"Look, Vipond," said IdrisPukke, "the Redeemers are clearly a brutal collection, but I can remember twenty years ago during the Mont
uprising there were all sorts of rumors about how, in each town they
captured, they'd collect all the babies, throw them up in the air in front
of their mothers and impale them on their swords. Everyone believed
it—but it was all bloody lies. None of it ever happened. In my experience, for every atrocity there are ten atrocity stories."

Vipond nodded. It had not been a productive meeting, and he felt
both frustrated and ill at ease about the stories from the East. But

something more trivial was also nagging him. He looked suspiciously at Cale.

"You've been smoking. I can smell it on your breath."

"What's it to you?"

"It's whatever I choose to make it, you insolent young pup." He looked over at IdrisPukke, who was still looking out of the window and smiling. Vipond turned back to Cale. "I would have thought you had more sense than to imitate IdrisPukke in anything. You should look to him as an example of how things should not be done. As for smoking—it is a childish affectation: a habit loathsome to the eye, hateful to the nose, harmful to the brain, dangerous to the lungs, causes the breath to stink and makes any man who takes it for long enough effeminate. Now get out, both of you."

25

*F*our hours later Cale, Vague Henri and Kleist were settling themselves into their comfortable rooms in Arbell Materazzi's quarter of the palazzo.

"What if they find out we don't know anything about being bodyguards?" said Kleist as they sat down to eat.

"Well, I'm not going to tell them," said Cale. "Are you? Anyway, how difficult can it be? Tomorrow we go through the place and make it secure. How many times have you practiced doing that? Then we stop anyone new from coming in and one of us stays with her wherever she goes. If she leaves here, which we discourage, she can't go outside the keep, and two of us plus a dozen guards go with her. That's all there is to it."

"Why didn't we just take a reward for saving her and get out?"

Kleist's question was a good one because it was exactly what Cale knew they should be doing, and if it wasn't for the way he felt about Arbell Swan-Neck, it was exactly what he would have done.

"We're just as safe here as we would be anywhere else" was all he said. "We'll get the reward we were promised and the money for taking care of business here. This job is money for old rope, and the truth is we've got an entire army guarding us from the Redeemers. If you've got somewhere better to go, be my guest."

And that was that. That night Arbell Swan-Neck slept with Vague Henri and Kleist outside her door. "We'd better be careful until we can make a plan of the place tomorrow," said Cale, planning all the while how he was going to make his entrance the next day as her all-powerful protector. He would show her his disdain for everything about her, and she would be cowed and afraid, and he would be delighted with himself as well as devastated.

It was nine o'clock the next morning when Arbell Swan-Neck emerged from her private apartment, having been told by the maids who'd brought her breakfast that there were two guards outside accompanied by two scruffy-looking herberts who they'd only seen before clearing out the stables.

Wearing her coldest face, she was put out to discover that, besides the two guards standing formally to attention on either side of the door, she was faced not by Cale but by two boys she'd never seen before either.

"Who are you and what are you doing here?"

"Good morning, lady," said Vague Henri affably.

She ignored him.

"Well?" she said.

"We're your bodyguards," said Kleist, controlling his urge to be bowled over by her staggering beauty and covering it with a look that signified he had seen any number of beautiful aristocrats in his life and he wasn't impressed, especially and particularly, with this one.

"Where's your . . ." She couldn't think of a word insulting enough. "Ringleader?" she said, at last, unsatisfied.

"Looking for me?" called out Cale as he turned the corner from a nearby passage accompanied by two men carrying several long rolls of paper.

"Who are these people?"

"These are your bodyguards. This one is Henri. The other one is Kleist. They have all my authority and you will please do as they ask."

"So, they're your familiars," she said, hoping to be as offensive as possible.

"Familiars? What's that?"

"Devils," she replied triumphantly. "Like the flies who go with Beelzebub whenever he leaves hell."

Unsurprisingly this put out Henri and Kleist but delighted Cale.

"Yes," he said, smirking at the two of them. "These are certainly my familiars."

"They're a little on the puny side for bodyguards, wouldn't you say?"

Cale looked at them regretfully. "I'm sorry about their condition—I wouldn't want to have to look at them all day myself. But as for puny? Perhaps you'd like to set a couple of Materazzi on them, then you'll see how puny they are."

"So they're killers like you?"

Henri was deeply offended by this, but Kleist clearly liked the insult.

"Yes," replied Cale easily, "killers exactly like me."

Unable to think of a reply, Arbell Swan-Neck walked back into her apartments and slammed the door behind her.

Ten minutes later there was a knock at the door, and Arbell Swan-Neck signaled her personal maid to answer it. When she did so, the maid was pleased to see that Cale's eyes widened with astonishment. It was Riba.

Riba's rise to such an exalted position had been as strange in its own way as Cale's. As soon as Anna-Maria had supervised Riba's ejection from Mademoiselle Jane's apartments, the old servant made her way quickly to the palazzo occupied by the Honorable Edith Materazzi, mother to Arbell Swan-Neck and the estranged wife of the Marshal. It should be said that since their arranged marriage twenty years before, they had never been anything *but* strangers, and the conception of Arbell Swan-Neck must have been one of the chilliest royal mergers in history. The Marshal's attempts to avoid his wife at all costs were often successful, but much less so his attempts to deny her all power or influence over the course of Memphis affairs. The Honorable Edith Materazzi was a woman who knew where the bodies were buried, and there was very little that took place in Memphis that was murky or underhand about which she was not, in some way, informed—or, when occasion demanded it, the origin of. Despite having no official power of any kind—something expressly seen to by the Marshal—the Honorable Edith Materazzi had influence backed up, often as not, by her knowledge of those skeletons and lapses prone to inhabit every family be they never so proud and great. So it was that within thirty minutes of Mademoiselle Jane's conniption attack over Riba, the Honorable Edith Materazzi knew of it from her spy, Anna-Maria, and had arranged for the angry if bewildered Riba to be a given a room in her own palazzo.

When Vipond heard what had happened and that Riba was now in the Honorable Edith Materazzi's clutches, he summoned Mademoiselle Jane immediately and gave his niece a most frightful bollocking. She emerged from his office, sobbing and wailing in terror, but there was nothing to be done but wait and see what the old witch was up to.

The Honorable Edith Materazzi did not waste time. She knew that something was up and that it involved her daughter. There had been wild rumors about her absence after visiting Lake Constanz three weeks before, rumors including a secret marriage and a secret birth. None of them so wild, however, as the truth itself. The Honorable Edith Materazzi had spent much time and money to get to the bottom of what happened but with little success—and little success was not something she was prepared to tolerate.

"Have they been treating you well?" asked the Honorable Edith Materazzi as she patted the sofa beside her and signaled with a warm smile that Riba should sit. Nervously, but also warily, Riba did as she was asked. She was already experienced enough in the social distinctions of Memphis to realize that something odd was going on—respect for the slightest difference in rank was insisted upon as if it had been ordained by God himself, and outsiders were treated with ridicule no matter what their status in the provinces. Riba had heard it said repeatedly of the Countess of Karoo, who had come to Memphis more than ten years ago, that she paid for the journey by selling her pigsty. This was a grotesque slander, as everyone well knew, because the people of the Karoo regarded swine as unclean. Why then, wondered Riba as she sat, was a woman of such eminence treating her with such kindness?

"First of all, my dear," said the Honorable Edith Materazzi, "I am sorry that you were subjected to so much unpleasantness by Jane. It's not an excuse, of course, but I was a friend of her late mother and there is no other word for it: she was spoiled, always given her way in everything. But, that's the way of things now, children get everything they ask for and you can see the result for yourself. But there it is," she said, sighing and patting Riba's hand. "And I'm sorry for it."

Riba was not certain what to say. "Yes, madam."

"Good," said the Honorable Edith Materazzi, as if pleased. "Now I want to ask you a great favor."

Riba could barely believe what she was hearing.

"I have a daughter too, you know," said the Honorable Edith Materazzi sadly. "And I worry about her." She turned to Riba. "You have seen her?"

"The Mademoiselle Arbell? Yes, madam."

"Ah." The Honorable Edith Materazzi sighed softly as if speaking of a distant memory. "She is so beautiful, isn't she?"

"Yes, madam."

Now the Honorable Edith Materazzi picked up Riba's hand.

"Now I want to take you into my confidence and also to help you because I feel that you are a girl with a kind heart and to be trusted with the concerns of a mother. Is that so, Riba?"

"Yes, madam, I hope so," replied the startled girl.

"Yes, I think so," said the Honorable Edith Materazzi, as if she had looked into Riba's soul and seen only kindness and a deep appreciation of maternal disquiet.

"We must speak of things that are difficult for me—but being a mother comes before pride, as I'm sure you'll discover for yourself one day." She sighed. "My husband hates me and does everything he can to stop me from seeing my daughter. What do you think of that?"

Riba's eyes widened in astonishment.

"I think it is very sad, madam."

"And so it is. He prevents my seeing her and poisons her against me. But I cannot defend myself, because if she were to take sides against the Marshal, it would destroy her future prospects. This I cannot do. So, Riba, I must endure. My own daughter, whom I love, I must endure her belief that I am cold and distant and care nothing for her. What do you think of that?"

"I . . ." Riba hesitated. "I think it must be terrible for you."

"It is. But you can help me."

Riba's eyes opened still farther, but she was unable to think of a reply.

"I have heard that you are an excellent companion and a beautifier of wonderful skill."

"Thank you, madam."

"Everyone talks about how your talents have transformed that ungrateful madam, Jane. She was no great beauty, if truth be told, but you have almost made her one."

"Thank you, madam."

There was a pause.

"Now, what I want you to do is this, and it will help you to a great place besides. I have arranged for you to become the beautifier to my daughter."

"Oh," said Riba.

The Honorable Edith Materazzi smiled.

"Oh, indeed. Is it not a great thing?"

"Yes, madam."

"I know you will do well. And all I ask of you are two things. It will be hard for you to do one of them because I can see you are a good girl and honest." She looked at Riba, who was already waiting for the catch in all this. "I'm asking you not to reveal to my daughter that you are coming to her through me." She clasped Riba's hand tightly as if she was desperately smothering an entirely natural protest. "I know this seems wrong and I understand, but it is only because she will refuse you otherwise. To do a great right it is sometimes necessary to do a little wrong. All I want from time to time is for you to come and tell me how she is, what she talks about, anything that worries her. Just the little things, the things that a daughter would tell a mother who loves her. Could you do that, Riba?"

Of course she could, and besides, what else was she to do? She entered into this contract with the Honorable Edith Materazzi, and if she did not entirely believe her, what difference did that make? There was no real choice for Riba, and they both knew it.

His Holiness the Redeemer Bosco sat on his balcony and looked down at the soldiers moving beneath him as far as the eye could see, filling the vastness of their Sanctuary. Men shouted, mules brayed, horses snorted and were sworn at by their handlers. The sights and sounds of so much preparation pleased him—the commencement, after all, of his life's ambition. He took another sip of his soup, a favorite: chickens' feet and a green vegetable known as asswipe in Memphis, where it was prized only for its usefulness and not its value as food.

There was a knock at the door.

"Come in."

It was Redeemer Stape Roy.

"You wished to see me, Your Devoutness."

"I want you to take twenty Redeemers and try to kill Arbell Materazzi."

"But, Your Holiness, that's impossible!" protested Stape Roy.

"I'm well aware of that. If it were possible, I wouldn't be sending you."

Irritated and afraid, Stape Roy nevertheless restrained an impulse to ask Bosco to say what he damn well meant.

"You are angry with me, Redeemer Stape Roy."

"I serve at your pleasure, Your Devoutness."

Bosco stood up and signaled to the Redeemer to come over to a table on which lay a map of the fortifications of Memphis.

"You were at the siege of Voorheis, weren't you?"

"Yes, Your Devoutness."

"How long did it take before it fell?"

"Nearly three years."

Bosco gestured to the map of the Memphis fortifications.

"How long, as an experienced man, do you think it would take to raze Memphis?"

"Longer."

"How much longer?"

"Very much longer."

Bosco turned and looked at him.

"We could waste ourselves, great as we are, trying to take Memphis by force, which is why it will not happen. Have you heard the rumors about why we attempted to kidnap Arbell Materazzi?"

Redeemer Stape Roy looked uneasy.

"It is sinful to listen to gossip and even more sinful to pass it on, Your Devoutness."

Bosco smiled.

"Of course, but in this instance I'm granting you a dispensation. The sin of spreading gossip is already forgiven you."

"It was mostly said that she was a secret convert to the Antagonists and was spreading their word and that she was a witch and she held orgies and corrupted men in their thousands, and made captured Redeemers defile themselves by making them eat prawns under torture."

Bosco nodded.

"A very formidable sinner, if true."

"I only repeated the rumors. I didn't say I believed them."

"Good for you, Redeemer," Bosco said and smiled. "The reason I had her kidnapped was because I wanted to force the Materazzi out from behind the walls of Memphis. To everyone in their empire she is a queen, idolized for her youth and beauty, a star in the firmament. Everywhere, even in the most flyblown collections of hovels in the empire, they talk about her exploits; no doubt many of them made up or exaggerated. She is adored, Redeemer, and not least by her father. When I heard that the abduction had failed, I was not, however, much concerned. Once it became known we had done something so heinous, my aim would have been fulfilled. The Materazzi would have come bounding out of Memphis full of piss and vinegar and ready to wipe us from the face of the earth." Bosco sat down and regarded the tough-looking man in front of him. "That didn't happen, of course, is what you're thinking, and so I must be wrong. You are merely too polite or afraid to say so. But you would be wrong yourself, Redeemer. Marshal Materazzi, on the contrary, agrees with me. It turns out that even if he is a loving father, he is not a sentimental one. He has kept the abduction a secret, precisely because he knows he would not be able to resist the people's desire for revenge. And this brings me to you, Redeemer. You have such a good relationship with that *thing* in . . ."

"Kitty Town, Your Holiness."

"I want you to persuade him to help you launch an attack using such a number of soldiers—thirty, perhaps fifty—as you decide fit. You will inform these soldiers that the rumors already widespread among the Redeemers as to her foul and sinful apostasy are true, and that they will be accorded martyrdom should they die . . . which they will. You will ensure that the captains you choose will each carry a certificate of martyrdom explaining why they are doing the Lord's work. With good fortune some of them will survive long enough for the Materazzi to torture the truth out of them. This time I do not want any possibility that our actions will be kept secret. Is that clear to you?"

"Yes, Your Devoutness," answered a pale Redeemer Stape Roy.

"You've gone quite white, Redeemer. I should tell you that your own death is not required. Quite the contrary. You should also use soldiers who have been disgraced in some way. What I ask is an evil thing, but necessary."

On his learning that the sacrifice of his own worthless life was not required, the color returned to Redeemer Stape Roy's cheeks. "Kitty the Hare," he said, "will want to know what he's being made a part of. He's not likely to think it's in his interests to get mixed up with something as dubious as this."

Bosco waved him away.

"Promise him anything you wish. Tell him that when we win we'll make him the Satrap of Memphis."

"He's no fool, Your Holiness."

Bosco sighed and thought for a moment.

"Take him the gold statue of the Lustful Venus of Strabo."

Redeemer Stape Roy looked astonished.

"I thought it had been broken into ten pieces and thrown into the volcano at Delphi."

"Just a rumor. Blasphemous and obscene though it is, the statue will stuff the ears of this creature of yours and make him deaf to any questions he asks himself, fool or no fool."

26

*O*ver the next few weeks Cale experienced all the self-defeating pleasures of making life unpleasant for someone you adored but hated. If truth were told, which it was not, he was getting sick of them.

He had never faced squarely what it was he expected by becoming Arbell Swan-Neck's bodyguard. His feelings about her—intense desire and intense resentment—would have been difficult for anyone to reconcile, let alone someone who was such a strange mixture of brutal experience and complete innocence. Perhaps charm might have done something to prevent her from cringing when he spoke to her—but where could charm come from in such a boy? Arbell's physical loathing of his presence was, understandably, of great offense to him, but all he knew how to do in response was to become even more hostile toward her.

This strange atmosphere between Cale and her mistress was the source of great trouble to Riba. She liked Arbell Swan-Neck, even though she had more ambition than to be a ladies' maid, no matter how illustrious the lady. Arbell was kind and thoughtful and, on discovering her maid's intelligence, was very easy and open with her. Nevertheless, Riba was devoted to Cale to the point of worship. He had risked his life to save her from something terrible not usually to be remembered except in nightmares. She could not understand Arbell's coldness toward him and was determined to put her mistress right.

The way she went about this might have seemed odd to an observer: she deliberately, pretending to have tripped, poured a hot cup of tea over Cale, having carefully ensured by adding cold water that it would not burn him too badly. But it was hot enough. With a cry of pain, Cale ripped off the cotton tunic he had been wearing.

"Oh, I'm sorry, I'm sorry," Riba fussed, grasping a mug of cold water she had deliberately placed nearby and pouring that over him too. "Are you all right? I'm sorry."

"What's the matter with you?" he said, but not angrily. "First you try to scald me, then you try to drown me."

"Oh," gasped Riba. "I'm so sorry." She continued to apologize, handing him a small towel and generally making a fuss of him.

"It's all right. I'll live," he said, drying himself off. He nodded toward Arbell. "I'll have to change. Please don't leave your chambers until I come back." And with that, he was gone. Now Riba turned to see if her ruse had worked—but as complicated ruses will, it had a complicated effect. What had drawn pity from Arbell, and of a kind she would never have imagined feeling for Cale, was that his back was covered in welts and scars. Barely an inch of his skin lacked the marks of his brutal past.

"You did that on purpose."

"Yes," said Riba.

"Why?"

"So that you can see all that he's suffered. And so, with all due respect, that you will not be so unkind."

"What do you mean?" said the astonished Arbell.

"May I speak frankly?"

"No, you may not!"

"I'll do it anyway, having come so far."

Arbell was not a pompous aristocrat by the standards of aristocrats, but no one, not just a servant, *no one* had ever spoken to her in such a manner except her father. Her astonishment made her speechless.

"You and I, mademoiselle," said Riba quickly, "may not have much in common now, but I was once almost completely indulged in everything and expected only a life of giving and being given pleasure. Well, all that came to an end in an hour, and I learned how horrible life is and how cruel and unbelievable."

She then told her wide-eyed mistress the details, sparing nothing of the fate of her friend and how Cale had risked everything, a death even more horrible, to save her.

"He always told me on the way through the Scablands that saving me was the stupidest and maddest thing he ever did."

"Do you believe him?" and the question really was spoken with a gasp. Riba laughed.

"I'm not sure. I think sometimes he means it and sometimes he doesn't. But I saw his back when we were washing in one of the water holes in the Scablands—God knows how he found it in that awful place. But Henri told me what they did to Cale. Ever since he was a little boy, this Redeemer Bosco singled him out for the slightest thing. He'd accuse him of anything, the more trivial the better he liked it—praying with his thumbs crossed, not putting a tail on the figure nine when he wrote it out. Then he'd drag him before the others and give him a ferocious beating—he'd punch him to the floor and give him a kicking. And then he turned him into a killer."

By now Riba had worked herself up into a fury of resentment—and not just against the Redeemers. "So it seems to me that it's surprising he'd bother to give you or me the steam off his piss—let alone risk his life to save us."

Arbell Swan-Neck's eyes, though it was hardly possible, widened even more at this startling figure of speech.

"So, mademoiselle, I think it's high time you stopped looking down your beautiful nose at him and showed him the gratitude and the pity he deserves."

By this time Riba had lost some of the purity of intention with which she had begun her rebuke and had begun enjoying her indignation and her mistress's discomfort. But she was no fool and realized it was time to stop. There was a long silence and a number of blinks from Arbell as she tried not to cry. She looked around the room with misty eyes, then back at Riba, then around the room again. She gave a long sigh.

"I didn't realize. Until now I never knew myself."

With that there was a knock at the door and Cale came in. Despite the completely altered mood in the room, he picked up nothing of the change that had taken place since he left. That change, however, was greater than either Riba guessed or even the young woman who was feeling it realized. Arbell Swan-Neck, the beautiful and most desired of all the desired, was touched by pity when she saw the terrible scars on Cale's back, but she was also touched by something less noble: a hunger as intense as it was unlooked for. Stripped to the waist, Cale was a complete contrast to the slender bodies of the Materazzi, strong and agile though they were. Cale's was wide at the shoulder and unnaturally narrow at the waist. There was nothing elegant about him. He was all muscle and power, like a bull or an ox. It was not comely; no one would have made a sculpture of this mass of sinew and scars. But just the sight of him like this had made something in Arbell Materazzi miss a beat—and it wasn't just her heart.

27

*W*ell, Redeemer," cooed Kitty the Hare, the nails of his hand stroking the wood on the table on which stood the golden statue of the Lustful Venus of Strabo. The faint sound of his voice felt to Redeemer Stape Roy as if something worse than you could possibly imagine was just about to softly crawl its way inside his ear. "This is all very strange," continued Kitty the Hare, staring at the statue. Or at least Redeemer Stape Roy thought he was staring—as always Kitty the Hare's face was covered by his gray hood, something for which the Redeemer was very grateful.

"The statue is yours if you help us. What do our reasons matter?"

The vague scraping of the nails along the wood continued, and then the Redeemer almost jumped as the scraping stopped and the covered hand reached forward to the statue and the gray cloth slid away from Kitty the Hare's hand—only it was not a hand. Think of something gray and furred, though lightly, a dog's paw but longer, very much longer, and with mottled nails, and yet this would not be close enough. The nails, softly, like a mother's stroking her baby's face, gently caressed the statue for a few moments and then withdrew.

"A beautiful piece," gurgled Kitty the Hare. "But I was told that it had been broken into ten pieces and thrown into the volcano at Delphi."

"Obviously not."

There was a long sigh that he could feel on his face, like the hot and wet bad breath of a large and unfriendly dog.

"You will not succeed," cooed Kitty the Hare.

"That's a matter of opinion."

"It is a matter of fact," said Kitty the Hare sharply.

"This is our business."

"You are trying to start a war and so it's my business also."

There was a long pause.

"As it happens," continued Kitty the Hare, "I have no objections to a war. They've always done well by me in the past. You'd be amazed, my dear Redeemer, at just how much money can be made from supplying poor quality food and drink and pots and pans for even the teensiest war. I will want a guarantee, written, that should you win, none of my possessions will be damaged and I will be given a protected passage to anywhere I choose."

"Agreed."

Neither believed the other. Kitty the Hare was certainly happy to make money from a war, but his plans went a good deal deeper than that.

"It will take some time," sighed Kitty the Hare, with another gush of hot, wet breath. "But I will have the plans ready within three weeks."

"That's too long."

"Perhaps, but that's how long it will take. Good-bye."

With that, Redeemer Stape Roy was led out of Kitty the Hare's private rooms and into the courtyard, then out into the town itself. A crowd had gathered to watch two men no older than sixteen being hanged from a gallows. Around each of their terrified necks was a sign that read: RAPIST.

"What's a rapist?" asked Redeemer Stape Roy of his guard, innocence and evil living quite contentedly together.

"Anyone who tries to get away without paying," came the reply.

It was a reflective Cale who made his way toward Arbell Swan-Neck's now carefully cordoned-off chambers. Despite his deep suspicion and resentment of her, even he had begun to detect a softening toward him. She no longer glared at him or flinched every time he came near her. At times he even asked himself if the look in her eyes (although he could not, of course, recognize it as pity and desire) might be of some significance. But he quickly dismissed such ideas because they made no sense. Still, something confusing was happening. Lost in these thoughts, he was barely aware of a group of boys about ten years old, at the edge of the practice field, looking shady and throwing stones at one another. As he came closer, he realized that one of them was much older, four- teen or so, as tall and slender and handsome as Materazzi boys were prone to be at that age. What was so odd was that the younger boys were throwing stones not at one another but at the older boy and that they were also shouting at him. "Pillock! Half-wit! Drooling gobshite! Flap-mouthed turd!" Then the stones. But despite his size, the bigger boy simply whirled around in fear and confusion as each stone struck him. Then one took him on the forehead and he collapsed in a heap. As the younger boys started to run forward to give him a kick, Cale ar- rived, clipped one of them round the ear, tripped up another and gave him a light kick as he lay on the ground. In a moment the gang were on the run, screaming insults as they went.

"If I see you little scum again," Cale called out after them, "you'll get the full benefit of my boot up your shiv!"

Cale bent down over the fallen boy.

"It's all right, they've gone," he said to the weeping lump beside him, his hand covering his face and curled up into a ball. There was no reaction. The boy just kept whimpering. "I won't hurt you. They've gone." Still there was no reaction. Somewhat irritated now, Cale touched him on the shoulder. The boy burst into life, lashing out with such speed that his hand cracked Cale on the forehead. With a cry of surprise and pain, Cale leapt back as the boy looked at him in utter astonishment and scrabbled backward toward a wall, looking around, terrified, for his tormentors.

"Shit!" said Cale. "Shit! Shit! Shit!" The boy had knuckles of iron, and it was as if he'd taken a glancing blow from a hammer. "What's the matter with you, you bloody maniac?" he shouted at the wild-eyed boy. "I was trying to help you and you nearly take my head off."

The boy kept on staring at him but finally spoke—only it was not speech but a series of grunts.

Because he was not used to the lame and the blind—they didn't live long at the Sanctuary—it took a while for Cale to realize that the boy was dumb. He held out his hand. Slowly the boy took it and Cale pulled him to his feet. "Come with me," he said. The boy stared at him. Deaf as well as dumb. Cale gestured to him to follow, and slowly, weeping with pain and humiliation, he did so.

Ten minutes later Cale was cleaning the boy up in the temporary guardhouse in Arbell Swan-Neck's quarters, when she came rushing in, attended by Riba. She gasped on seeing the bleeding boy sitting in front of Cale, and cried out, "What have you done to him?"

"What are you talking about, you mad bitch?" he shouted back. "He was being given a hammering by a gang of your little charmers and I ran them off."

She stared at him, full of remorse for having undone the good work of the last few days.

"I'm sorry. I'm sorry," she said, so pitifully and clearly stricken with regret that Cale felt an intense pleasure. For once he had an advantage in her presence. He gasped with dismissal, however. "I am so very sorry," she repeated, then went up to the boy, all anxiety and worry, and kissed him. Cale had never seen her show this kind of concern for anyone. He looked on, amazed. The boy almost instantly began to calm down. Arbell Swan-Neck looked at Cale as she stroked the boy's hair.

"This is my brother, Simon," she said. "Most people call him Simon Half-Wit—though never in front of me. He's deaf and dumb. What happened?"

"He was on the practice field. A group of younger boys were throwing stones at him."

"Monsters!" she said, turning back to her brother. "They think they can get away with anything because he can't tell on them."

"Doesn't he have a guardian?"

"Yes, but he wants to be on his own, and he's always escaping to the practice field because he wants to be like the others. But they hate and fear him because he's slow. They say he's possessed by a devil."

Happier now, Simon began pointing at Cale and grunting, acting out the stone throwing and his rescue.

"He wants to thank you."

"How do you know?" replied Cale, rather too bluntly.

"Oh, well. I don't know, but he has a good heart, even if he is simple." She took Simon's hand and formed it into an open palm and held it out for Cale to shake. Once Simon realized what he was to do, it took Cale some time to stop the energetic pumping of his hand. All the while the blood was soaking the temporary bandage Cale had placed on Simon's wound. He gestured for the boy to sit and, anxiously watched by Arbell, peeled it back. It was a nasty gash nearly two inches long.

"The little bastards could have had his eye out. It'll need stitching."

Arbell Swan-Neck looked at him in astonishment. "What do you mean?"

"It'll need stitching, just like you mend a shirt or a sock." Cale laughed at what he'd said. "Obviously, not like *you* do."

"I'll get one of our doctors."

Cale snorted with derision. "The last Materazzi doctor to treat me would have killed me given the chance. It's not just that he'll have a huge scar—a jagged wound like this won't heal. Ten to one it will get infected, and then, God knows. Three or four stitches will close it up and you'll barely know it's there."

Arbell Swan-Neck looked at him, completely at a loss.

"Let me get a doctor to look at him first. Please try to understand."

Cale shrugged. "Suit yourself."

An hour later two doctors had been called and after loudly arguing with each other had failed to staunch the bleeding and, if anything, had made it worse by their poking and prodding. By now Simon was so confused and in such pain that he'd had enough and refused to let the doctors near him, all the while bleeding profusely from his head wound.

After a few minutes of this, Cale had left, returning half an hour later to find Simon standing in the corner and refusing to let anyone touch him, not even his sister.

Cale pulled the distraught Arbell to one side. "Look," he said. "I've got some yarrow from the market to stop the bleeding." He nodded at the drama going on in the corner. "This isn't doing any good. Why don't you ask your father what he thinks?"

Arbell Swan-Neck sighed.

"My father refuses to have anything to do with him. You have to understand—it's a terrible shame to have a child like this. I can make the decision."

"Then decide."

Within a few moments the doctors had been dismissed and the room cleared but for Cale and Arbell. Simon stopped yelling but eyed the two of them suspiciously from his corner. Cale made sure Simon could see as he undid the curled paper of yarrow powder and poured a little into the palm of his hand. Cale pointed at the powder and then at Simon's wound and then at his own forehead. He paused for a second and then carefully approached Simon and knelt down, showing him his open hand with the yarrow powder as he did so. Simon looked at him, suspicion changing to wariness. Cale took a pinch of the yarrow and slowly brought it up to Simon's head. He then leaned his own head back and gestured to Simon to do the same.

As leery as you like, the boy did so, and Cale sprinkled the powder on the still-bleeding wound, repeating this six times. Then he stood back and let Simon relax.

Within ten minutes the bleeding had stopped. Now calmer, Simon let Cale approach him again so that Cale could clean the yarrow powder out of the wound. While this was clearly painful, Simon was patient as Cale delicately did his work, all the while watched by Arbell Swan-Neck. When he'd finished, he coaxed Simon back into the middle of the room and onto the table. Then, watched still leerily by Simon, he took out a small fold of silk material from an inside pocket and opened it on the table. It contained several needles, some of them variously curved, with short lengths of silk already through the eyes. The suspicion returned to Simon's eyes as Cale took one of the needles with its thread and held it up to show him. He tried various pantomime shows of what he wanted to do, but all that showed on Simon's face was a deepening alarm. Every time he tried to begin stitching the wound, the uncomprehending Simon shouted and screamed in terror.

"He won't let you. Try something else," said the distraught Arbell.

"Look," said an exasperated and increasingly irritated Cale, "the wound's too deep. I told you it's going to get infected—then he'll really have something to scream about—or it'll just shut him up permanently."

"It's not his fault—he doesn't understand."

It was impossible to disagree and Cale simply stood back and sighed. Then he stepped back again, took out a small knife from his inside pocket and, before either Simon or Arbell Swan-Neck could react, cut a deep gash into the palm of his left hand, just at the fleshy point leading to the thumb.

For the first time for many minutes there was silence. Both Simon and his sister stared in shock and awe at what they had just seen. Cale put the knife away, and as the blood poured from the wound, he took a bandage from the table and pressed it hard into the cut. For the next five minutes he said nothing and the other two just stared at him. Then carefully he pulled away the bandage and saw that the wound had stopped bleeding freely. He moved slowly to the table, picked up the needle and thread and showed it to Simon, as if he were about to perform a magic trick. Then he placed the needle carefully next to the wound and began pushing it through from one side of the cut to the next. He pulled it taut with an expression of concentration on his face as if he were darning a sock. Then he tied it off in a knot, reached for another threaded needle in his pack and repeated the action three more times until the wound was tightly closed. Then he held the stitched wound up to Simon's face so that he could examine it carefully.

When he had finished, Cale looked him in the eyes, nodded and waited. Simon, now pale with apprehension, took a deep breath and then nodded back. Cale took another needle from his pack, held it to the boy's wound (he thought of him as a boy, even though they were the same age) and pushed.

The five stitches were duly done but not, understandably, without a good deal of yowling and screaming from Simon. When he finished, Cale smiled and shook Simon's hand, and while Simon had gone as white as Melksham milk, he had endured the pain of hell. Cale turned to Arbell Swan-Neck, now almost as white and shaking as her brother.

"He's got the right stuff," he said to her. "There's more to your brother than people think."

Cale's shameless showing off was having the effect he had hoped for. As she stared at the extraordinary creature in front of her, Arbell Materazzi, dazzled, shocked, afraid and astonished, was now very nearly half in love.

The Guelphs—a people of notoriously ungenerous disposition—have a saying: no good deed goes unpunished. Cale was soon to discover the occasional truth of this miserable proverb. Unfortunately for him, he had not been brought up to police the behavior of nasty little boys with their childishly cruel ways—he had been brought up to kill. Moderation in violence was a deeply unfamiliar notion, and sadly the kick he had delivered to one of Simon's tormentors had been harder than he had intended and had broken two of the boy's ribs. By unfortunate coincidence the boy's father was Solomon Solomon, who already wanted his revenge on Cale for having thrashed five of his best students and who now was beside himself with rage at his son's injury. As is often the case with murderous brutes, Solomon Solomon was a kind and indulgent parent. Nevertheless his anger, which was incandescent, had to be contained. It was not possible to challenge Cale to a duel when the reason for doing so was that the injury to his boy had been caused while the little monster was attacking Marshal Materazzi's son. Mortified and ashamed as the Marshal might be at having a half-wit for a male heir, he would be furious at the attack on his family honor, and for all his importance and martial skill, Solomon Solomon would find himself shipped off to some dump in the Middle East to supervise burials in a leper colony. To an already festering anger against Cale was added a murderous hatred just waiting for an opportunity. The opportunity would not be long in coming.

It was not surprising that Simon Half-Wit, as he was universally known when not in the hearing of his father or sister, took to spending as much time with Cale, Kleist and Vague Henri as he could. Surprisingly, this addition to their company of someone who could neither speak nor hear was not as irksome to the three of them as might be imagined. Like them, he was an often maltreated outsider, but they also pitied him because he was so near to having everything that would have seemed to them like heaven—money, position, power—and yet so unreachably far from it. In addition, he wasn't allowed to become a nuisance. It was true that his behavior was erratic and emotionally wild, but that was only because no one had taken the time to instill in him what the boys considered polite behavior. This they did by shouting at him whenever he annoyed them—which, being deaf, made no difference to him—and giving him a swift kick up the arse, which did. Most useful of all, as they quickly came to realize, was to ignore him completely when he went into one of his unintelligible rants or otherwise misbehaved. He hated this more than anything, and he soon learned the basic social skills of the Redeemer acolyte. These, while they may not have been of much social benefit in the drawing rooms of Memphis, were still the only proper skills for dealing with people anyone had ever taught him.

Arbell told Cale that Simon had been given the very best teachers, and nothing had come of it—but the boys had one advantage over even the best teachers in Memphis. The Redeemers had developed a simple sign language for the various days and weeks during which they were forbidden from speaking. The acolytes, who were forbidden from speaking even more often, had developed the sign language further. Having tried unsuccessfully to get Simon to speak a few words, Cale started teaching him some of their signs, which he quickly picked up: water, stone, man, bird, sky and so on. Three days after they'd started, Simon had pulled Cale's sleeve as they were walking through a garden with a large pond and a couple of ducks and had signaled "waterbird." It was then that Cale began to think that perhaps Simon might not be entirely slow-witted after all. Over the following week Simon absorbed the Redeemers' sign language as if it was water poured onto a parched sponge. It turned out that, far from being a half-wit, he was as sharp as a tack.

"He needs someone," said Cale as the four of them sat in the guard-room eating their dinner, "to invent more words for him."

"What's the good of that," said Kleist, "if no one else knows what he's signing? What good's it going to do him?"

"But Simon isn't just anybody, is he? He's the Marshal's son. They can pay for him to have someone to read his signs and speak them aloud."

"Swan-Neck will pay," said Vague Henri.

But this wasn't in Cale's plan. "Not yet," he said, looking at Simon. "I think he deserves revenge on his father and everyone else but Swan-Neck. He needs to do something big, something to really show them. I'll find someone and pay them."

While this was certainly a true account of his reasons, it was not wholly true. He was well aware that Arbell Swan-Neck had changed her attitude toward him, but not by how much. He was not, after all (and why should he be?), very skilled in such matters as the feelings of a beautiful and much-desired young woman for someone who still frightened the life out of her. He felt he needed something dramatic to impress her, and the more astounding the better.

And so it was that the next day, along with IdrisPukke, his advisor in this matter, Cale found himself in the office of the comptroller of the Buroo of Scholars, an institution widely known as the Brainery.

Here were trained the many bureaucrats needed for the administration of the empire. The most important postings were, of course, reserved for the Materazzi—not just the governors of this or that province but also any job of power and influence. However, it was understood, if not publicly acknowledged, that insufficient numbers of them had enough wit or general good sense to run so large a dominion efficiently or, indeed, at all. Hence the foundation of the Brainery, a place that operated on strict principles of merit so that the administration of things did not quickly fall into incompetence and chaos. Wherever there was an idiot son or profligate nephew of the Materazzi appointed governor of this or that conquered state, there was always a significant number of graduates from the Brainery to make sure there was a limit to how much damage he could do. It was therefore solely out of aristocratic self-interest that a wisdom had been born that ensured that the clever and ambitious sons of merchants (though not the intelligent poor) had scope for their ambitions and a stake in the future of Memphis. This kept them out of involvement in the kind of conspiracy against the order of things that has ruined many an aristocracy before and since.

The comptroller eyed IdrisPukke, a man whose up-and-down reputation went well before him, with some suspicion. This suspicion was not allayed by the vicious-looking young ruffian beside him whose reputation was even worse—if somewhat more mysterious.

"How may I be of help?" he asked as unhelpfully as he could.

"Lord Vipond," said IdrisPukke, taking out a letter from his inside pocket and placing it on the table in front of the comptroller, "has asked that we are given your best assistance."

The comptroller eyed the letter suspiciously, as if it might perhaps not be entirely authentic.

"We need your best scholar as an equerry to an important member of the Marshal's family."

The comptroller cheered up—this might be useful.

"I see. But isn't that kind of position normally something kept within the Materazzi?"

"Normally," agreed IdrisPukke, as if this utterly and irrevocably cast-in-stone tradition was of no real significance. "On this occasion we need an equerry with intelligence and skill—language skills, that is. Someone flexible, capable of thinking for himself. Do you have such a person?"

"We have many such persons."

"Then we'll have your best."

And so it was that two hours later a stunned Jonathan Koolhaus, hardly believing his luck, made his way up through the keep and was taken, with the deference due to a Materazzi equerry, into the palazzo quarters of Arbell Swan-Neck and then to the guardroom.

If Jonathan Koolhaus had not heard the dictum of the great General Void—"No news is ever as good or as bad as it first seems"—he was about to learn the truth of it. He had been expecting to find himself in a grand apartment, the waiting room to a grand life, something he felt that was no less than his talents deserved. Instead he found himself in a guardroom stacked with numerous beds against the wall along with numerous vicious-looking weapons of one kind or another. Something was not quite right. Half an hour later in walked Cale with Simon Materazzi. Cale introduced himself and Simon grunted at the now bewildered scholar. Then he heard what was expected of him: he was to use his skills to develop a proper sign language for Simon and was then to go everywhere with him and be his translator. Imagine the galling disappointment of poor Jonathan. He had been expecting a glorious future at the very peak of Memphis society, only to discover that in reality he was to be the mouthpiece for the Materazzi equivalent of the village idiot.

Cale had a servant show him to his room, which wasn't much better than the one he'd had at the Brainery. Then he was taken to Simon's rooms, where Vague Henri was waiting to take him through the basic signs of the Redeemers' silent language. This at least gave the despondent Koolhaus something to take his mind off his disappointment. His reputation as someone with a natural talent for languages was deserved, and he quickly decided there wasn't much to this sign language business. In two hours he had all the signs written down. Slowly he became intrigued. Inventing, rather than learning, a new language might be interesting. No news is as good or as bad as it first seems. At any rate there was nothing to do but get on with it, even if he did lament the fact that all he had to work with was a half-wit.

During the next few days Koolhaus began to revise this opinion. Simon had been more or less left to his own devices throughout his life and was wholly undisciplined, never having been brought under control by any system of education or good behavior. Two things made it possible for Koolhaus to teach him: Simon's fear and worship of Cale and his own desperate desire to learn to communicate with others now that he had experienced this wonderful pleasure, even if only at the simple level afforded by the limited silent language of the Redeemers. This combination made Simon a more promising pupil than he at first appeared, and they made swift progress, albeit interrupted at least twice a day by tantrums brought about by Simon's frustration at not being able to understand what Koolhaus was doing. The first time Simon had one of these outbursts, an alarmed Koolhaus sent for Cale, who shut Simon up by threatening to give him a good thrashing unless he behaved himself. Simon, who, after the stitching incident, believed Cale capable of anything, did as he was told. Cale made a performance out of handing over his authority to Koolhaus to deliver horrible but unspecified punishments, and that was that. Koolhaus got on with his teaching, and Simon, who beyond anything wanted to please Cale, got on with learning. Koolhaus was not under any circumstances to tell anyone what he was doing, and his presence was explained away by letting it be known that he was Simon's temporary bodyguard.

Though unaware of Cale's bigger ambitions for her brother, Arbell Swan-Neck was well aware of what else he was doing for him. There were no games in the Sanctuary—play was an occasion of sin. The nearest thing to it was a training exercise in which two sides, separated only by a line neither side was allowed to cross, attempted to hit mem-

bers of the other side with a leather bag on a string. If this seems harm-
less enough, you should know that the leather bag was filled with large
stones. Serious injury was common; death was rare but not unknown.
Realizing the three of them were getting flabby from the easy life of
Memphis, Cale revived the game but with sand instead of rocks.
Though it was still intended only as a training exercise, they were
amazed to discover that without the threat of constant serious injury
they were laughing and enjoying themselves. Lacking a player, they let
Simon join in. He was awkward and without the grace of other Materazzi, but full of energy and so much enthusiasm that he was constantly hurting himself. He never seemed to mind this. They made so
much noise, laughing and jeering at one another's failure and incompetence, that Arbell could not fail to hear them. Often she would stand
watching at the window high over the garden as her brother laughed
and played and belonged for the first time in his life.

This too sank deeper into her heart—along, of course, with the
strange power and strength of Cale, his muscle and his sweat as he ran
and threw and chased and laughed.

One day, after he had been outside her room for an hour or so, she
had Riba call him in. While she carefully prepared herself in her bedroom
to appear casually beautiful, Cale waited in the main chamber. As this was
his first opportunity to look around on his own, he began a systematic
check of everything, from what books were on the tables to the tapestries
and the large painting of a couple that dominated the room. He was in-
specting this closely when Arbell entered behind him and said, "That's my
great-grandfather and his second wife. They caused a great scandal by
actually being in love with each other." He was about to ask why she had
a portrait of these two on the wall when she changed the subject.

"I wanted," she said, softly and shyly, "to thank you for all you've
done for Simon." Cale did not reply, because he didn't know how and
because this was the first time the object of his confused adoration had
spoken to him in such a kindly way since he had first seen her and been
struck down by love. "I've seen you playing your game, is what I mean.

He's so happy to have people to . . ." She was going to say "play with" but realized that this alternately brutal and kind young man might take this the wrong way. "Be friendly to him. I'm very grateful."

Cale liked the sound of this very much.

"That's all right," he said. "He picks things up quickly, once you can explain what's going on. We'll toughen him up." As soon as he said it, he realized that it was not quite the thing to say. "I mean, we'll teach him how to look after himself."

"You won't teach him anything too dangerous?" she said.

"I won't teach him to kill anyone, if that's what you mean."

"I'm sorry," she said, crestfallen at having offended him. "I didn't mean to be rude."

But Cale was not as touchy around her as he used to be. He realized there had been a considerable warming toward him.

"No, you weren't rude. I'm sorry for always being so quick to take offense. IdrisPukke told me to remember I'm just a hooligan and to be more careful around people who were properly brought up."

"He didn't," she said, laughing.

"He certainly did. He doesn't have much respect for my sensitive side."

"Do you have one?"

"I don't know. Do you think it would be a good thing?"

"I think it would be a wonderful thing."

"Then I'll try—though I don't know how. Perhaps you could tell me when I'm behaving like a hooligan and tell me off."

"I'd be too frightened," she said, her eyelids fluttering slowly up and down.

He laughed. "I know everyone thinks I'm no more good-natured than a polecat, but I draw the line at killing someone just for telling me off about being a thug."

"You're much more than that." Her eyes still fluttered.

"But still a thug, all the same."

"Now you're being oversensitive again."

"You see. You've told me off and I haven't killed anyone—and I'll keep trying to do better."

She smiled and he laughed, and yet another step was taken deeper into the chambers of her baffled heart.

Kleist was teaching Simon and Koolhaus how to fletch an arrow with goose feathers. This was Simon's third failed effort, and he was so furious he broke the arrow and threw the two pieces across the room. Kleist looked at him calmly and signaled to Koolhaus to translate.

"Do that again, Simon, and you'll get my boot up your shiv."

"Shiv?" asked Koolhaus, wanting to show his distaste for such coarseness.

"You're so clever, work it out for yourself."

"Guess what I've found in the cellar under here?" said Vague Henri, coming into the room as if someone had given him jam on his bread as well as butter.

"How, in God's name," said Kleist, not looking up from the table, "am I supposed to guess what you've found in the cellar?"

Vague Henri refused to allow his excitement to be diminished. "Come and look." His joy was so obvious that now Kleist was curious. Henri led them down to the floor under the palazzo and along an increasingly dark corridor to a small door that he opened with difficulty. Once in, a high-up casement window gave them all the light they needed.

"I was talking to one of the old soldiers, who was telling me all his war stories—interesting stuff, as it happens—and he mentioned that about five years ago he'd been on a scouting duty in the Scablands looking for Gurriers and they came across a Redeemer juggernaut that'd got separated from the main wagon train. There were only a couple of Redeemers standing about, so they told them to get lost and confiscated the juggernaut." He went over to a tarpaulin and swept it to one side. Underneath was a huge collection of relics: holy gibbets of various sizes in wood and metal, statues of the Hanged Redeemer's Holy Sister, the blackened toes and fingers of various martyrs preserved in small, elaborately decorated containers—one even had a nose in it, at least that was what Vague Henri thought it was; after seven hundred years it was hard to tell. There was Saint Stephen of Hungary's right forearm and also a perfectly preserved heart.

Koolhaus looked at Vague Henri. "What is all this? I don't understand."

Vague Henri held up a small bottle three-quarters filled and read the label: "This is 'Oil of sanctity that dripped from the coffin of Saint Walburga.'"

Kleist had lost patience and the pile of relics had stirred up bad memories. "Tell me you didn't bring us down here for this."

"No." He walked over to a smaller tarp and this time whisked it away like the climax to the magician's reveal they had seen in the palazzo upstairs the week before.

Kleist laughed. "Well, now at least there's some point to you."

Lying on the ground was an assortment of light and heavy crossbows. Vague Henri picked up one of them with a rack-and-pinion winding system. "Look, an arbalest. I bet you'd get something special from this. And this . . ." He picked up a small crossbow with what looked like a box on top. "I think this is a repeater. I've heard about them but never seen one."

"It looks like a kid's toy."

"We'll see once I can get some bolts made. None of them have got any bolts. The Materazzi probably left them behind—didn't know what they were."

Simon made a few finger passes at Koolhaus.

"He's worried about what you said about Henri."

Kleist looked puzzled. "I didn't say anything."

"About there not being a point to him. He wants you to apologize or you'll feel his boot up your shiv."

It was easy for Simon not to understand the way the boys spoke to one another. Before he met them, he was used only to outright insult or outright toadying. Kleist looked at Simon. Koolhaus's fingers raced as he spoke.

"Vague Henri is what the Materazzi call . . ." He lost the word and began searching. "A *cecchino* . . . a hit man. The crossbow is all he ever uses."

It was two hours later before Cale turned up in the guardroom, and the news of the crossbows immediately put him in a bad mood.

"Did you tell Simon and Koolhaus to keep it callow?"

"Why would we need to do that?" said Kleist.

"Because," replied Cale, now really irritable, "I can't see any good reasons for anyone knowing Henri is a sniper."

"And the bad reason?"

"What they don't know can't hurt us. The less they know about us the better."

"That's rich coming from someone who made such an exhibition of himself in the summer garden," said Kleist.

"Look, Cale," said Henri, "how could I have got the bows out or done anything with them without someone finding out? I'll need to get bolts made and I need to practice."

By then it was too late in any case. Two days later the three of them were summoned to see Captain Albin. He seemed amused as much as anything.

"You don't seem like the murderous type, Henri."

"I'm not a murderer. I'm just a sniper."

"Jonathan Koolhaus said you were a *cecchino*."

"You don't want to listen to Koolhaus."

"So you're a sniper who doesn't kill people. What's the point of you, then?"

Vague Henri, aggrieved, refused to rise to the bait, but the upshot of it all was that Albin demanded a demonstration.

"I've heard about this contraption. I'd like to see one at work."

"It's not one contraption; there are six of them."

"Very well, six. Will the Field of Dreams be all right?"

"How long is it?"

"Three hundred yards or so."

"No."

"Then what do you need?"

"About six hundred."

Albin laughed. "You're telling me you can hit something at six hundred yards with these things?"

"Only with one of them."

Albin looked doubtful. "I suppose we could close off the western edge of the Royal Park. Five days, then?"

"I'll need eight. I've got to get some bolts made and all the bows need to be restrung."

"Very well." He looked at Kleist. "Koolhaus tells me you're an archer."

"He's got a big gob, that Koolhaus."

"Not withstanding the size of his gob, is it true?"

"Better than you've ever seen."

"Then we'll have a demo from you as well. How about you, Cale, do you have any more party tricks you've been keeping under your top hat?"

Eight days later a small gathering of Materazzi generals, the Marshal, who had invited himself, and Vipond met behind large canvas screens usually used for herding deer past society women who wanted to do a little hunting. Albin, as relentlessly cautious as Cale, had decided it might be better to keep the demonstration quiet. He could not have said why, but the three boys were always hiding something and therefore unpredictable. And there was something about the boy Cale that always promised havoc. Best to be on the safe side of sorry.

Within five minutes of the start of the demonstration, Albin realized that he had made a dreadful mistake. It is not easy to accept, not deep in the deepest recesses of the soul, that by reason of birth other people less able, hardworking, intelligent and willing to learn, should always have the first opportunity to stick their snouts in what the poet Demidov calls "the great pig trough of life." Having had so much to do with Vipond—a hardworking man of intelligence and with outstanding ability—the sense of childish justice still hidden in Albin's soul had willingly overlooked the fact that aristocratic Vipond could easily have been chancellor had he been a complete dunce. The generals waiting for the demonstration to begin were no more or less able as generals than any other group selected by virtue of their relatives. Bakers, brewers, stonemasons in Memphis, all observed the rights of birth as rigidly as any Materazzi duchess. *You are an idiot,* thought Albin to himself, *and deserve this humiliation.* It was not merely that these three were children—if pretty odd, as children go—but that they weren't even common. It was possible to respect a stonemason, an armorer; even to be rude to a servant was regarded as vulgar by most Materazzi. But these boys were without identity, part of nothing, migrants, and, most important, one of them had gone too far. It was not that the generals would have condoned the matter of bullying by the Mond and Solomon Solomon—widely acknowledged to be a boor—it was that putting it right was a matter for the Materazzi themselves. Such things as injustice to members of the underclass were to be settled quietly, but if they were not settled, then they were not settled. It was not for the offended against in such circumstances to take matters into their own hands and in such an effective and humiliating manner. That Cale should have resolved his own grievances was a painful threat. *And perhaps they're right,* thought Albin.

First up was Kleist. Twelve wooden soldiers, usually used for sword practice, had been set up three hundred yards away. The Materazzi were familiar with bows but used them primarily for hunting: they were elegantly and beautifully made composites imported at great expense. Kleist's bow was the nearest thing to a broomstick they had ever seen. It seemed impossible to bend such an ugly-looking item. He placed the bottom of the bow on the ground, bracing it with the instep of his left foot. Holding the bowstring just under the loop, he started to bend the bow. Thicker than a fat man's thumb, it slowly curved to his great strength and then he delicately lifted the loop into the notch. Turning to the semicircle of arrows stuck into the ground behind him, he pulled one, notched it onto the bowstring, drew it back to his cheek, aimed and fired. All this was done in one flowing movement, one arrow loosed every five seconds. There were eleven identical *thwacks* as the arrows hit—and one silent miss. One of Albin's men ran from behind a protective wall of wooden beams and confirmed the score by waving two flags: eleven of twelve. The Marshal applauded enthusiastically; his generals followed his guidance, not enthusiastically.

"Oh, well done!" said the Doge. Miffed at the lack of response from the generals, Kleist gave a resentful nod in acknowledgment and stepped away for Vague Henri to show what he could do.

"There are three basic types of crossbow," he began brightly, convinced that his audience would share his enthusiasm. He held up the lightest of two resting in their cradles in front of him. "This is the one-foot crossbow—we call it that because you put one foot in here." He put his right foot in the stirrup at the top of the crossbow, hooked the string with a claw attached to a belt around his waist and pushed down with his foot and straightened his back at the same time, letting the trigger mechanism grab the string and hold it in place.

"Now," said Vague Henri, cheerfulness diminishing as he became aware of the disapproving looks of the generals, "I put the bolt in place, then . . ." He turned, took aim and fired. He grunted with relief at the *thwack!*—loud even from three hundred yards away—as the bolt hit its mark. "Oh, good shot!" said the Doge. The generals stared at Vague Henri not just unimpressed but sullen and disdainful. Having expected the power and accuracy of his shot to impress, he instantly lost confidence and started to become hesitant. He turned to the next crossbow, much bigger but with much the same design. "This is the two-foot crossbow—called that because you put . . . um . . . two feet in the stirrup . . . and . . . uh . . . not just one. This means," he added lamely, "it . . . um . . . gives you even more power." He repeated his previous moves and loosed the bolt into the second target, but this time it hit with such force it split the head of the wooden soldier in two.

The disapproving silence grew as cold as the ice on the top of the great glacier of Salt Mountain. Had he been older or more experienced in the art of presentation, Vague Henri might have stopped and cut his losses. But as he was neither, Henri blundered on to his last great mistake. To one side Henri had draped a large object with one of the tarpaulins from the palazzo cellar. There was no excited magician's brio this time. With Cale's help he slid the tarpaulin aside to reveal a steel crossbow twice the size of the last one but bolted onto a thick post set firmly into the ground. A large winding mechanism was attached to the back end of the crossbow. Vague Henri began cranking the mechanism and shouting over his shoulder. "This is too slow for the battlefield, of course, but using a windlass and steel for the bow, you can hit a target at up to a third of a mile."

This claim at least produced a reaction other than icy disapproval. There were outright snorts of disbelief. Because he had not shared the possibilities of his new discovery with either Cale or Kleist, they were equally dubious, though silent. This skepticism now cheered up Vague Henri. He was still young enough, foolish enough, innocent enough, to believe that when you proved people wrong, they would not hate you for it. He signaled to one of Albin's men to raise a flag. There was a brief pause; then another flag at the far end of the park was raised in turn and a second tarpaulin was pulled from a white-painted target about three feet in diameter. Henri put his shoulder to the crossbow butt, paused for effect and fired. There was a tremendous *twang!* as the half ton of power locked into the steel and hemp let loose. The red-painted bolt shot away as if impelled by its very own devil and vanished from sight toward the white target. Ingeniously, Henri had covered the bolt in red powder paint, and as it hit the target the powder sprayed dramatically over the white surface. There were gasps and there were more grunts. Even, or especially, from Kleist and Cale. It was certainly an outstanding piece of marksmanship—although it was not as outstanding as it seemed. It had taken Vague Henri many hours to fix the windlass crossbow exactly and firmly in place and tune the bow to the exact distance.

There was a long silence, which the Marshal tried to conceal by walking over to Vague Henri and asking a great many questions. "Really?" "Goodness me!" "Most extraordinary!" He called his generals over and they proceeded to examine the crossbow with all the enthusiasm of a duchess asked to inspect a dead dog.

"Well," said one of them at last, "if we ever need someone murdered from a safe distance, we'll know where to come."

"Don't be like that, Hastings," scolded the Marshal like a disapproving but still jovial uncle. He turned to Henri. "Don't pay him any mind, young man. I think this is fascinating. Well done."

That said, it was over and the Marshal and his generals were gone.

"You're lucky," said Cale to Henri, "that he didn't chuck you under the chin and give you a Spanish gobstopper."

"That crossbow," said Kleist, nodding at the steel giant bolted to the post. "How many hours did it take to get it to do that?"

"Not long," lied Henri. There was a brief silence.

"I learned a new word in Memphis market the other day," said Kleist: "Balls."

"There's no reason," said Vipond to the three boys in his office the following day, "why you should understand the way things work amongst the Materazzi, but it's time you started to learn. The military are a law unto themselves subject only to the Marshal. While I advise him on matters of policy, I have much less influence when it comes to the business of war. Nevertheless, I must take an interest in war in general and a further interest in your considerable talents for violence in particular.

I am ashamed to say," he continued unashamedly, "I may have a need for your talents from time to time, and this is why there are certain things you need to understand. Captain Albin is an excellent policeman, but he is not one of the Materazzi, and in allowing the generals to witness your demonstration he failed to show an understanding of something he now grasps and which it would be wise for the three of you to grasp as well. The Materazzi have a deep repugnance for killing without risk. They regard it as something utterly beneath them, the province of common murderers and assassins. Materazzi armor is the finest in the world, and it is for precisely this reason that it's so appallingly expensive. Many of the Materazzi take twenty years to pay off the debt incurred for just one suit of armor. It is beneath them to fight those without their armor and training. They pay these huge sums in order to fight men of equal rank whom they can kill or be killed by and maintain their status even in death. What status is to be won slaughtering a pig-boy or a butcher?"

"Or to be slaughtered *by* them," said Cale.

"Precisely so," said Vipond. "See things from their point of view."

"We're not pig-boys or butchers but trained soldiers," said Kleist.

"I don't mean to be offensive, but you're of no *social* significance. You use weapons and methods that defy everything they believe in. To them you are a kind of heresy. You understand heresy, don't you?"

"And what difference will that make?" said Cale. "A bolt or a dog arrow doesn't know or care who your grandfather was on your mother's side. Killing is just killing—just like a rat with a gold tooth is still just a rat."

"Fair enough," said Vipond, "but you don't have to like it to understand this has been the Materazzi way for three hundred years, and they're not going to change just because you think they should." He looked at Kleist. "Can one of your arrows pierce Materazzi armor?"

Kleist shrugged. "Don't know—never shot any Materazzi all dressed up. But it would have to be damned good to stop a four-ounce arrow at a hundred yards."

"Then we must see what we can do so that you can test it out. This steel bow of yours, Henri. Do the Redeemers have many?"

"I only heard of them before; I never saw one. My master had only seen two, so I don't think so."

"I saw how long it took to load. The Materazzi were right to discount it for the battlefield."

"I said that when I showed it you," protested Vague Henri. "A bolt from one of the other crossbows could go through armor. I've seen it. I've done it."

"But Materazzi armor?"

"Let me try it out."

"In due course. I'm going to send one of my secretaries to you tomorrow and one of my military advisors. I want everything you know about Redeemer tactics put on paper, understand?"

The three of them looked shifty at this but did not dissent.

"Excellent. Now go away."

28

*I*n the history of duels there must often have been pressing reasons that led to the slaughtering of one man by another. What they were, however, is rarely recorded. Those reasons that are known to us consist of minor insults, real or imagined, differences of opinion over the beauty of a woman's eyes, remarks held to have slighted the honesty of another's dealing at cards and so on. The notorious duel between Solomon Solomon and Thomas Cale began over the question of precedence in choosing cuts of beef.

Cale had become involved with this matter because the cook hired to feed the thirty men needed to guard Arbell Swan-Neck night and day had complained about the terrible quality of the meat being delivered. Raised on dead men's feet, the three boys had not really noticed that the meals they'd been eating were not very good. The soldiers had complained to the cook, and the cook then complained to Cale.

The next day Cale went to see the supplier, and for want of anything better to do, Vague Henri went with him. If Kleist hadn't been on duty, even he would have gone. The thing is that guarding a woman twenty-four hours a day, however beautiful the woman, was extremely boring, especially if you knew that the danger she was in was almost entirely invented. It was different for Cale because he was in love and spent the hours with Arbell Swan-Neck either just looking at her or putting into action his plan to make her feel the same.

His plan was working—even as Cale and Vague Henri wandered into the market to sort out the meat supplier. Back in her quarters Arbell Swan-Neck was trying to prize stories about Cale from a reluctant Kleist. This reluctance flowed from the fact that he was perfectly aware that she wanted desperately to hear anecdotes of Cale's past that showed him in a pitiable or generous light, and he, almost as desperately, didn't want to give Cale the satisfaction of providing them for her. She was, however, an extremely capable and charming interrogator and very determined. Over several weeks she had winkled out of Kleist, and the much more cooperative Vague Henri, a great deal about Cale and his history. In fact Kleist's reticence served only to convince her more of the truly terrible past of the young man with whom she was falling in love—his tense and reluctant confirmations of Vague Henri's stories acting only to make them more plausible.

"Was it true about the brutality of that man Bosco?"

"Yes."

"Why did he pick on Cale?"

"I suppose he had his number."

"Please tell me the truth. Why was he so cruel to him?"

"He's a lunatic, specially where Cale was concerned. I don't mean he was like your usual lunatic, raving and ranting—in all the years at the Sanctuary I never heard him raise his voice once. But he's as mad as a sack of cats for all that."

"Is it true that he made him fight to the death with four men?"

"Yes—but the reason he won is just because of how that hole in his head means he can tell what you're going to do."

"You don't like Cale, do you?"

"What's there to like?"

"Riba told me he saved your life."

"Seeing he was the one who put it in danger in the first place, I'd say we were even."

"What can I do you for, young man?" asked the cheery butcher, shouting above the racket of the marketplace.

Cale shouted back equally cheerfully: "You can stop sending the meat from dead dogs and cats up to the guardroom in the West Palazzo."

The butcher, now very much less cheery, picked up a vicious-looking club from under the counter and started to walk round it toward Cale. "Who do you think you are, you little shite, talking to me like that?"

He moved toward Cale surprisingly quickly, given his size, swinging the club as he came. Cale ducked as the club lashed past the top of his head, unbalancing the butcher, who was helped on his way into the mud as Cale clipped his heels. Then he stood on the butcher's wrist and twisted the club out of his hands.

"Now," said Cale, bouncing the end of the club gently up and down on the back of his attacker's head, "you and me are going to go into wherever it is you store the meat and you're going to choose the very best, and every week you're going to send me stuff just as good. Do we understand each other?"

"Yes!"

"Good." Cale stopped bouncing the club on the butcher's head and allowed him to get to his feet.

"This way," he said, his voice full of repressed bile.

The three of them made their way into a storeroom behind the stall full of haunches and sides of meat, beef and pork and lamb as well as a corner devoted to the smaller carcasses of cats, dogs and other creatures Cale did not recognize.

"Choose the best," said Vague Henri.

The butcher had started lifting the best of the rump and sirloin from their hooks when a familiar voice called out, "Stop!"

It was Solomon Solomon with four of his most experienced soldiers. If it seems odd that a man of Solomon Solomon's rank should be out choosing meat for his men, it should be pointed out that soldiers will endure death, injury, privation and disease much more readily than bad food. Solomon Solomon made a great deal of the business of providing his men with the best eats when such was possible, and he made sure his soldiers knew it.

"What do you think you're doing?" he asked the butcher.

"I'm setting aside cuts for the new guard at the palazzo," he replied, nodding at Cale and Vague Henri, both of whom Solomon Solomon pretended not to see. He walked over and curiously inspected the sides of meat and then looked around the storeroom.

"I want everything here delivered to the Tolland Barracks by this afternoon. Though not that shit in the corner." Then he looked down at the meat intended for Cale. "This is to be included."

"We were here first," said Cale. "This is already spoken for."

Solomon Solomon looked at Cale as if he had never seen him before.

"I have precedence in this matter. Do you dispute that?"

Though warm outside, it was cold in the storeroom, built deep into the rock, with the corners stacked high with thick slabs of ice—but the temperature fell still further with Solomon Solomon's question. There could be no doubt that something dreadful hung on Cale's reply. Seeing this, Vague Henri tried to be sweetly reasonable with Solomon Solomon.

"We don't need much, sir—only enough for thirty men."

Solomon Solomon did not look at Vague Henri, and indeed seemed not to have heard him.

"I have precedence in this matter," he repeated to Cale. "Do you dispute that?"

"If you like," replied Cale.

Very slowly, letting Cale see exactly what he was doing, Solomon Solomon raised his right hand in what was clearly a ritual, and with the palm open struck Cale almost tenderly on the cheek. Then he lowered his hand and waited. Cale also then raised his hand, again slowly, and brought it carefully to Solomon Solomon's face, but at the last moment he flicked his wrist with all his strength so that there was a *clap!* that rang in the intense silence like a holy book slammed shut in a church.

The four guards, furious at Cale's blow, started forward.

"Stop!" said Solomon Solomon. "Captain Gray will call on you this evening."

"Oh, yes?" said Cale. "Why's that?"

"You'll see."

With that he turned and left.

"What about our meat?" called out Cale jovially as he left.

He looked at the wide-eyed butcher, astonished and afraid at the murderous drama that had just played out in his storeroom. "I don't suppose you can be relied on to deliver my order."

"It's more than my life's worth, sir."

"Then we'd best take some of it with us." He lifted a huge side of beef onto his shoulder and walked out.

29

As when lightning strikes a tree in a parched forest and then quickly engulfs the rest, the hullabaloo that resulted from the meeting in the butcher's storeroom raged in every house in Memphis. Marshal Materazzi swore fit to be tied when he heard. Vipond cursed. They both sent for Cale and demanded he refuse to fight.

"But I'm told that if I refuse, anyone has the right to kill me on sight. Without warning."

It was difficult to argue with him on this, because it was true. Cale played the innocent party in this, and it was impossible not to agree. So then it was Solomon Solomon who was hauled before the Marshal and his chancellor, but despite a fearful torrent of abuse by the former, and clear threats by the latter that should he go through with it he could expect a career spent burying lepers in the Middle East, Solomon Solomon was unmoved. The Marshal was furious.

"You will put a stop to this or you will hang," shouted the Marshal.

"I will neither stop nor hang," shouted back Solomon Solomon. And he was right; not even the Marshal could prevent a duel where blows had been struck, nor could he punish the participants. Vipond tried appealing to Solomon Solomon's snobbery.

"What could killing a fourteen-year-old boy bring you except dishonor? He's a nobody. He doesn't have even a mother or father, let alone a family name worthy of a trial by combat. What on earth are you thinking by lowering yourself in this matter?"

This was a telling point, but Solomon Solomon dealt with it simply by refusing to answer.

So that was that. The Marshal barked at him to get out, and full of solemn rage, Solomon Solomon did so.

Cale's meeting with Arbell Swan-Neck was as distraught as might be imagined. She begged him not to fight, but as the alternative was so much worse, she soon turned to a furious diatribe against Solomon Solomon and then rushed off to see her father to demand he put a stop to this.

During the tearful reunion with Arbell, Cale had made sure to bring Vague Henri to back up his version of events. After the distraught young woman had left, Cale saw Vague Henri looking at him and clearly not thinking anything generous.

"What's your problem?"

"You are."

"Why?"

"Why are you trying to pretend you didn't know exactly what was going to happen when he asked if you disputed his right to choose ahead of you?"

"I was there first. You know that."

"You're going to kill or be killed for what—a few cuts of meat?"

"No. I'm going to kill or be killed over the fact that he thrashed me a dozen times for nothing. No one is ever going to do that to me again."

"Solomon Solomon isn't Conn Materazzi, and he's not a handful of half-asleep Redeemers who didn't see you coming. He can kill you."

"Can he?"

"Yes."

"I hope he agrees with you that I'm stupid—because then he's going to be even more surprised when I break him like a plate."

30

The Opera Rosso is a magnificent semicircle of a theater with a view of the Bay of Memphis to astonish even the most widely traveled. It rises so steeply from the arena itself that overexcited members of the audience have been known to fall to their deaths from the upper tiers. But the purpose of Il Rapido, as this vertiginous rise is called, is to enable the crowd of thirty thousand to gather around the field it encloses and yet feel as if they can touch the action even from the topmost seats.

Duels were of two kinds: duels simplex and duels complex. In the first, just the drawing of blood could lead to the fight ending; in the second, one of the combatants had to die. The Marshal's opposition to duels complex was driven not so much by compassion, though in old age he found no pleasure in such murderous spectacles, as by the enormous trouble they created. The feuds, squabbles and revenge murders that a deadly quarrel stirred up caused so much general grief that the Marshal had taken to bringing every power he had, formal and informal, to making sure they did not take place. Fights to the death were something that could only cause trouble in general and encourage disrespect for the ruling classes in particular. These days the Red Opera was where Memphis came only to see bullfighting and bearbaiting (though this was becoming unfashionable). Professional boxing matches and executions were also staged there. The opportunity, therefore, to see their betters—and no one knew any different about Cale—murdering each other in public was not to be missed. Who knew when the chance would come again?

From early in the morning of the fight, the huge plaza in front of the Opera Rosso was already packed. The queues for the ten entrances were already thousands deep, and those who soon realized they would

not get in milled around in the markets and stalls that appeared on
these big occasions like a tented city. There were peelers and riot gen-
darmes everywhere, watching for thieves and trouble, knowing that
disappointment could turn into an ugly fight. All the spivs and gangs of
the city were there—the Suedeheads with their gold and red waistcoats
and silver-colored boots, the hooligans in their white braces and black
top hats, the rockers in their bowlers, monocles and thin mustaches. The
girls were out in force too, the Lollards with their long coats and thigh-
high boots and shaved heads, the Tickets with their shaped red lips like
a cupid's bow, their tight red bodices and long stockings black as night.
There was the calling and shouting and booing and laughing—bursts
of music, fanfares as the young Materazzi turned up to be gawped at
and envied. And of every penny earned, half ended up with Kitty
the Hare.

At executions the hoi polloi used to throw dead cats at the condemned. While this was considered entirely fitting for criminals and
traitors, such behavior was strictly forbidden on an occasion like this—
disrespect involving one of the Materazzi was on no account to be allowed. However, such bans did not prevent the locals trying, and as the
morning wore on, large piles of dead cats, along with weasels, dogs,
stoats and the occasional aardvark, grew outside the ten entrances.

At twelve a blast of fanfares for the arrival of Solomon Solomon.
Ten minutes later Cale, along with Vague Henri and Kleist, made his
way unrecognized through the crowd, only causing attention as the
peelers overseeing the queues halted the moving lines and watched
with morbid curiosity as the boys passed into the Opera Rosso.

In the shadowy rooms underneath the Opera kept only for the Materazzi about to try to slaughter each other, Cale sat in silence with Vague Henri and Kleist, brooding on what was to come. Until two days ago his thoughts had been of uncomplicated rage and revenge—all powerful but entirely familiar to him. But then everything had changed as he had lain in bed naked with Arbell Swan-Neck under rich cotton sheets and understood for the first time in his life the astonishing power of bliss. Consider what it was like for Cale—Cale the starving, Cale the brutalized, Cale the killer—to be wrapped in the arms and legs of this beautiful young woman, naked and desperately passionate as she stroked his hair and kissed him over and over again. And now he was waiting in a dim chamber smelling slightly of damp while above him the Opera was filling with thirty thousand people expecting to see him die. Until two days ago what had driven him was the will to survive: deep, animal, full of rage—but always part of him had not cared at all whether he lived or died. Now he did care, and very deeply, and so for the first time in a long time he was afraid. To love life is, of course, a wonderful thing, but not on this day of all days.

So the three of them sat, Vague Henri and Kleist alike catching the completely unfamiliar sense of dread coming from someone they had come, like him or not, to see as untouchable. Now with each muffled shout or cheer, with each thud of huge doors and lifts, unseen machines clanking and echoing, expectation and belief were replaced by doubt and fear.

With half an hour left there was a soft knock on the door, and Kleist opened it to let in Lord Vipond and IdrisPukke. They spoke softly, daunted by the strange mood in the dark room.

Was he all right?

"Yes."

Did he need anything?

"No. Thank you."

And then the silence of the sickbed descended. IdrisPukke, witness to the terrible slaughter of the Redeemers against all odds at the Cortina pass, was baffled. Chancellor Vipond, so wise and crafty, who knew he had never met such a creature as Cale before, saw now a young boy going to a hideous death in front of a bellowing crowd. These duels had always seemed to him merely reckless and unwarranted; now they were grotesque and impossible to accept.

"Let me go and talk to Solomon Solomon," he said to Cale. "This is criminally stupid. I'll make up an apology. Just leave it to me."

He stood up to leave, and something surged in Cale, something to him that was astonishing and that he'd thought he could never feel again. *Yes, let it stop. I don't want this. I don't.* But as Vipond reached the door, something else, not pride, but his deep grasp of the reality of things, caused him to call out.

"Please. Chancellor Vipond. It won't do any good. He wants my hide more than life itself. Nothing you can say will make any difference. You'll give him the advantage over me for no gain."

Vipond did not argue with him, because he knew he was right. There was a loud rap on the door.

"Fifteen minutes!"

Then it opened. "Oh, the vicar's here to see you."

A strikingly small man with a gentle smile entered the room dressed in a black suit and with a white band around his neck that looked something like a dog collar.

"I've come," said the vicar, "to give you a blessing." He paused. "If you'd like me to."

Cale looked at IdrisPukke, who fully expected him to throw the man out. Seeing this, Cale smiled and said, "It can't do any harm." He held out his hand and IdrisPukke took it.

"Good luck, boy," he said and left quickly. Cale nodded at Vipond and the chancellor nodded back, leaving just the three boys and the vicar.

"Shall we get on?" said the vicar pleasantly, as if he were officiating at a marriage or a baptism. He reached into his pocket and took out a small silver container. He opened the lid and showed Cale the powdery contents. "The ashes from the burned bark of an oak tree," he said. "It's thought to symbolize immortality," he added, as if this was a view to which he, of course, attached little credibility. "May I?" He dipped his forefinger in the ash and spread it in a short line on Cale's forehead.

"Remember, man, that thou art dust and unto dust thou shalt return," he intoned cheerfully. "But remember also that though your sins are like scarlet, they shall be white as snow, though they be as red like crimson, they shall be like wool." He snapped the lid of the silver container shut and put it back in his pocket with the air of a job well done.

"Um . . . oh . . . good luck."

As he made for the door, Kleist called after him. "Did you say the same to Solomon Solomon?"

The vicar turned and looked at Kleist as if trying to remember.

"Do you know," he said, smiling oddly, "I don't think I did?" And with that, he was gone.

There was one more visitor. There was a faint knock, Henri opened the door, and Riba slipped into the room. Henri flushed as she briefly squeezed his hand before passing on into the room. Cale was staring at the ground and appeared lost. She waited for a few moments before he looked up, surprised.

"I came to wish you good luck," she said, speaking quickly and nervously, "and to say sorry and to give you this." She held out a note. He took it and broke the elegant seal.

I love you. Please come back to me.

No one spoke for a minute.

"What do mean about being sorry?" asked Cale.

"It's my fault you're here."

There was a snort of derision from Kleist, but he didn't say anything. Cale looked at her as he handed the note to Vague Henri for safekeeping.

"What my friend here is trying to say is that this is all my own doing. I'm not being kind. It's the truth."

As might any of us in her situation, she wanted to be sure of her absolution and so she pushed her anxiety too far. "I still think it's my fault."

"Have it your own way."

She looked so crestfallen at this that Vague Henri instantly took pity on her, put his hand in hers again and led her out of the room into the even darker corridor outside.

"I'm such an idiot," she said, in tears and angry at herself.

"Don't worry. He meant it about it not being your fault. He's just got to give his attention to this now."

"What's going to happen?"

"Cale's going to win. He always wins. I have to go." She squeezed his hand again and kissed him on the cheek. Henri stared after her, feeling many strange things, then went back into the waiting room.

With ten minutes left, Cale had begun, silent and automatic, to do his exercises before a fight. Kleist and Vague Henri joined in—arms milling, legs stretching, grunting softly with the exertion in the dim light. Then the loud knock on the door.

"Time, gentleman, pleeeease!"

The boys looked at one another. There was a short pause then a loud *rap!* as the bolt slid across a second door at the far end of the room. It groaned open slowly, and a ray of light bit through the gloom as if the sun itself waited just outside for Cale, the bright light arcing across the once dim room with all the weight of a blast of wind wanting to push them back into the safety of the dark.

As he started forward, Cale could hear her last words. "Run away. Leave. Please. What does any of this mean to you? Run away."

In a few strides he was at the threshold and then out into the two o'clock sun.

Along with the second blast of light, the bear-pit roar of the crowd, like the end of the world, assaulted his eyes and ears. As he moved forward ten, then fifteen, then twenty feet and his eyes adjusted, he made out not the wall of the faces of the thirty thousand moving and booing, cheering and singing, but at first only the man waiting in the center of the arena holding two swords in their scabbards. He tried not to look across to Solomon Solomon, but he could not stop himself. Solomon Solomon, thirty yards to his left, walked straight, eyes fixed on the man in the center of the arena. He was huge, far taller and broader than Cale remembered, as if he had doubled in size since Cale had last seen him. Cale was astonished at himself as terror drained him of the strength that had made him invincible for nearly half his life. His tongue, dry as sand, stuck to the roof of his mouth; the muscles in his thighs hurt, barely able to support him; his arms, oak strong, felt as if to lift them would be an impossible feat; and there was a strange burning in his ears, louder even than the noise of the crowd, the booing and cheering and snatches of song. Along the amphitheater wall several hundred soldiers were standing at attention every four yards or so, alternately looking in at the crowd and out into the great ring itself.

The high-hatted hooligans sang joyfully:

> NOBODY LIKES US, WE DON'T CARE
> NOBODY LIKES US, WE DON'T CARE
> BUT WE LOVE LOLLARDS AND
>   HUGUENOTS
> DO WE? DO WE? DO WE? DO?
> OOOOOOOH NO, I DON'T THINK SO
> BUT WE DO LOVE THE MEMPHIS
>   AGGRO . . .

Then they raised their hands high over their heads and clapped in time to the beat of a new song, raising their knees up and down as they did so:

> YOU'LL HAVE TO LIVE,
> OR ELSE YOU'LL DIE
> YOU'LL HAVE TO LIVE,
> OR ELSE YOU'LL DIE
> YOU'LL HAVE TO LIVE,
> OR ELSE YOU'LL DIE
> YOU'LL HAVE TO LIVE,
> OR ELSE YOU'LL DIE

Trying to outperform them and taunt the participants at the same time, the baldy Lollards chanted happily:

> HELLO, HELLO, WHO ARE YOU?
> HELLO, HELLO, WHO ARE YOU?
> ARE YOU A RUPERT? ARE YOU A FRED?
> IN A MINUTE YOU'LL BE DEAD.
> WHO ARE YOU?
> OH WE DON'T LIKE TO SAY, WE DON'T
>   LIKE TO BLAB
> BUT SOON YOU'LL BE LYING ON A
>   MARBLE SLAB
> LYING ON A SLAB COVERED BY A
>   WREATH
> MISSING YOUR PRIVATES, MISSING
>   YOUR TEETH
> HELLO, HELLO, WHO ARE YOU?

Each step forward dragged Cale further down, as if weakness and fear, alive in him for the first time in years, ran riot in his guts and brain.

Then finally he was there and Solomon Solomon beside him, his rage and power burning alongside him like a second sun.

The master-at-arms gestured them to his left and right. Then he called out:

"WELCOME TO THE RED OPERA!"

With that, the crowd, almost as one, rose bellowing to its feet—except for the section reserved for the Materazzi, where the men cheered and the women applauded indifferently. This was not, in any case, the top drawer of Materazzi society, who would not readily associate themselves with something as vulgar as either this occasion or the not-quite-one-of-us Solomon Solomon, who, though respected for his power in the military hierarchy, was the great-grandson of a man who had made his fortune in dried fish. This is not to deny that a few of the choice of Materazzi society had come late, including a deeply reluctant Marshal, and were watching from carefully recessed private boxes while eating that morning's catch of prawns. In the section reserved for the Mond, the blazing hatred they felt for Cale erupted in a sea of arms jabbing toward him and a chorus of derision.

"BOOM LACALACALACA BOOM LACALACALACA TAC TAC TAC."

From high up on the West Bank some skillful thug or hooligan, having escaped the searches of the peelers, threw a dead cat in a massive arc, the body thudding into the sand only twenty feet from Cale, to a roar of delighted approval from the crowd.

Panic ran riot though Cale's wilting soul, as if some reservoir of fear had been dammed up in him for all these years and now had burst its banks and swept away all nerve and guts, all gall and the will to power. His very spine shook with cowardice as the master-at-arms handed him his sword. He could barely now raise his hand to pull it free, so weak had he become. It was so heavy that he let it fall to hang loosely at his side. Everything now was just sensation—the bitter taste of death and terror on his tongue, the bright and burning sun, the noise of the crowd and the wall of faces. And then the master-at-arms raised his hands. The crowd hushed. Then he dropped his arms to his sides. The crowd bellowed as if one beast, and Cale watched as the man who was about to slaughter him raised his sword and cautiously, thoughtfully, moved toward the trembling, panic-stricken boy.

From deep inside, something in Cale called for protection, begging to be saved: *IdrisPukke save me, Leopold Vipond save me, Henri and Kleist save me, Arbell Swan-Neck save me.* But he was beyond all help except the help of the man he hated most in all the world. It was Redeemer Bosco who rescued him from the sickening blow and the red blood spilling on the sand; it was the years of violence at his hands, the daily dread and fear—those were what delivered him. Beginning in his chest, the waters of terror began to freeze. As Solomon Solomon quickly circled, the coldness spread downward through Cale's heart and guts and into his thighs and then his arms. In only a few seconds, like a miraculous drug suppressing an agonizing pain, the old familiar, numbing, lifesaving indifference to fear and death was back. Cale was himself again.

Solomon Solomon, wary at first of Cale's immobility, was moving in quickly for his attack, sword raised, eyes intent, controlled, the skillful emissary of violent death. He moved within striking distance, then held for a moment. Both stared into each other's eyes. The crowd hushed. All sights seemed to come to Cale as in a tunnel—an older woman in the crowd was smiling at him like a kindly grandmother while pulling her finger across her throat, the dead cat so stiff on the ground it looked like a badly made toy, the young dancer at the arena's edge, her mouth wide open in alarm and fear. And his opponent shuffling in the sand, the grating noise much louder than the crowd, who seemed to be so far away. And then Solomon Solomon gathered his strength—and struck.

Cale ducked and moved under his arm, stabbing downward as Solomon Solomon's sword tried to cut him in two. Then both had swapped places—the crowd roared, desperately excited and confused. Neither of them had been touched. Then something began to drip from Cale's hand and then it poured. The little finger on his left hand had been severed and lay on the sand, small and ridiculous.

Cale stepped back, the pain now hit, horrible, intense and agonizing. Solomon Solomon stood and took in carefully the blood and pain, the job not finished but the work of killing seriously begun. As the crowd started to see the blood on the sand, a slowly growing roar rippled around the Opera. There were boos from some of the hoi polloi, now rooting for the underdog, cheers from the Materazzi, more chattering mockery from the Mond. Then slowly the crowd went silent as Solomon Solomon, knowing that everything was now in his control, waited for the loss of blood, the pain and the fear of death, to do its work for him.

"Stay still," said Solomon Solomon, "and perhaps I'll finish you quickly. Though I can't promise anything."

Cale looked at him as if slightly puzzled. Then he moved his sword around in his hand, as if testing the weight, and made a lazy and slow pass at his opponent's head. Years of instinct to counterattack such a weak attempt drew Solomon Solomon into striking at Cale, his great thighs pumping him forward like a sprinter. But with his second step he fell as if he had been struck by one of Henri's bolts, crashing to the sand on his face and chest.

The crowd breathed in as if one creature—a great sigh of astonishment.

Cale's stab downward in the first attack had not missed its mark at all. As Solomon Solomon's first stroke took his finger, Cale had cut downward, severing the tendon in his opponent's heel. This was why, along with the agony of the pain in his hand, he had been so puzzled that Solomon Solomon had been apparently untouched. That was why he gestured so carelessly with his second stroke—he simply wanted to make him move.

Despite his fear and astonishment, Solomon Solomon had instantly rolled onto the knee of his good leg, lashing out at Cale to make him keep his distance.

"You dirty little bag of shit!" he said in barely more than a whisper. Then he shouted in a huge burst of anger and frustration.

Cale kept back out of reach and waited. Another burst of rage and humiliation from Solomon Solomon. Cale simply watched as he began to accept that he had lost.

"Very well," said Solomon Solomon—bitter and angry. "You win. I surrender."

Cale looked at the master-at-arms.

"I was told that this had to continue until one of us is dead," said Cale.

"Mercy is always possible," said the master-at-arms.

"Is it now? Because I don't remember anyone bringing it up at the time."

"A defeated opponent may ask for mercy. It need not be granted, and no one may reproach the victor if he refuses. But I repeat that mercy is always possible." The master-at-arms looked at the kneeling man. "If you wish to have mercy, Solomon Solomon, you must ask for it."

Solomon Solomon shook his head as if a great struggle were going on inside him, which indeed it was. What was going on inside Cale was at first puzzlement and then a huge and growing indignation.

"I ask you for your—"

"Shut up!" shouted Cale, looking back and forth between his beaten opponent and the master-at-arms.

"You hypocrites! You drag me here on a rail, and when it suits you, you think you can bend rules because things haven't worked out to your advantage. That's all your camel shit about the nobility amounts to— that you have the power to make everything suit yourselves. Everything about you is just a pack of bloody lies."

"He is obliged," said the master-at-arms, "to pay you ten thousand dollars to redeem his life."

Cale lashed out, and with a cry Solomon Solomon collapsed on the ground, a deep gash in his upper arm.

"Tell me," said Cale, "are you worth more now or less? You beat me without reason or mercy, but now look at you. This is childish. How many dozens have you butchered without giving them a second thought, and now that it's your turn, you're whining for an exception to be made for you?" Cale gasped in astonishment and disgust. "Why? This is your fate; one day it will be mine. What's your beef, old man?"

And with that Cale stood over Solomon Solomon, pulled his head up by the hair and dispatched him with a single blow to the back of the neck. He dropped the now slack body onto the sand, face upward, eyes open and sightless, a trickle of blood still pumping from his nose. Soon it stopped, and that was that for Solomon Solomon.

Throughout the final seconds of Solomon Solomon's life, Cale had been aware of nothing else, not the pain in his left hand or the crowd. Rage deafened him to everything. Now the pain and the crowd returned. The sound of the crowd was an odd one—no cheering but for a few small sections too drunk to know what they were a witness to, some shouts and boos, but mostly amazement and disbelief.

From the bench where they had been told to wait, Vague Henri and Kleist watched on in a state of shock. It was Vague Henri who realized what Cale was going to do next.

"Walk away," he whispered to himself. And then shouted to Cale, "Don't!" He tried to move forward but was prevented by a peeler and one of the soldiers. In the middle of the Opera Rosso, Cale flipped the body on its back, dropped his sword onto the stomach of the dead man, then pulled his sprawled feet together and started to drag his body through the dust toward the enclosure filled with the Materazzi.

It took him about twenty seconds, the arms of the dead man spread out behind him, his head bouncing on the none too even surface and the blood from the corpse leaving an irregular bright red smear. The master-at-arms signaled the troops in front of the crowd to move closer together. The Materazzi women and men and the young Mond looked on in an almost stupefied silence.

Then Cale, still holding Solomon Solomon's legs under his arms, stopped, looked over the crowd as if they were worth ten cents and dropped the feet—a thud onto the ground.

He stretched his arms high above his head and bellowed at the crowd in malevolent triumph. The master-at-arms signaled the peeler to let Henri and Kleist pull him away. As they ran to Cale, he started walking up and down in front of the soldiers and the crowd they were protecting, looking like a polecat searching for a way into the chicken coop. Then he began beating his chest heftily with his right hand three times, each time shouting with delight, *"Mea culpa! Mea Culpa! Mea maxima culpa!"* It was incomprehensible to the crowd, but they needed no translation. They erupted in fury and seemed to sway forward like a single living thing, baying their hatred back. Then the two boys caught up with him and eased their arms around his shoulders.

"That's right, Cale," said Kleist as he squeezed him carefully. "Why don't you take on every one of them?"

"It's time to go, Thomas. Come with us."

Screaming defiance at the crowd all the way, he allowed himself to be guided back to the door of the waiting room, and within thirty seconds it had closed behind them and they were sitting in the dim light, dazed by horrible wonder. It had been ten minutes since they had left.

In her palazzo, Arbell Swan-Neck waited for news in an unbearable frenzy of terror. She could not bear to go to the Opera and watch him die, for she was sure he would. Every intuition screamed at her that she had seen her lover for the last time. Then there was a strange scramble outside her door; it burst open and a wide-eyed and breathless Riba rushed into the room.

"He's alive!"

You can imagine the scene when they were alone that night—the thousand kisses of delight showered upon the exhausted boy, the caresses, the torrent of professions of love and adoration. If he had been through the Valley of the Shadow of Death that afternoon, he had been rewarded that night with a sight of heaven. Hell was with him also—the pain from his missing finger was intense, much worse than from more serious injuries he had taken. He could concentrate only on his delirious reception once Vague Henri had managed, at great expense, to find a small amount of opium that quickly reduced the pain to a dull ache.

Late on in the night, he tried to explain to Arbell what had happened to him before the fight with the late Solomon Solomon. Perhaps it was the opium, perhaps the sheer strain and horror of the day, the closeness to stark death, but he struggled to make sense. He wanted to explain himself to her but feared to do so. In the end she stopped him out of pity for his confusion and horror, and also perhaps for herself. She did not want to be reminded of her strange lover's pact with killing.

"Least said, soonest mended."

Ejected from her rooms before the dawn guard came on duty, Cale left (though after many more kisses and professions of love) to find Vague Henri on guard, alone.

"How are you?" said Vague Henri.

"I don't know. Strange."

"Do you want a mug of tea?" Cale nodded. "Then get it on the boil. I'll join you when I've handed over the watch."

Ten minutes later Vague Henri joined Cale in the guardroom just as the tea had finished brewing. They sat in silence, drinking and smoking, the pleasures of which Cale had introduced to both Vague Henri and Kleist, who now was rarely to be seen without a roll-up between his lips.

"What went wrong?" said Vague Henri after five minutes.

"I got the shits. Bad."

"I thought he was going to kill you."

"He would have done if he'd been less wary. He thought the reason I wasn't moving was some sort of trick."

They sat in silence for a while.

"So what changed?"

"Don't know. It went in a few seconds—like someone poured ice-cold water over me."

"Luck, then."

"Yes."

"What now?"

"I haven't really thought about it."

"Perhaps you'd better."

"Meaning?"

"We're finished here."

"Why?" said Cale, shifting and pretending to concentrate on making another roll-up.

"You killed Solomon Solomon, then dumped his body in front of the Materazzi and dared them."

"Dared them?"

"To do their worst, was that it?" Cale didn't reply. "I imagine their worst could be pretty bad, don't you? And it won't be face-to-face next time. Someone will drop a brick on your head."

"All right. I get the point."

But Vague Henri was not finished.

"And what about when they find out about you and Arbell Materazzi? All you've got to protect you is Vipond and her father. What do you think he's going to do when he finds out—arrange a marriage? Do you, Arbell Materazzi, with all your airs and graces, take this, the apprentice pig-boy and all-round troublemaker Thomas Cale, to be your lawfully wedded husband?"

Cale stood up wearily. "I need to sleep. I can't think about this now."

Cale fell into a black sleep just as the sun was coming up and with the grim words of Vague Henri ringing in his ears. He woke up fifteen hours later with the church bells doing the same thing. But the sound wasn't a melodious peal calling to the mostly halfhearted faithful of Memphis on a holy day but a wild and raucous clanging of alarm. Out of bed and through the door he rushed bare-legged along the corridors to Arbell's apartments. Outside there were already ten Materazzi guards and another five coming from along the corridor from the other direction. He banged on the door.

"Who is it?"

"Cale. Open up."

The door was unlocked, and a frightened Riba appeared with Arbell easing her aside and coming out.

"What's going on?"

"I don't know." Cale gestured to the Materazzi guards and turned her back into the room.

"Five of you in here. Keep the curtains closed and stay out of sight. Keep them in the corner of the room away from the windows."

She stepped into the corridor again. "I want to know what's going on. What if it's my father?"

"Get back inside," shouted Cale to this perfectly reasonable fear. "And do as you're bloody well told for once. And lock the door."

Riba gently took the appalled aristocrat's arm and led her back as the five guards, startled at hearing Arbell addressed in such a fashion, followed them inside. Cale nodded to the guard commander as the door lock clacked behind him. "I'll send news as I get it. Someone give me a sword." The guard commander signaled one of his men to hand over his weapon.

"How about some trousers as well?" he added, to much amusement from the other soldiers.

"When I come back," said Cale, "you'll be laughing on the other side of your face." And with this sour reply he was off and running. He grabbed his clothes from his room and in less than thirty seconds was down two flights of stairs and out into the courtyard of the palazzo. Vague Henri and Kleist had already set guards around the walls and, armed with bow and the one-foot crossbow, were about to join them.

"Well?" said Kleist.

"Not much," said Henri. "An attack somewhere past the fifth wall—men wearing what sound like cassocks. Could be wrong."

"How in God's name could Redeemers have come this close?"

The explanation was simple. Memphis was a trading city that had not been attacked in decades and was not likely to be. The vast array of goods bought and sold every day in the city needed to flow freely through six inner walls designed to do the exact opposite during a siege, the last of which had been raised fifty years ago. The inner walls had become a damned nuisance in times of peace and had been gradually penetrated by numerous exits and entrances, access tunnels for refuse and water and urine and excrement, so that their role as a barrier was much diminished. A sewerage superintendent had been blackmailed by Kitty the Hare—sins of the cities of the plain were almost as severely punished by the Materazzi as they were by the Redeemers—and it was he who had led the fifty or so Redeemers behind the fifth wall. Any link to Kitty the Hare, however, was not to be allowed. As the attack was launched against the palazzo, the superintendent of sewerage was lying upside down in a dustbin with his throat cut. It was in this way that Bosco's attempt to provoke an attack from the Materazzi at the cost of a few undesirables and perverts led to a desperate fight right in the most guarded heart of Memphis. The attack behind the fifth wall had been a feint by ten of the Redeemers, but the remaining forty had made their way under the palazzo and up into the courtyard through a manhole cover. As they were emerging like a swarm of sewer beetles in their black cassocks, Cale was sending Vague Henri and Kleist onto the walls, bow-armed, and wondering what to do with the twelve Materazzi around him. It was then that, openmouthed, they all at once saw the forty Redeemers spreading like a stain toward them.

"A line! A line!" called Cale to his men, and then the Redeemers struck. There was a shout by Cale for Kleist, but as blow and counterblow were struck, the fight was too close to risk a shot. But then a band of the Redeemers tried to spill around the line of Materazzi and head for the door of the palazzo. The sawfly zip and buzz of bolt and arrow struck as the Redeemers cleared the lines and Henri and Kleist could take clean shots. The scream of one of them, clawing at his chest as if a tiger wasp was trapped in his shirt, caught Cale's attention, and he stepped back out of the line and ran toward the palazzo door, slashing one Redeemer through the tendon of his heel, the same to a second, but with the third ahead of him taking an arrow in the upper thigh. The man staggered backward, crying out as a thrust from Cale, mistimed, hit him in the mouth, severing his lower jaw and spine. Then Cale was through the crowd, had reached the front of the palazzo and turned to face the attacking Redeemers. Cowed by the bolts and arrows, the attack had already stalled as they sheltered behind a waist-high wall that led in a V-shape toward the palazzo. Cale stood in front of it, waiting for them to come to him. The Redeemers trying to get to him could now crouch against the dreadful rain coming from the walls, and on hands and knees they slowly made their way toward Cale. He reached into a six-foot pot that held an old olive tree that decorated the entrance, picked up the fist-sized pebbles artfully arranged inside and started throwing them. This was not a child throwing sticks: these stones cracked against teeth and hands and forced the Redeemers up and into the bolts and arrows from above. Desperate now, the unwounded five Redeemers rushed at Cale. He elbowed, kicked and bit, and as he fought, they fell, but even in the middle of the fight for life a part of him was thinking that there was something odd. The feeling grew stronger as he stood like some hero from a storybook, sending his opponents to their deaths as if they were nothing but tall grass and weeds—the punch, the block, the slash, the killing stroke, and then it was done. The Materazzi guards, reduced only by three, had pushed their opponents back—then the priests lost heart and tried to run, cut down either by the chasing Materazzi swords or Kleist and Henri as they turned from protecting Cale to picking off any Redeemer who looked as if he might make it to the manhole and escape.

Now for Cale the after-battle surge, the beating heart and rush of blood. The courtyard before him seemed to move, now closer now farther away: the dying look of horror on a Redeemer's face, a Materazzi guard holding his stomach trying to keep his guts from falling on the floor; the almost whispered "Yes! Yes!" of another celebrating the fact of life, of winning, that he had come through without disgrace, and the young face of a Redeemer, his skin as pale as holy wax and knowing he was about to die as a Materazzi came to stand over him. And still for Cale the sense of something utterly wrong. He tried to call out for the Materazzi guard to stop the blow of grace, but all that emerged was an exhausted squeak that could not prevent the hideous cry and the foot shivering in the dirt.

"Are you all right, son?" said a guard. Cale gasped and breathed in deeply.

"Tell them to stop." He pointed at the Materazzi going among the wounded and finishing them off. "I need to talk to them. Now!" The guard shouted and moved off to do as he was told. Cale sat on the low wall and stared at a moth settling on the edge of a black puddle of blood, testing it carefully and, finding it satisfactory, beginning to feed.

"What's your problem?" said Kleist as he swaggered up to Cale. "You're still alive, aren't you?"

"Something's wrong."

"You forgot to say thank you."

Cale stared at him. "Go and see if there are any survivors."

Kleist was about to ask him what his last slave died of, but there was something odder than usual about Cale and he thought better of it.

Vague Henri had already started checking the bodies, counting the bolts and hoping to God that his victims were dead. He noticed that Kleist was doing the same, although the Materazzi had quickly finished off anyone who was still moving.

"Cale! Come and see," shouted Kleist as he turned over a body with one of his arrows in its back. Vague Henri watched as Cale approached but hung back, uneasy. "Look," said Kleist. "It's Westaby." Cale stared at the dead face of an eighteen-year-old he had seen every day at the Sanctuary for as long as he could remember. "Here's one of the Gaddis twins," said Vague Henri. There was a short silence as he pulled a body next to it onto its front. "And his brother." From the far end of the courtyard, near the manhole cover, there was a burst of shouting and four Materazzi began kicking and punching a Redeemer who'd been lying low. The three boys rushed over and started pulling them off, but the Materazzi kept trying to shove them aside until Cale pulled his sword and threatened them with vile dismemberments if they didn't back off. Kleist and Vague Henri dragged the Redeemer away as the Materazzi looked on in a bad temper. The evil mood was broken by another Materazzi guard who walked up to the four holding a sword bent into an L-shape. "Would you look at this?" he kept saying. "Would you look at this?" Slowly Cale backed away and went over to Kleist and Henri, still keeping his eye on the four Materazzi.

Cale, Kleist and Vague Henri stood over the Redeemer lying unconscious with his back against the palazzo wall, his face swollen, lips fat, teeth missing.

"He looks familiar," said Vague Henri.

"Yes," said Cale. "It's Tillmans, Navratil's acolyte."

"Redeemer Bumfeel?" said Kleist, looking down at the unconscious young man more closely. "Yeah, you're right. It *is* Tillmans." Kleist snapped his fingers in Tillmans's face twice.

"Tillmans! Wake up!" He shook him by the shoulders and then Tillmans groaned. Slowly his eyes opened, but they were unfocused.

"They burned him."

"They burned who?"

"Redeemer Navratil. They roasted him over a griddle for touching boys."

"Sorry about that. He was decent enough, all said and done," said Cale.

"As long as you kept your back to the wall," said Kleist. "He gave me a pork chop once," he added, a memorial as close to a eulogy as Kleist was ever likely to give a Redeemer.

"I couldn't bear the screaming," said Tillmans. "It took nearly an hour to finish him. Then they told me they'd do the same to me if I didn't volunteer to come here."

"Who was watching you on the way?"

"Redeemer Stape Roy and his cohort. They told us when we got to this place, there'd be God's spies to fight with us, and if we did well, we'd get a fresh start. Don't kill me, Boss!"

"We're not going to hurt you. Just tell us what you know."

"Nothing. I don't know anything."

"Who were the others?"

"I don't know—just like me, not soldiers. I want . . ."

Tillmans's eyes started to move oddly, one losing focus, the other looking over Cale's shoulder as if he could see something in the distance. Again Kleist snapped his fingers, but this time there was no response, except that Tillmans's gaze became more unfocused and his breathing more erratic. Then for a moment he seemed to come to—"What's that?" Then his head fell to one side.

"He's not going to last the night," said Vague Henri. "Poor old Tillmans."

"Yeah," said Kleist. "And poor old Redeemer Bumfeel. What a way to go."

He had been told to report at three to the chancellor's office and keep his mouth shut. When he was finally shown in, Vipond barely looked at him.

"I have to admit that I had my doubts when you predicted the Redeemers would try an attack on Arbell in Memphis. I wondered if perhaps you weren't making it up in order to give yourself and your friends something to do. My apologies."

Cale was not used to anyone in authority admitting they were wrong—especially when they were right—and so he just looked shifty. Vipond handed Cale a printed leaflet—on it was a coarsely drawn picture of a woman with her breasts exposed and above this the headline: THE WHORE OF MEMPHIS. The leaflet went on to describe Arbell as a notorious defiler and shaved-headed whore who prostituted herself and all innocents in mass orgies of devil worship and sacrifice. *She is a sin,* declared the leaflet finally, *crying out to heaven for vengeance!*

There were hammers working in Cale's brain trying to figure all this out.

"The attackers outside the walls left these pamphlets all along their trail of attack," said Vipond. "There'll be no keeping a lid on it this time. Arbell Materazzi is widely considered to be whiter than snow."

While this was clearly no longer entirely true, the grotesque lies of the pamphlet were as deeply puzzling to Cale as to Vipond.

"Any idea what this is about?" asked Vipond.

"No."

"I heard you interrogated a prisoner."

"What there was left of him."

"Did he have anything to say?"

"Only to tell us what was already pretty clear. This was never a serious attack. They weren't even real soldiers. We knew about ten of them—field cooks, clerks, a few soldier types who slacked off once too often. That's why it was so easy."

"You're not to repeat that anywhere else. The form all around is that the Materazzi have delivered a great victory against a cowardly attack by the pick of Redeemer assassins."

"The pick of Redeemer pig-boys."

"There is outrage at what has happened and great regard for our soldiers' skill and heroism in repelling them. Nothing must be said to contradict that claim. You understand?"

"Bosco wants to provoke you into an attack on him."

"Well, he's succeeded."

"Giving Bosco what he wants is a stupid idea. I'm not lying about this."

"That makes a change. But I believe you."

"Then you have to tell them that if they think taking on a real Redeemer army will be anything like this, then they've got another think coming."

For the first time Vipond looked straight at the boy in front of him.

"My God, Cale, if you only knew with what little sense the world is run. There has been no disaster visited on mankind that was not warned of by someone—never, not in all the history of the world. And no one who ever gave such warnings and was proved right ever got any good out of it. The Materazzi will not be told by anyone in this matter, and certainly not by Thomas Cale. That's how the world is, and there is nothing an insignificant nobody like you, or even a significant somebody like me, can do about it."

"You're not going to say anything to stop them?"

"No, I am not, and neither will you. Memphis is the heart of the greatest power on earth. Some very simple forces, Cale, hold that empire together: trade, greed and the general belief that the Materazzi are too powerful for it all to be worth the risk of defying us. Waiting behind the walls of Memphis while the Redeemers lay siege to us is not an option. Bosco can't win, but we can lose. All it requires is for us to be seen to be hiding from him. We could wait out a siege in Memphis for a hundred years, but it wouldn't be six months before revolts would have sprung up from here to the Republic of Pisspot-on-Sea. It's war—so we'd just better get on with it."

"I know how the Redeemers will fight."

Vipond looked at him, exasperated. "So what do you expect? To be consulted? The generals who are planning the campaign have not only conquered half the known world. They either fought with or were trained by Solomon Solomon, even if most of them didn't care for him much. But *you*—a boy . . . a *nothing* who fights like a starving dog. You can forget it." He waved Cale away impatiently, adding so as to send him away with a flea in his ear, "You should have let Solomon Solomon live."

"Would he have done the same for me?"

"Indeed he would not—so all the more reason to have exploited his weakness. If you had let him live, you could have won yourself golden opinions from the Materazzi and made him look like nothing. Force is as pitiless to the man who possesses it as it is to its victims—the second it crushes, the first it intoxicates. The truth is that nobody really possesses the kind of power that you have for long. Those who have it on loan from Fate count on it too much and are themselves destroyed."

"Did you make that up or was it someone else who never had to stand in front of a mob, barking to see them gutted for something to do of an afternoon?"

"Self-pity, is it? You need never have been there and you know it."

Irritated, not least because he had no good answer, Cale turned to leave.

"By the way, the report on what happened last night will diminish significantly your contribution and that of your friends. You will not complain about this."

"And why's that?"

"After your performance at the Red Opera, you are much loathed. Think about what I've just told you and it will become clear enough. Even if it does not, you will say nothing about what happened yesterday."

"I couldn't care less what the Materazzi think one way or the other."

"That's your problem, isn't it, that you don't care what people think? But you should."

Over the next week Materazzi from their estates came pouring into Memphis. It was barely possible to move for knights, their men-at-arms, their wives, their wives' servants and the vast number of thieves, histers, tarts, gamblers, bagmen, hot prowlers, loan sharks and ordinary traders all after the opportunity to make the large amounts of money to be had from a war. But there was wheeling and dealing other than that concerning money. There were complicated matters of precedence to be settled among the Materazzi nobility. Where you were placed in the order of battle was a sign of where you stood in Materazzi society—a Materazzi battle plan was partly a military strategy and partly like the seating arrangement at a royal wedding. Opportunities to give and take offense were endless. So it was that, despite the pressing business of war, the Marshal spent most of his time throwing dinners and gatherings of one kind or another solely in order to smooth dangerously ruffled feathers by explaining that what looked like a slight was in reality an honor of the greatest significance.

It was at one of these banquets to which Cale had been invited (at Vipond's request, as part of his attempt at rehabilitation) that events, yet again, took an unexpected turn. Despite the Marshal's general desire not to have Simon in his presence, and particularly not in public, it was not always possible, particularly when Arbell had begged that Simon be invited.

Lord Vipond was a master of information, true and untrue. He had a considerable network of individuals at all levels of Memphis society, from lord to lowly bootblack. If he wished something to be widely known, or at least widely believed, these informers would be given a story, true or untrue, and then they would spread the word. Such a means of disseminating useful rumors and denying damaging ones has, of course, been used by every ruler from the Ozymandian King of Kings to the Mayor of Nothing-upon-Nowhere. The difference between Vipond and all these other practitioners of the black art of rumor was that

Vipond knew that, for his informers to be believed when it really mattered, nearly everything they said had to be true. The result was that any lies that Vipond did want generally accepted were nearly always swallowed whole. He had used up some of his valuable capital on Cale because he was only too aware of the spirit of revenge that had been fired in those related or close to Solomon Solomon. His assassination was a near certainty. Vipond, despite what he had said to Cale, had it put about that Cale had fought bravely alongside the Materazzi in helping to save Arbell, and thus the immediate threat to Cale of poison or a knife in the back in a dark alley had been much, although not completely, diminished. Unusually, had Vipond been asked why he was spending so much time on someone of no significance, he would not have been able to say. But then there was no one to ask him.

Vipond and Marshal Materazzi had been meeting together for several hours in a frustrating attempt to create a battle plan that took into account all the complicated questions of status and power posed by putting the Materazzi into the field. The truth was that they were missing Solomon Solomon, whose heroic reputation as a soldier had made him invaluable as a man who could negotiate and deliver compromises between the various Materazzi factions struggling for precedence in the line of battle.

"You know, Vipond," said the Marshal miserably, "as much as I admire the subtleties of the way you deal with these matters, I have to say that, when all's said and done, there are few problems in this world that can't be solved by a large bribe or by shoving your enemy over a steep cliff on a dark night."

"Meaning, my lord?"

"That boy, Cale. I'm not defending Solomon Solomon—you know I tried to stop it—but if the truth be known, I didn't think the boy had a chance against him."

"And if you had realized?"

"There's no point in putting on that high-and-mighty tone; don't tell me you always do the right thing rather than the wise thing. The point is we need Solomon Solomon; he could have smoothed things over and whipped these bastards into line. It's simple—we need Solomon Solomon and we don't need Cale."

"Cale saved your daughter, my lord, and very nearly lost his own life in the process."

"You see, there you go—of all people, you should know I can't take things personally. I know what he did and I'm grateful. But only as a father. As a ruler, I'm pointing out that the state needs Solomon Solomon a lot more that it needs Cale. That's just the obvious truth and there's no point in you denying it."

"So what do you regret, my lord? Not having him thrown over a cliff before the fight?"

"You think you can embarrass me into backing down? First of all, I would have given him a large bag of gold and told him to bugger off and never come back. Which, incidentally, is exactly what I intend to do when this war is over."

"And what if he'd said no?"

"I'd have been pretty damn suspicious. Why is he hanging around here, anyway?"

"Because you gave him a good job in the middle of the most protected square mile in the entire world."

"So it's my fault? Well, if it is, I'm going to put it right. That boy is a menace. He's a jinx like that fellow in the belly of the whale."

"Jesus of Nazareth?"

"Yes, him. Once this business with the Redeemers is sorted, Cale is gone and that's all there is to it."

What also had the Marshal in such a foul temper was the prospect of having to sit with his son for an entire evening—the humiliation was almost more than he could endure.

As it turned out, the banquet went well. The nobles present seemed ready and even willing to set aside old resentments and squabbles and present a united front in the face of the threat from the Redeemers to Memphis in general and Arbell Swan-Neck in particular. Throughout the dinner she was so sweet and yet gently amusing and so astonishingly beautiful that she made the Redeemers' grotesque portrait of her seem an increasingly powerful reason to put aside petty differences and face the threat that these religious fanatics posed to all of them.

Throughout the banquet she tried desperately not to look at Cale. So intensely did she love and desire him that she felt sure it would be obvious even to the most thick-skinned. Cale, for his part, was in a sulk because he interpreted this as her avoiding him. She was ashamed of him, he could see, embarrassed to be around him in public. The Marshal's fears, on the other hand, that he would be mortified by Simon seemed to be groundless. True enough, the boy sat there inevitably saying nothing—but his habitual expression of alarm and terrified bewilderment had vanished. Indeed, his expression seemed entirely normal: now a look of interest, now one of amusement. The Marshal felt increasingly irritable as he had been unable to shake a tickly cough, probably caused by having to yap so much to his endless petitioners.

Another thing annoying the Marshal was the young man beside Simon. He did not recognize him and he said nothing all evening, but throughout dinner he endlessly twitched his right hand in a maddening series of small pointings, tiny jabs, endless circles and so on. In the end it started to get on the Marshal's nerves so much that he was about to order his manservant, Pepys, to tell the young man either to stop or get out, when the young man with Simon stood up and waited for silence—an action so astonishing in such company that the buzz of laughter and conversation almost slowed to a halt.

"I am Jonathan Koolhaus," announced Koolhaus, "language tutor to Lord Simon Materazzi. Lord Simon wishes to say something." At this, the room went quiet, more out of astonishment than deference. Simon then stood up and began moving his right hand in exactly the same peculiar style as Koolhaus had been doing all evening. Koolhaus translated:

"Lord Simon Materazzi says, 'I have been sitting opposite Provost Kevin Losells for the entire evening and during that time Provost Losells has on three occasions referred to me as a gibbering half-wit.'" Simon smiled, a broad and good-humored smile. "'Well, Provost Losells, when it comes to being a gibbering half-wit, as the children say in the playground: it takes one to know one.'"

The burst of laughter that followed this was fueled as much by the sight of Losells's bulging eyes and red face as it was by the joke. Simon's right hand flicked busily back and forth.

"Lord Simon Materazzi says, 'Kevin claims it is a great dishonor to him to be seated opposite me.'" Simon bowed mockingly to Kevin and Koolhaus did likewise. Simon's right hand moved again. "'I say to you, Provost Losells, that the dishonor is all mine.'"

With that, Simon sat down, smiling benevolently, and Koolhaus with him.

For a moment the table stared on in astonishment, though there was some laughing and clapping. And then, as if by some strange unspoken agreement, the guests all decided they would ignore what they had just seen and pretend it hadn't happened. With that, the buzz of laughter and conversation reignited and everything went on, at least on the surface, just as before.

In due course the evening came to an end, the guests were ushered out into the night, and the Marshal, accompanied by Vipond, almost ran to his private chambers, where he had ordered his son and daughter to wait for him. He was barely through the door before he demanded, "What's going on? What sort of a heartless trick is this?" He looked at his daughter.

"I don't know anything about this. It's as much a mystery to me as to you."

During all this, an astonished Koolhaus was thrashing his fingers about to Simon as discreetly as possible.

"There, you—what are you doing?"

"It's, ah . . . It's a finger-language, sir."

"What do you mean?"

"It's very simple, sir. Each gesture of my finger stands for a word or an action." Koolhaus was so nervous and spoke so quickly that it was barely possible to understand him.

"Slow down!" shouted the Marshal. Koolhaus, trembling, repeated what he'd said. The Marshal stared, disbelieving, as his son signaled to Koolhaus.

"Lord Simon says . . . uh . . . you are not to be angry with me."

"Then explain what this is."

"It's simple, sir. As I said, each sign stands for a word or an emotion." Koolhaus touched himself on the chest with his thumb.

"I."

Then he made a fist and rubbed it in a circular motion on his chest.

"Apologize."

He raised his thumb out of the fist, pointed it forward and made a hammering motion.

"For making."

He pointed to the Marshal.

"You."

He snapped his wrist and fist back and forth.

"Angry."

Then he repeated the gesture so quickly that it was barely possible to distinguish anything.

"I am sorry for making you angry."

The Marshal looked at his son as if looking would reveal the truth. Disbelief and hope were both of them clear on his face. Then he took a deep breath and looked at Koolhaus.

"How can I know for sure if it's my son speaking and not you?"

Koolhaus began to regain something of his usual balance.

"You never can, my lord. Just as no man can ever be sure that he alone is a thinking and feeling creature and everyone else a machine that only pretends to feel and think."

"Oh my God," said the Marshal. "A child of the Brainery if ever I heard one."

"Indeed I am, sir. But for all that, what I say is true. You know that others feel and think as you do because over time your good judgment tells you the difference between the real and the not real. Just so you'll see if you talk to your son through me that, while he is untrained and woefully ignorant, he has as keen a mind as you or I."

It was hard not to be impressed by Koolhaus's insulting sincerity.

"Very well," said the Marshal. "Let Simon tell me how all this was arranged from the start to this evening. And don't add anything or make him seem wiser than he is."

So for the next fifteen minutes Simon had his first ever conversation with his father and the father with his son. From time to time the Marshal would ask questions, but mostly he listened. And by the time Simon had finished, tears were pouring down the Marshal's face and that of his astonished sister.

He finally stood up and embraced his son. "I'm sorry, boy, so sorry." Then he told one of his guards to fetch Cale. Koolhaus heard this command with decidedly mixed feelings. The explanation given by Simon had, in Koolhaus's opinion, been unfairly biased in favor of Cale's idea of teaching Simon a simple sign language and had insufficiently taken into account that Koolhaus had turned it from a crude and simple-minded series of gestures into a real and living language. Now it looked as if that yob Cale was going to steal all his thunder. Cale had, of course, been almost as taken aback by what had happened as the rest at the banquet, having had no idea of the advances Koolhaus and Simon had made, mainly because the former had sworn the latter to secrecy with the intention of pulling off a brilliant surprise and taking the credit.

Cale was expecting a bollocking and was somewhat confused at being hailed as a savior both by Arbell and the Marshal, guilty about his ungrateful but not necessarily misguided decision to get rid of Cale.

But Arbell too was feeling guilty. In the days after the terrible events at the Red Opera, she had spent lascivious nights with Cale, passionately devouring every inch of him, but days listening to her visitors discussing the horrors of Solomon Solomon's death. As she had expressed only distaste for her mysterious bodyguard in the past, no one felt awkward about describing what had happened in all its unpleasant details. Some of this could be dismissed as gossip and bias in favor of one of their own, but when even the honest and good-natured Margaret Aubrey said, "I can't think why I stayed. I felt so sorry for him at first. He seemed so small out there. But, Arbell, I never saw a colder or more brutal thing in all my life. He talked to him before he killed him. I could see him smiling. You wouldn't treat swine like that, my father said."

After hearing this, the feelings of the young princess were in a great moither. Certainly she was aggrieved at the insult to her lover, but had she not also seen that strange murderous blankness for herself? Who could blame her if a quietly suppressed shudder did not make its way into the deepest recesses of her heart, there to be locked away? But all these dreadful thoughts were banished by the discovery that Cale had as good as brought her brother back from the dead. She took his hand and kissed it with both passion and wonder—and thanked him for what he had done. Not even the fact that he offered the credit to Koolhaus made much difference. Koolhaus felt betrayed, conveniently forgetting that it had been Cale who had spotted the hidden intelligence of Simon Materazzi and who had seen the way to unlock it. Cale's attempt to include him in the general mood of congratulation and indebtedness was just his way, Koolhaus began to think, of backing into the light and nudging him out of it. So on a day Cale finally won around two of his doubters, he balanced this by making another enemy.

33

*T*hat night Arbell Materazzi held Cale in her arms, having banished all reservations about him. How brave he was and how ungrateful she had been to harbor any doubts—and now he had worked this miraculous change upon her brother. How generous toward others it made him seem and how clever and full of insight. She was almost burning with adoration as she made love to him that night, worshipping him with every inch of her lithe and exquisite body. What graceful magic this worked on Thomas Cale's abraded soul, what joy and astonishment it brought him. Later, as he lay wrapped in her elegant arms and endless legs, he began to feel as if the deepest layers of his icy soul were being touched by the sun.

"No harm can come to you. Promise me," she said after nearly an hour of silence.

"Your father and his generals have no intention of letting me anywhere near the fight. I have no intention of going anyway. It's nothing to do with me. My job is to look after you. That's all that interests me."

"But what if something happened to me?"

"Nothing's going to happen to you."

"Not even you can be sure of that."

"What's the matter?"

"Nothing." She held his face in her hands and looked into his eyes as if searching for something. "You know that picture on the wall in the next room?"

"Your great-grandfather?"

"Yes—with his second wife, Stella. The reason I put it up there was because of a letter I came across when I was a girl, rooting around in some old family bits and pieces I found in a trunk. I don't think anyone had looked inside for nearly a hundred years." She stood up and walked over to a drawer on the far side of the room, naked as a jaybird and enough to stop the heart of any man. *How is it*, he thought, *such a creature loves me.* She rooted around for a moment and then returned with an envelope. She took out two pages of dense writing and looked at them sadly. "This is the last letter he wrote to Stella before he died at the siege of Jerusalem. I want you to hear the last paragraph because I want you to understand something." She sat down at the foot of the bed and began reading:

My very dear Stella,

The indications are very strong that we shall attack again in a few days—perhaps tomorrow. Lest I should not be able to write you again, I feel impelled to write lines that may fall under your eye when I shall be no more.

Stella, my love for you is deathless, it seems to bind me to you with mighty cables that nothing but God could break; if I do not return, my dear Stella, never forget how much I love you, and when my last breath escapes me on the battlefield, it will whisper your name.

But, Stella! If the dead can come back to this earth and move unseen around those they loved, I shall always be near you; in the garish day and in the darkest night—amidst your happiest scenes and gloomiest hours—always, always; and if there be a soft breeze upon your cheek, it shall be my breath; or if the cool air fans your throbbing temple, it shall be my spirit passing by.

Arbell looked up, tears in her eyes, "That was the last time she ever heard from him." She scrabbled closer to Cale from the foot of the bed and held him tight. "I am bound to you too. Always remember that, no matter what occurs, I will always be near, always you'll be able to feel my spirit watching over you."

Blasted and bowled over by this beautiful and passionate young woman, Cale did not know what to say. But in a short time words were no longer necessary.

34

*W*ilfred "Fivebellies" Penn, watchman of the city of York, a hundred miles to the north of Memphis, stretched his eyes wide to keep himself awake as he looked over the city walls. Another beautiful sun rose over the woods that surrounded the town, and Fivebellies thought, dreary and dull as the night watch always was, this was a time of day that, no matter how often seen, made you wonderfully glad to be alive. It was then that he noticed something so odd that its strangeness, its impossibility, puzzled rather than alarmed him. It could not, what he thought he saw, be happening. From behind the tree line about a mile and a half away, a large black object had risen from the forest and was soaring into the reddish blue sky as it moved toward the city. The black object got bigger and seemed to move ever faster until, stunned as an animal before slaughter, Fivebellies watched as a large rock the size of a cow flew over him not twenty feet away, lazily turning on its axis. It curved into the city below, destroying four large town houses as it bounced through a shattered collapse of stone and dust and came to rest in the Municipal Garden of Nightingales.

During the next two hours the four mobile Redeemer trebuchet siege engines launched another ten rocks and, having found their range, were able to do great damage to the walls. The designs were new and untried on the battlefield, and two of them snapped along the great lever arms. The Pontifical Engineers who had accompanied the Fourth Army of Redeemer General Princeps duly made their measurements and assessments of the weaknesses of their new mobile designs and within the hour had packed up the broken arms and started the long return march to Shotover.

In the afternoon it was so hot that, while no birds sang, the sound of cicadas was almost deafening. There was a brief attack at three o'clock by two hundred and fifty light cavalry from the city, designed to draw a response that might give the garrison commander some idea of what he was up against. A volley of arrows from the trees caused them to swerve away, and all the Materazzi got for their trouble was two dead, five wounded and ten horses that had to be destroyed. The Redeemers holding the tree line watched the cavalry retreat. All of them could feel a hideous tension in the air, as if something dreadful was holding its breath and about to strike. Then they all started laughing as the threatening hush was broken by the creatures who were the cause. The grasshoppers, silenced by arrival of the horses and calmed by their disappearance, started up their racket in an instant, as if they were one creature instead of a million.

That night the real dirty work began as Master-Sergeant Trevor Beale and ten of his men went on patrol into Dudley Forest, as leerily reluctant as you might expect. By dawn Beale and seven of his men were back inside the walls with two Redeemer prisoners and giving his report of the night's work to the Governor of York.

"What in God's name are the Redeemers attacking us for?"

"No idea, sir," said Master-Sergeant Beale.

"That was a rhetorical question, Master-Sergeant, one asked solely to produce an effect and not to elicit a reply."

"Yes, sir."

"What about numbers?"

"Between eight and sixteen thousand, sir."

"Can't you be any more precise?"

"We were buggering about in thick woods in pitch black in the middle of a well-guarded army, so no, sir, I couldn't be more precise. I doubt if it's less, I doubt it's more."

"You're very insolent, Master-Sergeant."

"I lost three men tonight, sir."

"I'm sorry about that, but it's hardly my fault."

"No, sir."

Three hours later Master-Sergeant Beale was back in Governor Agostino's office.

"All we can get out of them—one of them, anyway," said Agostino, "was his guess how many of them there were. Before he shut up for good, the prisoner said there were about six thousand in the forest but that the army had split up three days ago—oh, and they're led by someone called Princeps."

"Give me an hour alone with them, sir."

"I doubt very much if you're better at mistreating prisoners than Bradford. That's his job, after all. Besides, I want you and three others to take a dispatch to Memphis. Go separate ways; you take the most likely to make it through the Redeemer pickets."

An hour after Beale and his men had left the city, the Redeemers attacked a breach in the south wall, and a brief but savage clash followed with the three hundred fully armored Materazzi who were waiting for them. They were repelled with the loss of twenty of their number, without, it first appeared, any Materazzi being seriously wounded. It was nearly an hour after the attack that it became clear that three Materazzi were missing.

Odder still was that a few hours later four plumes of smoke started rising into the blue summer sky from the sites of the Redeemer siege engines. A group of scouts returned shortly afterward to tell the governor that the Redeemer army had withdrawn and that they had burned the four siege trebuchets that had cost them so much effort to bring to York.

When Beale reached Memphis three days later, the city already had news of the other half of Redeemer General Princeps's Fourth Army and were no less baffled by what they heard from Beale. The second Redeemer force, instead of attacking the three walled cities in their way, all of them at least as strategically important as York, had simply passed them by and headed for Fort Invincible. The standing joke among the Materazzi was that Fort Invincible wasn't a fort, but that this didn't really matter because it wasn't invincible either. It was, in fact, a place of wide expanses and gently rolling downs that came abruptly to a halt to be replaced by narrow canyons and rocky passes. Together these two contrasting geographies represented the best and the worst terrain in which cavalry and men in full armor could operate. As such it was the best possible place to train the Materazzi who flowed in and out of Fort Invincible from all over the empire. The result was that there were never less than five thousand cavalrymen and men-at-arms there at any one time, many with years of experience. For the Redeemers to attack Fort Invincible made no kind of military sense: it was to challenge Materazzi military might at one of its points of greatest strength on ground where they practiced daily. Four thousand Redeemers had set up in battle formation on the gentle downs in front of the fort and dared the Materazzi to attack them. This they did. Unfortunately for the Redeemers, a force of a thousand Materazzi cavalry returning from an exercise at the same time caught them in the rear, and the result was a bloody mess for the Redeemers in which they lost nearly half of their number. Fighting their way out, the remaining two thousand beat a retreat to the Thametic gorges and rejoined the four thousand Redeemers waiting there. Here the terrain was much harder for horses, and there was no bad luck for the Redeemers this time. The resulting first day's battle was vicious but inconclusive. There was no second day. When the Materazzi woke up, it was to find that the Redeemers had withdrawn into the mountains, where the cavalry could not follow. What baffled the Materazzi generals in Memphis was what the attack on Fort Invincible could possibly have been meant to achieve.

The news that arrived in Memphis the day after was puzzling in a very different way, if "puzzling" can be said to include horror and disgust. At seven o'clock on the eleventh day of that month the Redeemer Second Mounted Infantry under Redeemer Petar Brzica rode into Mount Nugent, a village of some thirteen hundred souls. There was only one witness to their arrival, a boy of fourteen who, sick for love of one of the girls in the village, had woken early and gone into the nearby woods to weep without exposing himself to ridicule by his older brothers. To the boy watching from the trees they were a strange sight, but the oddness of three hundred soldiers heading for Mount Nugent was much softened by the fact that they were wearing cassocks, something he had never seen before, and that they were mounted on small donkeys and so jiggling up and down in a way that looked rather comical and not at all like the magnificently threatening troop of Materazzi cavalry he had gawped at in awe on his only visit to Memphis. By the time the Redeemers left the village eight hours later, all of its occupants were dead except for the boy. The description of the massacre by the county sheriff was based on his account and arrived on Vipond's desk along with a linen bag.

> The Redeemers quickly roused the villagers and instructed them by means of a voice trumpet that this was only a temporary occupation and that if they cooperated they would not be harmed. Males and females were separated, as were children under the age of ten. The women were taken to the village grain store, which was empty as the fields had not yet been harvested. The men were held in the meeting hall. The children were taken to the Town Hall, the only three-story building in the village, and were held on the second floor. When we arrived we found that the Redeemers had erected a post in the center of the village and on that post was the device enclosed with this report.

Vipond opened the linen bag. Inside was a glove of sorts, but fingerless, rather like the kind worn by market traders in winter to keep their hands warm but their fingers nimble. The material here was of the strongest thick leather, and emerging from the thickest part along the edge of the palm was a blade about five inches long, curving round gently at the end so as to follow the turn of the human neck. On the blade was an inscription, "Graviso," after the place of manufacture. Just inside the interior of the glove was a name tag, like those attached to the clothes of schoolchildren, with "Petar Brzica" neatly stitched in blue. Shaking, Chancellor Vipond returned to the report.

> *Beginning with the women, the Redeemers led them out singly. They were made to kneel. Then a single Redeemer wearing the device sent with this dispatch came from behind, pulled their heads back exposing their throats and drew the blade, clearly curved for that purpose, across the victim's throat. The bodies were then dragged out of sight and then the next victim would be taken from the building in which they were being held. We could find only one living witness—a boy. According to him, each one of these murders would take no more than thirty seconds from beginning to end. Not knowing their fate, the victims seemed fearful but not terrified and their deaths were carried out with such speed that none cried out, nor indeed did so at any point during the day. In this way the Redeemers had killed all the women (391) by one o'clock. (The witness could see the clock tower on the Town Hall.) The men of the village were then dealt with in the same manner (503). However, when it came to the (304) children under the age of ten, they lost all concern for keeping their actions secret. In ones and twos the children were thrown from the highest balcony in order to break their necks. Not even the youngest baby was spared. In all my life I never saw such a thing. Upon completion of his testimony, and before we could prevent it, the witness ran off into the forest, swearing revenge upon the attackers.*
>
> *Geoffrey Menouth, Sheriff of the County of Maldon*

During the hours of daylight for three days Cale had been in the woods that edged the Royal Park, watching the Materazzi army training in full armor. He had tested the weight of a suit left in a corridor while its owner installed himself in one of the rooms of Arbell's palazzo. He must have been someone of serious significance because the city was already packed with Materazzi to the point where neither love nor money nor the rank that was more important than either could get you a decent bed. He guessed the suit must have weighed around seventy pounds. On the face of it he couldn't see how such a burden could allow any of the speed and flexibility he took for granted, no matter how much protection it gave. But having watched them practice, he realized he was completely wrong. He was astonished at how quickly they could move, how light they were on their feet and how the armor seemed to flow with their every move. They could jump on and off their horses with an ease that astonished him. Conn Materazzi even climbed a ladder up the reverse side and then flipped himself over to scramble onto the tower he was pretending to take. The blows they landed on each other would have cut an unarmored man in two, but they seemed able to shrug off even the most hideous strike. There were some vulnerable spots—the top and inside of the thigh for one—but it would be hugely risky taking one of them on. This would need thinking about.

"BOO! Caught you," said Kleist, emerging from behind a tree with Vague Henri and IdrisPukke.

"I heard you all coming five minutes ago. The fat women in the ice cream parlor would have made less noise."

"Vipond wants to see you." For the first time Cale looked at them.

"Did he say why?"

"A Redeemer fleet under that shit-bag Coates attacked somewhere called Port Collard, set fire to half of it, then left. One of the soldiers told me that the locals call it Little Memphis."

Cale shut his eyes as if he had heard very bad news. He had. When he finished explaining why, no one said anything for some time.

"We should leave," said Kleist. "Now. Tonight."

"I think he's right," said Vague Henri.

"So do I. I just can't."

Kleist groaned.

"For God's sake, Cale, how do you think you and Lady Muck are going to end up?"

"Why don't you take a long walk off a short pier?"

"I think you should tell Vipond," said IdrisPukke.

"We're done here. Why can't any of you see that?"

"Blab this to Vipond and all three of us'll end up at the bottom of the Bay of Memphis feeding our kidney suet to the fishes."

"He could be right," said Vague Henri. "We're about as popular as a boil at the moment."

"And we know whose fault that is," said Kleist, looking at Cale. "Yours, in case you were wondering."

"I'll tell Vipond tomorrow. You two leave tonight," said Cale.

"I'm not leaving," said Vague Henri.

"Yes, you are," said Cale.

"No, I'm not," insisted Vague Henri.

"Yes, you are," said Kleist, equally insistent.

"Take my share of the money and go," said Vague Henri.

"I don't want your share."

"Then don't have it. There's nothing to stop you going on your own."

"I know there isn't. I just don't want to."

"Why?" said Vague Henri.

"Because," said Kleist, "I'm afraid of the dark." With that, he took out his sword and began lacerating the nearest tree. "Shit! Shit! Shit!"

It was in this roundabout way that the three of them agreed both to stay and that IdrisPukke would go with Cale to tell Vipond.

This time Cale did not have to wait when he turned up at Vipond's offices, but was shown straight in. The first ten minutes were taken up with Vipond's account of the three Redeemer attacks and the massacre at Mount Nugent. He handed Cale the glove left on the post in the center of the village.

"There's a name inside. Do you know this person?"

"Brzica? He was the summary executioner at the Sanctuary. He was responsible for killing anyone not meant to be an Act of Faith. 'Public executions for the religious contemplation of believers.'" The tone in which he said this made it clear it was something learned by heart. "They were carried out by holier Redeemers than him. I never saw him use it, but Brzica was known for the speed at which he could kill with this thing."

"I have made it," said Vipond quietly, "my personal responsibility to find this man."

He sat down and drew a deep breath. "None of these attacks seem to make much sense. Is there anything you can tell me about the strategy the Redeemers are using?"

"Yes."

Vipond sat back and looked at Cale, picking up the odd tone in his reply.

"I know these tactics because I was the one who drew them up. If you show me a map, I can explain."

"Given what you've just told me, I don't think showing you a map would be wise. Explain first."

"If you want my help, I'll need the map to explain what they're going to do and work out where to stop them."

"Give me the sum. Then we'll see about the map."

Cale could see that Vipond was more skeptical than mistrustful—he didn't believe him.

"About eight months ago Redeemer Bosco took me to the Library of the Rope of the Hanged Redeemer, something I never heard of a Redeemer doing for an acolyte, and gave me free run of all the works there on Redeemer military tactics for the last five hundred years. Then he gave me everything he had personally collected on the Materazzi empire—and there was a lot of it. He told me to come up with a plan of attack."

"Why you?"

"For ten years he'd been teaching me about war. There's a Redeemer school just for this. There are about two hundred of us—we're called the Workings. I'm the best."

"Modest of you."

"I am the best. Modesty has nothing to say about it."

"Go on."

"I decided after a few weeks to rule out a surprise attack. I like surprises—as a tactic, I mean—but not this time."

"I don't understand. This *is* a surprise attack."

"No, it isn't. For a hundred years the Redeemers have been fighting the Antagonists—mostly it's trench warfare and mostly now it's stalemate. The trenches have stayed pretty much where they are for a dozen years. It needs something new to break the stalemate, but the Redeemers don't like anything new. They have a law that allows a Redeemer to kill an acolyte on the spot if he does something unexpected. But Bosco is different; he was always thinking, and one of the things he thought was that I was different and he could make use of me."

"How will attacking us break the stalemate with the Antagonists?"

"I couldn't really work it out either. So I asked him."

"And?"

"Nothing. He just gave me a good beating. So I got on with what he told me to do. The thing is, why I didn't think surprise would work against the Materazzi is because they don't fight like anyone else—not like the Redeemers, not like the Antagonists. The Redeemers don't have cavalry to speak of, and no armor. Bowmen are central to the Redeemers. You barely use them. Our siege engines were huge and clumsy, each one built on the site of every siege. You must have four hundred towns and cities with walls five times thicker than anything the Redeemers were used to."

"Two of the siege trebuchets used at York failed, but they burned all four. Why?"

"They broke through the walls on the first day, isn't that what you said?"

"Yes."

"They tested a new weapon in a real battle against a new kind of enemy a long way from home. So even if two broke down, the other two worked."

"But two didn't."

"Then make them better—that's what all this is for."

"Meaning what?"

"There's no point in surprising your enemy on their terms and in their territory if you can't be sure of destroying them quickly. Bosco was always beating me because he said I took too many unnecessary risks. Not here. I knew the Redeemers weren't ready, that we"—he corrected himself—"that *they* needed to wage a short campaign, learn as much about how the Materazzi fought, how good their weapons and armor were, and then withdraw. Show me a map."

"Why should I trust you?"

"I'm here and I'm telling you what happened, aren't I? We could have just legged it."

"Suppose this, what you're telling me, is just fake honesty, and Bosco is pulling your strings and has been all along."

Cale laughed. "That's a good idea. I'll use it one day. Show me the map."

"Nothing," said Vipond after a moment, "is to leave this office."

"Who'd listen to me but you anyway?"

"A good point—but for the avoidance of doubt, if anyone else finds out that you were a part of this, you'll get a rope for a reward." Vipond went over to a shelf on the far side of the room and removed a roll of thick paper. He looked at Cale very directly as he came back to his desk, as if this would make any difference to someone who had spent his entire life hiding his thoughts. Then he made up his mind for good or ill and unrolled it on the desktop, weighing down the edges with Venetian glass paperweights and a copy of *The Melancholy Prince,* of all books his favorite. Cale looked over the map with an intense concentration quite different from anything Vipond had seen from him before. For the next half an hour he answered Cale's detailed questions about the sites of the four attacks and the strengths and dispositions of soldiers. Then he stopped and for ten minutes studied the map in silence.

"I want a drink of water," said Cale. The water was duly brought and he drank it in one go.

"Well?"

"The Materazzi have walled towns and cities. I knew that without much lighter siege engines that could easily be moved from city to city we might just as well blow trumpets and expect the walls to come tumbling down. I told Bosco that the Pontifical Engineers would need to build something much lighter than we had and make them easy to put up and take down."

"And you designed this yourself?"

"Me? No. I don't know anything about that stuff. I just knew what was needed."

"But he didn't tell you he agreed, that he was actually going to put your plan into action."

"No. When I heard about the attacks at first, I thought I was going . . . you know . . ." He made several circling motions around his head. "A bit loony."

"But you're not."

"Me? Sound as a bell. Anyway, they learned what they needed to learn at York and that's why they left and took the three Materazzi with them—they wanted the armor, not the men. It'll be halfway to the Sanctuary by now, with the engineers waiting to give it a good going over."

"You took a beating at Fort Invincible."

"Not me, the Redeemers."

"You refer to them as *we* sometimes."

"Force of habit, Boss."

"All right, then, your plan took a hammering at Fort Invincible."

"Not really—just bad luck. The Materazzi didn't intend to attack them from the rear, they just happened to be returning at the wrong time—for the Redeemers, anyway. If you want to make God laugh, tell him your plans—isn't that what the Memphis moneylenders say?"

"You're supposed to have a parole to get into the Ghetto."

"Nobody told me."

"You're so sharp you'll cut yourself."

"I'm still alive, if that's what you mean."

"I still say it all went wrong at Fort Invincible."

"No, it didn't."

"How so?"

"How many Redeemers dead?"

"Two and a half thousand—thereabouts."

"They fought your cavalry twice and the rest of them got away. They were there to see what you were made of, not to win a battle."

"And Port Collard."

"You call it Little Memphis. Why is that?"

"It was built in a natural harbor very like the bay here. The city was built along the same lines. The layout worked once—provincials like to copy things . . ." He stopped in midsentence. "I see. Yes." He sighed heavily and sneezed. "Excuse me. So what happens next?"

Cale shrugged.

"I know what was in the plan next—it doesn't mean that's what they're going to do."

"Why shouldn't they? It's been reasonably successful so far."

"Better than that—just successful. They've got everything I planned for."

There was an unpleasant silence. Surprisingly it was Cale who broke it. "I'm sorry; the sin of pride is very great in me, according to Bosco."

"Is he wrong?"

"Probably not."

"Do you know this Princeps?"

"I met him once. He was the military governor along the northern seaboard then. There's no trench warfare there. It's all mountains and stuff. That's why he's running this campaign, because he's the best they've got at fighting with an army on the move—and he's thick with Bosco, though from what I can gather he's not too popular elsewhere."

"Do you know why?"

"No. But I've read all his campaign reports. He fights as if he thinks for himself. That kind of thing makes the Office of Intolerance nervous. Bosco protects him, that's what I hear."

"So why does Princeps need you to tell him what to do?"

"You'll have to ask Bosco." Cale gestured at the map. "Where are they now?"

Vipond pointed to a spot about a hundred miles from the Scablands at their northernmost tip.

"The view is that they're going to cross the Scablands to the Sanctuary."

"It looks like it. But it's too risky taking an army, even a small one like this, across the Scablands in summer."

"That's not part of your great plan, then?"

"It's exactly part of my great plan that they should *look* as if they're heading for the Scablands through the Forest of Hessel and so you'll try to get there first and wait for them to come on to you. But once they're in the forest, they'll turn west and cross the river here at Stamford Bridge and head for Port Erroll on the west coast here. The fleet that burned Little Memphis will take them from the harbor. Failing that, from what I read in the library, the beaches are shallow to this side. They can bring in the rowing boats if need be." He pointed to a pass on the map. "Even if the weather's bad and the fleet is delayed, once they're through the Baring Gap a few hundred Redeemers could hold off even a large army for days."

Vipond looked at him for so long without saying anything that it began to make Cale uneasy and then annoyed. He was about to speak when Vipond asked him a question.

"Do you expect me to believe you, that someone of your age, whatever that is, would be asked to prepare a plan of attack of this kind and then that plan would be carried out in exact detail? I'd have credited you with something more plausible."

At first Cale simply went blank, a kind of dead expression that made Vipond begin to regret the tone of his frankness and remember the cold delight with which Cale had dispatched Solomon Solomon. *This boy is barely sane,* he thought. But then Cale laughed, a short and sudden bark of amusement. "Have you seen the moneymen playing chess in the Ghetto?"

"Yes."

"There are lots of old men playing but also kids, I mean much younger than me. One of these kids always wins—not even the old rabbite with all the ringlets and the beard and stuff and the funny hat can beat him. So the rabbite says—"

"It's rabbi, I understand."

"Oh. I wondered about that. Anyway, so this rabbi, he says that chess is a gift from God to help us see His divine plan and this kid who can barely read is a sign to us to believe in the order that lies under everything. Me, I've got two gifts: I can kill people as easy as you could break a plate—and the other thing I can do is look at a map or stand in a place and I can see how to attack or defend it. It just comes at me like the game comes to the boy in the Ghetto. Though I don't suppose it's a gift from God. If you don't believe me, tough. Your loss."

"And how would you stop them?" He paused. "If you were going to."

"For one thing, don't let them reach the Baring Gap or they'll be away. But I need a more detailed map from here to here," he said, pointing at a section of some twenty square miles, "and two or three hours to think about it."

Should he believe this strange creature in front of him or leave well enough alone? It had been a much-loved joke of Vipond's father that when it came to a crisis, half the time it was better to wait: "Don't just do something," he would say, "stand there."

"Wait in the room next door and I'll bring the maps to you myself. Stay away from the windows."

Cale stood up and walked over to the private office, but as he was about to close the door behind him, Vipond stopped him. "The massacre, was that part of your plan too?"

Cale looked at him oddly, but whatever kind of expression it was, it was not one of offense.

"What do *you* think?" he said quietly and shut the door.

Vipond looked at his half brother. "You were very quiet."

IdrisPukke shrugged. "What's there to say? You either believe him or you don't."

"And do you believe him?"

"I believe *in* him."

"And the difference is?"

"He's always lying to me because he can't bring himself to take more risks than he has to. Being too secretive is sometimes a mistake, and it's one he's still making."

"I'm not sure it's that much of a fault myself," said Vipond.

"But, like Cale, you're also a secretive person."

"What about now?"

"I think he's telling the truth," said IdrisPukke.

"I agree."

Once he had made the decision to intervene, Vipond became increasingly tense and impatient to see Cale's plan, one that took not three hours but more than three days to complete. "Do you want it good or do you want it now?" said Cale in reply to Vipond's repeated demand to see something at least of his ideas. If he was uncharacteristically impatient for such a cool-headed thinker, it was because he had been deeply upset at the deaths of the villagers and what these deaths said about the strange reports from the few Antagonist refugees coming out of the north. Something about Brzica's glove had set his nerves on edge, as if all the malice and vindictiveness in the world had been made physical in the care that had gone into its design, the quality of the stitching and the way the blade was attached with such fine workmanship to the leather. He was all the more uneasy because he had thought himself to be a man of the world, almost a cynic, certainly a pessimist. He had come to expect little of people and was rarely surprised in his expectations. That there was murder and cruelty in the world was no news to him. But this glove was a witness to the possibility of something so terrible that could not be imagined, as if the hell he had long ago dismissed as a terror for children had sent a messenger not with horns and a cloven hoof but in the shape of a carefully crafted leather glove.

It was no easy matter for Vipond to influence the tactics of the Materazzi, who were jealous of their preeminence in such things to the point of hysteria. Vipond was not a soldier but he was a politician, both equal grounds for suspicion. There was also the problem that Marshal Materazzi had become increasingly unwell: the irritating problem with his throat had become a debilitating chest infection, and he was less and less able to appear at the innumerable meetings called to discuss the campaign. Vipond must deal with a new, if temporary, reality. He managed, however, with his usual skill. When the Materazzi scouts lost track of the Redeemer army in the Forest of Hessel, there was no great alarm, given that they expected them to emerge heading for the only passage into the Scablands.

It was then that Vipond had a secret meeting with the Marshal's second-in-command, Field General Amos Narcisse, and informed him that his own network of informers had news about the real intentions of the Redeemers, but that for many complicated reasons he had no wish to be seen in the matter. If Narcisse were to present this information to the Materazzi council as his own, then this would reflect considerable glory on the field general, as would the battle plan that Vipond would also offer for the general's consideration if he so wished. Vipond realized that Narcisse was a worried man. He was not a fool, but neither was he more than competent, and he was alarmed to find that with the Marshal's poor health he was effectively in charge of the whole campaign. He would not admit it to anyone, but he did not in his heart believe he was the man for the job. Vipond encouraged his complete cooperation with veiled but clear promises of changes in the taxation law that would hugely benefit Narcisse and an offer to ensure the end of a long-running dispute concerning a vast inheritance in which Narcisse had been involved for twenty years and looked like losing.'

The field general was not entirely venal, however, and even he would not agree to a strategy that put the empire in danger. He spent several hours poring over Vipond's plan, which is to say Cale's plan, before seeing that his financial interests and his military conscience were one and the same thing. Whoever thought up the plan, he told Vipond, knew what he was doing. He made not entirely convincing sounds about not taking another man's credit, but Vipond assured him that it was the work of a number of people and that the real skill would in any case be in the leadership abilities of the man executing the plan. It was, in effect, really Narcisse's plan when all was said and done. By the time he had presented and defended it to the council, this was no more than the truth, the clincher for the council being that the missing Redeemer army had turned up precisely where Narcisse predicted it would.

It was once famously said that it is as well that wars are so ruinously expensive, else we would never stop fighting them. However well said, it seems also to be endlessly forgotten that, while there may be just wars and unjust wars, there are never any cheap wars. The problem for the Materazzi was that the most expert financiers in their empire were the Jews of the Ghetto. The Jews, on the other hand, were deeply wary of other people's wars because they frequently spelled disaster for them whatever the outcome. If they lent money to the losing side, there was no one to pay them back, but if they financed the winning side, all too often it was decided that the Jews had been in some way responsible for the war in the first place and should be expelled. As a result it was no longer necessary to pay them back. So the Materazzi insincerely reassured the Jews that the war debts would be settled, while the financiers of the Ghetto equally insincerely claimed that credit was hard to come by in such vast amounts and only at prohibitive rates of interest. It was during these negotiations that Kitty the Hare saw his opportunity and resolved the problem by offering to finance all the Materazzi war debts. This came as an immense relief to the Jews, who regarded Kitty Town as an abomination before God. It was well known that they would not do business with its owner under any circumstances, not even at the price of expulsion. Kitty was more concerned with the Materazzi. For all his bribery, blackmail and political corruption, he knew that public opinion in Memphis was growing against the disgusting practices that went on in Kitty Town and that a move against him was more or less inevitable. He calculated that a war, particularly one where public feeling was running so very high, would trump what he considered to be a temporary flush of moral disapproval over his place of business. By funding what he thought would be a short campaign, Kitty the Hare felt reasonably confident that bankrolling the whole enterprise would secure his own position in Memphis for a long time to come.

Now at last the Materazzi were ready to move against the Redeemers, and with Narcisse's great plan to guide them, forty thousand men in full armor left the city to the cheering of huge crowds. It was put about that Marshal Materazzi was finishing his strategy for the war and would join his troops later. This was not true. The Marshal was extremely poorly because of his chest infection, and he was unlikely to take any part in the campaign.

The Redeemers, however, were in a significantly worse position because of an outbreak of dysentery that killed few but had weakened a great many. In addition, the plan to fool the Materazzi into waiting for them in front of the Scablands while they headed in the opposite direction had clearly failed. Almost as soon as they had emerged from the Forest of Hessel, an advance force of Materazzi two thousand strong had begun to shadow them from the other side of the River Oxus. From that moment on, every movement that the Redeemer army made was observed and the details relayed to Field General Narcisse.

To the surprise of Princeps, no attempt was made to delay his army, and in less than three days they had traveled nearly sixty miles. By then the effects of dysentery had considerably weakened more than half his force and he decided to rest for half a day at Burnt Mills. He sent a deputation to the town's defenders threatening to massacre all its inhabitants as he had done at Mount Nugent, but if they surrendered immediately and provided his men with food, they would be spared. They did as they were told. The next morning the Redeemers continued their march toward the Baring Gap. Now Princeps, seeing the terror that the massacre had created in the local population, sent a small force of two hundred men ahead using the same tactic to provide his still weakened men with a continuous supply of food, most of it much better than they were used to, something that cheered them up a good deal.

The campaign plan provided by Cale for an exploratory attack on the Materazzi empire had so far proved effective, but the territory they were entering now had only been vaguely mapped in the documents from the library in the Sanctuary. One of the most important aims of the plan had been to bring twenty cartographers and send them in ten separate groups to map in as much detail as possible the terrain they were to attack the following year. The three groups mapping the way ahead had not returned, and now Princeps was moving into a landscape about which he had only the most general idea. On the following day Princeps tried to take his army across the Oxus at White Bend, but the army shadowing him on the other side had now grown to five thousand. He was forced to abandon the attempt and move on into country where the going was hard and where the few villages they might have used to resupply had been evacuated by the Materazzi and everything of use and value removed.

For the next two days the Redeemers pushed on, looking with increasing desperation for a way across the river, something that the Materazzi on the opposite bank were equally determined to prevent. With each passing hour, the Redeemers grew more weary and weak from lack of food and the effects of dysentery, and were capable of covering only ten miles a day. But then their luck changed. The Redeemer scouts had captured a local cowman and his family. Desperate to save them, the cowman told them of an old ford, now disused, where he thought even a sizeable army would be able to cross. The scouts returned with the news that the crossing would be difficult and the ford needed considerable repair, but that it could be made passable. It was also completely unguarded. Their luck improved still further. Extensive marshes on the other side of the Oxus had forced the Materazzi guard to move well away from the river and out of sight. Having almost despaired, the Redeemers now felt a great rush of hope. Within two hours a bridgehead had been established on the other side of the Oxus, and the remaining Redeemers set to repairing and building up the crossing with stones from the surrounding houses. By midday the work was done, and the crossing of the Oxus by the main army began. As the sun went down, the last of the Redeemers had crossed safely to the opposite bank. Although small numbers of Materazzi turned up at a safe distance to watch the final hour of the crossing, they did nothing but continue to send back messages to Narcisse.

Three miles into their journey the next day, the Redeemers came across a sight that caused Princeps to realize that his army was finished. The muddy roads were churned up like badly plowed fields and the bushes ten yards to either side squashed flat—tens of thousands of the Materazzi had been there before them. Realizing that an army many times the size of his own must be waiting between them and the Baring Gap, Princeps did what he could to secure the remaining information that had always been the central purpose of Cale's plan. The surviving cartographers traced as many copies as they could of the maps they had made, and then Princeps dispatched them in a dozen different directions in disguise, in the hope that at least one of them would make it to the Sanctuary. He took a short Mass and then they marched on. For two days they caught neither sight nor sound of their enemy beyond the river of mud the Materazzi trailed behind them. Then it began to rain heavily in hideously cold sheets. In the face of wind and rain, the army climbed a steep hill, and this they managed in good order, but as they emerged over the crest of the hill and onto the flat terrain before them, they saw the Materazzi army drawn up and waiting for them, in huge numbers. To either side, streaming out of the valleys, more were arriving all the time. The rain stopped and the sun came out, and the Materazzi unfurled their flags and pennants, which fluttered cheerfully, red and blue and gold, the sun shining on the soldiers' silver armor.

A battle, for all the efforts of Redeemer General Princeps to avoid it, was now inevitable. But not that day. It was now nearly dark, and the Materazzi, having put the fear of death and damnation into the watching Redeemers, stood down and withdrew a little to the north. Seeing this, the Redeemers also drew back a short distance and found what little shelter was available to them, though not before Princeps had ordered each of his archers to cut himself a six-foot-long defensive stake from the trees on either side. Fearing that the Materazzi might attack by night, Princeps decreed that no fires be lit, in order to prevent any such attackers from making out their camp. Wet and cold and hungry, the Redeemers lay where they were, taking confession, hearing Mass, praying and waiting for death. Princeps walked among them handing out holy medals of Saint Jude, patron saint of lost causes. He prayed for his soul and the souls of his men with everyone from the specialist cesspit diggers to the two archbishops charged with commanding the men-at-arms. "Remember, men," he said cheerfully to each priest and soldier, "that we are dust and unto dust we shall return."

"And we'll all be returning by this time tomorrow," said one of the monks, at which, much to his archdeacon's surprise, Princeps laughed.

"Is that you, Dunbar?"

"It is," replied Dunbar.

"Well, you're not wrong there."

Most of the Materazzi were less than half a mile away; their fires were burning bright and the Redeemers could hear snatches of songs, assorted shouts of abuse at the Redeemers themselves and, in the still air as the night wore on, the odd phrase of ordinary conversation. Master-Sergeant Trevor Beale was even closer. Seconded to Narcisse's staff, he was lying low less than fifty yards away and looking to see what he might profitably do.

Miserable, wet, cold, hungry and full of fear at what was to come, Redeemer Colm Malik made his way to one of the few tents the Fourth Army had brought with them. *Still,* he thought, *it's your own fault. You insisted on volunteering when you could have been safe in the Sanctuary, arse-kicking acolytes.*

He ducked in through the flap of the tent to find Redeemer Petar Brzica looking down at a boy, perhaps fourteen, sitting on the floor with his hands tied behind his back. The boy had an odd expression on his face—pale-faced terror, which was understandable, but something else also that Malik couldn't quite put his finger on. Hatred, perhaps.

"You asked to see me, Redeemer."

"Malik, yes," said Brzica. "I wonder if you might do me a service."

Malik nodded with as much of a lack of eagerness as he thought he could get away with.

"This boy here is a spy or an assassin chosen by the Materazzi, because he tells me he was a witness to the action at Mount Nugent. He needs dealing with."

"Yes?" Malik was puzzled and not merely being obstructive.

"Just before the pickets caught him and brought him to me, I received a full absolution for all my sins from the archbishop himself."

"I see."

"Obviously you don't. Killing an unarmed person, however much deserved, subsequently requires a formal absolution. I can't kill him myself and then ask the archbishop for another shriving—he'll think I'm an idiot. Have you confessed?"

"Not yet."

"Then what's the problem? Take him into the woods and get rid of him."

"Can't you get somebody else?"

"No. Now get on with it."

So it was that Malik led the terrified young boy through the drizzle-sodden camp, past the numerous mumbled Masses the monks were giving for one another and out past the picket lines into the close-at-hand woods. With each step Malik's heart sank deeper into his wet boots: arse-kickings and beatings were one thing, but to cut the throat of a boy who had already been witness to something that had sickened Malik to be a part of was more than he could bear. Tomorrow he would have a personal meeting with his maker. Once they were out of sight and into the bushes, he grabbed the boy and whispered, "I'm going to let you go. You keep running in that direction, you hear, and you never look back. Understand?"

"Yes," said the terrified boy. Malik cut the rope at the boy's wrist and watched as he stumbled, weeping, away into the dark. Malik waited for several minutes to be sure that in his terror the boy didn't blunder back into the picket line. By tomorrow, if anyone found out, it wouldn't matter. And so, hoping that this act of charity might weigh against his many other sins against the young, Malik turned back to the camp and straight onto the knife of Master-Sergeant Trevor Beale.

Cale was up long before first light, and as the sky slowly brightened he was joined by Vague Henri, then Kleist and, last of all, at dawn itself, by IdrisPukke. They were standing at the top of Silbury Hill, from where they had a clear sight of the battlefield. Silbury Hill was not a true hill but a huge mound that had been built for reasons now lost by a people long forgotten. Its flat top provided an excellent viewing platform, not just for lookouts to spy the movement of the enemy—though the field of battle was clear enough wherever you stood on the Materazzi side—but for the numerous hangers-on from the court: ambassadors, military attachés, important persons of a nonmilitary sort and even important Materazzi women. One of these was Arbell Swan-Neck, who had insisted on being present despite the deep opposition of her father and Cale, both of whom had pointed out that she was a prime target for the Redeemers and that in the fog and confusions of a battle, no one's safety could be assured. She had argued that the presence of other Materazzi women would make her absence shameful, especially since this war was being fought to save her life. These men were risking death on her behalf, and only cowardice would explain her absence. This argument had continued right up until the day before the battle, the Marshal relenting only when Narcisse confirmed both the wretched condition and small size of the Redeemer army and the safety offered by Silbury Hill. It was too steep for an easy assault and simple to defend with a quick and safe line of escape. Cale was overruled, but he had already planned that at the first sign of danger he would remove her, and by force if necessary. Once he could see the battle lines drawn up early that morning, his anxieties were much relieved.

The field of battle was a triangle. He was on Silbury Hill at the left-hand corner of the base, and the Materazzi army of some forty-five thousand spread in a thick line to the right-hand corner. The Redeemers occupied the sharp end of the triangle. On either side were thick and almost impenetrable woods of bluish black and in between a large field, most of it recently plowed but with a strip of brilliant yellow stubble marking out the Materazzi position. They guessed the distance between the armies was about nine hundred yards.

"How many do you think?" said Cale to Vague Henri, nodding at the Redeemers.

He did not answer for a good thirty seconds.

"About five thousand archers. Maybe nineteen hundred men-at-arms."

"You have to hand it to Narcisse," said IdrisPukke, yawning. "The Redeemers can't retreat, and if they attack against such odds he'll cut them to pieces. I'm going to get some breakfast." Kleist went with him over to an old servant blowing into a fire, his face as red as a lobster, next to him a plate of brown eggs and a smoked ham the size of a horse's leg.

As they stood and watched, a red setter belonging to one of the Materazzi women joined them, wagging its tail and hoping to be included in the coming meal.

In the Materazzi camp below, no one else was handing Narcisse anything except for a considerable amount of grief. While there was widespread support and admiration for his general plan, and this from men who were highly experienced and skillful warriors, for twenty years they had been used to Marshal Materazzi having the last say about matters of precedence in the line of attack. His unfortunate absence from the battlefield allowed the reemergence of long-buried rivalries with no very clear way of resolving them. In addition, Narcisse had been obliged to change his battle plan on three occasions—something that even great generals were often obliged to do. This meant that noblemen of royal blood who had once been assigned important roles in the front line were now being asked to accept undistinguished but still vital commands in the rear guard. To them it looked like a dishonorable demotion in lives that had been devoted to, and whose very meaning was defined in terms of, military glory and prowess. The cleverness of the plan in trapping the Redeemers in a narrow field now became itself the problem in that there were too many nobles of great experience, skill and courage and not enough places in which to put them all. Each one of them was convinced besides, and with good reason, that he was the best man for the job, that to step aside in order to merely preserve a consensus was a compromise too far that could harm the empire all were honor bound and willing to die to protect. Each man had his argument for inclusion, and there were few that were not good ones. It would have taken all of Marshal Materazzi's diplomatic skill and years of authority to have forced a conclusion and, competent though he was, Narcisse had neither. In the end he decided that all the most powerful nobles could each lead a section in the front line, and only those he felt he could afford to offend were ordered into secondary roles. It made the chain of command horribly complicated, but it was the best solution he could come up with, and the situation was becoming more convoluted by the hour as large numbers of fresh arrivals also demanded their proper place in the great scheme of things. Narcisse comforted himself by considering that while Princeps's problems were infinitely simpler, they were also infinitely worse. Pretending that he had to survey the deployment of the enemy, he left the White Tent and its arguments behind, but as he did so, he noticed Simon Materazzi dressed in full armor and being made a great fuss of by a dozen men-at-arms as he demonstrated his newly acquired sword strokes. Narcisse pulled one of his equerries to one side and whispered quietly to him.

"Have the Marshal's half-wit taken to the rear immediately and keep him under guard until this is all over. All I need is for him to start wandering into the battle and getting himself killed." To be on the safe side he even waited to see it done, to Simon's incandescent but impotent fury. Koolhaus had gone to get himself a drink of water and saw nothing of this.

Cale and Vague Henri stayed watching and figuring, but however much they discussed what they would do in Princeps's place, neither of them could fault IdrisPukke's summary of the case. Their anxieties began to ease.

"It's your plan really," said Vague Henri as he looked admiringly over the splendidly laid out ranks of armored men and colorful pennants.

"It's my *idea*. What's down there is Narcisse's doing. It looks all right. Bit crowded, though. Still." He considered with satisfaction the dismal future that lay ahead of the Redeemers below.

Nevertheless, it was with unwelcome feelings of hatred mixed with fear that the two of them continued looking out over the Redeemer army as it began shaping itself into blocks of men-at-arms, cut into three separate units by two small blocks of cavalry. On either side, left and right, were two further blocks of archers.

For all their grim feelings about the Redeemers, Cale and Vague Henri could see how bad their position was. By now they had little or no food and they were cold and wet—as the sun shone a little and they began to move about, you could see the steam rising off them. For those suffering the squits, matters would have been worse—there was no chance to leave the field and they must shit where they stood. And all of this in front of an army that was well supplied, well fed and vastly outnumbered them. It was a satisfyingly unpleasant prospect.

Below them the Materazzi had been very roughly drawn into four groups of men-at-arms, fully armored (though many were not yet fitted) and each group eight thousand strong. On either side and behind these four lines were armored cavalry numbering about twelve hundred. The front lines of the Materazzi were still unformed—many had sat down to eat and drink, and there was a good deal of shouting, cheering and laughing as well as a good deal of unofficial pushing in and jockeying for position in the front line. Sheep were being roasted as well as a horse, with long lines of steam coming from the boiling kettles. Those too excited to sit and eat, with their still unarmored legs tucked under them on the light yellow stubble, buckled up, took up their position and tried to get closer to the front with more heavy shoving, though none of it was so undisciplined as to descend into anything more violent.

Two hours later and nothing had happened. A pale Arbell Swan-Neck joined them, accompanied by the now well-fed IdrisPukke, Kleist and also Riba. For all her loss of plumpitude during the preceding months, she was still and always would be a striking contrast to her mistress. She was shorter by nearly eight inches, dark, with brown eyes, and still as curved and abundant as Arbell was sinuous and blond and slim. They were as different to look at as a dove and a swan.

An anxious Arbell asked them what they thought would happen, and all agreed that the Materazzi were right to stay put because sooner or later Princeps would be forced to attack. However Cale looked at it, the Redeemers' position was satisfyingly desperate.

"Has anyone seen Simon?" said Arbell.

"He'll be with the Marshal," said IdrisPukke. These days Simon and the Marshal were inseparable. "Almost like father and son," joked Kleist, out of Arbell's hearing. Still worried, she was about to dispatch two servants to check on her brother when a group of five mounted soldiers approached them. One of them was Conn Materazzi. He had not been this close to Cale since their fight.

"I have been sent by Field General Narcisse to see if you're safe."

"Quite safe. Have you seen my brother?"

"Yes. I think so—about an hour since. He was in the White Tent with the nerk who translates for him."

"You've no right to talk about Koolhaus in that way. Look for Simon and please make sure he's sent here." Then she turned to her two servants and sent them down to the White Tent with the same instructions.

For the first time Conn Materazzi looked at Cale.

"You should be safe up here, I'd say."

Cale said nothing. Conn turned his attention to Kleist. "How about you? If you've got more courage than to sit up here and let us do your fighting for you, I'll arrange a place for you in the front line."

Kleist looked interested.

"All right," he replied agreeably. "There's one or two things I have to do here, but you go ahead and I'll join you in a few minutes."

Conn lacked much of a sense of humor, but even he realized he was being made fun of.

"At least your soapysam friends out there have the courage to fight for themselves. The three of you are just standing up here and letting us do it for you."

"What's the point," replied Kleist, as if explaining to someone of diminished understanding, "of having a dog and barking yourself?"

But Conn wasn't so easy to mock, or rather it made less impression on him because he had been born to regard himself as of immense worth.

"You've more reason to be in this fight today than any of us. If you think that's amusing, then I don't need some buffoon's last word for anyone to see what you really are."

And having had the last word himself, he turned his horse away and was gone. The truth was that this had little effect on Vague Henri, none at all on Kleist, but scraped a sore spot on Cale. His victory over Solomon Solomon had shown him that his skill was dependent on a terror that might come and go at any moment. What was the good of such gifts if panic could obliterate them? He knew that what kept him on top of the hill was that it was not, strictly speaking, his fight, that he was bound by duty as well as love to protect Arbell Materazzi, but also the remembrance of the trembling, the weakness and his dissolving guts—the horrible funk of being afraid and weak.

Now there was another visitor to the top of Silbury Hill and one whose appearance caused a fascinating stir from the very important persons gathered there. Although he had arrived at the foot of the hill in a coach, he had transferred into a completely covered sedan chair of the kind used by Materazzi ladies to travel in the narrow streets of the very old town where a carriage could not be used. Eight men, clearly exhausted by the climb, carried the chair and another ten watched over it.

"Who's that?" Cale asked IdrisPukke.

"Well, I can't say I'm often surprised, but this *is* a wonder."

"Is it the Ark of the Covenant?"

"Look down, not up. If the devil himself were ever possessed, this is the creature who could do it. It's Kitty the Hare."

Cale was suitably impressed and for a moment said nothing while he looked over the ten guards. "They look handy."

"So they should. Laconic mercenaries. Must cost a bob or two."

"What's he doing here? I thought he was heard of but never seen."

"Mock on. You cross Kitty and you'll regret it. He's probably come to keep an eye on his investment. Besides, today is a chance to see history being made and be safe doing it."

Then the door of the sedan opened and a man got out. Cale groaned in disappointment.

"That's not Kitty," said IdrisPukke.

"Thank God for that. Beelzebub should look the part."

"I forget sometimes that you're still a kid. If you ever get the chance to meet that one," IdrisPukke added, gesturing at the man, "remember, Mister Wet-Behind-the-Ears, to find a pressing engagement somewhere else."

"Now you've made me scared."

"You're a cocky little sod, aren't you? That's Daniel Cadbury. Look in *Dr. Johnson's General Dictionary* under 'henchman' and you'll find his name. See also 'assassin,' 'murderer' and 'sheep stealer.' Quite a charmer, though—so obliging you think he'd lend you his arsehole and shit through his ribs."

While Cale was puzzling out this interesting claim, a smiling Cadbury made his way over to them.

"It's been a long time, IdrisPukke. Keeping busy?"

"Hello, Cadbury. Just dropped in on your way to strangle an orphan?"

Cadbury smiled as if genuinely appreciating the malice in Idris-Pukke's voice and, a tall man, looked down approvingly at Cale.

"He's a card, your friend, isn't he? You must be Cale," he added in a tone that implied that being Cale meant something. "I was at the Red Opera when you put out Solomon Solomon. Couldn't have happened to a nicer chap. Quite something, young man, quite something. We must have lunch when all this unpleasantness is over." And with a bow that showed Cale respect but as if from an equal who was worth having respect from, he turned and went back to the sedan.

"He seems very nice," said Cale, meaning to be aggravating.

"And will be, right up until the moment when he is obliged, with the greatest regret, to cut your windpipe."

There was a shout from Vague Henri. There was movement in the ranks of the Redeemers. In a line about ten deep the five thousand archers and the nineteen hundred men-at-arms slowly moved forward. Fifty yards farther on, at the edge of the plowed field that stretched nearly as far as the Materazzi, they stopped and the front rank knelt down.

"What in God's name are they up to?" said IdrisPukke.

"They're taking a mouthful of earth," said Cale, "to remind themselves that they are mud and will return to mud."

With that the first rank stood up and walked onto the plowed field. The rank behind them moved forward, knelt, took a mouthful of earth, followed them, and so on. Within less than five minutes the entire Redeemer army were back in their loose battle rank, walking at no more than a stroll and out of step on the rough surface. All there remained for the Materazzi and the observers on Silbury Hill to do was wait and watch.

"When will they quicken for the assault?" asked IdrisPukke.

"Not at all," said Vague Henri. "The Materazzi use no archers, so the killing range is what? Six feet? There's no need to rush." It was now about ten minutes into the advance, and when the Redeemers had covered about seven hundred yards of the nine hundred to the Materazzi front rank, a shout went up from the Redeemers' centenars, each one of whom controlled a hundred men. The advance stopped.

There was more muffled shouting from the centenars, and the archers and men-at-arms began to step to the left and right and make space so that the line now filled the width of the battlefield. In less than three minutes they had finished rearranging their battle order and were now about a yard apart. The seven lines behind the front row were staggered checkerboard fashion, so the archers could see and shout more easily over the heads of the men in front of them.

For a few minutes it had been clear that each Redeemer was carrying what looked like a spear about six feet long. Now that they had stopped and were much closer, it was plain that whatever they were carrying it was too thick and heavy to be a spear. There was another order from the centenars and their use became obvious. There followed a long period of hammering as what were now clearly defensive stakes were driven at an angle into the ground with the hefty mallet each archer also carried.

"What are they preparing a defensive line for?" asked IdrisPukke.

"I don't know," replied Cale. "You?"

Kleist and Vague Henri both shrugged.

"It doesn't make sense. The Materazzi have caught them cold." Cale looked at IdrisPukke anxiously. "You're sure the Materazzi won't attack?"

"Why would they throw away such an advantage?"

By now the Redeemers were busy sharpening the ends of the stakes.

"They mean to try and provoke them into attacking," said Cale after a few moments. He turned to IdrisPukke. "They're within bow-shot. Five thousand archers, six arrows a minute—do you think the Materazzi will put up with twenty-four thousand arrows coming at them every sixty seconds?"

IdrisPukke sniffed and considered.

"Two hundred and fifty yards is a hell of a long way. I don't care how many there are. Every one of the Materazzi is covered head to toe in steel. The arrow isn't made that can get through tempered steel from that range. I can't say I'd fancy being under a shower like that myself—but the Redeemers will be lucky if one in a hundred finds a mark. And they won't have enough arrows—a couple of dozen each—to keep that rate up for long. If that's their plan . . ." IdrisPukke shrugged to indicate how little he thought of it.

Cale looked across at a group of five Materazzi signalers also watching the Redeemers from the vantage point of Silbury Hill. One of them was leaving with news of the defensive stakes being driven into the ground, something it would have been difficult to see from the front lines of the Materazzi. It had taken them some time to work out what the Redeemers were doing with the stakes and whether it was significant enough to send a messenger.

Having watched the messenger disappear over the edge of the hill, Cale turned back toward the Redeemers. A dozen bannermen, holding white flags with the figure of the Hanged Redeemer painted in red, were raising the colors. The order to take aim went up from the centenars, too indistinct to hear precisely but obvious as the thousands of archers pulled the strings back on their bows and aimed them high. A short pause, then a shout from the centenars and the banners fell. Four clouds of arrows arched a hundred feet into the air, streaking toward the Materazzi first line.

Three seconds passed and then they hit the Materazzi, heads bowed to deflect the points. The five thousand arrows struck, pinged and clattered, ricocheted over the armored line; the Materazzi bent into the steel rain as if they were leaning into wind and hail. From the flanks there were the screams of horses hit. But already another five thousand arrows had struck. Ten seconds later, another. For two minutes this rain continued on the Materazzi. Few died, only a few more were wounded—IdrisPukke was right that the armor covering the Materazzi men-at-arms would do its work. But consider the noise, the endless metal clanking, the short wait, the arrows again, the screams of the horses, the cries of unlucky men hit in the eye or neck, and that none of them had ever endured such a hostile, terrifying strike. What sense did it make just to stand and take an arrow from some cowardly Holy Joe without any breeding or skill or the courage to fight hand-to-hand?

It was the cavalry on either side who broke, the left side first, unsure when two of their own bannermen fell—was it a signal?—so hard to know among the screams of wounded horses, their own steeds panicking and ready to bolt and only an eye slit through which to see the picture unfolding around them. Three horses started forward, spooked. Is it a charge? No one wanted to show their cowardice by holding back. Like athletes in a race, watching and tense when one man jumps the start, the whole line goes. Shouts from the back to hold the line are lost among the noise—and then the arrows land again.

Then suddenly the horses on the left flank move ahead—impatience, fury, fear and confusion start them off.

Narcisse, watching from the White Tent, swears as if to bust. But soon he realizes they cannot be recalled. He waves his ensigns to signal the right flank of cavalry to attack as well. Only then does the messenger arrive from Silbury Hill to warn him of the hedgehog of stakes dug in among the archers on the flanks.

Up on Silbury Hill an appalled Cale stares in disbelief as the cavalry move forward, the riders spurring their horses to form a line—swiftly they merge at three rows deep and knee to knee, three hundred yards across to match the line of archers facing them. At first they keep a speed not much faster than a man can jog, standing in their stirrups, lances under their right arms, left hands holding the reins. For two hundred yards and forty seconds they keep this pace, enduring the flight of twenty thousand arrows as they charge. Then the last fifty yards—two thousand points of man and beast and steel spurred on to ride the archers down.

The archers, still tasting the mud mixed with fear, let loose one more flight. More horses scream and fall, crushing their riders, breaking backs, taking their neighbors with them as they crash. But the line draws on. And then the shock of the clash.

No horse will willingly ride down a man or take a barricade it cannot jump. No man in his right mind will stand against a charging horse and spear. But men will choose death where a beast will not. They can be trained to die.

As the horses seemed about to break over them like a crushing wave, the archers stepped back and moved quickly into the thicket of sharpened stakes. Some slipped, some were too slow and were crushed or lanced. Horses arrived on top of the stakes too quickly and could not refuse. Impaled, their screams were like the end of the world, their riders thrown, their necks broken. As they lay in the mud and flapped like fish, Redeemers finished them with mallet blows, or another held them down as oppos stabbed between the armored joints, making the brown mud red.

Most of the horses refused. Some of them slipped, throwing their riders; others held on as the great charge stopped in a moment, turning on itself, horse crashing into horse, some flying off the sides into the woods. Men cursed, horses screamed, turned in their fear like creatures half their size and weight, and fled back toward the safety of the rear.

Riders fell in their hundreds, and within a moment archers darted out from behind the stakes and battered the heads and chests of the stunned and fallen riders with crushing blows from their hammers. Three Redeemers in their muddy soutanes to every thrown Materazzi cavalryman staggering to his feet, trying to draw his sword as he was pushed and slipped and tripped and stabbed through eyeholes and joints. Farther back among the hedgehog stakes, angry and now free from fear, archers let loose at the retreating riders. More wounded horses fell, others driven into a frenzied bolt.

Worse was to come. To support the cavalry, as he was bound to do, Narcisse was forced to send the front line of his men-at-arms to back the charge. Eight thousand strong and eight men deep, they were already halfway toward the Redeemers' ranks when the returning cavalry, the horses terrified and maddened by fear and injury, crashed into the ranks of the advancing Materazzi men-at-arms. Because they were crowded together and prevented from moving by the thick woods to either side and ranks of armored men behind, it was impossible to move aside to let the charging horses through. Desperate to avoid the killing clash as the bolting horses fled into their ranks, the soldiers shoved sideways into one another, thrusting and barging to clear a way, grabbing their neighbors, setting up waves that spread backward and to either side as each man fell and clutched at his mate to stop himself from falling.

So all around the advance was halted and broken up—men slipped in the much-churned mud and cursed and pulled one another down. The Redeemer archers, now with the time to organize themselves again, let fly with their remaining arrows. But this time, with the Materazzi standing still and barely eighty yards away, the arrow points could make their way even through the steel of armor if they struck it right.

Even though only a few hundred men were crushed by the fleeing horses or wounded by arrows, the thousands left began to bend behind one another before the sergeants and the captains, shouting and screaming, heaved them back into line and the advance began again. Though they were vexed by disorder and the walk in sixty pounds of armor on three hundred yards of muddy plowed field, the might of their attack now built. Fifty yards. Twenty. Ten, and over the last few feet they broke into a run, aiming their spears to drive the points home into their opponents' chests.

But at the moment of the clash, the Redeemers, as if they were one, rushed back a few yards, wrongfooting the stepping thrust of their enemies. And yet again along the Materazzi line there was a staggered halt as some advanced and some held back; and so, in fits and starts, the great momentum of the charge was stalled again.

Now, though, for all the confusion of the attack, the Materazzi knew with certainty that they must win—armored, the greatest soldiers in the world and finally face-to-face and four-to-one. Convinced of victory, they pressed ahead. Now the air, besides the shouts and screams of men, was filled with the clatter of spears and the grunting heave of the Materazzi—but now further squeezed and twenty deep in places, with all of them shoving and pushing to get to the place of action and honor. But only the Materazzi at the front could fight—fewer than a thousand men could strike a blow at any given time. Fewer in number, the Redeemers had space to move in and out of the killing zone of only a dozen feet or so. Unable to advance, the Materazzi at the front were shoved and pushed by their comrades just behind and, worse, a dozen back—those at the rear knew nothing of what was happening at the front and kept on pressing forward, those in the middle likewise. The pressure began to build, one man pushing into another and another and another. As the Redeemers hacked at them, those at the front were trying to dodge and sidestep or retreat but found no room. Then the pressure from behind, impossibly strong, shoved them forward into the thrusts of spears and hammer blows. Some fell, wounded; others, unable to keep their feet in the pressure and the axle-greasy mud, slipped and caused the man behind, pushed from the rear, to fall himself—and then another and another. Wanting to get to grips, the middle Materazzi ranks tried to step over the fallen men in front. But whether they willed or not, the pushing from the back from men who couldn't see forced them to step on their fellows—many slipped and fell themselves, falling in the mud or unable to keep a balance as they stepped on the squirming and flailing men beneath their feet. What use armor now without room to move, only an encumbrance as they tried to gain their feet or climb over the bodies two or three deep? And always the stabbing from the front and hefty blows.

Even if the Redeemers also fell, they could rise easily or be pulled free. In three or four minutes, walls of the fallen Materazzi formed at the front, protecting the Redeemers and impeding the attack—and still the pressure from the rear, so deep that none of them at the back could see what was happening at the front. The men at the rear thought that each collapse of the forward line was an advance and were only further encouraged to push. Few of the Materazzi lying in piles were dead or even wounded to any great degree, but in the thrust and shove and mud a single knight found it hard to rise once he had fallen to the ground. With a second on top of him, it was almost impossible to move. A third and he was as helpless as a child. Imagine the rage and fear—the years of training and the many fights and scars, and to be reduced to being squashed to death or waiting, lying in the mud, for some peasant with a mallet to crush your chest or stab through the eye-slit in your helmet or the joint under your arm. What anguish and terror and helplessness. And all the while the terrible pushing from behind as twenty ranks of Materazzi heaved, convinced of victory and desperate to make their mark before the battle was won. Messengers stationed around what was now the rear of the battlefield, anxious for news, unable to see the disaster at the front and that the battle was already lost, sent back reports that victory was almost theirs and called for reinforcements to finish the day.

Within the White Tent there was conflicting news from Silbury Hill, where the collapse at the front could be clearly seen by the observers. But even here it was only the boys and IdrisPukke who appreciated fully the calamity unfolding in front of them. The observers, unsure and uncertain, could not countenance advising the Materazzi to withdraw. It was itself unthinkable, and they could so easily be wrong. And so they wrote alarming messages but hedged by doubts and ifs and buts. Narcisse was receiving signals from the front demanding reinforcements to finish the day, contradicted by the bleaker observers' reports from Silbury Hill, though hedged by caution and unwillingness to face the evidence that the battle was already lost. Against his better judgment Narcisse had staked most of his forces on a single throw against an enemy that was sick and weak and underarmed, fighting the greatest army in the world, which hadn't lost a battle for more than twenty years. Defeat did not make sense. And so, for all his alarm about the messages from Silbury Hill, the field general quickly gave the order for the second and third ranks to move to the attack.

Up on the hill, when the boys and IdrisPukke watched the second and third lines move toward the battlefront, a cry went up from all of them of disbelief, astonishment and rage.

"What's happening?" said Arbell Swan-Neck to Cale. Her lover raised his hand and groaned.

"Can't you see? The battle is already lost. Those men are going to their deaths, and who's going to protect Memphis once their bodies are rotting on the field down there?"

"You can't be right. Tell me it's not so. It can't be that bad."

"Look for yourself," he said, gesturing toward the battle line. Already thousands of Redeemer archers were swarming around the sides and even to the back of the Materazzi, hacking them down with pole and mallet, causing collapses as each one that fell took another three or four with him to the ground. "We have to leave," Cale said softly. "Roland," he called out to her groom. "Get her horse—and now! My God!" he cried in dreadful anguish. "I wouldn't have believed it if I hadn't seen it for myself."

He nodded to Vague Henri and Kleist, who started to move back toward the tents. But as they moved, a limping figure out of breath headed toward them. "Wait!" he called. It was Koolhaus, flushed and agitated.

"Mademoiselle, it's your brother, Simon. He gave me the slip while we were at the rear looking at the cavalry. I thought we'd just lost each other in the crowd, but when I got back to his tent the armor your father gave him for his birthday was gone. He was with that shit-bag Lord Parson an hour ago, and he was joking about Simon coming with him in the first attack." He stopped for a second, then quietly said, "I think he's down there in the battle."

"How could you have been so careless?" Arbell screamed at Koolhaus. But instantly she turned to Cale. "Please find him. Bring him back."

Cale was too stunned to say anything, but Kleist was not.

"If you want both of them dead, that's as good a way to go about it as I can think of." Kleist gestured for her to look at the battle. "There are going to be thirty thousand men down there in a couple of minutes, all squeezed into a potato field. The Redeemers have won already. All we're going to be seeing for the next two hours is men being killed. And you want to send him into that? It'll be like looking for a piece of hay in a haystack. And one on fire at that."

But it was as if she heard nothing, just looked into Cale's eyes, desperate and pleading.

"Please, help him."

"Kleist is right," said Vague Henri. "Whatever happens to Simon, there's nothing we can do about it." Again she did not seem to hear, still looking into Cale's eyes. Then slowly, hopelessly, she dropped her gaze.

"I understand," she said.

It was that, of course, that pierced him as if she had stabbed him through the heart. To him it was the sound of lost faith and it was unendurable. He felt he'd become a kind of god in her eyes, and it was simply impossible to give up her adoration. All through this the wide-eyed Riba had kept her mouth shut, hoping that she could rely on the others to stop Cale. But she knew that when it came to Arbell, he had lost all sense. Much as she held her strange savior in a kind of dread, and brusque and usually indifferent to her as he was whenever she passed by him in her daily tasks, she had seen for months that when it came to Arbell there was a kind of madness in him.

"Don't do this, Thomas," she said, stern as a mother. Arbell looked at her as much shocked as furious at her servant contradicting her in such a way. But with so many against her in this, she could not tell Riba to be quiet or, indeed, say anything. But it made no difference. It was as if Cale hadn't even heard.

Cale looked over his shoulder at the disintegrating battle below him, his heart sinking. He looked at Vague Henri and Kleist. "Cover me as best you can but don't leave it too late to get out yourselves."

"I wasn't going to," said Kleist.

Cale laughed. "Remember, if one of you hits me, I'll know who it was."

"Not if it's me you won't."

"Head back to Memphis with her guards. I'll follow when I can."

They ran to the tent to fetch their kit. Cale took IdrisPukke to one side. "If things go badly, head for Treetops."

"You don't want to go down there, boy," said IdrisPukke.

"I know."

Vague Henri and Kleist returned firm-handed and began to set up. IdrisPukke told one of Arbell's equerries to take off his official vestments, a shirt covered in blue and gold dragons on which was embroidered the Materazzi family motto: "Sooner Dead Than Changed." IdrisPukke handed the shirt to Cale. "Go down as you are and everyone will be taking a hack at you. At least the Materazzi won't go for you if you're wearing this."

"And if you're captured," said Arbell, "they might realize that you'll be worth a great ransom."

At this Kleist started to cackle as if it were the funniest joke he'd ever heard.

"Leave her alone," said Cale.

"You want to be worrying about yourself, mate. She'll be fine, I should think."

With that Cale started for the edge and disappeared over it, sliding down the steep hillside at almost running pace. In thirty seconds he was on the battlefield. Ahead of him the second rank was already moving into the brutal shambles of the first attack, another eight thousand men crammed into a space too small for half that number. Already the Redeemers were spilling around the sides, penning the new arrivals in—the reinforcements merely giving them more immobile soldiers they could take their time to hack and trip.

The packed ranks of soldiers had split here and there as they pushed and shoved, and huge piles of bodies, some as high as ten feet, caused the scrum to flow around them like the sea around rocks. Cale took up a fast trot, and within two minutes he was moving around the Materazzi rear of the fight. In contrast now to the overview from the hill, he had no sense at all of what was going on. Some of the soldiers at the rear were hanging back, uncertain; others were pressing forward. Only because of the view from the hill did he know that, at the front and moving down the sides, a massacre was going on. Here there wasn't even much noise, just groups of soldiers moving to go forward, changing direction as each one saw a gap or, following another collapse at the front, surged forward, thinking they had made another break in the Redeemers' ranks. And so thousands of men a little impatient, hoping that they would not miss out, went slowly to their dreadful deaths.

Cale raced along the line at the rear looking for Simon, a task as hopeless as Kleist had said it would be. But if he had been deluding himself when he started down Silbury Hill, now there was only despair. He would never find Simon, even if he were not already dead. All that would happen is that he would die down there or return a failure in Arbell's eyes. Even if she accepted that there was nothing he could do, he did not want her to accept such a thing. He did not want to give up what it meant to be adored.

Then he had other things to be worried about. Around the side of a line of Materazzi pressing forward, two dozen Redeemers appeared. In groups of three they attacked any men-at-arms looking for a way to get to the front of the fight. One tripped them with a long billhook, a second hit them with one of the hefty mallets they had used to bang in their wooden stakes and a third stabbed them under the arm or through the eyehole of the helmet. With the stragglers down, they even started to use the billhooks to pull back the legs of the men pushing in line to get to the front. In the crush and mud, and not expecting an attack of this kind, soldiers who would have been almost invulnerable anywhere else slipped and fell and were dispatched waving and struggling in the mire, helpless as newborns.

Then a group of Redeemers saw Cale and moved to take him from three sides. An arrow struck the one to his left in the eye, a bolt the one on his right. The first fell silently, the second screaming and scratching at his chest. The third still had a look of astonishment on his face as Cale struck at his neck and cut his throat deep into his spinal cord. He fell thrashing in the mud beside the Lord of Six Counties he had slaughtered only seconds before. Then Cale stepped into a second fight, holding the arm of his attacker to one side, crashing his forehead into the Redeemer's face and stabbing him skillfully through the heart. A billhooker went down openmouthed to one of Henri's bolts, but Kleist's arrow only took the mallet-wielder in the arm. His luck lasted two seconds as Cale, slipping in the mud, missed the fatal stroke and took him in the belly. He fell crying out, and lay where it would take him hours to die. Then another wave of men-at-arms pushed back the Redeemers that remained, and Cale stood, covered in blood and impotent, not knowing whether to turn this way or that. All his great skill was nothing in the press and the confusion—now he was just a boy in a crowd of dying men.

And then, just as he was about to turn away, there was another collapse. Sixty men deep ahead of him, the biggest yet, and a split going far toward the front opened up. For a second, terrified, he hesitated, knowing this breach was the very jawbone of death opening up for him. But fear of failure in his lover's eyes drove him into the briefly widening gap, and able to run far faster than the slipping armored men around him, he made it to within a dozen feet of the front. But all that met him was an impenetrable wall of dead and dying Materazzi. No one in front of him had a wound; they had simply collapsed on top of one another and were being crushed by the weight of those above them and pushing from behind. For a few moments there were only the piles of dead and a strange, low groaning. The helmets of some had come loose; others, trapped but with a hand free, had removed them in a desperate bid for air. Their faces now were purple, some were nearly black—a few groaning in a horribly wheezing effort to fill their lungs—but nothing could enter their horribly crushed chests. Even as Cale looked, the breathing stopped and the mouths gaped like fish on a riverbank. Several spoke to him—horrible whispers. "Help! Help!" He tried to pull a couple free, but they might as well have been set in the rice flour and concrete of the Sanctuary walls. He turned away and scanned the piles of the dead and dying moaning around him.

"Help!" creaked a voice. He looked down at a young man, his face a dreadful purple blue. "Help!" Cale looked away. "Cale. Help!"

Astonished, Cale turned back. And then he recognized him, even beneath the puffed-up black and blue of his face. It was Conn Materazzi. An arrow shot past Cale's right ear and pinged as it hit one of the armored dead. He ducked down next to Conn.

"I can finish you quickly. Yes or no?"

But Conn didn't seem to hear. "Help me! Help me!" he said—a horrible soft and rasping sound. Once again, more powerful now with the appalling sight of someone he knew, Cale felt the awfulness of being here—and how useless. Looking anxiously over his shoulder, he could see the gap that had let him so near the front begin to squeeze to a close as the Redeemers forced the Materazzi on the edges back into the middle. He stood up to run for it. "Help me!" Something in Conn Materazzi's eyes froze the hairs on his neck—the dreadful horror and despair. Cale reached into the pile of dead and heaved with all the strength he had, doubled by rage and fear. But Conn was pinned, one below and three on top, by a thousand pounds of dead weight and sheet steel. Again he heaved. Nothing. "Sorry, chum," he said to Conn. "Time's up."

Then he was sent sprawling to the ground by a hefty shove in the back. Frightened and surprised, he slipped on the mud as he tried to pull his sword and scramble free of his attacker.

It was a horse. It looked at him and snorted expectantly. Cale stared at the animal—its rider dead, it was looking for someone to lead it away from the battlefield. At once Cale grabbed the rope fastened to the saddle, knotted it around the hefty pommel then rushed to tie it round Conn's chest and under his armpits. His face was black now and eyes sightless. Luckily the rope was thin but very stiff, more ceremonial than practical, and easily pushed under one arm and then the other. Cale tied it, howling in rage as he fumbled it twice, and then fell over in the mud trying to jump into the saddle. More desperate than ever now, he grabbed the pommel and, seeing the gap closing, screamed in the horse's ear. Startled, it set off, slipping and flailing in the mud, almost falling but finally getting a purchase as it pulled with all the strength of a large hunter used to carrying three hundred pounds on its back. At first nothing moved, then with a rush and the snap of Conn's right leg, he was pulled free of the pile of dead men crushing him. With this rush of movement the horse nearly fell again and Cale almost lost his grip on the saddle. Then they were off, the three of them heading for the gap at no more than four or five miles an hour. But the horse was strong and well trained and it moved, happy now, for all the disaster around it, that it had a rider on its back. The instinct that had kept the horse safe in its wanderings around the battlefield for more than fifteen minutes in the middle of a massacre now kept it safe again. Cale held his body as flat to the horse's back as he could, ready to pull his knife and cut Conn free if he threatened to pull them over. But the mud that had caused the death of so many Materazzi, and was to kill many more, was

Conn's savior. Unconscious, he slumped easily in whatever direction he was pulled, almost like a sled in snow. Cale kept his head down and urged the horse on with his feet, not seeing the two Redeemers coming to meet the slowly moving animal. Nor did he see them fall, crying out in their horror and distress as if one man, cut down by the dreadful watchfulness of Kleist and Vague Henri.

Within less than three minutes the horse had made its way through the mass of men who were being pushed into the center of the field and, without drama or fuss, left the battlefield, carrying the rattled Cale and dragging the unconscious Conn into a narrow path between Silbury Hill and the impassable woods containing the battle. Once out of sight, Cale stopped the horse and got down to look at Conn. He looked dead, but he was breathing. Quickly Cale stripped off his armor and with great difficulty manhandled him, stomach down, over the saddle. All the while, unconscious, Conn groaned and cried out from the pain of his broken ribs and right leg. Cale led the horse on and within five minutes the sound of the battle faded and was replaced by the sound of blackbirds and the wind moving through the leaves of the woods.

An hour later Cale was overcome by an abrupt wave of exhaustion. He looked for a way into the woods and, failing to find an entry through the mass of briars and thorns between the trees, had to cut a way in, though he was slashed over his face and arms as he did so. Once past the edge, however, the thickets gave way to a mulch of dead leaves. He tied the horse and eased Conn carefully to the ground. He stared at him for a couple of minutes as if unable to understand what had brought them to this place together. He set his leg as gently as he could and strapped it with two branches he cut from an ash tree. Then he lay down and immediately fell into a deep and terrible sleep.

He woke up two hours later when the nightmares became unbearable. Conn Materazzi was still unconscious, now white as death. Cale knew that he had to find water at least, but he was drained and exhausted still, and for ten minutes he just sat as if in some dreadful trance.

Soon Conn began groaning and moving restlessly; he woke up to find Cale staring down at him. He cried out in horror and confusion.

"Calm down. You're all right."

Wide-eyed and terrified, Conn tried to move back and away from Cale. He screamed in pain.

"I wouldn't try moving around," said Cale. "Your thigh bone's broken."

For a couple of minutes Conn said nothing as the terrible pain in his leg only slowly ebbed away. "What happened?" he said at last. Cale told him. When he'd finished, Conn said nothing for some time. "The thing is," he said when he finally spoke, "I never saw one—a Redeemer, I mean. Not one. Is there any water?" Conn's utter hopelessness and misery, just the terrible state of him, began to move Cale to both pity and irritation.

"I saw some smoke just before we came in here. I thought I heard yesterday something about a village near the hill. I'll be back as soon as I can." He stripped the armor off the horse and cut away as much as he could of the mailed padding on its back and flanks and then led it out onto the path. He mounted and stroked the top of its head.

"Thank you," he said to the horse, and then rode it on.

35

*W*ithin three hours Conn Materazzi had been collected by a local farmer, put to bed and had his leg reset and rigidly splinted with four hazel sticks and eight leather straps. He'd passed out again and groaned pitifully during the hour or so it took Cale to straighten the leg satisfactorily, and had not yet regained consciousness. Indeed, he was so deathly white at the end that it didn't look as if he ever would.

"Cut his hair," said Cale to the farmer, "and bury his armor in the woods in case the Redeemers come. Tell them he's a laborer. If I make it to Memphis, they'll send people for him. They'll pay you. If not, he'll pay you when he's well enough."

The farmer looked at Cale. "Keep your advice, and your money." And with that he left them alone together. Shortly after this, Conn woke up. The two of them stared at each other for some time.

"I remember now," said Conn. "I asked for your help."

"Yes."

"Where is this place?"

"A farm, two hours from the battle."

"My leg hurts."

"It'll need to stay like that for six weeks. No telling if it will heal straight."

"Why did you save me?"

"I don't know."

"I wouldn't have done the same for you."

Cale shrugged. "You never know about things like that until they happen. Anyway, I did—and that's all there is."

Neither of them said anything for some time.

"What are you going to do now?"

"I'll head for Memphis in the morning. If I make it, I'll send someone."

"And then?"

"I'll take my friends and go somewhere the soldiers aren't mad and stupid. I didn't think it was possible to lose a battle from such a position. I wouldn't have believed it if I hadn't seen it."

"We won't make the same mistake again."

"What makes you think you'll get the chance? Princeps won't hang around at Silbury admiring himself in the mirror; he'll be kicking your arse all the way to the gates of Memphis."

"We'll regroup."

"With what? Three out of every four Materazzi are dead already."

Conn could say nothing in reply, but lay back miserably and closed his eyes.

"I wish I were dead," he said at last.

Cale laughed. "You need to make up your mind—that's not what you said this morning."

Conn looked, if such a thing were possible, even more dispirited.

"I'm not ungrateful," he muttered.

"Not ungrateful?" said Cale. "Does that mean you're grateful?"

"Yes, I'm grateful." Conn closed his eyes again. "All my friends, all my relatives, my father, every one of them is dead."

"Probably."

"Certainly."

This was probably true, so Cale could think of nothing to say.

"You should sleep. There's nothing else you can do anyway but get better and pay the Redeemers back in whatever way you can. Remember: revenge is the best revenge."

And on this wise note he left Conn to his miserable thoughts.

The next morning at first light he left, riding the horse and having decided there was no need to say good-bye to Conn. He had, he thought, done more than enough for him and was now somewhat ashamed of having risked his life for someone who, by his own admission, would not have done the same for him. He remembered a remark made by IdrisPukke when they had been smoking together one night under the moonlight at Treetops: "Always resist your first impulses. They are often generous." At the time Cale thought this was just another of IdrisPukke's black jokes. Now he realized what he'd been driving at.

Despite his anxiety to get back to Memphis to be sure Arbell Swan-Neck was safe, Cale started out heading northeast in a wide arc away from the city. There were going to be too many Redeemers and Materazzi wandering about in the confusion, and none of them too particular about who they killed. He avoided towns and villages and bought food only from such isolated farms as he came across. Even so, news of a great battle had reached all of them; though some talked of a great victory others spoke of a great defeat. He said that he knew nothing about it and moved on quickly.

On the third day he turned west and headed for Memphis. Eventually he hit the Agger Road that ran from Somkheti to the capital. It was deserted. He waited in the trees above the road for an hour and, when nothing passed by, decided to risk using the road directly. This turned out to be his third mistake in four days. A strange unease had grown over him the closer he got to Memphis. Within ten minutes a Materazzi patrol came around a sharp corner and he had no opportunity to avoid them. At least they weren't Redeemers, and he was relieved, if surprised, to see that the man leading them was Captain Albin. Though what the head of the Materazzi intelligence service was doing out here puzzled him. But puzzlement turned to alarm as the twenty men with Albin drew their weapons. Four of them were archers on horseback, their arrows pointing directly at Cale's chest.

"What's the problem?" said Cale.

"Look, it's out of our hands, but you're under arrest," said Albin. "Don't cause a fuss, there's a good boy. We're going to tie your hands."

Cale had no choice but to do as he was told. Probably, he thought, the Marshal was angry about his having left Arbell with Kleist and Vague Henri. An alarming thought struck him.

"Is Arbell Materazzi all right?"

"She's fine," said Albin, "though perhaps you should have thought more about that before you buggered off to wherever it was you buggered off to."

"I was looking for Simon Materazzi."

"Well, it's nothing to do with me. Now we're going to blindfold you. Don't be a pain about it."

"What for?"

"Because I said so."

In fact it was a sack, heavy and smelling of hops, the hessian so thick that it cut out almost as much sound as light.

Five hours later and he could sense the horse under him straining as the going suddenly became steep. Then through the sacking he could hear the hollow sound of horseshoes on wood. They were going through one of the three gates into Memphis. Despite the sacking, he expected to hear much more noise now that they were in the city, but though there were occasional muffled shouts, only the continued sense of going uphill indicated that they were heading for the keep. His anxiety over Arbell began to form a knot in his stomach.

At last they came to a halt.

"Take him down," said Albin. Two men reached up on his left side and pulled him over, gently enough, then stood him on his feet.

"Albin," said Cale from under the sacking, "take this off."

"Sorry."

The two men took him by either arm and pushed him forward. He heard a door open, then he sensed he was inside. He was led along what sounded like a corridor. Another door creaked open and again he was carefully pulled along. Within a few yards he was stopped. There was a pause and then the sack was pulled off his head.

A mixture of dirt in his eyes and having been in complete darkness for so many hours meant that he could not see at first. With his
bound hands he rubbed his eyes free of the specks of hop dust and
looked at the only two men in the hall. One he could tell immediately
was IdrisPukke, gagged and with his hands tied—but as he recognized the other man standing beside him, a terrible surge of fear and
anger made his heart miss a beat. It was the Lord Militant Redeemer
Bosco.

After the first few seconds of shock and hatred, Cale felt like sinking
to his knees and weeping like a child. And would have done but for the
fact that hatred rescued him.

"And so, Cale," said Bosco, "God's will brings us back to where we
began. Think about that while you gawp at me like a bad-tempered
dog. What have all your anger and divagations brought you?"

"What's happened to Arbell Materazzi?"

"Oh, she's quite safe."

Cale was unsure for all his deep shock whether to ask about
Vague Henri and Kleist. He said nothing.

"Not concerned about your friends?" asked Bosco. "Redeemer," he
called out loudly as a door opened at the far end of the room and Vague
Henri and Kleist, gagged and with hands tied, were led into the room.

There wasn't a mark on them, although they were clearly terrified.

"There are a number of things I am about to tell you, Cale, and I
would like to waste as little time as possible with conventional expres-
sions of disbelief. Have I ever lied to you?" he asked.

He had beaten him savagely every week of his life and made him
kill on five occasions, but now that he had been asked the question, he
had to admit that Bosco had, as far as he was aware, never told him an
ordinary lie.

"No."

"Remember that as you listen to what I'm about to tell you. You
must be sure that the importance of what I'm going to say lies far be-

yond such kinds of pettiness. And to make my good faith clear to you
I am going to let your friends go, all three of them."

"Prove it," said Cale.

Bosco laughed. "In the past such a tone of voice would have proved
painful."

He held out his hand, and Redeemer Stape Roy handed him a
thick leather-bound book. "This is the *Testament of the Hanged Redeemer.*" Cale had never seen one before. Bosco placed the palm of his
hand on the cover.

"I swear before God at the cost of my everlasting soul that the
promises I make now and everything I say today is the truth and the
whole truth and not anything but the truth." He looked at Cale.
"Are you satisfied?"

The mere fact that, among all the other atrocities Bosco had visited
on him, perjury wasn't one of them certainly didn't prompt Cale into
believing him. But an oath was of central importance to Bosco. And,
besides, he had no choice.

"Yes," said Cale.

Bosco turned to Redeemer Stape Roy. "Give them what they need,
within reason, and a warrant of passage, then let them go."

Stape Roy walked over to IdrisPukke, grabbed him by the arm and
shoved him toward Vague Henri and Kleist. Then he pushed all three
of them toward the door. Cale was reassured that Bosco might be telling the truth: his instructions not to give the three too much and the
casual roughness of their treatment seemed genuine—anything more
generous or less churlish would have been suspicious.

"What about Arbell Materazzi?"

Bosco smiled. "Why so determined to discover just how deluded
you are about the world?"

"What do you mean?"

"I'll show you. Though you must allow yourself to be gagged as well
as bound and agree to stay behind that screen in the shadows there and
make no fuss, no matter what you hear."

"Why should I promise you anything?"

"In exchange for the life of your friends? That doesn't seem unreasonable."

Cale nodded, and Bosco gestured for one of his guards to take him behind the small screen at the back of the room. Just before he reached the screen, Cale turned back toward Bosco.

"How did you take the city?"

Bosco laughed, almost self-deprecatingly. "Easily and without a fight. Princeps sent news of the Fourth Army's great victory to Port Erroll within three hours and ordered the fleet to withdraw and attack Memphis without delay. Here the entire population went into the most Godless funk. Fifty miles out the fleet saw a panic of ships heading away from Memphis. We simply landed without any fuss. Quite surprising, all in all. But very satisfying. Stay quietly back there and you will see and hear everything."

With that Bosco waved him behind the screen. The guard took a gag out of his pocket and showed it to Cale.

"We can do this the easy way or the hard. I don't mind which."

But Cale was anxious to see Arbell and did not resist. There was a pause of a few minutes, Bosco's presence and the strangeness of his manner creating growing uneasiness in Cale. He watched as a table and three chairs were placed in the center of the room. Then the door opened and the Marshal and his daughter were shown in.

Cale did not know that it was possible to feel relief of such depth—a powerful, joyous surge of happiness. She was white and terrified but seemed unharmed, as did her father, though his eyes were gaunt and his face haggard. He looked twenty years older, and a sick twenty years at that.

"Sit down," said Bosco softly.

"Kill me," said the Marshal. "But I ask you in all humility to let my daughter live."

"My intentions are far less bloody than you imagine," said Bosco, still softly. "Sit down. I won't ask you again." This uneasy mixture of benevolence and menace cowed the two of them even further and they did as they were told.

"Before I begin, I want you to try to grasp that the requirements and zeals of those who serve the Hanged Redeemer are not to be understood by the likes of you. I neither want nor seek your understanding, but it is necessary for your sake to appreciate how things stand." He nodded to one of the Redeemers, who pulled back the third chair, and then Bosco allowed himself to be seated. "Now I will be unequivocal. We are in complete control of Memphis and your army now consists of no more than two thousand trained soldiers, most of whom are our prisoners. Your empire, vast though it is, is already beginning to fall apart. You agree this is so?"

There was a pause.

"Yes," said the Marshal at last.

"Good. I will return the city of Memphis to your control and allow you to rebuild a standing army to reinstate the lines of power in your empire—subject to certain taxes and conditions, the details of which you will agree to at a later date."

The Marshal and Arbell stared at Bosco, eyes wide with hope and suspicion.

"What conditions?" said the Marshal.

"Don't misunderstand," said Bosco, so gently that Cale could barely hear. "This is not a negotiation. You have, of course, nothing with which to negotiate. You are utterly powerless and you have only one thing that I want."

"And what's that?" asked the Marshal.

"Thomas Cale."

"Never. Not for anything," said Arbell passionately.

Bosco looked at her thoughtfully.

"How interesting," he said.

"Why would you do that?" asked the Marshal.

"Swap a boy for an empire? It hardly seems likely, I agree."

"You want to kill him," said Arbell.

"Not so."

"Because he killed one of your priests doing something unspeakable."

"Well, you're right: he did kill one of my priests and he was doing something unspeakable. I knew nothing of these heretic practices until the day that Cale ran away. All of those who were subsequently found to have been involved were cleansed."

"You mean killed."

"I mean cleansed and then killed."

"Why did Cale think you were responsible?"

"I'll ask him when I see him. But if you think that I would give away an empire in order to execute Cale for killing a murderous heretic and pervert . . ." He paused, looking sincerely puzzled. "Why would I do such a thing? It makes no sense."

"You could be lying," said the Marshal.

"I could be. But I don't really need to. I'll find Cale sooner or later, but I would prefer it were sooner. You have the means to give me what I want, but I only have so much patience, and once that's gone, you have nothing."

"Don't listen to him," said Arbell.

"And why are you so very concerned?" said Bosco. "Is it because you are lovers?"

The Marshal stared at his daughter. There were no indignant demands to be told the truth, no condemnations for having tainted royal blood. Just a long silence. At last he turned back to Bosco.

"What do you want me to do?"

Bosco drew in a deep breath.

"There's nothing you can do. There are not many people, if indeed any at all, Cale trusts, and certainly not you. Except for your daughter, of course, and for reasons now acknowledged by us all. What I require is for her to write a letter to Cale that she will give, as it were, secretly to one of his friends. In this letter you will ask him to meet you outside the walls at an appointed time. I'll be there and with such numbers that he must surrender."

"You'll kill him," said Arbell.

"I will not kill him," said Bosco, raising his voice for the first time. "I will never do so, and for reasons that I will explain to him when he can see that I'm telling him the truth. He has no idea what I have to say to him, and until he knows, his life will be as it has been since he left the Sanctuary—violent, angry, a life that can bring down only pointless destruction on the heads of everyone he has anything to do with. Consider the havoc he has brought to your lives. I alone can save him from this condition. Whatever you think you feel for him, you cannot understand what he is. Try to save him, which you can never do, and all you will achieve is to bring ruin upon your father, your people, yourself and, above all, on Cale."

"You must write the letter," said the Marshal to his daughter.

"I can't," said Arbell.

Bosco sighed sympathetically. "I know what it means to wield authority and power. The choice you have to make now is of a kind no one would envy. Whatever you do will seem wrong to you. You must either destroy an entire people and a father you love, or a single man you also love." She stared at Bosco as if transfixed. "But though this choice is harsh, it is not so harsh as you fear. Cale will come to no harm at my hands and I will find him sooner or later in any case. His future is too bound up with the will of God for him to be anything but one of us—and a very special part." He sat back and sighed again.

"Tell me, young lady, for all your love for this young man, a love I can see now is certainly genuine . . ." He paused to let her swallow this sugary poison. "Haven't you felt something"—he paused again, searching carefully for the right word—"something fatal?"

"You made him like that with your cruelty."

"Not so," replied Bosco reasonably, as if he understood the accusation. "The first moment I saw him when he was very young, there was something shocking about him. It took me a long time to put my finger on what it was because it simply didn't make sense. It was dread. I dreaded this little boy. Certainly it was necessary to mold and discipline what was already there, but no human being could make Cale what he is. I am not so boastful. I was merely an agent of the Lord to incline his nature for our common good and in God's service. But you have seen this in him and it frightens you—as well it might. The kindnesses in him that you have sometimes seen are like the wings of the ostrich—they beat but will not fly. Leave him to us and save your father, your people and yourself." He paused a moment for effect. "And Cale."

Arbell started to speak, but Bosco held up his hand to silence her. "I've nothing more to say. Consider it and make your decision. I will send the details of the time and place when we will meet Cale. You will either write the letter or you will not."

Two Redeemers who had been standing by the door moved forward and gestured for Arbell and her father both to leave. As she went through the door, Bosco called out to her as if reluctantly sympathetic to her plight. "Remember that you are responsible for the lives of thousands. And I promise never to raise my hand to him again, nor allow anyone else to do so." The door closed and Bosco said softly to himself: "For the lips that to him now are as luscious as honeycomb, shall be to him shortly as bitter as wormwood, and as sharp as a two-edged sword."

The Lord Militant turned and gestured Cale forward into the light. The guard removed the gag and led him over to Bosco.

"Do you really think she'll believe you?" said Cale.

"I can't think why not: it's mostly true, even if it's not the whole truth."

"Which is?"

Bosco looked at him as if trying to read something in his face, but with an uncertainty Cale had never seen before.

"No," Bosco said, at last. "We'll wait for her reply."

"What are you afraid of?"

Bosco smiled. "Well, perhaps a little honesty between us would be no bad thing at this stage. I fear, of course, that true love will conquer all and she will refuse to deliver you into my hands."

✠

Back in her palazzo, Arbell Swan-Neck was suffering the terrible pangs of private desire and public obligation, the dreadful and impossible betrayal involved in either choice. But it was worse than it seemed because in her heart of hearts (and the yet more secret one that lay within that heart) she had already decided to betray Thomas Cale. Understand her loss, the numbing shock of witnessing all she had ever known collapse in front of her. Then understand the dreadful power of Bosco's words that echoed her most fearful thoughts in almost every way. Thrilling though Cale was to her, it was the same strangeness that roused her that also roused distaste for him. He was so violent, so angry, so deadly. Bosco had seen right through her to the other side. How, given who she was, could she be other than refined and delicate? And, make no mistake, this refinement and delicacy were what Cale adored; but Cale had been *beaten* into shape, hammered in dreadful fires of fear and pain. How could she be with him for long? A secret part of Arbell had been searching for some time for a way to leave her lover—although she was unaware of this, it is only fair to record. And so as Cale waited for her to save him while he worked out a way of saving her, she had already chosen the bitter but reasonable path of the good, of the many over the one. Who was there, after all, to say otherwise? Not she. Surely even Cale himself would understand in time.

36

Nearly six hours later Bosco entered the locked room in which Cale had been confined. He was carrying two letters. He handed one of them to Cale. Cale read it without expression, apparently twice. Then Bosco offered him the second.

"She asked me, tearfully, to give this to you after we had taken you prisoner. It asks you to believe how hard it was to deliver you into my hands and to try and forgive her."

Cale took the offered letter and threw it on the fire.

"I dreamt something wonderful," said Cale. "Now I'm awake I'm angry at myself. Say what you have to say."

Bosco sat down behind a table that made up the only other furniture in the room.

"Thirty years ago, when I went into the wilderness to fast and pray before I became a priest, the Hanged Redeemer's mother, peace be upon her, appeared to me in three visions. In the first, she told me that God had waited in vain for mankind to repent for killing His son and had now despaired of its nature. The wickedness of man was great in the earth, and every imagination of the thoughts of his heart was continually evil. He repents that He had ever made him. In the second vision, she told me that God had said: 'The end of all flesh is come before me; every living man and woman that I have made you will destroy from the face of the earth. When you have accomplished this the world will end, the saved will enter paradise, and men and women will exist no more.' I asked her how it would be possible to do this, and she told me to fast and wait for a third and final vision. In the third and final vision, she brought with her a small boy carrying a hawthorn stick, and from the end of that stick dripped vinegar. 'Look for this child, and when you see him, prepare him for his work. He is the left hand of

God, also called the Angel of Death, and he will bring about all these things.'"

Throughout all this it seemed as if Bosco had become transfixed, as if he were not in a room in Memphis but back in the deserts of Fatima thirty years before, listening to the Mother of God. Then it was as if some light had been put out and he was back. He looked at Cale.

"As soon as I saw that boy brought into the Sanctuary ten years ago, I knew him." He smiled at Cale in the strangest way, a smile of love and tenderness. "It was you."

A week later a procession paused briefly in the keep. Among those on horseback were Lord Militant Redeemer Bosco and by his side was Cale. Among those gathered to watch them leave were Marshal Materazzi, Chancellor Vipond and such of his senior men who had survived the battle at Silbury Hill. Between them were two lines of Redeemer soldiers, there to make sure that the now free but unarmed Cale did nothing untoward. It suited Bosco for the time being to keep the Marshal where he was. However, he thought wiser of provoking Cale by having the girl present, and he had ordered her in person, much to her relief, to stay away from the official humiliation being handed out to her father and everyone else in Memphis. Instead she was to watch and listen from a nearby window. She needed no warning not to make her presence known. Despite his precautions, Bosco wondered if he had been wise to let Cale go unrestrained. Cale pulled his horse up and stared at the Marshal over the heads of the guards. Standing next to him, distraught, was Simon. Cale did not seem to be aware of him. When he began speaking, it was so softly he could barely be heard over the noise of the restless horses.

"I have a message for your daughter," said Cale. "I am bound to her with cables that not even God can break. One day, if there is a soft breeze on her cheek, it may be my breath; one night, if the cool wind plays with her hair, it may be my shadow passing by."

And with this terrible threat he faced forward and the procession started once more. In less than a minute they were gone. In her shady room Arbell Swan-Neck stood white and cold as alabaster.

Quickly and silently the Marshal and his people left to dwell on their mortification. As Vipond returned to his palazzo accompanied by Captain Albin, he turned to him and said quietly, "You know, Albin, the older I get, the more I believe that if love is to be judged by most of its visible effects, it looks more like hatred than friendship."

Half a day later the procession had cleared the outer reaches of Memphis and turned toward the Scablands and the Sanctuary beyond. During this time Lord Militant Redeemer Bosco and Cale had not exchanged a single word.

From a small cloud of trees some distance from the road, Vague Henri, Kleist and IdrisPukke watched the procession pass out of sight. Then they began to follow.

ACKNOWLEDGMENTS

First, my thanks to Alex Clarke, my editor at Penguin, who has been a heroic champion of this book. Also thanks to Ben Sevier of Dutton, my American editor. They are a pleasure to work with. Thanks too to my agent, Anthony Goff, endlessly determined, and Alexandra Hoffman for her good sense. Without Lorraine Hedger's uncanny guesswork while typing the illegible manuscript, it would have taken twice as long. Jeremy O'Grady was a reassuring long stop. My gratitude also to the rights department at Penguin: Sarah Hunt-Cooke, Kate Brotherhood, Rachel Mills and Chantal Noel.

This book draws on endless bits and pieces of everything I have ever read or heard, from the Book of Judges to *The Duchess of Malfi* to a line from an old children's film—too many to mention individually. Some borrowings are crucial: I am indebted to John Keegan's brilliant *The Face of Battle*, and not just for his description and analysis of the Battle of Agincourt. *Agincourt* by Juliet Barker was immensely useful in its detail of the complex days leading up to the battle itself, as was Matthew Strickland and Robert Hardy's *The Great Warbow*, from which I took precise details of the use of the bow and crossbow. For IdrisPukke's philosophy of life, I stole heavily from Arthur Schopenhauer's *Essays and Aphorisms* and *On the Suffering of the World*; for Chancellor Vipond's, La Rochefoucauld's *Maxims* set the tone. Scattered here and there are lines from Robert Graves's great translation of Homer, *The Anger of Achilles*. The letter on page 309 is based on one written by Sullivan Ballou in 1861. There are two or three descriptive sentences from Tolstoy near the end—good hunting.

ABOUT THE AUTHOR

Paul Hoffman studied English at New College, Oxford, before becoming a senior film censor at the British Board of Film Classification. He lives in the United Kingdom.

Read on for the next installment in Cale Grimperson's story

THE LAST FOUR THINGS

Available in hardcover from Dutton in August 2011.

Kleist was singing wildly, happily off-key.

> "The buzzing of the trees and the cigarette bees
> The soda water fountains
> Where the bluebell rings
> And the lemonade sings
> On the big rock candy mountain
> In the big rock candy mountain
> the priests all quack like ducks
> There's a five-cent whore at every door
> At dinner there is always more
> and never was heard a discouraging word.
> In the big rock candy mountain."

He reached down, casual-like, to check the knife sheathed in a pocket of the horse's saddle, and went on bawling not with much respect for tunefulness.

> "There's a lake of stew and whisky too
> You can paddle all around it in a big canoe
> In the big rock—"

Then he was off, pulling the knife with him and running for a patch of blackberry briars. He leapt into the middle, his speed and weight carrying him, thorns scraping his skin red as he went. But the tangle of shoots was thicker than he'd realized and the older suckers in the middle were tough and thick-barbed and his headlong flight was painfully brought to a halt.

Powerful hands grabbed him by the heels and dragged him backward out of the briars. They had to tug hard and it gave Kleist a couple of seconds to decide. He dropped the knife in the briars and then he was free and being dragged into the open.

Other hands grabbed his wrists as he kicked and wriggled. Once he was held fast, he knew there was no point and stopped struggling.

One man stood in front of him, his precise features hidden by the sun in Kleist's eyes.

"We're going to search you, so don't move. Any weapons?"

"No."

Two hands, swiftly and cleanly, skillfully frisked him.

"Good. If you had lied to us, it would have been the last thing you ever did. Get him up."

Kleist was pulled roughly into a sitting position, and all four men, knives and short swords pulled, let him go in disciplined order. These people knew what they were doing.

"What's your name?"

"Thomas Cale."

"What are you up to out here on your own?"

"I was heading for Post Moresby." A hefty blow landed on the side of his head.

"Say 'Lord Dunbar' when you speak to Lord Dunbar."

"All right. How was I supposed to know?"

Another blow to teach him not to be lippy.

"What would you do there?" said Lord Dunbar.

Kleist looked at him—he was scruffy, dirty and badly dressed in an ugly-looking tartan. He didn't look like any lord Kleist had ever seen.

"I want to get on a boat and get as far away from here as I can."

"Why?"

"The Redeemers killed my family in the massacre on Mount Nugent. When they took Memphis, I knew it was time to go away where I'd never see one of them ever again." This was half true as far as it went.

"Where did you get the horse?"

"It's mine."

Another blow to the head.

"I found it. I think it was a stray from the battle at Silbury Hill."

"I heard about that."

"Perhaps the Redeemers would pay cash for him," said Handsome Johnny.

"Perhaps they'll string you up when you try," said Kleist, getting another clip on the ear.

"Lord Dunbar!"

"Lord Dunbar, all right."

"Handsome Johnny," said Dunbar, "search his horse." Dunbar squatted down beside him.

"What are these Redeemers after?"

"I don't know. All I know is they're a bunch of murdering bastards, Lord Dunbar, and the best thing to do is get away from them."

"The Materazzi haven't been able to catch us in twenty years," said Lord Dunbar. "It doesn't much matter to us who's trying to hunt us down."

Handsome Johnny came back and laid an armful of Kleist's possessions on the ground. There was a good haul. Kleist had made sure that however basic the purpose of anything he took from Memphis, it was all of the highest quality: the swords of Portuguese steel, inlaid with ivory at the handle, a blanket of cashmere wool, and so on, then the money—eighty dollars in a silk purse. This cheered the five men considerably. For all Dunbar's boasting, the pickings were pretty scant if their clothes and ragged state were anything to go by.

"All right," said Kleist. "You've got everything I own. It's a pretty good drag. Just let me go."

Another blow.

"Lord Dunbar."

"We should shallow the cheeky little sod."

Kleist didn't like the sound of that.

"Let me take him back there," said Handsome Johnny. "I'll save any trouble."

Lord Dunbar glared at him. "I know what beastliness you want to do before that, Handsome Johnny," he shouted. He looked back at Kleist. "Get up." Kleist got to his feet. "Give us your jacket." Kleist took off his short coat, one he'd stolen from on a hook in Vipond's attendance room, soft leather and simply but beautifully cut.

"You've been lying to me, and I like that in a man," said Dunbar, admiring the jacket and mourning the fact that it was too small. "But you're right about fair dos." He pointed to a roughish path. "That'll take you in the general direction out of the woods. After that you're on your own. Now bugger off!"

Kleist didn't need to be told twice. He passed by Handsome Johnny, who watched him go with resentful lasciviousness, and vanished into the woods with nothing but half the clothes he'd been wearing five minutes before.

"You can't replace three hundred men carefully chosen for their great qualities and bound to you with hoops of steel with those degenerates in the House of Special Purpose."

"How else are we going to replace them? Do we have ten years?"

Bosco was not so green that he was unaware this was the first time Cale had spoken of them both in this way, and that he was being charmed. Still, that he was making an effort to be deceptive was encouraging.

"No, we don't."

"Are there any records?"

"Oh, each Redeemer has a tally codex. Everything about him is recorded there."

"Do you have one?"

"Of course."

"I'd like to read it."

"This idea won't work."

"It *might* not work. They're standing on the edge of death followed by eternal Hell, where devils every day will disembowel them with a spade or swallow them alive and shit them out for all eternity. Save them from a fate like—those are the hoops of steel that'll bind them to me."

"These are deviants. The very boilings of moth and rust."

"If they don't come up to snuff, I'll return them for execution. These are trained men abandoned by everyone. At least give me their tallies." Cale smiled, the first time in a long time. "I don't even believe you disagree."

"Very well. We'll both read the tallies. Then we'll see."

"Tell me about Guido Hooke."

There was a knock at the door, which opened immediately, followed by a Redeemer who nodded obsequiously to Bosco and dumped a large file in a box, marked *INTRO*. He nodded again and left.

"Hooke," said Bosco, "is a nuisance to me and of no real concern to you."

"I want to know about him."

"Why?"

"A hunch. Besides, I thought I was to know everything."

"Everything? You see that file Notil just bought in? That's just a day's paperwork—a slack day. Stick to what you're good at."

"Tell me."

"Very well. Hooke is a know-all who thinks he can understand the world by the book of arithmetic. He is a great inventor of engines. He is brilliant in the way of the best of such people, but he has struck his gonk once too often into things that he had much better not have done. I've left him alone because I admire his mind, and for ten years. But his declarations about the moon contradicted the Pope. I warned him to leave and suggested the Hanse might be willing to employ him. While I was in Memphis, he went to Fray Bentos to take ship but was caught by Gant's men in a hotel waiting to embark."

"Why didn't they take him to Stuttgart?"

"Because in Stuttgart he wouldn't be my responsibility. Now I must either make an Act of Faith of him or be seen to defy the ruling of the Pope."

"But you said the Pope was wrong."

"You are being deliberately slow."

"What kind of engines?"

"Blasphemous engines."

"Why?"

"A machine for flying—if God had meant us to fly he would have given us wings. A wagon cased in iron—if God had meant us to have armor, we would have been born with scales. And for all I know, or care, a machine for extracting sunlight from cucumbers. Most of the drawings he's made are fantasies. His idea for a hopiocopter that flies is twaddle. It doesn't look as if it could move along the ground, let alone fly through the air. But I have made use of his water gate in the east canal."

"If God had intended there to be water gates, wouldn't He have made water flow upward." Bosco would not rise to the bait.

"If you want to know about him, read his tally. He's a dead man, whether you do or don't."

Kleist had been forced to hang around until the next day before Lord Dunbar and his men left and he could collect the knife he'd dropped in the bramble bush. He thought carefully about what to do next. He was not interested in revenge, not being the indulgent type—it was dangerous, and Kleist did not believe in risk. On the other hand, he was in the middle of some bumhole wilderness with no horse, no chattels, no money and few clothes. All in all he decided he had to follow them, but he wondered repeatedly over the next three days if he hadn't made a mistake. He was cold and hungry. He was used to that, but though the surroundings were green enough, he came across no standing water. Weakness from lack of water could take you quickly, and once he lost touch with Dunbar, he was finished. He had one break: he found some bamboo—spindly but good enough. Probably. He cut himself a section five feet long and a dozen thin poles, and hurried to catch up. Following for the rest of the day, he found a small puddle of green-and-brown water and decided to risk it. He'd tasted worse but not often. Dunbar and his men stopped an hour before darkness, and Kleist had to work quickly in the fading light. The bamboo was still green, which made it easy to cut it into thin lashings to twist and use for a bowstring. Then he split the bamboo down the middle into three staves, each one shorter than the last. By the time it was dark, he'd bound one stave on the other with the lashings like the leaf spring of a cart. He slept little and badly when he did. The next day he began work as soon as it was light, following as they moved off, and finished the bow as they stopped for a couple of hours at midday. He would like to recurve the ends for more power but there wasn't time—it was a complicated process. The sun came out and tormented him with thirst, but while it desiccated him, it did the same to the bow, drying it fully and binding everything archer-tight. There was flint enough lying around, and it took only ten minutes to make an arrowhead.

A maggoty crow provided the feathers for the fletch, but crow feathers were hard to work, and he'd wasted most of the best getting the technique right. Binding them accurately with the bamboo and twine was a bastard. Still, while Redeemer Master Arrowsmith Hart would have given him a good hiding for the results, they weren't too bad, all considered. Good enough as long as he could get in close to cause some serious evil. He was exhausted, thirsty, hungry, and in a foul temper. A few quick practice shots out of sight eased his weariness with a mixture of satisfaction at his skill and a dose of malice. But he'd let them get too far away and, thinking he'd lost them, almost walked into the camp they'd hidden in a thickish cloud of trees. In the light that remained, he only had the time to crawl around half of the campsite and see what was what. By then he had placed four of them but not the fifth. Sunset meant that the hoped-for attack would have to be delayed. He would have preferred to wait out the night where he was so as not to risk a reapproaching in the morning. But the failure to spot the fifth man meant he thought it better to withdraw a few hundred yards. Tricky either way and a bloody nuisance.

Nine hours later and with a splitting headache, he was back and watching. Still only four men, but the one missing yesterday was back and Lord Dunbar was gone. Frustration and excitement and fear made the hammering in Kleist's brain seem like it would break his skull but he didn't dare do a thing until all five were together. And then, around eight, Dunbar crawled out of what looked like a large bush at the edge of the camp. In a few seconds he was urinating at the edge of the camp and shouting orders for them to strike it. Arrow into bow, string pulled, the huge power of his right arm and shoulder and back tensed and a deep breath and then loose. A scream from Dunbar as the arrow took him in the left hip. Three-second pause—the four stared. "What?" called one.

Another arrow hit Handsome Johnny in the mouth, and he fell back, waving his arms. A third raced off, slipping and sliding in terror to the cover of the trees. An arrow, pulled badly, hit him in the foot, and he hopped the last few yards, shouting in pain, and vanished into the trees. Another, unscathed, raced out of the camp in the other direction. The fifth man in the almost center of the camp did not move. Kleist took aim, the bow creaking with the bend, and let loose into the middle of his chest. A dreadful gasp of anguish. He bowed another arrow and drew it back, carefully and quickly making his way into the camp, moving the point back and forth over the points of threat. Handsome Johnny wasn't going to be any trouble. The man kneeling with his head bowed was still groaning, but there was now a strange whistling sound alternating with each indrawn breath. No one could fake that noise. He wasn't going to be any trouble either. Kleist just wished the sound would stop. Dunbar, lying on his side, was a dreadful white color, lips bloodless.

"I should," said Dunbar softly, "have killed you when I had the chance."

"You should have left me alone when you had the chance."

"Fair enough."

"Any weapons?"

"Why should I tell you?"

"Fair enough." Nervous, Kleist kept watching the trees. This was too risky.

"This could take hours. Finish me."

"So I should, but it's easier said than done."

"Why? You did for those two without much problem."

"Yeah, but I was angry then."

"When all's said, I let you go. Finish it."

"Your men will be back. Let them do it."

"Not for hours. Maybe not at all."

"Well, I don't want to, see."

"You'd best be."

There was a loud *THWACK!* as Kleist loosed the bow almost point-blank into Dunbar's chest. His eyes widened, and he breathed out for what seemed like minutes but was only a few seconds. Fortunately for both of them, that was that.

Behind him the man on his knees still groaned and whistled. Kleist dropped to his knees and heaved. But there was nothing in his stomach to come out. It was not easy to keep on retching and keep an eye on the trees. He dropped the bow—he needed his hands free to search his new possessions and claim his old. He stood up slowly and screamed.

Standing five yards away was a girl. She looked at him wide-eyed and then threw herself into his arms and burst into tears.

"Thank you! Thank you!" she sobbed, hugging him as if he were a lost parent, her hands clutching him with desperate relief and gratitude. She kissed him full on the lips, then pushed herself into his chest, her hands squeezing his upper back as if she would never let him go. "You were so brave, so brave." She stepped back to examine him, eyes brimming with admiration.

It would not have taken a talented student of human nature to have read Kleist's not only astonished look but also the deep shiftiness of his expression as she looked adoringly at him. He watched the understanding that he had not arrived to rescue her move over her face like a fast sunrise. The admiration washed out and her eyes began to become wet with tears. It was not often that Kleist felt mean-spirited.

She stepped back rather more than the emotion of her discovery warranted and produced the knife she had lifted from Kleist's belt while she was so gratefully hugging him.

The look of astonishment and anger on Kleist's face was so comic in its effect, the girl burst into laughter.

His face went red with anger, which only made her laugh harder. Then he stepped forward, knocked the knife out of her hand, and punched her in the face. She went down like a sack of coal and fetched her head a nasty blow. He picked up the knife, keeping his eyes on her; then he gave a quick scan of the trees. The status of things was getting out of control. Her expression now was one of shock and pain at her bloody nose. She sat up.

"Laughing on the other side of your face now."

She said nothing as he backed away and started examining the bundles around the camp for his own stuff and anything else portable. The man on his knees was still moaning and his punctured lung still whistling.

The girl started crying. Kleist carried on searching. In what must have been Lord Dunbar's pack, he found his money. Otherwise the pickings were scant. Their lives as robbers couldn't have been up to much. And they had only three horses, including the one they had stolen from Kleist. The girl's crying became louder and more uncontrollable. Along with the groan and whistle of the kneeling man, it was getting on Kleist's nerves. But more than that.

The tears of a woman are an alcahest to the soul of man, Redeemer Fraser had once said to him. A tearful bitch can dissolve all a man's good judgment in its liquid gerrymandering.

At the time this warning had seemed of dubious relevance, given that he had no memory of ever having seen a woman. His experience in Memphis, though it had very much expanded his experience of women in some ways, was not helpful when it came to tears, the whores of Kitty Town not being given much to weeping.

"Shut up," he said.

She reduced the sound to a grizzling and the occasional heavy sob.

"What the hell were you doing with these desperadoes?"

She could not answer at first, trying to bring herself under control with wet gasps of emotion.

"They kidnapped me," she said, which was not true or not entirely true, "and they all raped me." His time in Memphis had made Kleist familiar with the term. He had heard a number of puzzling amusing stories about rape and had caused even more laughter by asking for an explanation. He was shocked by the answer and did not approve. She was clearly a liar, but she looked as distraught as even Kleist would have expected. But then a few minutes ago, she'd been laughing at him.

"If you're telling the truth, I'm sorry."

"Let me have one of the horses."

"That would mean you could keep up with me. I don't think so."

"You'll have the best horse—the others are just kick-bags."

This was true enough.

"I could sell them in the next town. Why should I give one to you when you're a thief? Or worse."

"They're both branded. They'll hang you for a horse thief if you try to sell them."

"Well, you look as if you'd know," he said, tying his newly filled bag onto his horse saddle.

"Please. Two of them are still out there."

"One of them isn't going to be following anyone for quite some time."

"But the other one could."

"All right. Just shut up. But you go in that direction," he said, pointing to the west. "If I see you again, I'll cut your bloody head off."

With that, he mounted his horse and set off, leaving the girl sitting on the forest floor, next to the kneeling man, who was still wheezing and whistling. If his actions in leaving the young woman in the clearing were ignoble, they were in the light of the appalling consequences of his only other experience of rescuing young women in distress at least understandable.